GRIFFIN

THE BILLIONAIRES OF WHISPERS
BOOK 6

SAMANTHA SKYE

Ebook: 978-1-923258-36-5

Paperback: 978-1-923258-37-2

Alt Paperback: 978-1-923258-38-9

Cover Design: Angela Haddon

Editor: Nice Girl Naughty Edits

Proofreading: Kimberly Dawn

Sensitivity Edit: Tina Catania

Cover Photography: CJC Photography

Cover Model: Tyler Gilson

1

———

SAVANNAH SHEPHERD

I'm sweating in areas that haven't sweat before.

That, combined with the fact that my hair's a mess, my hands are wrinkled from all the suds, my nails are chipped and my back aches, has me feeling all the seven months pregnant that I am.

So, of course, that's when the front door chimes, and I look up from where I'm on hands and knees, scrubbing the floor, to see one of the most devastatingly handsome men I think I've ever laid eyes on in real life.

"Hope I'm not interrupting?" He steps in, all towering muscles, looking down on me with a furrowed brow.

With my hands still wet with suds, I blow out a sharp breath to move the hair that's dangling in my face and wonder how the heck I'm going to get off this floor to greet him like a normal person.

"No... not at all." I quickly wipe my hands on my overalls, the pair of secondhand threads that are starting to fit a little more snug than usual due to my expanding belly. Although, I'm still carrying small, and the bump is barely noticeable to most people. "Welcome to Betty's Bakery." I try to stand, thanking God above when I succeed in that task.

"I'm Tanner Whiteman..." He pauses, and it has the effect he was hoping for. Everyone around here knows who Tanner Whiteman is. This guy might as well own Whispers. It's one of the reasons I moved here. Whispers is a sleepy little town, yet the businesses do a roaring trade, all thanks to his rich friends and his amazing distillery. My heart races, knowing the man in front of me could close me down before I even serve my first customer.

"I'm Savannah. Savannah Shepherd. Owner of..." I raise my hands to gesture around and try to smile. There's so much work to do; it'll be a miracle if I get it all done and the bakery opens before my little cherub arrives. When I submitted the paperwork to open the bakery here in Whispers, I thought the process would be quick. I needed it to be. But the interest in Whispers has intensified in the past few years and local government shuffling paperwork seemed to take months. Hence why I'm about to pop and open a bakery at the same time. But I trust God's plan.

"I came to welcome you to town. It's nice to have new people invest here, and opening a bakery is a welcome addition to Whispers."

Great, he's good-looking *and* kind. I also happen to know that he's very, very taken so I put my hormones in check.

"Thank you. Everyone's been really nice so far. I love it here in Whispers." My smile is genuine. Compared to where I came from, Whispers might as well be a luxury destination, not the small town it is. I'm still finding my feet, but I've never felt so free. Probably because I never was. My family's increasing fanatical religious beliefs were so suffocating, I'm surprised I survived it at all.

"Is it just you or..." Tanner looks around, seemingly

obvious to how much work needs to be done here. Probably expecting a man to pop out. But my father disowned me, I have no brothers, and the man who contributed to my bump made it clear that he wasn't interested in me beyond the gratification he gained from putting me in this situation. He skipped town almost immediately, leaving me to face the community and our families on my own.

"Yeah." I wipe my hands on my legs again, the familiar sense of loneliness sweeping through my body. "It's just me."

Tanner's eyes flick back to mine, and his frown deepens.

"I mean, I have a help wanted sign in the window. I'm looking for a part-time employee who can assist when I'm not here." I try to convey that I'm an organized business-woman, even though I don't look like it. But this bakery has been a dream of mine for forever. Something I never thought possible, and I'm making it happen.

"When do you think you'll be up and running? I'd like to talk to you about supplying my distillery." My eyebrows shoot to my hairline.

"Ahhh, supplying?" I'm not deaf, but I do have baby brain so I don't trust myself to believe my ears at times.

"Yeah, well, I have a restaurant at the distillery. They need fresh bread daily, pastries, that kind of thing. My accommodations will be opening soon. I like the idea of providing a fresh basket of local produce to every visitor, of which your bakery can provide for as well." He nods, like it's a done deal. Excitement blooms. My first real customer already! This conversation almost makes all the months of anguish I've endured worth it.

Biting my lip, I look around, seeing the mess of the place. Secondhand professional mixers in the back that I'm still trying to get used to. The old oven needs to be cleaned, but it's in working order. The floor is now almost sparkling, the dust and grime something that had built up for many years. I also need to paint the walls, fix the counter, and install some new display cabinets here at the front, and then I should be able to open it to the public while perfecting the rest at night.

"I'm hoping to be open in a few weeks. I still have all this to fix up." I wave my hand around. It should feel impossible, but I'd rather be here than back with my family.

"Who's doing your carpentry?" I look back at Tanner quickly, my brain scrambling.

"Oh... me?" I don't know how to repair a countertop or how to build the cabinets, but I'll watch some videos online and figure it out. That's pretty much what I've been doing since I got here. My family made it clear what they thought of me when I unexpectedly fell pregnant. Kept me inside, with their fear of community backlash at the forefront. More concerned about my actions tarnishing their good name in the religious community we were a part of than they were about what I was going through. They were adamant I would stay hidden, place my baby for adoption, and then just enter the world again like nothing happened. But I have other plans. Although going through it alone feels harder every day.

Tanner's eyes move down to my belly, then back to my face. I'm not sure if he can tell that I'm with child, since I kind of look like I ate a huge bowl of pasta, but these overalls don't hide it.

"I have a builder. He can help." As soon as the words leave his mouth, he nods. Again, like it's a done deal.

"Uh... I... um..." My grandmother left me some money when she passed, which is how I ended up here, with this bakery and all the secondhand equipment. But the little funds I have left need to see me through the birth and until the bakery can start bringing in a solid, consistent income.

"Sounds great, but my budget doesn't extend to builders' fees, so I'm okay. I'm figuring it out as I go." I smile, hoping he doesn't think I'm being ungrateful.

"My builder's the best. He'll have this done in a few days. No charge."

Back aching, I stand rooted to the floor in shock. Blinking wordlessly at him. *No charge?* Like the miracle inside of me knows I'm staring, the baby kicks, helping me to get my mouth working again. But as generous as his offer is, nothing is free. Everything comes at a price, and I start to feel unsettled.

"Why would you help me?" I didn't always suspect people of having ulterior motives. I went through life thinking everyone was kind and genuine and honest. But that all changed a few months ago when those closest to me showed their true colors. Now I doubt everyone.

Tanner's face blanches for a moment before he looks me in the eye.

"This town likes to see people succeed. A thriving bakery like this gives a place for tourists to stop, somewhere that can cater for the diner or my distillery. We help each other out here. Not sure what you've experienced before"—brow furrowed, he looks down at my belly again—" but here, in Whispers, we don't leave our people to fail."

I take in a small breath, still not agreeing to anything. I'm not sold on the idea of accepting so much free help. Especially from a man I just met. Regardless of how good-looking and rich he is.

"We could always barter?" he suggests, clearly noticing my hesitation.

My head tilts at that. "Barter?"

"I'll get my builder to help fix this place up. You supply me a fresh loaf of bread every morning until you've paid back the fee."

"But that could take a year. Or longer!" I'm astounded. A man I've never met, offering to give me essentially a loan and allowing me to pay him back in gluten.

"I know a good investment when I see it. And my builder will too." His eyes twinkle, like he knows something I don't. But as I look around my bakery, spotting the chipped counter and the cupboard doors almost off their hinges, I know I could use the help.

Something deep within tells me I can trust this man. That he isn't someone who's going to push me out of town or bury me out in the large acreage of forest on the outskirts that I saw on the map recently—apparently, locals call it Serial Killer Forest. Yikes. I get a chill just thinking about it. Actually, from what I've read, Tanner Whiteman is one of the most wealthy and upstanding members of not only this town and this state, but I dare say, most of the country.

Maybe this is the small break I've been hoping for. Maybe this is part of God's plan. Maybe Grandma is looking down on me from above, giving me the helping hand I need. I take a deep breath, praying that I don't make the wrong decision.

"Do you like sourdough or...?" The corners of my lips start to curve. I need to learn to trust again. I have to lean on someone to make this bakery a success. For me and my little one.

"Sourdough will be just fine." He grins, offering me his hand again, and I shake it, sealing our agreement. Completely unaware of how much this deal will change my life.

2

GRIFFIN PATTERSON

I sip the warm coffee, wondering how Rochelle gets it so flavorful. I have coffee all over the country, and never once has another cup come close to the quality that Delish Diner offers.

"Good, you're still here." Tanner strides into the diner like he owns it, heading in my direction and taking a seat in the booth opposite me without an invitation.

"Not for long. Just grabbing lunch, then flying out to Colorado." I've spent the past few days here with him at the new distillery accommodations we're building, of which we've had plans drawn up for a while now. I have a team at the distillery who are almost finished with the structural build. We're at the fit-out stage, so I flew in this week to check on it. I've also had meetings with Victoria, Tanner's wife, and my interior's contractor about what she has finished for my new place that I've built here at Billionaire Boulevard. I don't have a home. I have houses. And I decided to build one here to add to my portfolio.

"I need a favor before you go."

I both sigh and grin. His favors are never small things.

Instead, always something like, *I'm building an extension; could you finish that in a few days.* Or, *build my ranch; I need it done yesterday.*

"I need you to go over to the bakery across the road."

Eyes narrowed, I look at him over the rim of my coffee cup, where it's stalled halfway to my mouth.

"Is it open?" I saw newspapers covering the windows, so I assumed someone was doing work over there. But commercial fit-outs aren't really my thing. Certainly not that small size. Give me a world-class distillery, and I can build your dreams, but a small bakery isn't worth my time.

"No. It needs a fair amount of work. The new owner seems to think they can do it all on their own."

I can tell by how his jaw clenches that he isn't happy about something. But while he's my closest friend, a bakery builder I am not.

"I gotta fly out today. I need to sign off on the plans for my new Colorado project before I hit Sundown Valley in the morning."

I'm a busy man. My construction company does luxury builds all around the country. Work is my life. I built my business from the ground up. Something I'm proud of. Something that gives me purpose. Keeps me busy. I need to be busy.

"Sundown Valley? What are you doing over there?"

I give Tanner a grin. "Winery. Stonemore's making some additions."

His eyebrows rise. He knows who I'm talking about. The Stonemore family has been around for a while and making a name for themselves. One of the best wineries in the country. I have no idea what it is about these men and their liquor, but Tanner Whiteman and Grayson Stonemore could be two peas in a pod. Both grumpy assholes, but they would give you their last dollar if you needed it.

"They're already the largest winery in the country. What the hell else do they want." Tanner frowns as he scrubs his chin. His distillery is on par with what the Stonemore family has. But they might get one up on him with this new fit-out.

"Yeah, well, they obviously have some things going on." I don't delve into the private lives of my clients too much. Tanner and the guys here at Whispers are an exception, since we've all become firm friends over the years. I built the distillery with Tanner decades ago, and it was one of my first big major projects that helped put me on the map. So the place he calls home is full of my own blood, sweat, and tears. My connection to it, to him, to this town, it's one I don't have anywhere else.

"What about your house here?" He frowns, not happy I'm leaving already. But I never stay in one place for long. I live a transient life. Always have. Growing up in foster care with quasi-parents who didn't give a shit about you will do that to you. Home is not where the heart is in my experience. Violence? Yes. Abuse? Also, yes. Love? Never.

I shrug. "It's here. Victoria will finish it off." Real estate is the one thing I invest my money into. Having not had a real home growing up, I collect them now like people collect stamps or coins.

Because I can.

But having a house here in Whispers will allow me not to live out of a suitcase when I come here so often. The decor will be comfortable, and I like Whispers. My friends are here. I hope to spend more time with them. But with no family, I have no roots. Nothing tethering me. So I continue to float around the country, building dreams for other people. My bank balance has never seen as many zeros as it does now. My needs are minimal. Social life is nonexistent. I can't even remember the last time I took a vacation.

"When can you take a look at it?"

I sip my coffee, wondering why the rush.

"The bakery?" I look at him like he's crazy. He knows how busy I am and that I don't have time to look at a fucking bakery.

"Yes, the bakery. They need help."

My mouth opens to respond, but I'm cut off before I can. "Are you talking about the bakery?" Rochelle slides up to the table, pouring a fresh cup of coffee for Tanner. That's the thing about small towns. Everyone knows everyone. Clearly a new person and a new bakery are talk of the town.

"Didn't think you were talking to me..." Tanner murmurs, looking a little remorseful.

"I'm not," she snaps at him, and I raise an eyebrow in question.

"I took Charlotte from her and gave her a job at the distillery," Tanner says with a sheepish grin. Charlotte Titan is his new Sustainability Officer who used to work here with Rochelle. She's making huge improvements on the distillery; so much so, I'm thinking she could come and consult with me on some builds. Not to mention, along with her movie star husband, Sutton Silvers, they're both my neighbors here on Billionaire Boulevard.

"My best worker!" Rochelle looks at Tanner with a huff, and I wonder if she'll pour the full coffee pot all over him. I'd pay money to see that.

"Fine. I'll go take a look..." I try to ease the tension. Besides, Tanner knows I can't say no to him.

"I'll ask Victoria to pop by as well. She might need help with the interior design." He scratches his chin again. It's not unusual for Tanner to take an interest in what happens in this town. But he sure is pulling out all the stops to help the bakery if he wants Victoria and me to be involved.

"She?"

"Yeah... she." Something in the way Tanner looks at me makes me think there's more going on, but he doesn't elaborate, and I don't care enough to ask anything more.

"I'll be in Sundown Valley for a few days, then back here. I'll pop in then," I offer. It's the best I can do. I have commitments. My jet gets lots of use. It's more a necessity than a luxury at this point.

"Fine. It won't take much; she just needs a hand. I'll pay for your time."

My head rears back as I look back at him quickly. "You're paying the bills? Shit, she must bake good bread." I laugh as Tanner sips his coffee.

"I haven't tried it. But I'm hopeful."

Bewildered, I shake my head at him. His love for this town runs deep. I'm jealous of it. To have ties to a place. To have people that you've known for a long time, who are all by your side each day. To have a bigger purpose in life than building a business and making money.

I had that once. But like everything else in my life. I lost it. And I lost a piece of my soul with it.

I shake my head to dislodge the thought as I take my final sip of the caffeine I desperately need. No point in remembering what I had. I swore to myself years ago to never hold on to someone like that again. And so far, I've kept myself away from everyone and everything that comes remotely close.

I live a transient life for a reason. And I'll continue to do so.

3

SAVANNAH

A frown pulls at my lips as I look at the measly box of baby items I have stored under my bed. I've been buying bits and pieces for months, not sure exactly what I'll need. The small expecting mother's handbook taking over the Bible in the top drawer of my bedside table has been my only nightly read for months. But each page I read is overwhelming.

I'm scared. Anxious. And I've been throwing myself into the bakery build so much that I have little time to concentrate on the life I'm creating. But the familiar flutters in my tummy bring me right back to my reality every time.

I pull in a deep breath. "We'll just work it out together." Rubbing my belly, I push the box back under the bed, knowing I need to visit the hardware shop in town to see if they stock blankets and baby clothes, the two things I think I do need more of.

I also need to book a doctor's appointment now that I'm settled here. I had one initially. When I felt different and wondered why I was so bloated, I visited the local doctor who informed me that one night from months earlier, when my boyfriend at the time said that it *felt better without a barrier* had resulted in a pregnancy.

So not only was I pregnant, but to everyone's shock and surprise, I was already thirteen weeks along. I don't remember the drive home. I barely remember the words when they fell from my mouth as I told my family. But I do remember my father's face turning red. My mother's tears of disgust. And that within ten minutes, despite being a twenty-three-year-old woman who can decide her own future, they had planned my life out for me without consultation.

Their plan was that I was to remain hidden at home for the remainder of the pregnancy. The baby would be adopted by my older and married sister who's been trying to conceive for years. She had plans to fake a pregnant belly. Spend more time at home to be away from people who would take too much notice. They wanted the whole thing to be secret and to pretend that Eden had been pregnant all along. Leaving me with nothing and no one.

I walked into my room that day in complete shock. Stayed like that for weeks until I felt the flutters and knew I needed an alternative. I wanted this baby. I wanted out of the house that felt like a prison and from the life that felt so controlling and constricted it was unhealthy.

Pulling myself up from the floor, I make my way down the stairs from my apartment to the bakery kitchen, knowing I forgot something.

As I hit the bottom and smell smoke, I remember what.

"The dinner rolls!" Frantic, I run around the bakery, grabbing a towel and flinging open the old ovens. Smoke bellows around me, making my eyes water, and I internally scold myself for being so forgetful. Clearly, the timers on the ovens don't work either. This baby brain I have developed isn't serving me well at the moment.

I look at the tray of dinner rolls I just pulled from the oven, my eyes now stinging with frustration and defeat. They're a little brown on the edges; although they look better than the burnt rocks I pulled out earlier. I need to start writing things down. I can't make mistakes like this.

"Hello?"

My breath catches as I turn quickly at the sound of a voice, my fingers catching on the hot tray.

"Ow!" I pull my hand back quickly, the burn instant.

"Shit." That same gruff voice comes from over my shoulder as the tray of burnt rolls falls to the floor. Their large hand grabs my wrist, the other fits on the small of my back, and I'm manhandled toward the sink.

"I... I..." My voice is half-breathy and half-panicked, and I can't get my words out.

While burns in my line of business are common, I know I need to get my hand underwater quickly. Add that to the fact that this baby is pushing right against my diaphragm, limiting my air intake, and I'm panting like I've run a marathon.

But all that combined isn't half of what I'm feeling. Because suddenly, I smell the most masculine scent of a pine cologne, and my hormones take over, my body becoming almost weak against it.

It has me quickly remembering that a strong, unknown male is at my back. Tall, if the way his chest connects with my shoulders is any indication. My skin prickles with the feeling of being touched. His hands are large and warm. It's been seven months since I've had a man's hands on my body, and even then, it wasn't memorable. The small human growing inside of me is the only link.

The man turns on the faucet, pulling my hand under it, and I breathe out in relief as the cool water hits my hand and the sting subsides. As does any lingering fear at being manhandled by a stranger right here in my kitchen. He led me to safety; it would be odd for him to now hurt me. Though I remain wary.

"Thank you... I—" I turn to see who's helping me, wanting to offer my thanks, but I still. At a loss for words all over again.

Brown eyes, hidden by dark eyebrows, look at me from under a deep frown. He hasn't moved, his body, strong and hard, leaning against my back as he ensures my hand is under the cool water. My eyes widen and heart pounds harder as I realize exactly how close we are.

He's like Heaven answered all my questions. I've never seen a man like him before. Sure, big, tall, gruff guys are common. But there's something in his eyes. Something that tells me he's the kind of strong and dependable man you only find once in a lifetime. That thought has my stomach doing somersaults.

Before I get too lost in my hormone-induced fantasy-land, the baby kicks, knocking some sense into me. I'm a pregnant woman. I may be single, but I'm no catch. I'm a commitment and shouldn't even be looking for a man in my state. My mother's words ring in my mind. *You've ruined yourself. The devil got into your soul, and now you're filthy.*

I swallow roughly as I look up at him. His gaze is roaming over my face, from my eyes to my lips and back again, like he's making sure I'm okay. Somehow, I feel safe.

"You make a habit of burning yourself?" Okay... there goes my fantasy. He sounds like a complete asshole.

"Part of the job," I sass back, yet I don't move from where I'm positioned between him and the sink. I've never talked back like this, but this is my bakery, my home, and my protective motherly instincts are already setting in.

His brow pinches slightly. "You should be more careful."

My anger rises at his condescending tone. I'm so sick of people telling me how I should do things. I thought I left all that back in Williamstown.

"Well, you shouldn't sneak up on people and scare them." I quirk an eyebrow, totally shocked by my tone. This is *so* not me. I'm meek, mild, well mannered. Seems like he's bringing something else out in me.

"You also shouldn't leave your front door unlocked. Any asshole could walk in here."

"Looks like one did," flies past my lips next, and my eyes widen. I bite my tongue not immediately apologizing.

He blinks quickly a few times, like he's coming back to himself. Clearing his throat, he steps back, giving me some space, yet my skin feels cold without him close. For some reason, I hate it.

"My name is Griffin. I'm a builder. Tanner Whiteman sent me over to see if I can help you with your carpentry." His Adam's apple bobs as he swallows, like he's as thrown off as I am. But then his eyes drop to my body before snapping back to my face. I don't know what he's looking at. I'm a mess. A long, flowing dress that hides my bump and almost hits the floor. My hair pulled back into a top knot. Not a scrap of makeup on.

But God, you could cut glass on his jaw and that five o'clock shadow is really doing something to my insides.

I'm quiet, distracted by how attractive I find this man, but then my brain connects the puzzle pieces. *Shoot.* This is awkward.

"Oh... *Oh.* Yes, Tanner did come by a few days ago." Is it hot in here? Did I leave the oven on? I can't remember the last time I was this flustered. "Oh my gosh!" From the corner of my eye, I see smoke leaking through the oven, and I run back to it and fling open the large oven door. Panic kicks in as I grab the tray of burnt croissants and start fanning the billowing smoke. Running to the small window, I whip it open, the screech of it almost deafening, and Griffin runs to the back door to do the same, but as he does, the screen comes off its hinges and falls to the ground outside, and I cringe.

"You'll be needing a new back door." Griffin's voice is tight. Angry, almost. Like this is the last place he wants to be. Like me and my bakery are a mere annoyance.

"I can fix it," I grit out. I hate being a burden to someone. Hate having people in my space who don't want to be here. Sure, Tanner was nice to offer, but I don't want to be a charity case.

"Your hand?" Griffin's frown is pinned to the red welt throbbing on my palm, but it's nothing I can't handle. He takes a step toward me before he pauses, like he thinks better of it. My heart trips over itself, not used to any care or attention from anyone, let alone a stranger.

"The downside of being a baker." I throw the towel on the counter, where my flour and butter still reside. Today was meant to be productive. Testing the new equipment and ingredients and baking goods that I could deliver to the diner down the street as a small gesture of goodwill. Apparently, that isn't working out. "This is the third batch I've burned already today. At least I now know the ovens aren't working as they should be."

"Or your smoke alarm." Griffin assesses my kitchen. I look up at the faint smoke still lingering at the ceiling and, sure enough, the smoke alarms aren't blaring as they should be.

"Another thing to add to my list." I scrub my face, trying not to feel overwhelmed that my list is getting longer and longer every day.

"Are you living upstairs?" he asks, his tone a bit softer.

I look back at Griffin, who's eyeing the staircase leading up to what is my current home. The small studio above the bakery is one of the reasons I took this building. I could have a business and a home all in one, making baking with a baby so much easier.

I nod. "Yes."

He's back to being serious. "Then the fire alarms need to be fixed today."

I swallow past a lump in my throat as his gaze moves around the room. *Is he worried about my safety?* I mean, there's no fire escape, so I'd need to jump out of the upstairs window if there was a fire. That jump would *not* be painless.

I watch him taking it all in, seeing his mind turning over, and I wonder what he thinks. Does he see the potential like I do?

"You'll need some new cupboards in here. A longer counter to work on. Stainless steel would be best, I think."

I glance at where my ingredients and materials are all gathered on top of each other, the space nowhere near enough to roll out the right sized batch of my famous chocolate chip cookies. But while the top-of-the-line bakeries all have stainless-steel counters, it's way too expensive for my budget.

"Oh, laminate will be fine."

He looks back at me. His face seems to be in a permanent scowl. I wonder if that old wives' tale is true, *never frown when the wind changes or it will stay like that.*

By the looks of this man, it potentially is. I'm almost tempted to ask when it happened and how strong the wind was. But my mom always said to mind my manners because God is always watching.

He nods to himself. "I'll get you stainless steel." I don't miss it as his jaw clenches a little under his stubble.

I have no idea what it is about Griffin that has my stomach in knots and lungs empty. But he's authoritative, brooding, and mysterious, mixed with a kindness that appears to be buried under a grumpy, dominant, rugged exterior. He's extremely magnetic to someone like me, who's opposite in every way.

Forcing my eyes off him, I look over to the side, where I plan to put the baby's things once it arrives. *The baby.* The little life in my stomach. The reason I can't be swooning over a very alpha male who stands right in front of me in my kitchen, wearing jeans that look like they fit all too well and a shirt that, for some reason, I want to unbutton.

"Out front is the priority... I mean, if that's okay?" I feel myself retreating. The years of subordination that have been drilled into me from my parents is what I revert to time and time again.

I can't afford a total renovation. My dream bakery will be one that's built over time, not all at once. I'll make do with what I have out here. But I need the front to be fixed, that's what people will see. I swallow down my embarrassment at not having this all done already.

His eyes drape over me again, like he's trying to figure me out.

"I have some time now. My tools are in my truck. I'll get started on the back door, because if you live upstairs, then security is important. Then I'll change your smoke alarms." He doesn't wait for a reply, seemingly ignoring my statement about focusing on the front, before he pushes off the doorway and strides out the front of the shop.

I suck in a breath, roll my head on my neck, and try to calm my insides. My hips hurt, my back aches, and I now need a cool drink of water. Not only did a man just swan in and offer to fix everything, but he left me feeling a certain way. A way I haven't felt in a long, long time. Or maybe ever.

Damn hormones.

4

———

GRIFFIN

I fixed the back door, then went to Bob's hardware and picked up new smoke alarms that are now all fitted and tested. I ripped up the front counter and sanded back some timber, ready to build some cupboards for her to display her baked goods in the shop front.

I've also measured and ordered a new stainless-steel workbench, something that has cupboards underneath for storage that will allow her to work freely. She thinks it will be laminate, which tells me that she's clearly on a budget. But I saw her eyes light up a little when I mentioned stainless, so that's what I'll make her.

I've been laser-focused all afternoon, trying to get as much done as possible. Because if I don't focus on work, I'll be focusing on her. She's here on her own, that much is obvious. No one else has come by to check in, no one has called. We've worked in relative silence, yet I notice no ring on her finger and no mention of a partner, business or romantic.

I've watched her move around the space, fixing this or that. She's graceful, reminding me of my mother. Memories swirl, which isn't a good thing. My mother was one of the only shining lights of the past I think of. Even if I only had her for a short time, every memory I have after her is nothing but dark and traumatic.

Nothing I want to revisit, especially not today.

So I look back at the new local baker and take my fill.

Sweet baby Jesus, she's beautiful. Round, soft, feminine. Wearing some kind of floaty summer dress that's alluring and sexy as hell. God, the thoughts I have of pulling up that material and sliding my hands up her thighs has my throat thick.

But it sure as hell isn't OHSA friendly. Not with the big ovens she has here. If I didn't think it would piss her off, I'd tell her to go change. Not because I don't love what she's wearing, but because she needs to be safe. Here, all on her own. The damn smoke alarms weren't even working. The entire thing pisses me off. My scowl is well dented on my face and has been all afternoon.

I wasn't sure what I was walking into when I came to Betty's Bakery today. I wanted to assess things, do as much as I can while I have the time, and then walk out. A favor to Tanner, that's all it is. But when I saw her... all I could think of was *Tanner who?*

She's been in the kitchen for the entire afternoon. Baking. Burning. A mixture of smoke and sweet pastries wafting through the air. The kind of home-cooked smell that I haven't experienced... ever.

My phone vibrates in my pocket. It has been since I arrived, yet I've ignored every call. Something I never do.

"Ahhh, Griffin?"

I look up at the sound of her sweet voice, her sparkling blue eyes twinkling as she walks toward me hesitantly with a plate of pastries. I stand to say something in response, but my heart is pounding so powerfully I can't think straight. When we first met earlier, she was full of sass and confidence. Now, she's more reserved and has barely spoken to me since I started working, approaching me like she isn't allowed to. I know I act and look like an asshole, but a woman scared to approach me is new.

"Can you do me a favor?" She stops in front of me, and her cheeks tint a little. "I mean, you already are, so I feel bad asking. I just…"

"What do you need?" I force my eyes to stay on hers and not flick down to her chest. I'm a breasts guy. Always have been. And the way her tits are sitting round, perky, and full has me feeling a certain way. A way I shouldn't be feeling. Fuck, it's been too long since I felt the love of a good woman.

"Can you… taste test these for me?" *I sure as hell want to taste something.* I frown at my own thoughts. I need to get it together.

Her eyes are almost pleading, like she really needs my help.

"Do you need a second opinion?" I ask, sounding rougher than I'd like.

"Yeah… I know these recipes by heart. I've baked ever since I was little, but my memory isn't good these days, and I'm sure I'm forgetting something. Maybe it's me. It doesn't help that my taste buds are off, too. They have been for a while, so I can't taste what ingredient I'm missing…" That confuses me. Not sure what would cause a baker to lose their sense of taste, but I don't pretend to know much about women, and I sure as hell don't know anything about this one.

Despite my best efforts to create distance, I find myself nodding before I reach out and grab a cinnamon roll. It's still warm. The smell of the spice hits me as I lift it to my mouth.

Not telling her that cinnamon rolls are my all-time favorite food, I take a bite. But this one... No, this one is shit.

It's dry, tasteless, and it's like chewing cardboard. Her eyes widen as she watches me, so I force myself to keep chewing, my jaw working double time to get through it before I swallow, feeling it move like a rock down my throat.

"Tastes great," I lie, and it was worth it as her shoulders lower and a small smile brightens her face.

"Really? I've been cooking them forever, a recipe my grandma taught me. But I haven't been able to test the taste of them for weeks. I have a constant metallic taste in my mouth lately, and I'm using all new brands of ingredients that I haven't used before. Plus, the mixers and ovens are all new to me, so I wasn't sure if they needed more or less cooking time." She shrugs and then yawns, and as she does, her breasts lift and lower teasingly. I shove the remaining roll in my mouth, forcing myself to concentrate on chewing and thinking about all the work I need to do. Anything to get my mind off her.

"You from town?" I start to finish up what I was working on, my attempt at small talk something I don't often do.

"Williamstown, the next town over. But they already have so many bakeries, so competition is fierce over there."

I nod, having only been to Williamstown a few times, so I see the appeal of Whispers.

"What about you? Local?"

I huff a little, because I don't know the answer.

"Not born here. Not raised here. But I seem to aways be here," I tell her honestly.

"Whispers seems to attract good people." As she looks at me pointedly, my eyes meet hers.

"Yeah. Yeah, it does."

She offers me a small smile, one that you wouldn't think could penetrate my hardened chest, yet it does. As she tries to stifle another yawn, I lift my gaze above her head to the clock on the wall. It's getting late. I could keep going for hours. I'm used to working around the clock. But something tells me this woman needs to rest. She's beautiful but I can tell she's weary.

"Tired?"

"Oh, sorry... I've been awake since five, and it's catching up with me. I don't sleep very well anymore."

I frown. "Five a.m.?" I thought I was the only one up at that hour.

"Yeah, life of a baker!" She laughs lightly, shrugging her shoulders, and I nod. It makes sense.

"I'll be back tomorrow. Early then."

"Thank you, Griffin. Truly." She looks around at what I've already achieved, and if I didn't know any better, I'd say her eyes are glassy. Women and tears, the two things I don't do well with, so I grab my things and focus on heading out.

She shuffles closer as I start to edge toward the door. "Oh, before you leave, I know Tanner said he was paying you, but I want to as well."

"I'm not accepting your money." I won't even accept Tanner's. I'm here. I'm capable. The constant work keeps my mind busy.

"I can pay in other ways," she says with a smile.

My eyebrows hit my hairline.

Seeing my reaction, her words rush out. "Oh, I mean with pastries..." Her cheeks tint bright pink, and I grit my teeth, mentally telling my dick to stand down.

I remain silent as I look at the container she stretches out to me, filled with cinnamon rolls, and my throat dries.

I'm not sure I can stomach it. But when I grab the container, her smile hits me straight in the chest.

"Oh, and here. I popped in an extra cupcake for later."

I nod because I have no words. I secretly hope the cupcake tastes better, but I doubt it.

"I'll see you tomorrow," I confirm, and she follows me to the door. Seeing this woman standing here on her own, in what's effectively a worksite, has me feeling protective. "Lock up after I leave."

She nods. "I will." There's something in her gaze that makes it hard to take another step away.

Snapping out of it, I head outside and load my truck. But unable to help myself, I pause and look back at her, where she's still standing at the shop entrance, like a woman I sure as hell shouldn't be looking at like I am.

I wait and watch as she closes the door, and once I hear the click of the lock, I jump into my truck and start the drive to my new place on Billionaire Boulevard.

The drive is quiet as I snake through the streets, my eyes moving from the road in front of me to the container next to me. Before I can think about it, I open it and shovel the dry and overly salted pastries into my mouth for the entire drive and force myself to like every single one of them.

Stomach be damned.

5

———

SAVANNAH

"Miss Shepherd?"

I look up, meeting the kind eyes of the local doctor.

"That's me." Heart thudding, I nod and stand.

"I'm Dr. Hamilton. Right this way." He smiles, and I follow him down the hallway to his office, ignoring the anxious swirls in my stomach. I haven't spent a lot of time in hospitals, so the strong smell of cleaning products isn't helping my nausea.

"How can I help you today?" The local doctor appears charming as we take a seat, and he looks at me with kind eyes. Yet another good-looking man in what is fast becoming a town of them. They should rename this town Handsome instead of Whispers, because the men in this place are next level.

"Ahhh, well, I'm new in town..." I wring my hands together, my palms sweating.

"The bakery, right?" He grins, and I nod.

"That's right. And... I thought it would be best to get a checkup. It's been a few months."

Prenatal care is something I take seriously. I always ensure I do my nightly reading to understand what my body is going through and how the baby is growing. I try to look at blogs and websites to get information without feeling overwhelmed about certain topics. Yet with everything that's been happening in my life, I haven't made it to a doctor to check on things in a little while. But I sleep, I eat all my vegetables, and I take my pregnancy vitamins. Plus, I feel the little one kicking almost every hour, so I know things are all okay.

He frowns, looking confused. "A checkup for what, exactly?"

"I'm due in about six weeks."

At that, he blanches. "You're pregnant?"

"Yes."

"Sorry, I just didn't even see it." He looks down at my stomach, complete surprise on his face.

"I've been carrying small. It just started to pop." I shrug because I have no other answer as to why I'm not showing unless I put it on full display.

Ever since I told my family, their unimpressed scowl burned into me, they were adamant that I didn't flout the fact that I was with child out of wedlock, and my mother forbade me from wearing anything remotely fitted. So now, in my flowing dresses and baggy tops, it wasn't even noticeable. I'm also a voluptuous woman naturally, so my curves do hide it well. But I know the little human is tucked in tight. My bruised organs are proof of that.

"Father?"

I shake my head. "Not in the picture."

"Family support?"

Clearing my throat, I swallow hard. "None of that either."

He nods. I don't have to tell him. It's like he already knows.

"Okay, well... with six weeks to go, it's a good time to see how things are going. Do you have your medical files from your previous doctor?" He starts tapping on his computer, setting up my file, I'm assuming.

He looks at me briefly when I don't respond, feeling uneasy, and I shake my head, but I offer no explanation. What is there to say? I grew up in a highly religious household that was part of a strict religious church. My parents told me I needed to give my baby to my sister and I wasn't to see a medical professional again? I know not everyone in Williamstown went to our church, but sometimes it felt like that, since my world was made up entirely of other church members. All I could think about from that point onward was escaping and doing things on my own for the sake of myself and my baby.

"I see..." He grabs his blood pressure cuff and slides it on my arm. I feel the tightening and try to relax. "Blood pressure is fine. How have you been feeling?"

"Fine. I mean, it's been a big few months, with the new business and moving to town, but aside from being tired and losing my sense of taste, I feel good."

"Sense of taste?"

"Yeah, not ideal as a baker. Is it common?"

"Very. Caused by fluctuating hormones usually. What vitamins are you taking?"

I tell him the brand and watch him think it over.

"Here, swap them out for this one." Reaching over, he grabs a bottle of pills from his cupboard. I look them over, familiar with the brand. They are the more expensive option.

"The ones you're using do have a small side effect that

will alter your sense of taste. This one has a slightly lower iron level, so you might find it helps." Making some more notes on his computer, he continues. "I would like to do a thorough workup. Urine samples to test for proteins to ensure we have no issues with preeclampsia. We can do an ultrasound today to check the baby's heart and formation. Do a thorough check of everything. Do you have insurance?" His smile is genuine. Warm. But his question leaves me feeling sick.

A sigh leaves me. "No. I-I don't."

His face falls a little before he brightens. "I have a new program here for prenatal care and new moms. I found that when I moved here to Whispers, there was a need to help support pregnant women, many who, like you, haven't had the care they needed due to work or other such commitments. What that'll mean is that you'll come and see me, and I'll help you here at the hospital with your pregnancy and delivery. We'll monitor you both and start a new file for you here at the hospital."

That all sounds too good to be true, and it makes me wary. "What's the catch?" I ask, sounding weaker than I'd like.

"Catch?" His eyebrows pinch.

"What will I need to pay?"

"Well, the program itself is funded by some local residents. It's a fully philanthropic program to ensure that Whispers is a town that will flourish with new children. It covers any hospital and birth related costs, but also meals, delivery of any medications, ongoing emotional support through connection with other women in the community. The program is completely free for you, however I'm also conducting research on how well it works, but you don't need to participate in the research. For those who do participate, I record their outcomes and use it for research purposes. All anonymously, of course. I'd include your data in a subset with other moms, so we can see the benefits of new babies in a small community and track if there are any commonalities among either medical or social outcomes."

I swallow roughly. "Anonymously?"

"One hundred percent. I use figures only, no names, no identifying information at all. It's a small study, one that I will probably collect data for quite some time before I publish any robust research. I'm using data from my own baby as well. I have a little girl; she keeps me on my toes."

For a moment, I sit with the information. Free healthcare is a game changer, especially for a new baby.

"Okay." I nod, feeling like I can take a full breath.

He smiles in a way that only assures me more. "Great! I'll start the paperwork. We're going to take good care of you, Savannah."

Free healthcare and a free builder... So far, things are looking up. Looks like moving to Whispers was the right decision, after all.

AFTER GETTING the all-clear from the doctor and seeing my baby on the small screen for the first time, I feel like I'm on cloud nine. To say that I got emotional when I heard the heartbeat and saw the tiny hands and feet would be an understatement. Tears fell quicker than I could catch them, but for once, they were happy tears. The baby is perfect. Healthy, happy, and everything is as it should be. Relief fills me and excitement builds.

He did say that my fundal height is smaller than expected, which explains why my bump is so small.

Although medically, there's nothing to worry about. I didn't find out the gender, deciding to keep it a surprise. All I cared about was looking at those ten little fingers and ten little toes. The doctor also mentioned how active the baby was, asking me if I was prepared to have one energetic child once they're born.

I was at the hospital all morning, which is why when I walk into the bakery, I'm shocked at what I see.

"Griffin?" I call out. He turned up early today, like he said he would. The now familiar frown on his face greeted me as I pulled out a fresh tray of cookies from the oven, the shape of which looked odd, telling me I obviously forgot yet another ingredient, before he got straight to work. I chose to ignore his scowl, as sexy as it was, since I wasn't sure what I did to prompt it. He's a conundrum I can't figure out.

I look over the new countertop and cupboard here at the front. All exactly how I imagined it to be. *He did all this?*

"You're back?" He pops out of the kitchen, and I look at him, open-mouthed.

"You've done all this while I've been gone this morning?" To him, as a professional, I'm sure this is a small job, but it would've taken me all week, if not longer. He's practically got it all how it needs to be apart from a bit of a clean.

He doesn't respond, instead asking, "You painted?" His eyes drill into mine, his tone accusing in a way that throws me off.

My head tilts. "Was I not supposed to?" After he left yesterday, instead of resting, like I probably should have, I continued with the work, painting the kitchen with a coat of stark white before I collapsed, exhausted. I have another coat to go tonight, but then it should be all done. The whole room looks sparkling now, compared to before. It's amazing the difference some paint can make.

"Thought you were tired."

Okay, angry and grumpy today, got it.

I have to refrain from rolling my eyes or throwing up my hands. "There's too much to do."

"I finished it," he says as I walk toward him in the kitchen.

"I can see that." I look over the new countertop, where I'll put the cash register and trays of cookies. It's a beautiful wood grain that's varnished and even prettier than I imagined.

"No, I mean, the painting."

My head shoots up, and I step into the kitchen, seeing the walls now with their second coat and a few specks of white paint covering Griffin.

"You painted?" Not only is the front practically done, but the walls in my kitchen are finished, the back door fixed, the smoke alarms new. *Oh, these damn hormones.*

"I've ordered a new counter here. It should arrive in a few days. I have to travel for work, but I'll come back when it arrives and install it."

I can't talk. I'm shocked. Eyes watering, my throat feels thick with emotion. I knew it wouldn't take him long, but this is amazing. I hold on to the old counter, feeling slightly dizzy. Overwhelmed. Completely taken aback. I'm sure Tanner is paying him well, but no one has ever helped me out so much.

"I... I don't know what to say." My words come out breathy, and he gives me a curious look.

"There're also a few new cupboards required in here, too. That spot over there, I thought I could build you some shelves for your flour and whatnot." He points to the area I had reserved for the baby. My heart skips a beat. *He wants to build me shelves?*

"Oh, that needs to stay empty."

Bringing his gaze back to me, he seems curious. He hasn't looked at my belly once, and I know I hide it well in these flowing dresses, especially as the doctor didn't even see it. But Griffin has been here for the past two days and hasn't mentioned anything, so I assume he either knows and doesn't care or has no idea.

"Empty?" he asks.

"I have some other plans for that area." I should tell him. But I'm hesitant. Within weeks, a new little baby will arrive and my life will change again. But right now, I like feeling like me. The girl who finally stepped out from under her family's rules, who chose this baby and this life. I'm scared that once everything changes again, I'll lose the parts of myself I only just found.

"How long have you been a builder?" I ask to change the subject. His work is good. Clean, thorough, high quality. My grandpa would be impressed.

"All my life."

I wonder exactly how long that may be. He's older than me, that's for sure. By at least a decade or two. He has thick dark hair, but there's a small sprinkle of gray at his temples. Not much, but up close, I see them. He also looks like a man with experience.

"Makes sense." I nod to myself.

"What does?" His eyes hold mine. He's a little guarded, almost like he wants to connect with me but can't for some reason.

"You did all this in less than a day. I've been building for about... a minute, and it would've taken me at least a week." I roll my lips, trying to lighten the mood, and I think I succeed when I see his lips quirk at the sides. It was small. A millimeter at most, but it happened.

"Who taught you to build?" He's humoring me, so I go with it. I'm enjoying talking with someone other than myself for a change. Being here on my own can be a little lonely sometimes.

"My grandpa. Every Sunday after church, I'd go to my grandparents' house. He taught me to hammer a nail, chop wood, change the oil in my car…"

"Sounds like a solid guy." Griffin nods in approval.

"Afterward, I'd go inside, and my grandma would teach me how to bake."

He nods slowly in understanding. "Betty?"

I smile. "Yeah. I named the bakery after her."

"It's a good name. Is she coming to see it?"

My smile falters. "No. They died. About a year ago now." The memory burns my eyes. They were the only ones ever in my corner. I was never the black sheep of the family, but I certainly wasn't the favorite. I had great grades throughout school, and I always did every chore and everything that was asked of me at home.

But I asked too many questions. I was always inquisitive, wanting to know why things were the way they were. Why the people coming to the church food pantry were not blessed by God with more? Why were girls and boys not treated the same? I loved books, often reading outside of the approved books which opened even more questions for me. I was seen as troublesome. As not being submissive enough. Throughout the years it was almost like all the love my parents had went into my older sister since she toed the line so well. So much so, there wasn't any left for me. My grandparents were the only ones to show me any kindness. No wonder I spent most weekends with them.

"I'm sorry."

"Yeah. Me too." I take a breath and shake off the emotion. "So where do you travel to?"

"This week, I'm heading to Sundown Valley over near Sonoma."

My eyebrows rise. "Sonoma? Wow, that sounds amazing. I haven't traveled much. I hardly ever left my small hometown."

"It's a beautiful part of the country. You should go sometime."

I sigh. "Yeah. It'll be a dream," I say absentmindedly. Because traveling is on my bucket list, but with my life now laid out for me, with a new business and a new baby, travel isn't going to happen for a long time.

Checking the time, he grabs his toolbelt off the counter. "I need to go. I fly out later tonight."

"Oh... oh, of course..." I pull myself together. *He has a life, Savannah. One that doesn't involve talking to you.*

As Griffin grabs his things, he pauses and looks at me, taking a few steps closer that have my heart beating faster.

"Do you have any more cinnamon rolls?"

"You liked them?" My grin is instant. I love it when people eat the food I make. I try to put so much love and attention into every roll, every bun.

"They were like nothing else I've eaten before."

Shifting over to where I left some goods to cool this morning, I tell him, "Here... I don't have any cinnamon rolls, but I made some fresh cheese pies this morning." I quickly put some in a container. They look a little different to how they normally do, but I hope they taste great, nonetheless. "Please... take these. It's not much, but I'm so grateful for all your help. I wish I could offer you more." My words rush out as I thrust the container toward him.

His face softens a little. "Are these as good as your cinnamon rolls?"

"I hope so..." I cringe, because I really don't know.

"I'll be back in a few days. Here's my number... in case you need anything." He passes me his business card, and I take it. It's thick. Glossy. Luxurious, almost. He takes the container, and as he does, his fingers graze my own. Prickles coat my skin, and my breath hitches.

He looks at where our hands connect, his scowl still etched across his face, and I blow out my breath. He's magnetic. And I'm pregnant. I pull my hand away quickly, like I've been burned. These stupid thoughts about my grumpy yet very good-looking builder are ridiculous.

"Thank you..." I roll his card over in my hands, gently, careful not to bend it.

He clears his throat and turns to walk out, his toolbox in one hand and my container in another. My eyes drop to his ass, filling out his jeans just right, making my heart race, the flush across my cheeks and chest instant. I'm going straight to hell, just like my mother said.

"Griffin!"

He halts, turning immediately and looking straight at me. I pause. For too long. My chest feels like it's heaving for breath as he watches me closely. All words leave my brain when he takes a step toward me, his eyes pure molten.

"Ahhh, safe travels..." Inwardly, I cringe at myself. His jaw pops, yet he gives me a small nod before he walks out, and I sigh. Scrubbing my face, I wonder if I could be any more foolish.

With him now gone, I pull on my apron and get to work cleaning out the front to make the shop sparkling for opening day. I push Griffin and his sexy scowl to the back of my mind, but I'm already planning to make an extra batch of cinnamon rolls for when he returns in a few days.

As I get busy, I hear a knock at the front door. I quickly wipe my hands and rush out.

"Hello?" I greet a woman who's standing at the entrance. "I'm sorry. We're not open yet."

She gives me a kind smile. "I know, but I saw the help wanted sign in the window, and I wanted to drop off my details."

Gleeful surprise takes over me. "Oh, of course. Come in." I open the door and invite her in, excited to talk with her. I've had that sign up for weeks now, and she's the first person to apply.

"As you can see, I'm still getting things organized. Hopefully I'll be open in a few weeks."

"Of course." She nods and looks back at me.

I wipe my dusty hands off on my apron. "I'm Savannah, owner of Betty's Bakery."

"I'm Melissa Thorton." She smiles, and we shake hands.

"So can you tell me a bit about yourself? Your experience?" I haven't hired staff before, so I'm not sure what to ask. But I need someone part-time to help out when I have the baby and during busy periods.

"Oh, well, I've lived in the area most of my life. My husband and I live farther out of town. I've been a housewife for many years and would like to start some work to bring in a bit of extra money. I cook at home, I bake, so I'm familiar with kitchens and baking in general, and when I was in town last week, I saw your sign and spoke to my husband, and... here I am." She seems nice. Friendly, personable. She'd be great on the register serving customers.

Being local, she'd know people from around here too, which would be beneficial.

"I don't need anyone with lots of experience or anything. The job would be casual, helping me out, serving customers and restocking the products. I'll need someone here when I run errands and have appointments, that kind of thing," I rush out, excited that someone actually applied.

She nods eagerly. "I'm happy to help out wherever's needed. The hours also work well for me. I don't have any other commitments that would prohibit me from coming in whenever you need."

This feels right. Feels good. Like another piece is slipping into place.

"Great! Well, how about we start in a week? You can help me set up the front, and we can go through the register system together because that confuses me more than anything. That way, we can see if it all works out before opening day."

"Oh, fantastic. I'm looking forward to getting out of the house a little more and seeing all the locals around town."

"Perfect. Well, I'll call you to set up the first day." With a grin, I walk her back to the door.

"Thanks so much," she gushes, clearly happy to have a job.

"Thank you! I'm so glad you stopped in." I watch her head out and down the street, glancing back to wave, before I close and lock the door.

Leaning back against the door, I take in the space. It's all coming together—the bakery, the business, this new life I'm building. I rub my belly, the skin pulling a little tighter each day. I need to get everything open before the baby comes. I need the income. I need the stability.

I walked away from my family with nothing but my small inheritance, and they've made their disappointment loud and clear. My sister was already buying baby clothes and picking out names for the child she thought I was going to give her, yet neither she nor my mother ever listened when I said I wanted to keep the baby. When I packed my bags and left home and reinforced that I was not giving them what they wanted, their shock quickly turned to anger.

So when this baby is born, I know I'll have a fight on my hands. And I need to be ready. I need to prove, to them and to myself, that I can do this. I can work. I can run a business. I can provide for my child.

6

GRIFFIN

"You're back a day early?" Tanner looks at me with a quirked eyebrow as we sit at his bar. Hudson is here too, the three of us meeting up for dinner.

"Got done in Sundown Valley early." I sip the whiskey in my hand. Tanner sure as hell makes a nice drop. I have stock of each of his releases in all my houses, so no matter where I am, I'm never without.

"Early? Is Stonemore a lighter build than you thought?" Tanner watches me carefully. They're not competitors as such. One in the whiskey game, one in wine. But they compete in the overall liquor market, so I'm careful with my words.

"Not by a long shot," I share. "The build we're doing for them is huge. Luxurious. It'll make the Stonemore brand the standout feature of the entire wine region. People will flock from everywhere to go to Sundown Valley to see it. A premier destination. One I'm grateful to be a part of."

Truth be told, I worked twenty-hour days, three days straight, just to get back here quicker.

"Just miss us, then?" Hudson chimes in with a cheeky grin.

"Never. I need to wrap up the bakery this week." I take another sip, needing the burn. I've done nothing but think of the beautiful baker since I met her. Outwardly beautiful, of course, but also determined, with a strong work ethic, if her long days and early mornings are anything to go by. Yet aside from me, there doesn't seem to be anyone else in that bakery to help her. She's all alone, which doesn't sit well with me. The fact that her back screen door was broken and her smoke alarms didn't work left me furious. Whispers is a safe place, but there are assholes everywhere.

"Ahhhh. Savannah tells me you like her cinnamon rolls." My eyes flick to Tanner. *He's seen her?* Jealousy coils deep within—a feeling I haven't felt before.

"Have you tried them?"

"Unfortunately..." he murmurs.

I know they're terrible, but when I saw her get all glassy-eyed while talking about her grandparents, I wanted to do anything to make her smile. So I asked for more. The cheese pies she offered me were like cardboard, yet I shoved every last one into my mouth when on my jet that night. They were so bad, I didn't shit for days.

"She's lost her sense of taste. Not sure why. But she wanted me to taste test them," I grumble, pissed that Tanner has eaten her goods now too.

"I mean, it's a common side effect," Hudson quips, and I look at him and frown.

"Side effect?"

"It happens in about ninety percent of women in their first trimester. Those in their third, like Savannah, it drops to about ten to fifteen percent of women."

My soul leaves my body. I feel it swoosh out from my legs down through my feet. Thank God I'm sitting down.

"Trimester?" My voice is like gravel. I look between Tanner and Hudson, both watching me, and I feel like I've been hit with a hammer.

"Savannah's pregnant," Tanner says, deadpan.

"Since when?" My pulse spikes. Chest tightens. I feel like I've been sucker punched.

"Yeah, I didn't see it at first either. But she only has a few weeks to go," Hudson confirms.

"A few weeks?" I nearly choke on my whiskey. "How the hell is that possible?"

"She's carrying small," Tanner says. "But it's there. You just weren't looking."

I wasn't. I was too damn focused on the curve of her smile, the way she seemed so incredibly grateful for the small amount of work I did for her. I also didn't miss the fire in her eyes when she talked about rebuilding that bakery. I saw her. But I didn't *see* her.

"I mean... she hasn't got a big belly or anything," I mutter, feeling like a complete idiot. But I've never been around pregnant women. No sisters. No mom. No clue. Tanner and Victoria have a kid, and I saw her belly, but she was waddling for weeks, though. Savannah is the opposite, up and down ladders, painting, baking. Not a waddle in sight.

"Women all present differently. Lacy was always on the go with our little one." Hudson grins, happier than ever with his little family of four.

"Victoria ate her way through her last trimester. I had to fly in so many fucking burgers and chocolate layer cakes from New York it was almost embarrassing." Tanner rubs his eyes, and I still sit there, dumbfounded.

"How did I not see it?" I shake my head, upset with myself that I didn't work it out.

Tanner's gaze sharpens. "She's a single mom-to-be, who's doing that bakery all on her own. Why did you think I called you in to help?"

"Fuck..." I scrub my face before I grab my glass and down the whole thing.

"Did you sign her up to the prenatal program?" Tanner looks at Hudson and I watch them both.

"You know I can't tell you that. Don't worry though, I'm taking good care of her." Hudson nods, confirming Tanners thoughts without saying as such.

"Prenatal program?" I have no idea what they're talking about.

"Hudson and I have jointly funded a program here in Whispers for women who are pregnant," Tanner tells me. Of course he has. Giving back to this town is one of his biggest jobs, I'm sure.

I nod, but I'm not hearing them anymore. My mind is spinning. She's pregnant. She's working herself into the ground. And I've been standing there like some dumb bastard, eating her cardboard cheese pies and pretending I wasn't affected by her.

"The father?" I ask, wondering if I want to know.

"Not in the picture." Hudson is careful with his words.

I grip the edge of the table, knuckles white, that old, familiar rage stirring. The kind I'd buried deep, the kind that came from years of watching people walk away from their responsibilities. From kids who deserved better. From me.

I'd seen it too many times in the system. Fathers who vanished. Mothers who gave up. Promises broken before they were ever made. I bounced around from home to home, not one adult giving a shit about anything other than the paycheck I could provide them. It's a miracle I'm still alive, really. Hit my mid-teens and found a life of petty crime, until one night, a foster father came home drunk, just like my bio dad used to, and started hitting the younger kids in his care. All I saw that night was red. I was their only hope of protection, and I made sure I didn't miss. Thankfully, I knocked him out; otherwise, I would've killed him. A short stint in juvie helped me get on the right path, and I never went back to that house. I have no idea what happened to him, and I don't care.

"Griff." Tanner's voice is quiet but firm. "You okay?"

"I don't get it. How does someone just leave her like that? How does someone know she's carrying their kid and not show up?" The feelings of abandonment I carry surface like a tidal wave. Scars from my fear of getting close to someone, just for them to be ripped away. This is why I work constantly or have my head in puzzles and crosswords. If I relax too much, if I get too close to people, I'll unravel.

Tanner doesn't speak. He doesn't have to.

"She's weeks away from having a baby," I say, more to myself than them. "And she's lifting heavy boxes, painting walls, walking upstairs, ladders, up early, finishing late." I grab the bottle of whiskey in the middle of the table and pour another glass. One which I down as fast as the first.

Hudson shifts beside me, but Tanner keeps his eyes on me.

"Well, the town is ready to support her, and I appreciate all the work you're doing to help her get up and running." Tanner nods to me, his words not putting me at ease.

I need to go. I need space to think. I haven't felt this mix of emotions in a long time.

"I gotta go." I stand abruptly, the chair squealing on the timber floor.

"You alright?" Tanner leans back, looking at me. Hudson's gaze is assessing as well.

"Fine. I had a few big days, and I need to sleep." Grabbing my jacket, I say a quick goodbye and stride out of the bar like it's on fire.

I slam my door as I jump in my truck. My hands grip the steering wheel tight as my breathing becomes labored.

"This is bullshit..." I grit out to myself, hating that I get so worked up about this.

My past feels like it's wrapping itself around my chest, heavy, black, and miserable. The raw feeling of being left alone, of being scared, unable to depend on anyone. I know what it's like to have no support, no genuine care. No love. It fucking enrages me that, even all these years later, there's still asshole parents in this world. A man who would leave his baby. Leaves the mother of his child alone, without help, without love.

Back when I was young, it was almost the norm. Not that it hurt any less, but the number of kids who were damaged from adults not providing them with the necessities of life was a situation I grew up in and know all too well. But seeing it still happen... Seeing society become bigger and better, yet still not providing for the kids of this country, leaves me hurt, angry, and bitter. One half of me wants to cry, while the other wants to hit something.

This is why I never get close. Never stay in one place for long. Never commit. Not just to women, but to people. Tanner's the only man I've known for longer than I remember. Even then, I keep some distance. Even if just geographically.

But there's something about this woman that has me

questioning everything I've ever done, and that almost frightens me more than anything else.

I suck in a breath and try to pull myself together, forcing myself to turn the ignition and drive. When I detour and drive past the bakery, as expected, the lights are still on, and I see her shadow moving about in the kitchen. The sight eases my pain a little, with a newfound respect for my local baker. Resilience is a hard muscle to build, but one I have a feeling she has had a lot of experience using.

I turn quickly and head to my place before I do something stupid, like go and knock on her door.

I'm her builder. She's almost a new mom. It needs to be that simple.

7

SAVANNAH

I chew the tip of my pencil, my eyes homed in. Three down, five letters: *"Something that slips away."* Time? Maybe. Or sleep? I stare at the empty boxes as if they might fill themselves, going almost cross-eyed since I barely slept last night, my growing middle making getting comfortable harder.

I sip my coffee and stall. Oh my God, my taste is coming back. It took a week since seeing the doctor and being on the new vitamins, but I breathe out a sigh of relief, grateful that I can now taste something other than metallic bitterness. My eyes prick with tears. It's nothing to cry over, but the waterworks are almost an hourly occurrence this week.

As I wipe my eyes, Griffin walks into the kitchen with what looks like a piece of stainless steel.

"What's wrong?" He nearly balks. He's been here since this morning. His scowl is deeper today than I've ever seen it, and he's barely said two words to me.

"Oh, it's nothing... it's just... a crossword." I lift the local paper as a poor excuse to cover my tears. He looks at me like he doesn't believe me, then puts his tools down and walks over, peering over my shoulder.

"Youth."

I frown, look back at the puzzle. Sure enough, *youth* fits.

"You do crosswords?" I'm surprised. He doesn't seem like the crossword type. I used to do them sometimes with my grandpa, an activity I still try to do regularly, particularly when I want to feel closer to him.

"They help quiet my brain." He steps back to his tools and resumes his tasks. I watch him, trying to work him out. He is a puzzle, this man, one I think no one else has managed to solve.

"Oh, before I forget, I got you a key cut." I pass the new key over to him. "I know you start early, and while I'm usually up, I thought a key would help you access the bakery at any time. I don't want to hold you up on your other jobs..."

I think this is what people usually do. And I trust him. Tanner Whiteman wouldn't just get anyone to help me. This I've come to learn.

"I'll keep it safe." He pockets the key as I slide off the stool, wanting to eat something to test my taste buds. "I think I got my taste back." I smile, and it's then I see it. His eyes drop down to my belly. *He knows.* "I can finally try one."

Stepping over to the cinnamon buns I baked this morning, I grab one, excited as they're still warm, and take a bite. I start to chew, then pause. The taste, the texture, it's all wrong. I look at Griffin, my mouth full, my eyes wide before I grab a napkin and spit it out.

"You've been eating this?" I'm horrified. It tastes like cardboard. Dry, not sweet at all.

He shrugs. "Yeah."

"Oh my God, why? They're disgusting!" I throw out the

one in my hand and then proceed to throw the entire tray in the trash.

"They're fine."

I look at him quickly, confused.

"They are far from fine. No, no, noooo, my grandma would be rolling in her grave." I slap my hand on my forehead, and I see his lips curve a little, his eyes not leaving me.

"With laughter?" He rolls his lips a little, and I can't help but grin.

"Yes, she would. Probably sitting up there, having a glass of sherry, taking great delight in my bakery mishaps... I'm so sorry you had to endure that. I swear, I'm not trying to kill you with my food." I cringe, because I gave a whole batch to Tanner a few days ago too.

"I'm sure if you were, I'd be dead already. You seem like the kind of woman who knows what she wants and is doing her best to get it."

I pause at his assessment. I've never thought of myself like that. But that's exactly what I'm doing. At first, it felt foreign, but now, it feels like it was always inside of me, just waiting to get out.

"Well, after these disasters, my career in this town will be over before it begins." I squeeze my eyes together, feeling a little helpless. Stupid. I always try to taste my products before I give them to anyone, and the one time I can't, they taste like feet.

He clears his throat, gaze softening. "It's not that bad..."

"But no one will buy from me again. No one will— Oh!" My hand moves swiftly to my stomach, the pain intense.

"Shit." Griffin drops everything in his hands and rushes over.

"Ow..." I wince as I hold my belly, the tightening pain entirely new.

"What is it? What's wrong?" I hear his panic, but I also feel his hand. Warm, large, solid, and comforting on my back.

Fear takes over, making my voice shaky. "I don't know..."

"Let's get you to the doctor."

"It's okay, I'll be— Ooow..." I wince again as my knees buckle.

"No, I'm taking you." Without asking, Griffin picks me up, the movement so quick, I barely have time to register what's happening as my feet leave the floor and he walks us out of the bakery.

"Griffin?" I grab on to him as he marches out into the street, straight to his truck.

"I've got you. It will be okay." His face is still hard set, but his voice soothes me.

He places me into his truck with precise yet gentle movements, which contrast completely with the man I see working in my bakery.

"Here. Let's get you settled."

I swallow as he reaches over, putting my seat belt on, and even though I'm panicked and holding my belly, I'm completely aware of his closeness.

I'm trying to breathe through the anxiety taking over as he closes the door and runs around to the driver's side and speeds us away from the bakery.

"It's too early... I have another few weeks. Something's wrong..." I say quietly, and his frown deepens.

"You'll be okay," he grits out.

"Maybe I did something I shouldn't have. Maybe I didn't—"

He cuts me off. "It's not your fault. Let's get Hudson to see you before you get yourself too worked up."

Nodding, I swallow hard as he looks at me, his eyes

running down and back up, like he's assessing me, and within five minutes, he's screeching into the hospital parking lot.

"I'm scared, Griffin. Ow..." I grab my belly tighter, like my hold will ease the pain, but it doesn't. Griffin's out of the truck and at my door before I've even had a chance to take off my seat belt.

"Come on." He pulls me from the seat, again carrying me into the hospital like I don't weigh the same as a whale.

"Hudson!" Griffin barks at the doctor so loudly I jump in his arms.

Dr. Hamilton looks up at us from where he's standing at the reception desk and immediately springs straight into action.

"Down here." The two men stride down a small hallway as I feel another pulse of pain rippling across my abdomen.

"Ahhhh..." I try to be quiet, gritting my teeth to contain the pain, but I can't help the whimper that escapes. I curl into Griffin a little more, gripping on to his shirt, wanting to hide in his chest.

His hold on me tightens. "It's okay, sweetness..." I barely hear his words, yet I feel them against my hair. I think he must have misspoke.

"What's happening?" Griffin places me on the bed and steps to the side as Hudson starts his assessment.

"Sharp pain... across here." I show the doctor.

"Griffin, give us a moment," Hudson tells him, and I look up, seeing Griffin watching me before his jaw tics and he nods, stepping out of the room as the doctor gets to work.

~

"Braxton Hicks. It's pretty common. About fifty percent of pregnant women feel them at some point. They're not dangerous as such, but they're a good indication that you need to start resting a little more. Keep your water intake up. Hydration plays a role."

I breathe out in relief. "Will they continue?"

The doctor writes a few things down in my file. "They're a little unpredictable. They could remain until you go into labor, or you might not experience any more. Again, I think you need more rest. You only have a few weeks to go, but the baby can decide to turn up at any time now, although I would prefer they stay inside a little longer. If they reoccur, or if you experience anything similar, come straight back here, and we can check you out. But as I said last time, I hope you're ready for one energetic baby." His wide smile puts me more at ease as I stand and walk toward the door.

I've been here for a few hours, and in that time, they've run tests and had a heart monitor on both me and the baby. The care and attention here is second to none.

"So is that what labor is going to feel like?" I gulp, waiting for his answer, because I'm not in a hurry to feel that pain again.

"I'm afraid it will be similar. But we have a variety of options to help you through it all. Different pain relief options, or even an epidural, if that's the path you want to go down."

I swallow, unsure. The pain, although I got through it, was intense. I hope this baby comes out quickly.

"I suggest you go home and put your feet up for the afternoon," he tells me as we walk down the hall.

"Oh, I've got a few more things—" I start to tell him but get cut off by a gruff voice I wasn't expecting.

"She'll rest."

My head whips around, and I see Griffin, standing there at the end of the hall like a big ogre ready to pounce.

"You're still here?" I look at him in shock as my eyes get glassy. No one has ever shown this kind of support to me, not ever. Not while pregnant, and apart from my grandparents, not throughout my life.

"I am. I'll take you home."

I stare up at him for what I'm sure is too long. Am I dreaming? I blink a few times, but he remains in my vision. I thought I might have had to call the local taxi to get home or something. I assumed he left hours ago.

"Make sure she rests for the remainder of the day. And don't forget Harvey's party tomorrow. Actually, why don't you bring Savannah," Hudson says.

I look at my doctor, confused.

"My son's birthday tomorrow. A big party. Lots of kids. Good way to get you prepared for your new role as a parent and to meet some more of the locals." Hudson grins, and I look back at Griffin, my brain not connecting.

"Oh, I'm..." I start to say I'm busy, because I still have cleaning to do, and now that I have my taste back, I should be baking all night.

"We'll be there," Griffin tells him without hesitation.

"Great. Take care." And just like that, my grumpy builder picks me up and walks me back out to his truck.

"I can walk, you know." My words are halfhearted because I'm exhausted. The early mornings, late nights, and all that poking and prodding at the hospital has my mind and body more than ready to rest.

"I know," is all he says as I lean into him a little, enjoying the feeling of being taken care of. He puts me in the truck quickly yet tenderly, ensuring I'm secure, and we get on our way.

He remains quiet for the entire drive back, silently brooding, and I feel my weariness deepen, yet glad to finally get back to the bakery and see it all still in one piece.

As the truck pulls up, I make a move to get out.

"Thanks, Griffin, I don't..." He's out of the truck and his door slammed mid-sentence. I sit, stunned for a moment, before my door whips open.

"Wha..." My words fail me as he scoops me up from the seat and carries me inside. Being in his embrace, my heart pounds. I didn't have time to think about it earlier, but now that I'm calmer, I feel his large hands wrap around me. I take comfort in his protective hold, and I swallow down the feelings building; they have no business popping up now, as my friendly builder gives me a helping hand inside.

"The doctor said to rest," he grits out as we step inside the bakery. I get ready to drop from his hold, but he keeps me in his arms tight, walking straight through the retail area and out the back to the kitchen.

"I need to remake the cinnamon buns." I start to wriggle so he'll set me down. Not wanting to embarrass myself because I can think of nothing I want more than to relax in his embrace and snuggle into his very hard and very masculine chest. My eyes snag on my baking trays. I want to make another batch. I want to make something for this party tomorrow.

"No, you need to rest. You also need to hire some help around here." He doesn't let go of me and his steps don't falter as he climbs the small staircase leading to my apartment.

"I have a local woman, Melissa, coming in to work with me. What are you doing?" If I could move, I would, but there's no way I can get my pregnant body out of his grip, and the longer I'm in it, the more comfortable it's feeling.

"Putting you to bed." He hits the landing and pauses. I look around to see what he's seeing. My small studio is open plan. It's just me, so it's not like I need much. My bed in the corner, a few cupboards, a small kitchenette, and then off to one side is the small bathroom with a shower. The one I'm already struggling to fit into. It's not much, but it's more than adequate.

"I don't need to sleep yet." But like my body is fighting against me, my mouth opens involuntarily, and a small yawn escapes.

"Yeah, sweetness, doesn't look like it."

Eyes wide, I look at him and blink. There's that name again. I thought for sure I imagined it earlier. Maybe I'm already asleep. Maybe I'm dreaming. It's my rampant hormones again, making me think I'm hearing these soft words from a sexy, gruff man who's manhandling my pregnant body like he's put on this earth for that exact purpose.

"I have to bake." My words come out strong, yet as he lays my body onto my bed, I immediately sink into the soft, old mattress and know I'm not going to get out of it in a hurry.

"Sleep. Doctor's orders. I'll work downstairs, and I'll lock up when I leave." He pulls a blanket over me before he turns and walks straight back out. I watch his back disappear and then hear his boots hit each step on his way down. I'm lost for words. I'm not his responsibility, and we're not friends. But today when I needed someone, he was there.

I lie there, looking at the ceiling, caressing my bump. I have a feeling Griffin is like a caramel. Hard on the outside, gooey on the inside. His eyes are brown, the same color as the candy too. I take a few deep breaths, trying to de-stress. Griffin and Hudson are right. I do need to rest.

"We'll be fine, baby. Just fine..." I tell my cherub, rubbing my tummy, and as my eyes slowly close, I start to dream of a hard but gooey caramel.

MY EYES PING OPEN, and I'm immediately awake as the light from beneath the curtains shines in on my face.

"Urghh." I start to sit up, the endeavor taking a little longer than usual. I'm already puffing before my feet hit the floor. I look at the clock, seeing it's four a.m. and need to blink a few times. *I slept for twelve hours? How is that even possible?*

"Wow, you're really taking all my energy these last few weeks, aren't you, baby?" I rub my belly as I head to the shower to get ready for the day.

I've always been an early riser. For years, I worked the early shift at one of the local Williamstown bakeries, which was located right near the church. Waking at four, baking all morning, offering fresh delights for everyone on their way to work or home from church. I think it's the quiet of it that I like so much. Before anyone else is awake, before the world starts, I get to work in my own little world, putting all my attention into the dough. But that was before I lost my job the minute the community discovered I was having a baby out of wedlock.

Once I'm fresh and clean, I throw on some clothes, put my hair back, and start my trek downstairs. I hit the kitchen, seeing the lights still on, and frown. As my eyes canvass the room, my head rears back. Right in the middle is now a long, professional stainless-steel bench, with custom-made cupboards underneath. My ingredients have been sorted and stacked, my baking trays are all itemized in size in what looks to be a customized rack, and all the drop sheets from the painting yesterday have been removed, and the floor mopped.

"Oh... my goodness..."

Griffin must have done it all. I reach out and grab my apron, putting it on as I walk tentatively through the space in awe. I run my fingers across the stainless steel. My kitchen now looks like a fully functional professional bakery. The only spot left is the small section to the side, where I plan to put the baby while I work.

He must've worked all night, and this is above and beyond anything I was expecting. My stomach flutters, but I blame it on my baby.

Inspired from my thoughts of him last night, I've decided to make some sweet caramels for the party. It was nice of Hudson to invite me. I know Tanner was welcoming, and Griffin is amazing, so I'm starting to think this small town is just inclusive like that. And I need to repay everyone for their kindness. Starting with the birthday party today.

I step out toward the front door, to ensure Griffin locked up after he left last night, but I take a few steps and stall. Because there on the floor, with a rolled-up sweater under his head, is Griffin.

He slept on the floor. He stayed with me for the entire night.

There goes that flutter again.

8

———

GRIFFIN

My neck and back are killing me, and as I roll over, I remember why. I slept on a hardwood floor for a few hours, right here in the bakery.

"Arghhhh." Moaning, I start to wake, sitting and stretching a little, smelling the sweet aromas of freshly baked goods wafting from the kitchen. It's the kind of smell love makes. From someone who spends time perfecting. That same sweet scent I breathe in whenever Savannah is nearby. It clings to her hair and her skin, like she's brushed herself with sugar before stepping into the world, subtly giving off a sweetness I really shouldn't be touching.

Rubbing my eyes, I swallow, trying to moisten my dry throat. I'm still tired after a big few days both here and in Sundown Valley. Standing gingerly, feeling older than my years, I walk toward the noise and smells of the kitchen, my night flooding back to me. I spent hours getting it ready for her. The kitchen, the retail space. All she needs to do is sort her things and she can open. I also didn't want to leave her. Not alone. At night. Not after her needing the doctor. It scared me, seeing her double over in pain and knowing she doesn't have anyone else. I sped to the hospital so fast; I'm surprised I didn't take out someone on the way.

I pause in the doorway to watch her. She looks vibrant as always. Her delicious curves are food for my eyes. She's been busy, clearly up for a while if the rows of cupcakes are anything to go by. I'm glad she hired some help, because I have no idea how she was going to manage all this when the baby is born.

She works quietly, yet diligently, not noticing me as she moves through the kitchen like she was born to do it. My eyes flick to the clock on the wall. Six a.m. Barely light out.

"Morning." No point in hiding. She obviously saw me sleeping.

"Oh... good morning." She turns at the sound of my voice, a smile pulling at her lips. "Here..." She pours fresh coffee from her percolator into a mug and walks it to me.

"Mmm. Thank you." I take the cup, ignoring the burn in my chest at her thoughtfulness, keeping the coffee hot, knowing I'd need one. My hands brush against hers, and a small rumble starts in my chest. One of contentment.

"I thought you might need it." Our eyes meet, and I keep my mouth shut, giving her a small nod. "Soooo, make a habit of sleeping on bakery floors?"

I take a sip of coffee and almost groan again. "First time." I'm not one for a lot of conversation. Especially when I first wake. I should've said good morning and left immediately. Yet here I am, feet rooted to the ground, watching her.

"Work late?" She swatches me for a moment before getting back to her baking.

"Somewhat. But I sure as hell wasn't leaving you here alone." My tone makes me sound like an asshole.

Her brow pinches as her eyes flick up to mine again. "I'm perfectly fine and capable..."

"You were in the hospital yesterday. As I said, I sure as hell wasn't leaving you here alone."

Nodding, she bites the inside of her lip. "Well... thank you. I appreciate your concern and thank you again for taking me to the hospital yesterday." She's cute when she's coy.

"What's that smell?" It smells like her. All sugar and sweet. I didn't mean to call her sweetness yesterday. But with her in my arms, holding her tight, that's all I could smell in her hair. The powdered sugar sweetness.

"Oh, I made a fresh batch of cinnamon buns. *These* are delicious. I taste tested them already, so they're safe." She puts one on a small plate and offers it to me along with a big smile, making me feel like the full sun's rays are shining on my face. "And I also made some cupcakes and caramels."

"Caramels?" I frown as I take a sip of coffee before I put it down, my stomach now growling.

"I didn't want to turn up to the kids' party today without something."

Fuck. The party. I wasn't going to go. Snotty little creatures will be high on sugar and excitement and probably want me to play with them, even though I always say no. I don't go to many of these parties; I've stayed well away for years, never wanting to get too close. I usually send the obligatory gift, something ridiculously expensive they'll never use. But when Hudson invited Savannah yesterday, it was a done deal. You can sure as hell believe I'll be taking her.

"That's nice of you." I swallow before I lift the cinnamon bun to my mouth, preparing my throat and stomach for the bland taste. But as the bun touches my lips, then the warm icing hits my tongue, my eyes almost roll into the back of my head.

"Are they good?" She watches me hesitantly, a small wince on her face, waiting for my verdict. Even if they weren't, I'd tell her they're perfect, but today, I don't need to lie.

"These are..." I take another bite. "These are... delicious." God, they almost melt in my mouth. I've eaten a lot of cinnamon buns in my time. These are by far the best.

"Really?" Her eyebrows rise like she can't believe it.

"Really," I confirm, and she grins even wider and lets out a little happy squeak before turning back to her baking.

From the back, she doesn't look pregnant. A little curvy in all the right places, but nothing to indicate she's carrying a child.

"The baby got a father?" My voice is still rough from sleep, and the words rumble out of me before I have time to rein them back in. I clench my jaw as her body stills for a moment before she moves to take out another tray from the oven.

"No. Not one who wants anything to do with either of us." She huffs a small laugh like I said the most ridiculous thing, the news causing my teeth to grind. "I thought he was the one. Dated for a while. He told me he was going to marry me. This"—she looks at her belly before continuing —"was a surprise. Not planned. It turned out he didn't want the responsibility, which did come as a big surprise to me. He skipped town as soon as I told him."

The bun I ate sits heavy in my gut as she grabs a piping bag and starts icing the cupcakes.

"No new boyfriend? Partner?" I find myself pressing, my voice like gravel. I shouldn't be asking. Have no idea why I am. There's no one here. She gets no visitors, no gentleman callers that I've noticed.

"Nope. None of those are interested in me either. As you

can see, I'm a real man magnet." Her sarcastic humor doesn't make me smile. I'm not sure how a woman like her can be single. My eyes drape over her again, unable to help myself. She's beautiful.

"So no one will mind me taking you to the party today, then. Good to know."

She turns and looks at me, and I sip my coffee, acting like none of that bothers me. Because outside of the asshole people she's had in her life, it doesn't.

"What about you? No wife? Girlfriend? Waiting for you to take them?" She's tentative with her words. The two of us asking the questions we want answers to. I take another sip to hide my grin.

I shake my head slowly, eyes on hers. "No. No one."

"Good to know." She passes my own words back to me, before turning back around and finishing off the cupcakes. I reach for another cinnamon bun, not able to stop at one.

9

———

SAVANNAH

My baking skills are back. After Griffin ate my cinnamon buns faster than ever before, I knew they were good. Now with two dozen cupcakes iced and packed, ready to go, along with two dozen small jars of caramels, I feel proud and a little tired from my morning activities.

But I had to keep myself busy. It's not every day you wake and stumble across a big, broad, good-looking man sleeping on your floor. I still feel like coffee and breakfast were not enough to offer him. I assumed he worked late and stayed, but when he mentioned not wanting to leave me alone, my stomach swooped and my knees weakened. I had to continue to move around my kitchen, pretending to fix my baked goods, to keep from thinking too hard about it. Sympathy. That's obviously what it is. Seeing me pregnant and all by myself, some people feel the need to help, and while I appreciate it, I don't need his or anyone else's pitying gaze.

I can do this. On my own.

While he left not long after finishing his coffee and a

second cinnamon bun this morning, needing to go home and shower, I'm refreshed and a little nervous about attending the birthday party today. But I know it's a good opportunity for me to meet more people and hopefully spread the word about the bakery. I need to make it a success. I need to ensure this plan of mine works. There's no way I'll be going home with my head hung low in defeat. I'll never step foot in Williamstown again.

After tidying the apartment, I slide my feet into my sandals, feeling instant relief and a small amount of accomplishment they still fit without issue. Tying laces and clipping buckles on my shoes is now harder to do. I feel useless even trying.

Now fully dressed, I head into the bathroom to ensure my hair is still how I left it. Down today. I usually wear it up, out of my face, so much so, it feels odd to have it down. But I'm trying to put my best foot forward with this town. And Griffin. I might be pregnant, but at least my skin and hair are glowing.

As I tap on a little lip gloss, my cell vibrates.

Mom.

I stare at her name on the screen for what feels like an eternity as my stomach coils, and I feel like I want to dry retch. But instead, I answer.

"Hi, Mom."

"Faith." Her tone has my shoulders lowering in disappointment. I haven't been called by my real name in months. I took on my middle name Savannah when I moved, wanting to leave behind all my history and start fresh. But I can tell by her tone she isn't calling to make amends. Isn't calling to say they were wrong to disown me for becoming pregnant and not wanting to hide it. I secretly hoped she might call to apologize and now want me to come home. Not sure why I even expect it at this point.

"Have you had the baby?"

Okay, straight to the point.

"No. Still waiting. It's not exactly something I can schedule."

I match her energy. I know her beliefs are so ingrained, there's no way she can move past the horror of me falling pregnant without being married.

"Honestly, Faith, the shame you've brought on this family. Pregnant, alone, no husband, no plan. It's disgraceful."

I hold back an exasperated sigh. "I have a plan. You know I have the bakery…"

"Oh, for heaven's sake. Your grandmother put too many ridiculous ideas in your head. You think you're equipped to raise a child? You think you can raise a child while working on your own? You haven't even repented for your sinfulness. What kind of example is that for a baby? That poor baby deserves better."

My heart aches, this whole conversation making me anxious.

"Your sister—"

"I'm not giving my baby to Eden," I cut her off immediately, my voice raised, my blood pressure rising.

I feel empathy for Eden's situation, not being able to get pregnant after so long of trying, but just because she can't have a child doesn't mean she automatically gets mine.

This isn't school, where Eden got a new prom dress and I had to get the secondhand one. This isn't college, where Eden got a new car and I had to take the bus. It also isn't youth group, where Eden could study late with all her friends, and I had to come home immediately to cook dinner for everyone before she returned. This is a new life. This is an actual human I'm growing. Not merely a new toy I need to give away.

This baby was created at a time when I should've been saving myself for marriage. From a young age I was taught that we're supposed to help men not be tempted by being modest and being strong when they struggle. But I caved to his pressure because I thought he would be my husband. I thought we were as good as married in the eyes of the Lord. Boy was I wrong. And while it's clear he was using me, this baby was *created* and I'm keeping my baby. I love it. I want it. And I can't wait to be a mother.

"She's more equipped than you. She's married. Stable. God-fearing. She's been trying for years. This is a blessing for her."

"It's not hers to be blessed with."

"You're being selfish. You think this is about you? You always think this is about you. It's about giving that child a proper life. Not dragging it through your mess."

"Mess? How can what I do be called a mess? I've worked hard all my life. I've volunteered. I've given back to my community. I put myself through school to live a dream of owning a bakery, and now I'm on my way to having exactly that. Just because I'm not married and am pregnant doesn't mean I'm a mess. I'm not giving up my baby, Mom. Eden has to find a different solution."

This same conversation has occurred numerous times. Only last time did it end in her slapping me across the face. That was the final straw. That was when I knew I had to leave. For my safety and for the safety of my baby.

"Pastor Greg said that—"

"I don't care what Pastor Greg says. It doesn't have anything to do with him," I snap, frustrated and hurt that she can't let me be. I'm not part of the family. I brought shame to them. I understand. Their faith is all-encompassing and always has been. I'm a disappointment. I get what I've done is less than ideal and not what they or anyone else wanted. But it happened. It's my responsibility and I'm owning it. I've moved away. I'm not in their face. I'm not flashing my pregnant belly in front of my sister or in front of the congregation.

"You'll regret it. Mark my words. God already told me this child isn't yours. I heard His small voice whispering in the quiet, and I submitted. You will too."

My stomach sinks even lower. "Thanks for the pep talk, Mom. I'm hanging up now."

"Don't you dare..."

"Goodbye, Mom."

I end the call, my hands shaking, my heart racing. I've never feared my family. I grew up doing everything they asked of me. I kept quiet, didn't talk back. Now, though, I know I was never really loved by them. I may technically not be a mother yet, but I already know a child is something that should be cherished, loved, surrounded by positivity and opportunity. And so for the first time in my life, I'm finding my voice as well as my own two feet and a new name. Doing my life on my terms, not only for me but for my child.

Getting away from them and their toxic brand of Christianity was the smartest decision I've ever made.

Bringing me out of my thoughts, I hear a loud knock on the door downstairs. Griffin is here. I look to the ceiling and blow out a breath before I take one last look in the mirror. Flowy dress on, hiding my bump as much as possible, because some habits are hard to break. Hair out, lips glossed, yet the tension still simmers across my shoulders.

But today, I'm meeting new friends. Today, I'm building

new connections. Ones I hope won't judge me for being a single mom. Ones I hope will support me with my new business. And I'm doing it with a man who seems angry twenty-four seven but is fast becoming a friend.

A man who sleeps on my floor and eats horrible baked goods and tells me they're nice. Who still feels more genuine and honest than anyone else I've had in my life.

10

GRIFFIN

We drive out to Billionaire Boulevard with what looks to be the Mount Everest of baked goods in the back.

"You baked all morning?"

I keep my eyes on the road. One look at her, and I'll forget I'm even driving. Her hair is down. First time I've seen it like that, and it's shiny, like a waterfall running over her back in soft waves. It's enticing. I want to run my fingers through it to feel the softness against my dry, hardened hands. She has on another flowing dress, and I realize she's hiding her bump. Not sure why. We all know she's pregnant. But I'm also not complaining, because these long, flowing dresses she wears have her breasts lifted like a feast for my eyes. The dress also sways when she moves, her body flirting as she walks. But even though she's beautiful, she seems different. Her usual sparkle is a little dull.

"Yeah. I enjoy it. I find it therapeutic. Plus, I didn't want to turn up empty-handed."

"You've left no doubt with what's on my back seat," I

grumble, taking the turn to where me and the other guys live.

"Did I go too far? I want to make a good impression. And after Tanner ate one of my terrible batches of buns, I feel like I need to redeem myself." Her words rush out. It means a lot to her to ensure her bakery is a success. If I didn't see it before, I see it now.

"You did fine." We pull up and park, and I jump out quickly, going straight to her door, helping her slide out of my truck, which is too high for her, especially in her current condition. "Easy," I warn her as she turns to slide down off the passenger seat.

She huffs. "I'm pregnant, not totally inept."

I tame my grin at her feistiness as I help her out, my hands holding hers. The feeling of her soft hands in mine is foreign, yet I like it. I've noticed she's increasingly coming out of her shell around me. Around the bakery, she works quietly, and after our initial meeting, she was somewhat reserved. Now she's found a little confidence. And it looks good on her.

"Let me get the goods," I tell her once she's on safe ground, not wanting her to lift a thing. Our eyes connect, and she doesn't give me any pushback.

"You're here. Welcome!" Hudson walks out to meet us, and a slew of kids follow him, chasing each other, throwing balls, and squealing. I cringe.

"Fucking kids," I mumble, and Savannah huffs a laugh.

"What did you expect at a kids' party?" Her lips quirk as she grabs one of the containers from my hands, as Hudson reaches out to grab another, and we follow him inside.

"Don't mind him. He's always the grumpy one," Hudson jests, and Savannah's smile almost has me stumbling over the entry steps as we walk inside.

As predicted, everyone's here, and it's a fucking circus. Kids screaming and running around. Parents mingling in different groups. There're a few faces I don't even know. Probably from school or sports or some shit. I pass the containers to Lacy, who has her toddler on her hip, her mom helping her in the kitchen. Meanwhile, Savannah is swooped up by the women; Victoria, Daisy, and Charlotte circle her like sharks who smell fresh blood in the water, all of them talking fast like a gaggle of geese, and I quickly move to the left out of their path before I get a headache.

"You turned up, huh?" Tanner comes to my side, passing me a drink. He's got his little girl on his hip. If I thought Victoria would make Tanner buckle, his little daughter has him completely on his knees. Amber, who I have no doubt is named after his liquor, is a toddler, with cute pigtails and big blue eyes like her mother, who also has her mom's unrelenting passion for the color pink.

"Uncy Gif." She giggles at me, and despite my solid frame, it does soften me a bit.

"Hey, kiddo."

She grins and claps as Tanner puts her down, and we watch her walk on wobbly legs over to the girls.

"Thought I better. I missed the last one." It's a fucking kids' monsoon in here. Squealing and giggling from the girls and the boys roughhousing and throwing balls.

"I see you went to the bakery first..."

I don't look at him, busy watching Savannah's face light up with all the attention at making new friends. Amber walks right up to her and giggles, cuddling her knees as all the women swoon. I can feel Tanner's gaze burning into the side of my head.

"She needed a lift." Though my response is true, it gives

me pause. I'm not even sure she has a vehicle, and I frown thinking about it.

"Are these ones safe to eat?" Connor leans in, grabbing a cupcake from the counter behind me, and I chuckle.

"Yeah, she has her taste back. Best I've ever eaten." I watch as he shoves a bite into his mouth and chews before his eyes widen comically.

"Oh, damn. Sooo good," he mumbles with his mouth full, and my chest puffs, pride shining through.

"Told you." I still haven't looked at Tanner, whose gaze hasn't moved from my face.

"Uncle Griff, come play, come play." The birthday boy, Harvey, runs up to me, a glove and ball in his hand. *Fuck.*

"Yeah, come! You never play!" Sawyer's boy, Kevin, backs him up. I take a deep breath. I usually say no. Playing with kids isn't really my thing. Kids in general aren't really my thing. Too loud. Too boisterous. Reminds me too much of my past, so much so, my heart hurts. But I look over to Savannah and catch her watching me, taking in all the kids who now surround me. Swallowing hard, I pass my drink to Tanner and roll my shoulders.

"Alright... let's go."

The kids yell in excitement, attracting the attention of everyone around us, and as I follow them outside, I meet Savannah's surprised gaze. I keep my face like stone as I walk past, yet I'm basking in the way she's looking at me.

"What the hell are you doing? You never play with the kids," Sutton, Hollywood celebrity, one of the newer locals and my neighbor here in Whispers, asks as I walk past.

I shake my head, having no real idea what the hell I've agreed to. My body still hurts from sleeping on the hardwood floor last night, my mind forgetting I'm not in my twenties anymore, my forties a whole different ball game.

"Batter up!" I yell as I grab one of the kids' baseball bats, and all the boys and girls run around and get into position. Tanner, Connor, and Hudson, along with Sawyer and Sutton, all stand at the side, watching me like I've grown a second head.

"Have you been drinking this morning?" Sawyer frowns.

"Just coffee."

"I think he's having a midlife crisis..." I hear Sutton say to his brother, and I roll my eyes before finally meeting Tanner's gaze, the silent intrigue making me move them away almost instantly.

Harvey throws the ball, and I hit it, the ball going for miles as we all watch it fly straight over to the fields. The kids screech and all run together to go and find it as I stand and watch, my friends all shaking their heads.

I last about thirty minutes, but it feels like all day as the kids decide Uncle Griff is their new plaything. Baseball is not my sport of choice; I prefer football, but it's easy enough, although my back may prove otherwise tomorrow.

"Alright, I'm done." I throw them the ball. I've had an audience the whole time. Probably because I never play with the kids for this long. I never partake in any kind of group activities. Rarely make an appearance at these kinds of parties.

"Noooo!" Harvey yells, running to me.

"Come back!" Preston shouts right behind him.

"Not yet!" Kevin races to me, and before I know it, Harvey, Kevin, Preston, and what feels like twenty of their friends jump on me, all trying to drag me back to the grassy lawn where they're playing. Kids hang off my arms and legs, and I walk slowly toward my friends, dragging all of them along the grass like I'm the Hulk, which seems to heighten their excitement and does little to help the stiffness in my back. *I'm too old for this shit.*

"Looks like you have some new fans." Tanner's analyzing my every move, unable to hide his amusement.

"What's up with you?" Sutton looks me up and down like he hasn't seen me before. He hasn't. Not like this.

"He's been working at the bakery..." Tanner drops, and Sutton looks over to the gaggle of women before he looks back at me and nods.

"Ah. Makes sense."

"What does?" The kids jump off me, no longer interested as they run toward the farm animals off to the side.

He narrows his eyes. "You're different. Trying to impress someone."

"Am not." My shoulders tighten.

"Oh, so she's available, then? Because my security guy Jackson is looking—"

"She's not his type." The words rush out quickly, and I don't miss when he rolls his lips. My frown deepens.

"Hmmm, alright... whatever you say..." Sutton grins, walking back inside, and Tanner and I follow. As I make my way toward Savannah, she looks up and gives me a smile, and I immediately stand ten feet taller, my back ache suddenly barely noticeable.

As the kids swarm me again, I feel out of my element. Sutton's right. This isn't me.

But her grin widens at the sight, so I find myself picking up Harvey, throwing him over my shoulder, and running back down to the lawn to play again.

All because it makes her smile. And the warmth I feel from her attention is one I haven't felt for decades.

11

SAVANNAH

"I'm surprised you're still walking." I try yet fail to hide the small smirk as Griffin and I walk out of the party to his truck. As the happy screams of the kids becomes more distant, my body also feels weary.

"Hmmm, I got my exercise. Here." Griffin opens the truck door for me as I make a weak attempt to reach up for the door grab handles and almost topple.

"Looks like your legs aren't working either..." His voice is a mere grumble, but I feel his breathy words on the back of my neck, my skin prickling at his closeness. I have little time to bask in it before his hands are on my waist and my feet leave the ground.

I can't help but laugh. "Whoa, give a girl some warning before you manhandle her." My cheeks flush immediately as he puts me in my seat. I have no idea how he's not breaking a sweat. I mean, I'm not a size two, and I have a bun in the oven.

As I look at him, he doesn't meet my gaze, but his jaw is tight, his permanent scowl not wavering as he leans inside and secures my seat belt across my body. With his face so close, my breathing stops as his chest almost hits my own.

Seeing him play with the kids did something to my insides. It made me all warm and gooey. His frown and scowls remained throughout the entire day, looking entirely unapproachable to anyone, but still, he kept playing, continuing to make the kids giggle and laugh. I wasn't the only person to notice; it seems his behavior was unusual, according to the girls I met today. But even through his grumpy façade, I could tell he had a good time.

Now as he leans across me to help buckle me in, I can smell his cologne, like wood, trees, and rain all combined. I close my eyes, wishing I could get these stupid feelings out of my mind. The last thing this man needs is his very pregnant baker lusting over him. God, it's almost embarrassing at this point.

"You want a warning next time, sweetness?" His voice is low, rough. "Fine. Next time, I'll tell you exactly where I plan to put my hands."

I still, my eyes popping wide, as does my mouth, before he slams the door and strides around the truck to the driver's side. I have exactly two seconds to close my mouth, take a breath, and tell my raging hormones to get back in their box. *Is it normal to get immediately horny when I'm so pregnant?* I mean, it has been a long time since a man touched me. A long time since a man even spoke to me like an equal, like I was someone worthy.

I rub my bump, acutely aware he's probably being kind because I'm with child. We've only just gotten to know each other, but I can already tell he's a man of his word. A man who has a strong sense of what's good and bad in the world. Maybe he feels sorry for me.

He jumps into his truck with ease, and I swallow

roughly, the tension thick as he starts the drive through Hudson's expansive ranch.

"Everyone seemed to like the baked goods?" I'm fishing to see if anyone commented to him, trying to ease my nerves of opening my bakery in a few days.

"They did. They were delicious. Are you ready for opening?" He doesn't look at me, his eyes remaining on the road. I sigh, feeling the pressure starting to mount on my shoulders with opening the doors to Betty's Bakery, hoping I get at least one customer on my first day.

"Well, I think I've gotten the hang of the ovens. My secondhand mixtures are working overtime, so I'm praying they last a few months before I need to invest in some new ones. But I hope I've redeemed myself after the terrible cinnamon buns I handed out weeks ago... I still can't believe you ate them."

I smile, and his lips twitch.

"I was hungry."

"I'm surprised you survived. They were truly terrible." I laugh at myself now and soften as his lips curve even more. God, if this man smiled, it would light up the whole town, I'm sure of it. Talking with him is easy. I haven't felt this comfortable talking to anyone before. It's almost like being near him eases everything else on my mind.

"Anyway, to answer your question, I have to prep a few more things, need to order some extra ingredients and firm up my offerings, but fingers crossed when I open in a week, it will all come together." I send a quick silent prayer up above that this bakery is a roaring success.

"I don't think you have to worry. I have a feeling the town will line up out the door."

I appreciate his positivity.

"I hope so. That would be fun to have a line of people

waiting. But I highly doubt the population of Whispers is in that much need of bread."

His eyes flick to me. "Did you see how fast those cupcakes went? And there were only a few caramels left, too."

I grin, rolling my lips, loving that he noticed. "I have a feeling you ate the most."

He remains quiet, which is how I know I'm right.

"You seemed to make some friends today?" He looks over at me from under his brow. Again, it's brief, a glance, but it lights me up inside.

"The women were all so warm and welcoming. We swapped numbers." I can't even tame my smile. I've finally made friends. It's been a long time since I've had to, even longer since I tried.

"Good."

"I mean, you could've given me a heads-up that there would be a Hollywood movie star there..." I chuckle.

"Sutton and Charlotte are my neighbors."

My eyes widen. "Surprisingly down-to-earth too. They talked about bees a lot..."

"Yeah, Sutton has an unhealthy obsession with them."

"It sure is a specific hobby. Probably okay as long as you're not allergic."

"Of which he is..." Griffin sighs and shakes his head, and I frown in confusion but let it be.

"It's beautiful out here." I lean my head back on the seat and look out the window in awe of the scenery, trying to get my mind on anything other than the mammoth of a man next to me and how good his hands felt on my body. I try to focus on the rolling green hills, the lines of trees for privacy, the grass so green it makes you want to stop and lie on it and bask in the sun.

"Mm-hmm. It is."

"You said you were neighbors with Sutton? Where do you stay when you're here?" I look at him, his eyes firmly on the road, not meeting my gaze. But I feel our connectedness. He's one hundred percent with me, not thinking of other things, not looking out and around trying to ignore me. He's totally present.

"My place is down the road, up the back behind the pines. I like my privacy." He nods, and I take another moment to drink him in. Shirtsleeves rolled to his elbows. Jeans fitting him just right. Thick arms, solid body. I don't think he works out as such, but being a builder has him lifting and moving around all day. His body is a byproduct of his job.

"If you weren't building mansions for billionaires, what would you be doing?" I'm interested to hear what a man like Griffin would want to do with his life if he could change it.

He shrugs, thinking about it for a few seconds. "Something quiet. Maybe restoring old cabins. No deadlines. No clients."

"That sounds... peaceful." I smile softly. I can see that about him. Wanting peace. Wanting space. After my upbringing, that sounds like it would be good for my soul too.

"What about you? If you weren't baking?"

I pull in a breath. No one has ever asked about what I like or what I want to do. I've always known. I always followed my passion. But no one else around me seemed to care enough to ask.

"I think I was always meant to bake. My grandma instilled it in me from a young age. I can't imagine my life without some type of baking. I like making something from nothing."

"I understand that." I suppose that's kind of what he does when he builds. He builds homes from basic materials. He houses people, and I feed them.

"Do you get lonely?" I feel like it would be. A big house way up here in the middle of nowhere. Always traveling, never settled. He looks out the window and thinks about my question, which gives me pause. I have a feeling Griffin keeps himself isolated. Not sure why. His friends seem amazing.

"I'm never here for long enough." He's right. He isn't. I know he's leaving town again tomorrow, having only been here a few days. He's always busy, always ready for the next destination. I get exhausted thinking about it.

The truck hums beneath us, the road winding through the trees. "You ever think about staying? Here in Whispers more permanently?"

He doesn't answer right away, but I wait. "Sometimes... But I don't know if I'd know how." Shifting his gaze to me, his eyes search mine for a millisecond, causing me to hold my breath. "What about you? Get lonely?"

"Hmmm, not really. I talk to my bump a lot. I guess in a few weeks, loneliness will be the furthest thing from my mind. Dare I say, sleeping will become a priority." I huff a laugh, not sure what to expect from my life when my baby arrives. But I know life's going to change. Again.

"You talk to your bump a lot?" I notice his lips quirk. Great, now he probably thinks I'm crazy.

"All the time. I think it's already sick of me."

He glances over, head shaking. "You're going to be a good mom."

I blink away some emotion at his sincerity, warmth blooming in my chest.

"I hope so..." I swallow past a sudden lump in my throat.

The pressure of trying to give my baby everything has me wringing my hands on my lap.

"You got a family that will be here to help you?" I almost laugh. My family? Help?

"No. They don't... approve of my situation. I didn't really have any choice but to leave them and do it on my own. So I did."

"Don't approve?" His frown back in full force.

"Yeah, well, I grew up in a religious household in a religious community. For the most part, it was okay. I always had my grandparents, you know. But they passed, and now I'm having a baby out of wedlock... It's seen as a sin. I'm a disappointment. A big one." I sigh heavily, resigned to the fact that no matter what I do, I'll never have my parents' approval.

"What about the baby's father?" His jaw works overtime. This is the most transparent I've been with anyone, and my heart rate increases when I think about sharing more. I haven't told another person my story, but for some reason, Griffin makes it easy.

"I met him at church, actually. You know the type. Slacks, button-down ironed to within an inch of his life. Turns out, he doesn't have a backbone. He left town the day after I told him I was pregnant. Doesn't want anything to do with me or my baby." It's sad, but it's my reality. I want to change the subject, so I put the question to him. "What about you? Got a family?"

His jaw tics as his eyes remain glued to the road ahead. I don't know why, but I feel like it's a sore spot. The silence stretches, and I'm about to apologize for asking, but he speaks.

"Had a few. Grew up in foster care. Wouldn't recommend it."

I can feel his hurt and anger rolling off him in waves. My heart breaks a little for the boy Griffin was and what he obviously had to endure.

"Any siblings?"

His eye twitches, and I feel like I'm pushing too far, but I wait.

"One. A younger brother. He passed." I watch his Adam's apple bob as he swallows, his hands gripping the steering wheel so tight his knuckles turn white.

"Looks like we're both trying to find our way..." My heart is nearly beating out of my chest, but I reach my hand out and place it palm up on the seat next to his thigh. He spots the movement, his eyes flicking down, before his gaze meets mine and his nostrils flare as he takes a breath. When he looks back at the road, I leave my hand there, hopeful. And as we pull onto Main Street, his posture softens, his hand leaves the wheel, and his palm finds mine. Our fingers lace, and he lifts my hand in his and rests it on his thigh. I feel his thumb then, strumming my skin where we're connected. It's a simple gesture, one of friendship, care, maybe a moment of solace in a world where we both feel so alone. My hand feels small in his, but his grip doesn't waver and neither does mine.

"I'm in Sundown Valley for a few days, then I'll be back. You've got my number. You call me if you need anything." He still looks straight ahead, but his tone is less grumbly than normal.

Smiling, I nod. "Sure. I'll be in a whirl of stress trying to get the bakery ready."

He gives my hand a squeeze. "Don't lift anything, don't rush, don't work late..."

"You know, you're bossy, but for a grump, you're surprisingly gentle," I murmur, watching our hands settle.

His lips twitch. "Don't get used to it."

I clamp my lips together so a smile doesn't take over my whole face. I'm enjoying this moment. Enjoying his touch. Feeling a little more at ease with life.

If only that feeling lasted.

12

—————

SAVANNAH

I frown at the register, frustration worming its way to the surface.

"What if we hit this button?" Melissa suggests, leaning in beside me. We've been staring at this thing for thirty minutes, both pretending we're not technologically cursed. She presses the button. The machine whirls, lights blink, and my shoulders drop in relief.

"Oh! I think it worked!" My grin is instant.

Melissa's been with me all morning. We've gone through the bakery process, kitchen guidelines, food handling, and hygiene. She's absorbed everything like a sponge, and somehow, we already click like we've known each other for years, not mere hours.

"I haven't used these newer systems much"—she taps a few more buttons—"but it's pretty straightforward."

And just like that, the screen settles into the home menu. Ready for opening day.

"Thank you," I breathe out. One less thing on my list. Opening is only days away, and my nerves are a tangled mess. Having Melissa here now makes everything feel a little less impossible, though.

"Of course! I'm so excited. And the smells in here..." She fans herself dramatically. "I'm going to gain ten pounds just by working near your pastries."

I laugh. It feels good. Light. I haven't had many real friends. Sure, there were girls at school, women at church, coworkers, but in Whispers, it's different. I get to start over. Like people here won't judge me before they know me.

Like Griffin.

He's been away all week, and every night, I've found myself rolling his business card between my fingers like a worry stone. Two mornings ago, I woke with it still in my hand. The urge to call him is stronger than it should be.

"Do you think you'll stay open every day once the baby comes?"

I nod without hesitation. "I want to. But I'm trying to be realistic. I could be recovering for weeks... or maybe I'll bounce back in a few days. I honestly don't know."

That's the part keeping me up at night. I need the bakery running before the baby arrives. I need income. I need to prove to my family, and to myself, that I can do this. That I can raise a beautiful human and still chase my dreams.

"I noticed the freezer is stocked." Melissa gestures in that direction, seemingly impressed.

"I'm baking extra every day. Freezing what I can. Just in case."

"That's a great idea. And once you give birth, I'm happy to come in and serve. I can't bake like you, but if you've got the supply, I can sell it."

Warmth spreads through me. "I'd love that."

I shift to stand, but wince, rubbing my belly.

Melissa's face softens. "Sit. Please. I'll finish wiping down the windows."

I hate feeling useless, but I lower myself onto the stool and watch her grab the cleaning spray as the front door chimes.

"Hello?" Tanner's wife, Victoria's, voice carries through the shop. I look up, smiling immediately as she walks in with Annabelle and Daisy, the new friends I made at the birthday party last week.

"Oh, hi!" I push off the stool and meet them at the counter.

"Wow." Daisy spins slowly. "This looks incredible." Daisy owns the yoga studio down the street and is the longtime girlfriend to Connor Whiteman. Co-owner of Whiteman's Distillery and Tanner's son.

"It's changed a bit since I took it over," I say with a laugh. "There were cobwebs older than me in here."

"It's beautiful," Annabelle adds. "You've done an amazing job." Annabelle's an amazing woman who owns an organic soap business here in town, and with a few kids of her own, she knows all about the juggling of tasks it takes to open a business with kids. She's also married to Sawyer, the local lawyer, so their business is not only super successful but also managed really well.

I smile at their reactions. "Thank you. We're almost ready."

Victoria waves at Melissa, who waves back before slipping into the kitchen to give us space.

"Griffin did a great job with the carpentry," Victoria says. "I'm not surprised. He's the best in the country."

I hum, my stomach fluttering at the thought of him and how much work he's put into this place for me. "I was lucky

Tanner arranged for him to help. I still don't know how to repay you all."

"Oh stop," Victoria says, brushing it off. "My husband eats a loaf of bread a day. Supporting you is basically self-preservation."

"You and me both; I walk past a bakery and I gain weight." Daisy rolls her eyes at herself, and we all laugh, the sound warm and easy. Something I've missed in my life before and something I hope continues to grow.

"We won't keep you long," Annabelle says, her eyes soft with concern. "We wanted to check on you. See how you and the baby are doing this week."

"I'm okay. My due date is closing in on me now, though, so I'm getting nervous."

"You're still carrying high," Victoria says. "I think you've got a little time."

"Just remember to rest," Annabelle adds.

I nod, even though resting feels like a luxury I can't afford.

"I brought you some soaps. They're lavender, so they're relaxing..." Annabelle offers me a small box, the fragrance hitting my nose immediately. It smells divine.

"And chamomile and lemon, straight from the distillery garden and made into a tea in case you want a warm cup before bed." Daisy passes over a few boxes, and my eyes sting for a moment at their generosity.

"Thank you all so much..." I'm almost overwhelmed with gratitude. "You've been so kind."

"Of course. Please call us if you need anything. We can't wait to see you opening day." Daisy smiles, leaning in to give me a hug.

"We'll be the ones buying all the cinnamon rolls... Unless Griffin eats them all first." Victoria laughs, and as we say goodbye and they step out into the afternoon sun, the shop falls quiet again.

Too quiet.

I stand there for a moment, their gifts still warm in my hands, and all I can think about is him. *Griffin.*

I shouldn't be thinking about him this much. I'm about to give birth, and I'm opening a business, trying to rebuild my life from the ground up. I don't have space for... whatever these feelings are. But my fingers are already drifting toward my apron pocket, brushing over the edge of his business card like it's a secret I'm not supposed to touch.

Maybe I should message him. To check in. Just to say thank you again. Just to... hear from him.

My heart gives a ridiculous little kick, stronger than the baby's, and before I can talk myself out of it, I pull out my phone. Once I add his number to my contacts, my thumb hovers over his name.

Don't do it, the sensible part of me whispers.

But the part of me that remembers the way he looked at me—steady, warm, like he saw more than I meant to show—wins out. If I want to be the woman I know I can be, then I need to leave the girl I was behind. That starts with confidence. Doing the hard things. Like moving to a new town, opening a new business, using a new name and maybe, just maybe, texting a guy first.

I type a message, then delete it. Then type another.

"It's a message, Savannah. Nothing more," I mutter to myself before my fingers start typing.

> Hey. Just wanted to say thank you again for all your help with the shop. It's really coming together, and I couldn't have done it so fast or so well without you.

I stare at it for a second, then hit send before I chicken out. The reply comes faster than I expect.

> You don't have to thank me. But I'm glad it's looking good. How are you holding up?

Another flutter moves through my chest this time.

> I'm okay. Tired. Nervous. Excited. All of it, I guess.

Three dots appear. Disappear. Reappear.

> You don't have to do everything alone, you know.

My breath catches. I shouldn't read into that. I shouldn't.

> I'm trying not to.

The dots appear again, then vanish. Then my phone starts ringing. His name lights up the screen, and my heart thumps once, hard. I hesitate, just long enough to feel ridiculous, then answer.

"Hey," I say softly.

"Hey." His voice is warm, low, and moves through my body like honey. "You sound tired."

"I am," I admit. "But the shop's almost ready. And the baby's... Well, the baby's on its own schedule."

He chuckles, and the sound slides right under my skin. "I figured. You need anything?"

"No," I say automatically. Then quieter, "I mean... I don't think so."

"Savannah." His voice drops enough to make me shiver in the best way. "You can call me. For anything. Even if it's because you're overwhelmed… or bored… or you want to hear something that isn't a bakery appliance."

A laugh slips out of me before I can stop it. "I don't want to be a burden."

"You couldn't be if you tried." The low certainty in his tone sends heat straight to my cheeks.

"I, um… I didn't expect you to call," I admit.

"I didn't expect you to message," he counters, and I can hear him smiling. "But I'm not complaining. You made my day a hell of a lot better."

My breath catches. God, he shouldn't say things like that. The baby shifts under my ribs, and I wince.

"You okay?" Concern filters into the question. Protective. Alert. "Savannah?"

"Yeah," I breathe. "Just my insides are running out of room, and the baby is pushing around, ensuring they're comfortable."

He chuckles. "I can imagine. Well… not really. But I'm trying."

The sound of his laugh does something to me, something I'm not ready to name.

"I'll be back in Whispers in a few days."

"Oh." I try to sound neutral, but longing creeps into my words anyway. "So… I guess I'll probably see you around then."

"You probably will."

I bite my bottom lip so my smile doesn't split my face. "See you then, Griffin."

"See you then, Savannah."

I end the call, but I keep the phone pressed to my chest, letting the warmth of his voice settle into the quiet shop.

I shouldn't be falling for him.

But he makes it far too easy.

13

GRIFFIN

I walk over the land at the distillery, enjoying the peace it brings. The new wind turbine sits tall and proud off to the side, its blades gently moving silently in the breeze. I'm amazed by how one tall thing like that can power this entire site. Yet it does.

"Happy with it?" Tanner steps toward me, the man who just spent millions upgrading his facilities, my team finishing off some key areas as Victoria's team starts putting the finishing touches on it.

"I think it's one of the best builds I've done." I'm proud. I work hard, I have original ideas, and the success of my business is testament to that.

After a few days in Sundown Valley, finalizing plans and stepping out measurements, I immediately came back here, my jet landing at the local airport about an hour or so ago. Tanner is my first stop. The bakery next.

"I love it. I can't believe we've built all this." Tanner stands taller, looking over his land.

"We've come a long way." I nod. Seeing the progress like this after years of work really is satisfying.

"We have... You give any more thought to spending more time here? I mean, this is almost finished, and you don't have another job here in Whispers lined up. Planning on sticking around?"

I clear my throat. "Maybe."

"She's a nice woman."

My eyebrow lifts, even as my heart beats a little faster. "I don't know what you're talking about."

I can't look at him, my gaze remaining on the horizon in the direction of town, where I know the bakery to be. I've done nothing but think of my baker since the day I met her. The phone call we had a few days ago was over too soon. I wanted to call her again just to hear her voice. But I didn't. With everything she's got going on, that was the last thing she needs.

"Oh, Griff, I think you do."

"I'm looking over the bakery project. That's all." I hate that he can see right through me. He's the closest I have to family.

"Bullshit. You're one of my closest friends, I know you're talking rubbish."

"She's pregnant." I'm starting to feel angry. At myself. For even having thoughts of a woman, but one who's pregnant with another man's baby.

"Mm-hmm. I know."

"I travel a lot." I can't get involved. I never get involved. I have no idea why I'm even entertaining it. Maybe I need a woman. A body. The hard-on I've had for the past week since she held my fucking hand in the truck is evidence of that. It's been a long time since a woman held my hand. Fuck, I can't even remember the last time I held something so soft.

"True."

I sigh. "There are a million reasons why I shouldn't even be here."

"Yet here you are."

I stand in the silence. Thinking.

"It's opening day tomorrow," I tell him, like he doesn't already know.

"Hmmm, she's been busy."

My head moves swiftly in his direction. "You been in?"

"Victoria and the girls popped in to see if she needed anything. I thought since you were gone, it might be nice for them to go over."

I nod. I'm glad there are others now watching out for her. "And?"

Tanner's eyebrows rise at my intensity. "And... she's killing it. The bakery looks amazing, and she's handing out free samples to everyone who drops by."

I smile a little, huffing out a laugh. She's so entrepreneurial. "She'll have people lining up the street." I told her that as we left the party last week, and I meant it. Her food is delicious. She's going to be a success, I know it.

"She's going to be great. Whispers is lucky to have her. And you."

My throat thickens with emotion I try to bury deep, and luckily my cell vibrates in the next second.

It's Savannah. Like a schmuck, I've been waiting for another text message, another call, so I grab it quickly. Too fucking eager.

"Savannah?"

Tanner watches me with a hint of amusement.

"Griffin!" She says my name in a way that has my feet moving.

"What's wrong?" I'm already running to my truck, Tanner hot on my heels.

"I'm... I'm..." She's crying, hiccupping, and I can't make sense of anything she's saying.

"I'm on my way. I'm five minutes away. Just take a breath..." My heart pumps harder at what could be happening.

"She alright?" Tanner asks.

"I'll let you know," I tell him as I jump in the truck, not waiting for him. I speed out of the distillery, the gravel in his driveway flicking out from beneath my tires as I race into town.

"Are you alright? Savannah!" I yell into the phone, driving one-handed. If the local sheriff was around, he'd pull me over for sure.

"I can't... I'm trying to..." She sniffs and cries, and I still can't make out a word.

"I'm here," I bark into the phone as I pull sharply into a parking spot right at the front of the bakery. I barely turn off my truck before I'm out, pocketing my phone and pushing my way through the door.

"Savannah?" I yell, feeling like I'm going to have a fucking heart attack. Looking around, I don't see her in the shop and have no time to admire how good it looks as I stride out the back to the kitchen and pause in the doorway.

She's on the floor, leaning against the wall. Tears coat her cheeks, her eyes red, and she looks even more beautiful than when I left her a week ago.

"Savannah?" I stride to her, sinking down on my knees, looking her over. She's intact. Not visibly hurt. Not grabbing her belly like last time.

"What happened?" My anger increases, ready to kill the person responsible for these tears.

"I can't tie my shoes!" she wails, and I still.

"What?" I frown, wondering if I heard her right.

"I can't tie my shoes... I wanted to walk to the diner... to drop off some new cupcakes... and I can't tie my shoes..." Her tears continue through hiccups, and my pulse starts to slow. Looking her over, I see that she's highly emotional, her hormones probably all over the place. She's likely over-tired from working so hard, too. I guess growing a kid and having a belly the size of a watermelon would do that to you.

"Your shoes?" I look down at her feet, seeing some running shoes half-on, laces undone.

"I can't even touch my toes... I used to be able to touch my toes. Now I'm so fat, I can't even see them." Her body is weary as she slumps against the wall.

"You're pregnant..." I tell her firmly as I lean over to gently wipe her cheeks with my thumb. As I do, I lower my hand to her chin and tilt her face so she's looking at me. "..and you're beautiful."

"You're here?" Her pout is cute. Like she just realized I'm in front of her.

"I am. Are you alright?" Her breathing has calmed now. Her tears have stopped.

"Aren't you still in Sundown Valley?"

I clench my jaw so I don't grin like a fool. I didn't tell her exactly when I'd be back, so her surprise is understandable. The relief is flooding me now knowing she's okay.

"Great!" She throws a cloth onto the ground. "Now I'm hallucinating," she grumbles, and I roll my lips so I don't laugh.

"I got back early. I wanted to be back for opening day."

Her gaze snaps back to mine, in awe, her big, beautiful, now glassy eyes widening. The same ones I try not to focus on because they draw me in so deep I'm scared I'll drown in them.

"You came for my opening day?" Blinking up at me, another tear trails down her cheek, and I wipe it away.

"I did. Are you okay?" I ask again, searching her face. She looks to be more settled now, but that tear has me concerned all over again.

"Yeah, sorry... I just... had a moment. I didn't know who else to call. My emotions are all over the place, and when you can't do something as simple as put on some shoes, I think my stress just overflowed. Sorry." She shakes her head, a little embarrassed, but I nod in understanding. I didn't mind her call. I know there's no one else here to help her. I feel honored that she feels so comfortable with me.

As she wipes her face, with more tears having escaped, I glance around the space. Everything looks amazing. She already has prepackaged jars of caramels ready to go. There are batches of sourdough proofing over on the side. She also has bowls and bowls of different-colored icing ready to apply to an assortment of baked delights tomorrow. She's been busy. No wonder she's exhausted.

"You've been pushing yourself. I think you need to rest." I lean over to scoop her up and lift her to me. I swear she's heavier than she was last week, but I don't falter as I stand, keeping her in my arms.

"I've got too much to do. I still need to ice the cupcakes..." She starts to wriggle, but it's futile, because I'm not letting her down.

"You need to rest. When's your new staff member starting?" I clench my jaw, hating her doing all this on her own, wanting to help her, yet also not wanting to get too close. Getting close to a woman like this is dangerous. I can't catch feelings. She's pregnant. She doesn't need a man like me walking into her life. A man who isn't worthy. Not for her or her baby. My past has proven I can't be. I can't be responsible for another person. Besides, she needs to concentrate on the baby and the bakery.

"Melissa has already started. She's great, but I have to do the cupcakes, Griff. Just the cupcakes..." She looks at me with pleading eyes.

"Fine. Show me how," I tell her, dropping her feet slowly to the floor.

Head tilting, she looks at me, unsure. "You want to learn how to ice my cupcakes?"

"Someone better. Who's going to ice them when you need to rest?" I ask, because as resilient as she is, I don't know if she fully understands how having a baby works. She isn't going to be able to be on her feet all day and night straight after birth.

"Okay..." she says tentatively, and she takes my hand, leading me to the counter.

"Cakes, icing, spatula. I make my own swirl design, like this." Grabbing her things, she takes a small dollop of icing and swirls it on the small cake. I frown, the flick of her wrist seemingly a quirk, giving her an extra little lift to the icing, making it look sophisticated and surprisingly decorative for such a simple thing.

"Here. You try." She pushes over a cupcake and the bowl, and I give it a try.

I make a mess of the first one, and the second. Dainty is something I'm not.

"Why don't you try this way?" She swaps the spatula and gives me a slightly smaller one, and it has the desired effect. I swirl on the icing like she does and turn my wrist at the right second and get the little lift.

"Got it." I'm surprisingly proud of myself. Clearly all those years of working with plaster and render is transferrable. I do a few more, happy that I've got the hang of it.

Her grin brightens her whole face. "Brilliant, only about a hundred to go."

"A hundred?" My eyebrows rise.

"Yeah, I'm doing extra-large batches. This batch here, I'll freeze, so when the baby comes, I don't have to bake so much."

I nod as we work side by side, glad she's thought about it.

"Making anything else? There might be a few days when you can't bake," I push, wondering if she has a contingency plan.

"Yeah, pies and buns are all things I'll make extra of as the days go on. I got a large freezer from Bob at the hardware store so that's come in handy. But I'm staying hopeful that my little one will let me get some baking time in at least the week after I give birth, whenever that is."

"Do you know if you're having a boy or a girl?" I ask, intrigued.

"No. I thought I would keep that as a surprise. A reward for all the hard work, you know." She smiles with a shrug.

The soft way she says it has me wanting to pull her into my arms. "I think that'll be quite the reward."

When I glance at her, she's already looking at me, something in her expression I can't quite place.

"How is Sundown Valley going?" I haven't had this before. Working and talking with someone you're getting to know. Them wanting to learn about me, and me wanting to learn about them.

I blow out a breath. "It's a big project. It's going to take months. A few new cottages on their estate, a larger winery to accommodate growing tourist numbers and tastings. They're a big family, with lots of money, and are growing rapidly. They have their eyes on global expansion. Just like Tanner here in Whispers, but bigger. They have lots of ideas, and a few of them are butting heads over it. There's always something going on."

She giggles, the sound shooting through my chest.

"Sounds like a sitcom."

"It feels like it sometimes. But the Stonemore family makes really fucking great wine."

"What do you prefer, wine or whiskey?"

"Whiskey. But I do love a deep red too and Stonemore makes a brilliant one," I tell her easily. The older I get, the more I appreciate the finer things of life, even though I grew up with none of them.

"As a kid, I remember sneaking into the church's supply room and stealing a sip of the communion wine," she admits as she ices three cupcakes to my one. I pause, looking at her, and her face is riddled with guilt and a small hint of mischievousness.

"Really?" I imagine her being a Goody Two-shoes, always on her best behavior.

Her face drops a little. "My sister dared me."

"And let me guess, you're not one to back down from a dare?"

"No. I also always wanted her approval. So I did anything she wanted me to. I got caught, though..."

"What happened?"

"I got five lashes and locked in the cupboard for three days."

I feel the life leave my body. "What?" I nearly bark.

"I was a small kid; I fit fine." She shrugs, like being abused was no big deal.

My eyes narrow. "Did that kind of thing happen a lot?"

"It always seemed to happen to me." She blows out a breath.

"Your parents?"

"Yeah, and Pastor Greg. The wine wasn't even real. It was grape juice. So disappointing. My sister laughed, though."

"What was her discipline?" I ask, wondering what she got for orchestrating it all.

"Her discipline?" Savannah stops icing and looks at me, confused.

"Yeah, what were the ramifications for her for putting you up to the task?"

She pauses, thinking about it a small frown coming to her brow. "She lied. Told them she caught me and was trying to stop me. They saw that as her setting a good example and she got elevated to the leader of Girl's Fellowship Group." Like the facts are just resonating with her, she blinks a few times.

I don't push, I don't bite, but my anger swirls. I know what it's like to grow up with people who didn't have your best interests at heart. Looks like Savannah had the same experience. She rubs her belly, and a small wince comes to her face.

"Alright, let's go." I drop the things on the counter and grab her arms gently and start to move her away from the counter.

"Griff? What, no, I need to finish." She immediately resists, but I'm not having it.

"Savannah. You and the baby need to rest; otherwise, there will be no opening tomorrow. Remember what Hudson said." She's quiet then, and I feel her body soften in my hold as I walk her up the stairs.

"Okay, fine..." she relents. This is now the second time I've walked her to bed. And I swear this time, she's almost asleep before I even get her there. Clearly, she overdid it these past few days while I was away.

I spot a bassinet over to the side that wasn't here last

time, along with a pile of children's clothes. Not many items. But a few.

"I'll lock up," I tell her quietly as I lay her on her bed, ensuring she's comfortable.

"Griffin..." she whispers.

I pull the blanket over her, taking in her pretty face. "Yeah, Savannah?"

Her eyes are closed, barely awake. "Don't sleep on the floor tonight. It's too hard... You can come up here..."

That offer makes my heart stutter. I stand here, looking down on her, her body already softening into the mattress, her breathing evening out.

"Sleep tight, sweetness," I whisper as I turn and walk down the stairs, making myself useful by finishing the cupcakes, all one hundred of them, before cleaning the kitchen, needing to move, to push out my anxiety, my frustrations, my fears.

I remain focused, keep my head down, and put her things away and lock the back door. I then move to the front and wipe down the counter, filling the napkin holders and mopping the floors, even though they look sparkling already. I wipe the windows, then double-check the signage, doing anything and everything I can think of to get the front retail space ready for customers tomorrow. I shoot Tanner a text so he isn't worried, and before I know it, it's dark. I stand in her kitchen and look at the base of her stairs. The ones that lead to her.

She's right. I'm not going home. I won't leave her. And I can't sleep on the hard floor another night. Before I think too much about it, I flick off the light and take the stairs one at a time.

14

SAVANNAH

It's dark when I feel movement to my side. *What's happening?*

I blink a few times, the movements and sound becoming a little more frantic before I hear a deep grumble.

Griffin.

I sit up, albeit slowly and extremely uncoordinated as he continues to move and mumble. He slept in the armchair next to my bed, a small blanket half draped over him, and it seems he's having what I think is a night terror.

"Griffin?" I say gently as I turn on the side lamp.

"No... no... NO!" he shouts and wakes himself up, and I gasp as he looks right at me, all wild-eyed, breathing hard, looking ready to kill. My heart thuds as we stare at each other for a beat.

"Are you..."

"Fine. Sorry. Shit..." Leaning over, he rubs his face. I look over him. His chest is moving rapidly, like he's been running. I spot the time, noting it's two a.m.

"It's okay if you..." I say softly.

"I said I'm fine." His words have a bite, and I swallow.

We're in close quarters, so I can almost feel the heat radiating from his body. I should feel uneasy, having a man right next to me while I was sleeping. My apartment is tiny, the armchair barely big enough for him. But I'm glad he came here to rest, and knowing he was here makes me feel safer.

He remains sitting forward with his head in his hands, not meeting my gaze. So I lower back down, keeping the lamp on and turning onto my side to face him.

"You know this bump is nocturnal too." I try a different tactic. He remains silent, so I continue.

"Moves and dances all night. I'm surprised, since I don't have a rhythmic bone in my body..." I huff a laugh at myself as I rub my belly on the side and feel a kick. "Oh... yep... there it is..." I grimace a little, and Griffin lifts his head quickly to look at me.

Without thinking any more about it, I reach out and grab his hand. "Here."

His body is rigid, like he's too scared to move. But he lets me hold his hand, and I move it slowly to come to my belly.

"Here... feel that?" I ask, watching his reaction.

His eyes widen as my baby kicks his hand. The little one is playing soccer or football in there.

"Does it hurt?" His voice is like gravel, but there's kindness in the way he asks. Even though his scowl remains deep, his eyes electrify me. Glassy, deep brown, looking right at me like he can see into my soul.

"Not hurt, just a little uncomfortable. I think it knows today is a big day..." I smile, and Griffin's body softens a little.

"You been doing some reading?" He nods toward the baby book on my nightstand.

"I can barely keep my eyes open some nights, but it tells me what to expect each week."

He leans over and grabs the book, flicking through the pages and lifting an eyebrow. "It says the baby is about the size of a melon?"

"It sure feels like it." I grimace as I rub my side, and he goes back to reading.

"Says that you will experience back aches, shortness of breath..." His voice trails off as I nod, feeling all those things and more.

"Have you packed your hospital bag?" He lifts his head to look at me, concern shining through.

"Not yet... I haven't had time." It's a poor excuse, but I don't have much to pack.

He frowns, obviously not liking the answer, then he closes the book and slides it back on my side table.

"Do you have a lot of nightmares?" I broach the subject again, tentatively, my head on the pillow, facing him. He scrubs his tired face, not meeting my gaze, yet his hand remains on my tummy, the baby continuing to move around. His thumb gently brushes across my skin tenderly, making me smile.

"Yeah," he answers honestly, his voice quiet.

"Do you remember them?"

He nods subtly. "Unfortunately."

"Want to talk about them?" I ask, seeing the pain in his expression.

He looks at me, and I see him swallow, his Adam's apple bobbing. I guess his silence means no. He doesn't like to be vulnerable. I guess no man does. So I take a deep breath and let him in on my own thoughts.

"What if I'm a bad mom?" I whisper my fears to him. Out of everything I've been through, that's my biggest fear.

"Not possible." He refutes it immediately, shaking his head.

"But what if everyone's right? What if I'm not the best person to raise a baby?"

"Who's everyone?" His body shifts so he's fully facing me, his hand remaining on my belly. It's intimate; we're close here in my bedroom. The closest I've been to another person in forever. But I don't move. I don't shuffle back or pull at the blanket. It feels like this is our secret spot. A place where we can whisper and no one will hear us. Where we can verbalize our deepest thoughts and there's no judgment.

"My family. They want me to give my baby to my sister. She's been trying for years... hasn't been able to fall pregnant," I whisper, shame running through me.

"You're going to be a great mom. The fact that you're even worried about it says so."

"Do you still see your biological mom?" I try to be tactful, not entirely sure of what happened to her.

"My mom died when I was a kid."

"I'm sorry." My heart hurts for this man. I haven't even given birth yet, and I already know leaving my child would be heartbreaking.

He's quiet for a while. I can hear him breathing. I sit up, reach my hand up and cup his jaw, brushing my thumbs against his lips. I feel his rough stubble under my palm, and his strong jaw tenses a little at my touch. He goes to talk, but nothing comes out. I can tell his wounds are deep, that he carries a lot. His body is heavy with the toll of trauma.

"How old were you?" My thumb moves across his cheek, slowly, consistently, ensuring he's still with me. A repetitive motion allowing him to just be.

"Twelve. Mom died. Dad went to jail. I went into the system. Let's just say, my upbringing wasn't what you'd ever want for your kid. That's how I know you're going to be an amazing mom."

"What was her name?"

"Monique."

"What was she like?"

His face softens then. "Beautiful. She had this long hair, kinda like the color of honey. She was kind. Warm. Funny. She loved to cook. A bit like you. She used to make me her sweet apple pie for my birthday every year. I haven't had apple pie like it since she last made it for me the year I turned twelve." As his eyes meet mine, I give him a small smile. "I still remember the smell and taste, the warmth of it fresh out of the oven..."

"She sounds like a wonderful woman."

"She was." He clears his throat, this conversation deeper than I was first expecting. "You should go back to sleep. We have a few more hours until daybreak." His eyes cloud over like I've lost him, and his gaze moves away from mine, back to the floor, my hand sliding from his face.

My chest hurts for him. My family is still alive, yet the pain I feel from never being accepted by them is sharp and gnawing. I can't imagine what he must feel, having lost his family at such a young age.

"That chair can't be comfortable. Come lie with me," I offer, moving over, creating some space for him. There's no way he can sleep in the small chair for the rest of the night. He looks ridiculous sitting in it.

"It's okay..."

"I won't take no for an answer. I can't afford your chiropractic bills, and I don't have insurance." I make light of it and see him pull in a breath before he stands and comes to bed. He lies on top of the blanket right next to me.

"Griffin?" My voice is a mere whisper.

"Hmmm?"

"I may not be a mom yet, but I already know your mom would be so proud of you."

He turns his head and looks at me, his gaze swirling with a mix of emotions.

Then I feel it. His hand reaching out to mine. He entwines our fingers, much like we did the other day in his truck. But this time, he brings our clasped hands to his lips, softly kissing my hand before lowering it to the mattress between us, not letting go.

"Sleep, sweetness." His voice rumbles, and I remain facing him as I close my eyes, our hands still entwined, the two of us having a more restful sleep. Just in time before opening day.

15

SAVANNAH

There was a line out the door this morning, and even though it's almost lunchtime, it isn't dissipating.

"That's a perfect combination," I hear Melissa say to the next customer while I whirl around her, restocking the cabinets, my cupcakes going fast. I have new batches made; I just haven't had time to ice them yet.

"Have a great day!" she sing-songs and the register chimes. I'm overwhelmed, but in the best possible way.

"Hey, we're almost out of dinner rolls and the cupcakes are a winner today," Melissa whispers to me, clearly as excited as I am that we're both run off our feet.

"I have some almost ready. I just need to sort out the cabinets," I murmur to her, knowing I need to get busy in the kitchen, yet there's a million different things I need to be doing out here. I spot the paper bags our products go in, the pile almost gone.

"Morning... Excuse me... Pardon me, ma'am..."

That voice. Low, gravelly, unmistakable.

I snap upright so fast I nearly drop the tray in my hands.

And there he is, the man who slept beside me last night, pushing his way through the crowd like a storm rolling into a cupcake shop.

"Griffin!"

He takes in the chaos, the line, the scent of cinnamon and sugar, and his eyebrows lift. "Wow. This is... impressive."

Pride blooms in my chest instantly and embarrassingly warm. "It's great, but I need to ice more cupcakes, I have to sort these cabinets, I need to find more paper bags..." The words tumble out of me in one breath, my panic showing.

"I can ice," he says, dead serious.

I blink. "You what?"

"I can ice. You taught me how last night." He reaches past me, grabbing a spare apron off the hook. His body brushes mine, solid, warm, steady, and for a second, I swear my knees wobble. "Where are they?"

He's already tying the apron around his waist. The apron is... Oh no. Oh no, no, no.

Blue gingham. Frills. Tiny. It looks like it was made for a Disney princess, not a six-foot-something lumberjack of a man.

"Aren't you busy? Aren't you heading to the distillery today?" I ignore the way my heart somersaults.

"Tanner can wait." He says it like it's nothing. Like he didn't rearrange his entire day because I look overwhelmed.

There are maybe three people in this town who can tell Tanner Whiteman to wait. Griffin is one of them.

"In the back," I finally answer.

"I'm on it." He disappears into the kitchen, and I stand there for a beat too long, staring after him like a lovesick idiot.

Melissa snaps me back to reality. "Found those bags yet? Also, pies are running low..."

"Right! Yes. Bags. Pies." But my eyes betray me, flicking toward the kitchen in time to see Griffin reappear, picking up a piping bag filled with pink frosting. Pink. Frosting. In those hands.

The dainty vanilla cupcakes look like toys in his grip. The apron is ridiculous. He doesn't even notice. He's too focused on helping me.

And something in my chest squeezes so tight it's almost hard to breathe.

He shouldn't look good like this. He shouldn't look... so right in my space. He shouldn't make me feel steadier just by being here.

But he does.

"Don't forget the bags and the hot pies ..." Melissa brings me back to the present, forcing me to peel my eyes from the brooding man with the dainty vanilla cakes looking comically small in his large hands.

"I'll grab them now. More pies are ready too." I rush around, running out the back around the kitchen, to the front and all around the bakery. I walk the line of customers, offering samples and tastings of the cinnamon buns while they wait, thanking everyone for coming to opening day. I'm then behind the register, fumbling my way through as Melissa takes a break, the adrenaline surging through me as I see my stock dwindling down, my fresh breads and rolls already sold out.

"Here." Griffin emerges again, carrying a full tray of perfectly iced cupcakes. Perfect. I don't know how he did that with hands that could probably snap a rolling pin in half.

He slides the tray into the cabinet as the next rush hits.

"You need me to do anything else?" He scans the room for the next task.

Before I can answer, Sawyer and Sutton step up to the counter, both staring at Griffin like he's sprouted wings.

"Oh, this has made my day," Sawyer mutters.

"You ordering?" Griffin grumbles, crossing his arms, which only makes the frilly apron look even more absurd. And somehow... adorable.

"Depends." Sutton smirks. "Do the cupcakes come with a side of midlife crisis?"

He snaps a photo, and Griffin's jaw tics. I bite back a laugh, rolling my lips to tame the grin.

"Charge these assholes double, sweetness." His hand brushes my lower back as he moves past me, and the touch is so gentle, so unexpected, my breath catches. His head lowers then, his lips brushing the hair near my ear.

"I'll go clean up. Then I've got to run. I'll be back later," he murmurs for only me to hear. And I shouldn't want that. I shouldn't want him here, in my space, in my day, in my thoughts.

But I do.

More than I should.

All I can do is nod, not trusting myself to say another word to him, before he walks away.

"Two cupcakes?" I bring my attention back to the two men, who are still grinning as I try to get my head back on work. While they look over their options, I look past them at the line and notice the customers in the store all looking at Sutton and whispering. It dawns on me then that he's more than Griffin's friend and neighbor. He's a Hollywood movie star, and I freeze a little. I've met him before, at the kids' party, but that was just briefly, and I didn't think too hard about it.

"Better make it a dozen. My kids will eat them all, and I need to save one for Annabelle; otherwise, she'll bury my body in her vegetable garden..." Sawyer says, and I roll my lips again, loving the banter these guys have.

"A pretty dozen coming right up." I get busy sorting the box of cupcakes and look up, noticing Sutton filming around the store.

"You don't mind, do you? Thought I'd put it out on my socials. These cupcakes look awesome..."

"Ahh, um... no, that's great!" Seriously. Am I in a dream right now? Sutton Silvers is in my bakery, filming my cupcakes for his social media. His following is into the millions. One post from him and my little bakery will be put on the map!

"I have these ones." I point out a smaller batch off to the side that have yellow frosting and a small fondant bumble bee on them. Given he makes honey, he might appreciate those the most.

"Oh yeah. They're awesome!" He grins, takes a photo, and orders a dozen yellow ones too.

I wrap the order quickly, offer them my thanks, and move on to the next customer and then the next.

But every time I glance at the kitchen door, I half expect Griffin to walk back through it.

Every time I catch a whiff of cedar and soap, my heart jumps.

Every time I see the hook where the frilly apron usually hangs, I smile like an idiot.

By the time we lock the door, I'm exhausted, aching, and nearly floating.

"We did it," I breathe.

"You did it," Melissa says. "This place is going to be huge."

I rub my belly, feeling the baby shift. Feeling the weight of everything I've built. Everything I'm still trying to build.

And somewhere in the back of my mind is the image of Griffin in that ridiculous apron, icing cupcakes like it was the most natural thing in the world.

The grin to my face instant.

I did it. I opened my very own bakery. Just how I always wanted.

I rub my belly, knowing the next hurdle now awaits, so I push off the door and get straight into cleaning up. Because I can't rest. Not yet. I still have the prep work to do for tomorrow, and by the looks of today, I'll need a lot more bread.

"Want me to stay?"

I look at Melissa, knowing one of us has to rest before we do it all again tomorrow.

"No. Go head home. Thank you so much. I'll see you back here in the morning?" I question, not blaming her if she doesn't turn up again after how busy we were.

She grins as she grabs her things and walks toward me. "I'll be back. See you then."

I open the door for her and watch her walk down the street before I close it and lean against it. I take a big breath before a knock startles me, and I turn to see Griffin.

He came back, just like he said he would.

16

GRIFFIN

I got up early and left Savannah to it and attempted to keep busy all day.

But the nerves I had for her opening never left. I saw the crowds gathering on my way to do another site visit at the distillery and decided to stop by. She was busy. Completely run off her feet. So I did what I thought I could do to help and iced some of her cupcakes. I've built houses, barns, decks, and half the damn distillery. I could fix anything with my hands. But apparently, the one thing I couldn't do was pipe frosting onto a cupcake without making it look like a toddler was finger painting.

Were they perfect? No. Not by a long shot. I ruined at least five cupcakes. Maybe six. It was hard to tell where the frosting ended and the crime scene began.

My spoilage rate alone probably doubled the second I touched a piping bag. But if ruining a few cupcakes meant she breathed easier, I'd ruin a hundred more.

The truth is... I don't care about the cupcakes. I care about her.

The way she'd looked this morning—overwhelmed,

breathless, trying to do everything at once—hit me harder than I expected.

So if I had to ruin a few cupcakes to make her day easier, then fine. Let the spoilage rate climb.

I'd fix anything for her.

After my first foray as a baker, I spent time at the distillery, looking over the new accommodation and talking with Victoria about a few new projects coming up before I decided to grab some materials from Bob at the hardware store. Needing to keep myself busy, I went to my place on Billionaire Boulevard and got to work.

I had to do anything to keep my mind off her. I probably should've flown to Sundown Valley. Or even to Colorado to look over a build my team is doing, but leaving after just getting back here feels wrong. Even though I've done it numerous times before.

It's not uncommon for me to be in three or four different states per week. The miles of air travel I have racked up is beyond anyone's wildest imagination. I'm always on the go. Always building, quoting, managing, reviewing. My workaholic nature has won me awards, made me millions. There's nothing I want for.

Until now.

I want Savannah to succeed today. I want the bakery to be amazing. I want her to smile, to laugh. I want her to sleep well. I want her to look at me with those big eyes and never stop. I want to hold her hand. Touch her. Be with her.

That's probably why I slipped into her bed last night. Refusing to leave her alone and refusing to attempt to fit myself into the poor excuse of an armchair she had at her bedside any longer. So I stayed on the top of the blanket and watched her sleep until slumber took me under.

My sleep was restless. It usually is. But it was also one of the more peaceful experiences I've had. Hearing her soft breaths and little snores all night had me feeling content like I haven't felt before. Despite the usual night terror that woke me.

It should've been weird sharing her bed. I don't share beds with women. I don't cuddle, don't caress. I sure as hell don't hold hands and touch baby bumps. But it felt right. I've got friends, acquaintances, but she's different. We click. It's easy with her. She doesn't pry, doesn't want more than I'm willing to give. She doesn't demand a thing from me, and because of that, I want to give her more of me than I've given anyone else.

Perhaps that's why, in the middle of the night, I shared more with her than I have with any other person. She didn't prod too much, didn't look at me any differently. I appreciated it.

Now with my new project at home underway, and not able to stay away from her for a minute longer, I knock on the bakery door, seeing her leaning against it.

"You're back!" Her smile is wide, and I puff out my chest.

"How did it go?" I walk in and shut the door behind me, turning the closed sign around and looking over her.

"Why do I feel like I spent the day in my mixer?" She's exhausted but happy if her soft smile and shiny eyes are anything to go by.

"Because your opening day was fucking phenomenal." I push off the door and move closer to her. The cabinets, which housed all the fresh pastries this morning, are now empty. She sold out.

"That was amazing." Her grin is wide, her eyes sparkling, and I'm proud of her.

"You should've seen the line at the door before we opened! I sold out of sourdough before noon. All the donuts and the cupcakes you iced were all gone by two, and the after-school rush cleaned me out of everything else. Thank goodness Melissa was here to help."

I saw her line. I drove past here so many times today to check on things, but aside from helping her for a little bit, I gave her space to do her thing. Yet here I am, right on closing. I'm turning into a man I don't recognize around her.

"And you. Thank you so much, Griffin..." She takes a step toward me. "You came to my rescue earlier." She lifts onto her tippy toes and places a small peck to my cheek. My hands move automatically, holding her waist. The urge I have to turn my head to put my lips on hers is strong, but I resist. She lowers back down, my hands moving from her waist, one lingering to her side, where I grasp her fingers, them curling into mine a little.

My heart pumps a little faster than usual, my chest feeling warmer at the contact.

"You need to put your feet up." I notice her cradling her bump, the one that seems to have doubled in size since I first met her over a month ago.

"Yeah right." She snorts a laugh. "I need to get things ready for tomorrow."

I frown, not liking that answer.

"Seriously?" I don't know too much about baking and owning a bakery, but I guess she does need to replenish.

"I need to get some more sourdough proofing, get the cookie dough ready, more icing and cupcakes..." She looks around, rubbing her belly a little in one spot.

"Are you in pain?" My frown deepens. Not liking it. Hudson told her weeks ago she needed to rest and she hasn't. I know she has a lot on her plate and not a lot of help, but she does need to take it easy. Her due date is almost here.

"No, just junior kicking my bladder again."

I'm amazed. When she moved my hand to her bump last night, and I felt the baby kicking, I was in awe. Never felt anything like it.

"What are you going to do with the baby once it arrives and you're here?" There's no way she can work and have the baby, especially if the bakery is as busy as it was today.

"Let me show you." Her grin is magnetic and she turns, her hold on my hand tightening as she pulls me into the kitchen.

"There," she says, pointing to the spare area in her kitchen currently housing boxes and a few other bits and pieces.

"What?" My brow pinches, not getting it.

"I plan to put in a bassinet, a soft mat, some shelves to hold all the baby things. The baby can sleep while I serve and bake. Melissa was so good today, so she will help more. I also have a carrier so I can wear him or her during the day."

"Wear?" I have no idea what she's talking about.

"You know, wrap it to my chest. Like a backpack, but on my front."

I still have no idea, but it seems practical.

"You haven't been around babies much before, have you?" Her head tilts, her smile like the sun.

I grew up looking after my baby brother when my mom worked and my dad was too drunk to do anything other than yell. When he died, I never wanted to look after another kid. It hurt too much.

"No."

"Hmmm, well, you'll learn. I have a feeling this little one is going to love Grumpy Griff." She grins, walking toward her bench and putting on a fresh apron as my eyebrow rises. *Grumpy Griff.*

She sighs, tired but happy. "I gotta get things ready before I fall into a heap."

I watch her move around the kitchen for a moment before I look back at the space where she wants the baby setup to go.

"I've got to pop out. Be back later."

"Okay." Her smile widens as she gives me a little wave, and I turn and walk out before I get too lost in it, another new project already on my mind.

I step out onto Main Street and pause. Besides the clothes, the baby book, and a small bassinet I noticed in her apartment, I haven't seen much other baby stuff around. I look up and down the street, not seeing a kids' store, apart from the toy store, and I know they won't have what she needs.

Fuck. I don't even know exactly what she needs. I spot Sawyer's law office across the street and stride over.

He has kids. He should know.

As I push through his doors, I'm greeted by silence.

"Hello?" My rough voice echoes before Sawyer pops out of his office down the hall.

"Hey, Griff, where'd the pretty blue apron go?" Sawyer grins at me like he doesn't have a care in the world. Meanwhile, I'm coiled tight, wanting to get everything perfect for Savannah before the baby comes.

"I need some help." Ignoring his quip, I'll get payback for that.

"I'm great, thanks for asking." I look at him, deadpan, and he only grins wider.

"Jeez, do you ever smile? I thought for sure after your customer service in the bakery today, you would be more attuned to smiling. Looks like Savannah did a roaring trade."

I nod. "She did. Sold out."

"So, what do you need? Planning permits for Tanner? Building contracts for Sutton?"

"I want to get some things for Savannah," I tell him, and he looks at me, confused.

"Things? Like what things?"

"Baby things." His eyebrows rise, surprise written all over his face.

"Baby things? You know you're in a law office, right?" His brow crumples, and I scrub my face.

"Well, you have kids, don't you?"

"Yes, Griffin. I do. Kids. Not babies. Not yet anyway."

"But you should know what they need, right?"

"I have no clue. I'm still trying to figure out how to make the perfect monster spray for Noah. Apparently, there's a science to the glitter to water ratio that I can't get right."

I look at him like he's crazy because I have no idea what he's talking about.

"Where do I go for baby stuff around here?" I sigh, frustrated.

"Probably Williamstown is the closest. Does she have babysitting set up? She'll need a hand with either the baby or the bakery, if not both. Especially after the line of people I saw down the street today. She won't have a moment to feed the baby, let alone change diapers or rock it to sleep."

"Yeah, she's got a local woman helping her out. Seems pretty good. They were both run off their feet today."

"Well, good that she has someone helping. Hey, didn't you say you were doing a new build in Colorado?"

I frown before I understand his meaning. "Mother Maven." I grumble my new client's name and start to walk out, my mission now sorted.

"Yeah, you're welcome!" Sawyer hollers as I leave, my cell

already in my hand, dialing my new client. Sandra Suiter, otherwise known as Mother Maven. The go-to woman in the baby and infant industry around the country. A CEO who owns over one hundred stores. How did I not think of her?

"Griffin. How are you?"

I take a deep breath, not used to asking people for help. Especially clients.

"Fine. I hope I'm not interrupting?" I pause on the street. People pass by, a group of women walking across the road to the diner all look at me before they giggle. I turn my back to them and look in the window of Daisy's yoga studio instead, pretending like it's the most interesting thing I've ever seen.

"Not at all. Just between meetings. How's the build? Everything going okay?"

"Yes, fine. I'm calling on another matter." I swallow.

"Oh, sure, What's up?"

"I have a... friend. She's due soon. I need to get some things for her and the baby."

"Oh... of course. What does she need?"

"I have no idea, but she doesn't have much, so I'm guessing she needs everything. I can get my jet to one of your stores tonight."

"Wow, she must be important. Leave it with me. I'll organize a personal shopper to gather everything and text you the pickup location. East or West Coast?"

I blow out a breath, feeling like I'm doing something right.

"Kind of in the middle. I'm in Whispers."

"Great. I'll get the team on it."

"No budget. I want the best," I tell her, because Savannah deserves that.

"Of course. Leave it with me. You'll have everything you need by tonight. She's a lucky woman to have you."

"I appreciate it. Thanks." I end the call, not agreeing with her. Lucky is not something people are around me. That's why I usually keep my distance. That's why I should be in Colorado overseeing her new ranch rather than standing on the street worrying about jumpsuits and pacifiers.

"Griffin? Are you okay?"

Daisy pops her head out of her studio, looking at me, and I frown.

"Fine. Why?"

"Well, you're making the women a little uncomfortable, standing there, watching their downward dogs through the window." Her gaze flicks inside, and it's then I realize she's holding a yoga class, and like the idiot I am, I'm planted at the window, glued to the view like it's prime-time TV, like some creep.

"Shit. Sorry." I step away immediately. Clearly my mind isn't on my surroundings.

"It's okay. See you later." She smiles, walking back inside, and I hightail it back to the hardware store, needing some timber for my new project. On my way, I call my pilot and get him ready. A jet full of baby equipment will be here in twenty-four hours.

You resting?

I SEND the text to Savannah before I think about it. I left her this afternoon, hands deep in flour for her to get things prepared for tomorrow. I hope she's resting already.

Yes, boss.

My eyes thin.

You need to rest.

My cell rings then, her name lighting up the screen, so I put my sander down and answer.

"You're not even here and you're still bossing me around." Her voice is full of jest.

"Mmmmm. You're looking after that baby and that bakery. I'm making sure you're looking after you too."

I brush my hand over the smooth timber, the soft curve of my project feeling just right. I've never built a crib before. I guess there's a first time for everything.

"I just locked up, and I'm upstairs in the apartment. I have sourdough everywhere, I have cookie dough ready, flour in my hair, and I can't even tell you how many macarons I've piped."

She laughs at herself, and I smile.

"Where did you get to today?" Her voice is soft. Like she cares. Feeling like a warm hug, like a safe space.

"I had to do a few things here at the house. You need me to come and check your locks? You alright?"

"I'm fine. You don't need to."

"What if I want to?" The words leave me before I can pull them back. My heart thuds, my chest tight. Fuck, what the hell am I doing?

"You know, I can't remember if I locked the back door or not..."

"I'll be there in five minutes."

"Okay." I swear I can hear her smile.

I end the call and blow out a breath. I have no idea what we're doing. Dancing around each other. Spending time together like we're friends. And we are. But there's an underlying tension simmering that I can't get a hold of. Fuck, I don't even know what the hell I'm thinking, getting all excited to see her like I didn't see her a few hours ago.

But I put my tools down and leave my shed, walking through my garden and heading inside to wash my hands. As I do, I look over my expansive lawn. Memories from roughhousing with the kids at the birthday party are vivid in my mind. I pause, staring at the space, imagining what it would look like with streamers and kids everywhere, celebrating a birthday.

Wondering if there's even a slither of possibility that kids around here would even be an option. My mind imagines a little one. Maybe two. Running around on shaky legs, giggling, tumbling on the grass like Tanner's little girl before I swoop them up and throw them in the air, hearing them squeal in delight.

I rub my eyes. I never daydream. Not sure why I'm starting now. Shaking my head, I stride to the house, pushing inside to the kitchen. Modern. Polished. Unused. The house is new, and I barely stay here. So I have no trinkets, no photos. Nothing personal. I don't even keep that kind of thing anywhere.

It feels empty. Hollow. Yet it's full of designer furnishings thanks to Victoria. But it's a house. Not a home. I need to remember that.

My cell rings, and I pull it out, thinking it's Savannah again, and answer immediately.

"Hey? You alright?" It's my go-to. My worry for her constant.

"Griffin?" the voice on the other end is eerily familiar.

"Who's this?" I'm immediately on alert, like my body knows exactly who it is, my mind not wanting to believe it.

"I guess it has been almost twenty-five years…"

I feel like a deer in headlights. It can't be. It can't be him. My heart thuds heavily in my chest and my body tenses. I breathe in and out of my nose, my jaw tight. Anger swirls inside of me like a tornado building, gathering every ounce of emotion that floats around my body and pulling in tight to create a storm so severe it's unavoidable. I can't stop it.

"Lose my number." I end the call and throw my cell on the kitchen counter, my body now vibrating in anger.

"Goddamn motherfucker..." I grit out to the empty stillness of my kitchen.

My cell chimes, and I swipe it from the counter, ready to crush it. But this time, I look at my screen and see Savannah's name again. Looking at the time, I've been standing here for too long; she probably thinks I've forgotten about her.

> I baked you something today...

Accompanying the text is a photo of a gingerbread man holding a hammer and wearing a scowl. He has a little lunch box in his other hand with the name Griffin on it. And just like that, she breaks my mood, and my anger starts to dissipate. My fingers move before I think too hard. The familiar, safe feeling I've had for years resurfaces, and I do what I always do. I run.

> Sorry, something came up. I can't come. Lock the doors. Rest up. I have to fly out early tomorrow. Not sure how long I will be gone.

I send the text to her before I change my mind. Then I send another one just as quick to get my jet and pilot ready for dawn, needing to leave, to go, to always be on the move as anxiety runs through my body like a full river after a storm. I swallow down the lump in my throat, hating myself for letting her down.

But it's for the best.

That dream of kids playing on the lawn... It's never going to happen. It can't. And I need to stop thinking about it.

SAVANNAH

I breathe deeply and try to relax as Hudson takes my vitals.

"So, the bakery is a roaring success. You must be happy?" He makes small talk as he types a few things into my file.

"Well, I've been open for over a week now, and the interest hasn't died down. Every night, I make more and more products, but every day, I continually sell out. It's better than I ever could have imagined." I can't help the grin. I'm proud. Exhausted, but proud. But I would be lying if I said I didn't feel a little hollow.

I haven't seen Griffin since opening day. The night he texted and said he was coming over yet canceled instead. I feel a little lost without him. He's been the most constant person in my life for weeks. A new friend. A man to lean on when I needed it. It was nice to have him close by. And I'm scared to admit it, but I miss him when he's gone. We went from sleeping next to each other and sharing secrets one night, to not seeing each other all week.

He's sent a few text messages. Short, simple ones to

check how I'm doing. But never anything that prompts conversation. Never anything that extends to talking on the phone like we had before.

"So, your due date is next week. Going over is not uncommon, but we don't want you going over for much longer than about a week or so."

Only I would open a new business so close to my due date. But I knew the chances of me opening after the baby was here would be harder, so I've pushed myself to this point. I needed to make it work. I needed the income; I needed to show my family and anyone else who ever doubted me that I could provide for my baby. And I have. I'm stressed, I'm not going to lie. It's either going to be the best thing I've ever done or the most foolish decision I've made. But deep in my bones, I know it was the right one.

"Oh, I feel this little one is tucked so tight that coming out is the last thing they want," I say with a laugh, trying to make light, but I'm secretly terrified. Labor, the pain, doing it all on my own. It's a lot.

"You could go into labor any day now, so take it easy." He pauses for a moment, then asks, "What do you plan to do when the baby arrives?"

"I'm hoping the baby will be a good sleeper, allowing me to still bake every morning and then serve throughout the day. But I have Melissa, who's been helping me. I know I sound naive, but I have no other options." I need to make it work.

"Well, good. But you also need to be mindful that carrying a baby for nine months and then delivering the baby will have some impact on you and your body. We all think we're invincible, me included, so please make sure you get adequate rest, take your vitamins, drink water..." He gives me a look of warning, and I offer a small nod in understanding.

"I am. I will. I plan to rest when the baby arrives. I'll probably close the bakery for a little while until I get the hang of things. The girls have all said they can help. Victoria is first on the list for babysitting duties." I grin, thinking about my new friends who have all been checking in on me.

"You have Lacy and me too, of course. That's the great thing about Whispers; there's a lot of helping hands. But... your bump still hasn't dropped like I would expect it to, so you might still have some time." The furrow to his brow isn't reassuring.

"Should I be doing anything?"

"Resting." Hudson is firm with that quick answer, and my lips thin.

"Aside from resting. Anything to help get the baby into position?"

"Movement can work. Walking, swimming..."

"Dancing?" I do love to dance. I haven't in a while because I'm so front loaded in weight. Plus, I'm not exactly a ballerina at the best of times. I trip over my own feet more times than not. But having music on and moving around the bakery is one of my favorite things to do. I just haven't done it in a while.

"Sure. I don't recommend anything too frantic, but yes, dancing would work. Some old wives' tales also suggest things like eating spicy food or even sex can help put things into motion."

Sex. I blink wordlessly at him as I feel my cheeks heat. My mind moves to one man and one man only. The one who isn't here.

"Oh, well, I'm sure I can make a curry or something." God, why am I flushed. "And I do love dancing to a bit of

Whitney Houston in the kitchen." I'm rambling now. But Hudson is a professional as he finalizes my notes.

"Okay, well, dance, spicy foods, rest. See how you feel over the next day or two. Call me any time of the day or night, the minute you start to feel some movement or pain."

"I will." I wring my hands together. My stress is high, anxiety crawling around my body like it's considering taking up permanent residence. Even though I know this baby has to come out, it's the coming out part I'm not looking forward to.

As I make my way from Hudson's office back to the bakery, I grab my phone, seeing the screen blank. No word from Griffin today. I have no idea how long he's away for, but my heart feels a little heavy from missing him. I hate the distance. Before I second-guess myself, I shoot him a text.

> Checkup with Hudson all done. I need to try to find some spices in Whispers to cook with. Apparently spicy food will help get the baby into position.

I see some bubbles dance on my screen from his reply, and I hold my breath.

> Only five percent of babies are born by their due date…

I frown. How does he know that?

> Really?

> That's what the app is telling me.

App? What does he mean?

> App?

I push through the door back to my safe haven of Betty's Bakery, going straight into the kitchen to see what I have for spices, which I already know is nonexistent. Sugar, yes. Yeast, also yes. Turmeric or cardamom? No. Definitely not.

> I downloaded a baby app. It tells me what you're feeling and what the baby is up to.

My heart stutters as I look at my phone. Then I dial before my brain can catch up to the action.

I talk before he can.

"You downloaded an app?" I'm in shock. I don't even have an app.

"I did," his deep voice rumbles. Safe. Steady. Strong.

"But when? Why?" My words rush out, feeling a little flustered.

"Well, I don't know much about babies, so I'm trying to educate myself. After seeing your book on your nightstand, I thought an app might help me understand a little more."

It's a really nice thing to do, actually. Just not something I ever imagined a man like Griffin to do.

"Okay... what else does it say?" I take a seat on the small stool at my new stainless-steel counter.

"Says the baby is now mostly fully developed and gaining weight."

I huff a laugh. "Oh, I feel that," I tell him, rubbing my bump, feeling the size of a house myself.

"It also says the baby's reflexes are ready to go, so it can suck and grasp and things."

"Kick. Push against my diaphragm like it's a competitive sport," I whine. I don't whine often, but at nine months pregnant, I feel like I'm allowed to whine a little.

"What did Hudson say?"

I smile. This is nice. Talking about it with someone. Someone who cares.

"Just that I need to eat spicy food. Apparently, it'll help the baby move into position. But I have nothing here at the bakery. I thought I could make some curry puffs or savory muffins, but I have no turmeric or cumin or anything. I don't even think the local grocery store here in Whispers will have anything. And I don't want to go to Williamstown. I never want to go back there." I shiver, feeling the need to stay away from the town I grew up in.

"Hmmm, pineapple juice can also help," Griffin offers, and I grin.

"Is that on the app too?" I tease.

"No, I'm researching online."

I feel warm all over, basking in his attention.

"Where are you?" I'm tentative. I never want him to think I'm tracking him. I have no claim over him, even if I do feel some simmering tension building between us. He's busy with work, and I'm busy with the bakery and cooking a human. But we have a connection, that much is clear.

"Just landed in Sundown Valley. I was in Colorado the last few days checking over my build."

"Are you okay?" My heart skips a beat. But his message and quick getaway out of town last week seemed sudden.

"I need to be asking you that."

"I'm fine. We're fine."

"Good. Not sure when I'll be back..." Disappointment fills me.

"Okay, well... Don't work too hard." It's all I can think to say that will prevent me from asking him to come back to Whispers. Back to me.

"Take care, sweetness." The call ends as quickly as it started, and I sigh, look around my kitchen, and decide to make some dough in case I stumble across some spices. If I can't, I'll make cherry puffs instead.

Four hours later, among the batches and batches of dough and pastry, there's a knock at the back door.

"Delivery!" a man yells, and I frown, not expecting anything.

"One minute." I wipe my hands and peek out the window. Sure enough, a delivery driver stands there, carrying a box.

"Hi," I greet him, opening the door. "Just on the counter, please."

He notices my bump and nods and walks inside, putting the box down for me and handing me a tablet to sign.

"Where's this from?" I ask him.

"India Imports. Urgent delivery."

My eyebrows rise as I pass the tablet back to him. "India Imports?"

"A bulk importer of spices and items from India. They organized a private flight here today for this. Must be pretty urgent, miss. Enjoy your evening." He gives me a wave and walks out, and I stand at the door, watching him leave.

He was right. The smell hits me immediately as I open the box. Large jars of fresh spices—turmeric, curry, chili, cumin, even saffron, which gives me pause, because it's the most expensive spice in the world.

My heart races as I pull out the paperwork, a small note included.

Found the spices for you. Griff x

"Oh…" I think I'm in shock. There'd be no way I could find this quality of spice here in Whispers or even in Williamstown. At best, I could probably find a small shaker that's been sitting on the shelf for months. This spice from

Griffin is top quality, directly imported and probably the freshest you could get outside of India.

I plop on the stool near the counter and take a minute to gather myself. The man is on the other side of the country, building mansions and ranches, yet he still downloaded a baby app, found authentic spices, and sent them to me within hours.

I have no idea who Griffin is, exactly. I don't know his past. But I do know he's an amazing man. One I'm grateful to have in my life.

I HAVE Whitney blaring on the speakers throughout my kitchen as I pull out the last tray of curry puffs from the oven. While I could make a curry or some type of laksa, the baker in me loves these pastry spice mixes and the town is loving them too. I've made them all week, ever since the spice delivery turned up. So I now have fresh curry puffs, savory vegetable pies, and spiced muffins all cooling on the counter, ready to go for tomorrow. Minus a few here and there that I gobbled as I danced.

None of it has helped, though. I have no pains, the baby is still firmly intact, my belly position remains high right under my ribs, yet I've swayed, twerked and salsa'd my way around this small space for days since my checkup with Hudson. No amount of spices or dancing is helping; this baby is holed up tight.

"Ohhh, I wanna dance with somebody..." I sing at the top of my lungs and shimmy across the floor to ensure the fridge is shut properly.

"I wanna feel the heat with somebody..." I shimmy back,

holding my bump, moving my hips from side to side as best I can.

"Yeah, I wanna da—" The words die on my lips as I turn and spot someone standing in my doorway, watching me. Eyes wide, expression unreadable. I turn down the music, my cheeks flaming under his burning gaze. "You're back?"

I swallow hard as he remains silent. His eyes trail down my body and back up again. Like he's ensuring I'm in one piece.

"Griffin?"

He still hasn't moved. Hasn't said a word. His eyes burn into mine. His hair is a little scruffy, like he's been pulling at it, his eyes a little dark like he hasn't slept much.

"This is your warning…"

"Warning?" I frown, confused.

"I'm going to put my hands on you." His voice is a growl as he strides forward, his gaze not leaving me as my eyes widen in understanding and my stomach flips.

"Oh," I whisper as this man stalks toward me.

"You alright?" His hand slides around my waist, settling at my lower back.

"Ahhh, yeah…" My mouth is dry as I look up at him, his eyes, then his lips, feeling a pull to get closer. *What's happening right now?*

"The baby?" he asks gruffly, yet there's a tenderness there that he only has with me.

I swallow, my heart thudding as his other hand sweeps over my jaw and cups my face.

"Fine." I can barely talk as he holds me tight. My hands now rest on his chest. It feels so nice to be held in his arms.

"Good. Come here." He tilts my head and lowers his, and before I know what's happening, his lips are on mine, and I swear I see stars.

18

GRIFFIN

I fucking missed her. I missed her smile, her tenacity, her body, her eyes on me. I missed her soft hands, her baking, her smell. Her sweetness the most.

As I walked into the bakery tonight after seeing the lights on, using the spare key she gave me weeks ago, I felt a little sheepish for being so absent. I ran. I ran away. Trying to outrun the past that always lingers, not wanting to tarnish her beautiful life with my dirty one. But on the way to my place from the airport tonight, I couldn't help but drive down Main Street to check on her. I sat outside in my car, debating with myself for over an hour. Debating on whether to see her, knowing exactly where it would lead, or drive away, keeping her at arm's length. It was an easy choice in the end. I couldn't stay away. I heard the music the minute I opened the front door and followed it like a moth to a flame, helpless and already burning.

Walking through her sparkling shop front, I saw everything clean and ready for tomorrow. But when I walked through the kitchen door, I paused and watched.

She was dancing. And God, she's beautiful. Swaying with her bump. One of her long dresses showcases her curves that I like so much. Pastries hot from the oven, smelling so good, I'm sure you could hear my stomach growl from hunger if the tunes weren't so loud. I haven't eaten much since being away. I get tunnel vision, pushing everything from my mind and focusing on work. I've done it for so long, it's now second nature. People, thoughts, feelings, emotions, hunger, pain. It all dissipates under the thud of a hammer and a nail.

I watched her for less than a minute before I knew I had to kiss her. I had to have her in my arms, had to have her lips on mine, and I walked straight to her like a man on a mission. One half of my brain wondering what the hell I'm doing, the other knowing I'd follow her anywhere.

Now as my lips touch hers, I feel like I'm right where I belong. I feel like I've finally found the piece of me that's been missing. I feel at peace.

Hiding myself in Colorado and Sundown Valley all week, I thought was for the best. I had the baby items from Mother Maven delivered straight to my place here and then tried to forget all about my sweet baker and her belly. But I couldn't. Every night, I'd lie awake, staring at the ceiling, wishing I was with her. Wondering if she was sleeping, resting. Wondering if and when the baby was coming. Every morning, I'd grab my phone to call her or text her, to check in. But I'd force my hand away before I could. I spent hours and hours poring over the baby app I downloaded. Wanting to know as much as possible about the very topic I had no idea of.

But then she texted me. Then called me. Told me about her checkup, and my chest burned, knowing I wasn't here with her when it's the only place I truly wanted to be.

When I got the mystery call last week, the voice I recognized immediately, it brought back so many emotions. I thought I was free. Free of his hold on me. But like the low-life scum of the earth he is, he still tries to pull me back under. I didn't want to tarnish Savannah. A beautiful woman growing a beautiful new life and starting fresh.

I'm a man with a dark past. I rarely show emotion. I don't do soft touches and sweet gestures. So I did what I always do. I got on my jet and went to work. But I couldn't stay away. There's a connection. A pull. A deep-seated need to protect, caress, have her. Be with her. And right now, kissing her, my lips demanding, taking, my hands not just holding her, but pulling her close. Fuck, I want this. Want her more than anything.

I growl onto her lips, feeling greedy as she kisses me back just as feverishly. She tastes as good as she feels. All soft, supple, feminine.

She moves her hands then. I feel her palms glide up my arms and cup my face, and they feel so nice. Like she's holding me. Caring for me. Looking after me. I pull back a little, the two of us panting for air.

Her big round eyes blink up at me.

"Welcome home." Two simple words. To her, probably no more than a simple greeting. But they hit me in my chest, burning through my skin like a brand, so hot I almost flinch.

"You're dancing? Are you okay to dance?" My voice is rough. I sound like an asshole. Like I'm berating her. Hell, I am an asshole. I walked into her space, watched her, and then put my mouth on her. Like I'm a fucking stalker. But my eyes narrow, looking at her. Wondering if the dancing is good for her and the baby. As much as I love to see it, I want her to be healthy.

"The baby still hasn't dropped into position yet. Hudson

said dancing may help. Plus, the spicy food." Her cheeks go bright pink. I see them clearly since I haven't let her go.

"You're using the spices?" I can smell that she is. There's a savory smell in here that I haven't smelled before.

"Yes. Thank you. You didn't have to go to so much trouble." Her eyes search mine, and I remain steady.

"I wanted to make sure you have what you need."

"Well, I do now..." Her voice is small, but her words are full of weight, and if I could, I'd wrap her up and never let her go.

"Wanna dance with me?" Her head tilts a little, and her lips quirk up at the sides. I swallow hard. Dancing isn't something I do, but she moves her hands from my cheeks and runs them back down my shoulders, pulling me in. I take the hint and drop my hand from her jaw and wrap it around her waist, meeting the other at the small of her back.

A slower song comes on, and she starts to sway, her hips moving from side to side. I don't move. I can't. My feet are rooted to the floor as I watch her in awe. She has a little flour on her cheek, her hair up, her breasts looking fuller since I last saw her. Her bump too. I can't believe how much she's changed in a week.

"I don't dance." I feel like I'm going to have a heart attack. I want to move. I want to give her what she wants. But it feels so foreign. So odd. So unnatural.

"Well, I'm not sure I'm technically dancing either... so just sway with me... You can do it." Her smile widens, and that's what has my feet moving. My eyes are glued to hers. The light's hitting her just right, her soft body moving under my hands. She runs her hands down my arms, stepping out from me and grabbing my hand to twirl around. I ensure I keep her close, not wanting her to slip and fall.

"How does this help the baby?" Here in her arms, there's nowhere for me to hide. I have a feeling she would see straight through it anyway. My feet shuffle like my shoes are made from lead. But I'm moving. I'm doing it.

"Well, Hudson said it could come any time, but it's not in position. Apparently, upright movement, hip swaying, and gravity all work together to open the pelvis, create more space, and gently guide the baby downward, ready for birth. And then I also made some curry and spicy pastries."

"Mmmm. I can smell them." My mouth waters. For her and her food.

"How long are you staying for?"

Forever. That's what I feel like saying. I move my eyes from hers and look at her belly. If she could go into labor any day now, then I want to be close.

"I might stick around for a week or so," I tell her and watch as her features soften.

"I'd like that," she says quietly, and I tighten my grip on her, pulling her closer to me, her belly squished into my own as I bury my face in her hair and we sway.

If this is what Heaven feels like? Then I'm ready to die, because holding her and her holding me feels like a dream. One I don't want to wake from. Yet like every night, it will no doubt turn into another nightmare.

Sweet kisses and soft dreams are not something a man like me gets in life. No matter how bad I want it.

"Actually... I feel like I might need a new mattress. Do you want to sleep over tonight and let me know what you think?" she murmurs against my chest, and I swear she'll hear my heart explode.

I know what she's really asking of course. Her mattress is fine.

"Thought it felt a little lumpy last time. Might be worth trying it again before you get a new one..." I offer, trying to tame the grin pulling at my life.

And just like that, I'm staying. Sleeping by her side, right where I want to be.

19

SAVANNAH

I step into the yoga studio and pause.

"Surprise!" the girls all yell, and I'm momentarily shocked into place.

"We wanted to put together a little party." Victoria looks at me, waiting, since I haven't moved a muscle since I stepped inside.

Snapping out of it, I smile wide and chest warm. "Oh my gosh... you did all this?"

"Victoria nearly hot-glued her fingers together trying to get those glittery signs on the wall." Lacy chuckles.

"It was one time," Victoria mutters. "And I stand by my commitment to glitter."

"A baby shower?" Tears prick my eyes as I look at the pink and blue streamers on the wall. The cute tables and chairs have replaced the yoga mats and the tables off to the side house a large cake and refreshments, along with a mountain of gifts.

"Yes. We know the baby's coming soon and wanted to make you feel special, before sleepless nights take over your entire personality." Annabelle comes to my side, giving me a small hug.

I'm lost for words. I've never really had a party before. Celebrations were never something I grew up with. I told myself it was too indulgent, that I didn't need the fanfare. But truth be told, I was always jealous when Eden had large birthday parties with her friends every year, and I was barely acknowledged on mine.

"Come on through here..." Daisy steps forward, placing a sash over my head saying *Mom-To-Be*.

"Oh, this is..." I'm trying to find the words while simultaneously trying not to cry.

"Now my cupcakes are not as good as yours, so be kind..." Rochelle, the lady who owns the local diner, teases, and I grin. "Honestly, if they taste terrible, just lie. I'm fragile today."

"You're always fragile," Charlotte snorts.

"Excuse me, I am a delicate flower," Rochelle says, flipping her hair.

"You're a cactus," someone mutters from the back.

"Sharp, but thriving," Rochelle fires back.

"Thank you. Thank you so much. This is all so beautiful..." I finally say, looking at all the women who have turned up. Some I've met a few times, and others I've only started to get to know.

"Well, now you're here, so let the games begin!" Lacy says, moving around, and I see everyone start to shuffle. "Who wants to start with Baby Bingo?"

Some of the older ladies all grab a card, shuffling to their seats as they chatter.

"Okay, ground rules," Lacy announces. "No cheating, no bribing, and no threatening the bingo caller."

"Why did you look at me when you said that?" Daisy

asks with a wide grin on her face.

"Because last time you tried to trade me a rose quartz for a win." Lacy laughs.

"It was a *good* rose quartz," Daisy argues.

Victoria leans in with a gentle smile. "Look around, Savannah. Every single woman here showed up because they adore you already."

I swallow hard, a tear escaping. "I'm still getting used to that."

"Well," she says, looping her arm through mine, "get used to it. We're not going anywhere." She leads me farther inside, where I sit with the ladies all afternoon. Wondering how I became so lucky.

"You haven't stopped smiling since we left."

Griffin and I walk hand in hand down the street, him having come to the yoga studio with the other guys to help pack up and take the girls home.

"It was amazing." My face hurts from smiling so much. "We played games, ate too much, laughed..."

"Well, Victoria knows how to throw a party." He nods, and I tilt my head up at him.

"You knew?" While the party was a complete surprise to me, the way Griffin's brows don't furrow as deep as they normally do gives away his knowledge.

"Maybe."

"And you didn't tell me?" I laugh, surprised.

"When Victoria first mentioned it, I thought it was a great idea. Seeing you smile now, I know I was right."

I lean into him as he gathers me closer to his side, our slow stroll down Main Street here in Whispers feeling nice in the warm afternoon sun.

"Tell me how I can eat all afternoon but still have a craving for pickles..." I murmur.

"Pickles?"

"Yeah, those really sweet green pickles." My mouth waters.

"You want me to go get you some?"

"Oh no. Believe me when I tell you, there's absolutely no space in my stomach for another thing after all the food I ate today. But this baby has me craving them all the same." I smile, rubbing my belly subconsciously.

"I've heard pregnancy can make you crave a lot of things."

"A good night's sleep, mostly..." I laugh. "Let's sit in the gardens here and watch the sunset," I suggest as we wander down toward the seats behind Sutton's law office, the area green and tranquil at this time of day.

"You feeling alright?" He watches me slowly take a seat, my walk turning into a waddle now the baby is almost here. As he sits, he stifles a yawn.

"I'm fine. But you didn't get much sleep last night."

He had another nightmare last night. He's had one each time he's stayed over.

"I never get much sleep." He rubs his eyes.

"You know I used to have them as a kid. I could never sleep. Always thought the devil was under my bed." I smile, swallowing a little, seeing if he'll open up.

"What stopped them?" He looks at me then, our gaze connecting before he leans back on the seat, lifting his arm up and around my back, encouraging me to lean in on him. And I do.

"My grandmother gave me her small pocket Bible. Told me to put it under my pillow and that it'd ward off the bad dreams. It worked." I shrug, thinking about my gran and how amazing she was. "Do you believe in religion?" I lift my head to ask him.

"Somewhat. We said grace as a family. Went to church about once a month or so as a kid. That kind of filtered out as I grew up and went into foster care. My mom always read the Bible, though, and I turned to it at different times in my life."

"It was such a big part of my life growing up."

"Is it something you're going to instill in your child?"

I sigh. Griffin asks a good question.

"I've been thinking about it. Thinking about what my faith means to me now. If I'll carry it through in my life and that of my child. I'll always cherish it, but I think my days of strict rules, attending church multiple times a week, and spending all my free time praying is over. I mean, how can you claim to have such strong beliefs and morals but turn me away when my life got hard? That's not what Jesus did. I know being unmarried and pregnant is not ideal. It certainly wasn't my plan either, but you can't force your daughter into hibernation and look at her in disgust. I don't see that written anywhere in the Bible."

It's cathartic to talk about. The heaviness I've felt with coming to this decision weighed more than I realized.

"I guess that's the beauty of it. You can have it in your life however much you want. Periodically, daily, never, always. The belief never goes; it just changes as your life changes..."

We sit silently for a while, me digesting his words, trying to reconcile my thoughts around it all.

"I've also been thinking about the future..." I say tentatively. "I've loved getting to know you. Spending time with you... I believe many of my prayers were answered when you turned up in my life. But..." I pause as I sit to face him.

"Griffin. I appreciate it all. I really do. But I'm pregnant, about to give birth any day now. I just opened the bakery. I love having you here. I love spending time together. But I'm not a catch. I can't offer you anything. I have no value to bring to your life. All I can offer you is a fat, emotional woman, sleepless nights, potentially a screaming baby and dirty diapers..." The words rush out of me, because he's handsome, successful, independent, wealthy, and one of the best men I've ever met in my life. What does he get out of this? Out of me? Before I can second-guess my words, I continue.

"The kissing, the dancing..." I swallow roughly before I continue. "I can't tie you down. You're a free spirit, and I don't want you to feel obligated to..."

When I meet his eyes again, they're flaming, his jaw tight.

"You think I'm here with you because I feel obligated?"

My heart thuds, confusion swirling, and he too sits forward, looking right into my eyes.

"I don't know what to think. My history proves that I'm not someone who is... well regarded." My parents had always told me no man would want to marry someone like me, even if I was a good cook. I know their idea of marriage is not mine, it's all about women submitting. But it's hard to let those thoughts go when they have been embedded in me for so long. I know I shouldn't think it. But I do.

"Neither does mine. My life was not cupcakes and fairy tales. I've seen more evil in this world than anyone should. I'm damaged. Not sure if I can even be repaired. Too damn old to be even considering it. I feel like just being around you, I'm bringing a shadow to your sunshine. I should stay away from you. And believe me, I tried. I left for a week, buried myself in work on the other side of the country. I fought hard to push you out of my mind, yet I couldn't stay away. But I'll leave if you want me to."

"No, I don't... I want you here," I whisper, my shoulders softening in acceptance and relief that he doesn't see me as a burden or an obligation. That he couldn't stay away from me, and that's the same way I feel about him.

"This is a little unconventional. You and me. But you're a strong woman. You're resilient. You're making something of yourself, pulling yourself through to ensure you provide. I don't feel obligated. I don't know what's brewing between us. But I know something is." He pauses, eyes steady. "You don't owe me anything. I'm not here out of obligation or because I feel sorry for you and your circumstance. I'm here because I see something in you. Something I want to be near."

"Okay..." I whisper, nodding. Griffin's gaze doesn't waver as his hand cups my cheek again.

"Okay." He nods before he leans down and places a chaste kiss to my lips, melting the tension away. Pulling back, his eyes have a little more light in them. Like my lips offer him energy he's never had before. "Come here." Sitting back on the bench, he pulls me into his side. I rest my head on his shoulder, and we sit in silence, looking at the sunset.

And for the first time in months, the future doesn't feel so terrifying.

20

SAVANNAH

I'm officially overdue and sick of myself. I've eaten so much spice, I feel like I would pass for a cardamom pod myself. So today, I switched back to my normal baking program. Although the curry puffs did sell out every day, and I now have a long list of orders for larger pies than I ever thought possible. All of which I have baked and stored in the freezer, ready for a supply I can sell after I give birth.

And as he said, Griffin has been here all week. At the bakery every morning, drifting in and out through the day, always finding some excuse to check on me.

He works from home, from the distillery, from the corner table in my shop... but he's here. With me. Sleeping beside me at night like it's the most natural thing in the world.

And I've let him. More than let him... I've wanted him here.

At night, we talk, kiss, laugh. He reads my baby book out loud, his voice low and steady, and we cross-check everything with the app he downloaded. I'm forty weeks now, so the book has run out of pages, but my pregnancy is still ongoing, and we're both on edge, waiting for the moment everything changes.

Having Griffin here brings comfort, yes, but it's more than that. Every day, my respect for him deepens. Every day, my feelings shift into something I can't pretend is simple. I've never had someone who shows up for me without being asked. Someone who notices when I'm overwhelmed. Someone who cares in a way that feels... safe. Solid. Real.

We're not just friends. We passed that line quietly, somewhere between the late-night conversations and the soft kisses and the way he watches me like he's memorizing every version of me.

If I wasn't pregnant with another man's baby, maybe we would've crossed into something more a long time ago. Maybe we would've stopped pretending we're taking this slow for any reason other than fear. Because the way he kisses me... It steals the breath right out of my lungs.

And I know, with a clarity that scares me, that Griffin is a man I could love. Not just for now. Not just because he's here when I need him. For a lifetime.

Now, as the last customers leave for the day, I sigh out a breath. My body is starting to feel tired and my mind matches it. Like I want to nap all the time, and my brain is starting to frizzle up. I've never been a napper; I've always been pretty good with my energy expenditure, but carrying a little human the size of a watermelon is tiring me out. My ankles have doubled in size, my face is puffy, my clothes are stretched. I couldn't feel any less attractive.

Before I can turn the closed sign over and lock the door, someone else walks in.

"Welcome to Betty's Ba..." My words die on my lips, and the smile falls from my face as the one person I was least expecting walks into my bakery. "Eden?" Shock coats my body as my older sister stands near the door, looking around before her eyes settle on me.

Her face is hardened, and my shoulders tense from her expression.

"So you did it."

I wish she had more pride in her tone. Maybe some empathy. But no. She spits the words out at me like they're poison. Giving a huff of a disgruntled laugh at the end.

"Opened the bakery, you mean?" My hand instinctively moves to my belly, shielding my child from the known enemy.

"Looks like you're not doing so well. No customers... Barely any stock in your cabinets." She folds her arms across her chest, looking down her nose at me like I'm a failure. I'm not sure when she went from being a caring big sister to one with such contempt. I swallow roughly. If I'm honest, a caring big sister wasn't something she ever was. I followed her around like a puppy dog waiting for any crumbs of compassion she'd drop for me. Of which never came. Spoiled by my parents from a young age, as the golden child, she got everything she ever wished for. Was never told no.

"It's closing time. I've sold out." I'm proud of what I've achieved. The lines out the door are not getting shorter. No matter how much I bake, I always sell out, and I've now got more money in my bank account than I ever had living at home. I'm not letting her rain on my parade.

"Still making excuses. You know, Faith, I pity you. Your boyfriend impregnates you, leaves you because he knows you're worthless. You embarrass yourself and us in our community with your"—she makes a show of looking at my bump like I'm contagious—"sin. You know Douglas and I have been trying for years. You know that baby is better off with me than you. Why are you being so selfish?"

My eyebrows rise in surprise. It's been a while since I heard my real name. So much so, it's jarring. Like I'm suddenly in a whole other world.

"Selfish?"

"Stupid too. You think I don't know that this silly little bakery is just a temper tantrum."

"Temper tantrum?" I repeat the words back to her, head shaking.

"You know you're going to end up with nothing. No one. Such a disgrace. No good Christian man will want you. You've ruined the family. You need to kneel at the feet of God and repent your sins. You know that you need to give me this baby. The baby I've been praying for. The baby *I* deserve. If you fully repent and realize you and your sinfulness have no place in this baby's life, our parents might consider taking you back, but that baby deserves a rich and loving life."

I swallow. She's crazy.

"Everything alright?" Griffin's voice rumbles into the bakery from behind me and soothes me instantly, as does his hand as it settles around my waist, his thumb rubbing softly across my skin.

"Oh, you are so shameful." Eden's face shrivels up when she notices the contact, and Griffin pulls me a little closer.

"Pregnant with one man's baby and another man has his hands on you. Have you no shame?" My sister raises her right hand in the air, as if overtaken by the Spirit to pray over me.

"Have you no shame?" Griffin steps forward, shoulders tight, and I grab his hand, squeezing it. Keeping him with me. I feel his anger and as he steps toward Eden, and I want to de-escalate the situation before it goes up in a ball of anger from both sides.

"You need to leave, Eden. You're not welcome here. You're not welcome in my life anymore." I'm trying to remain calm and mature. Not wanting to stress the baby or Griffin. The fierce defensiveness thrumming from his body beside me makes me feel protected.

"That baby deserves better than to be raised by a woman who isn't saved and refuses to repent to Christ. What kind of future is that?" Eden spits, her face screwed so tight like she tasted something disgusting.

Griffin doesn't flinch, but I feel his hand grip mine tighter.

"I think you've said enough." His voice is low but firm.

Eden's eyes narrow at me, ignoring Griffin completely. "You think God smiles on this? This is sin parading as comfort." She's almost to the point of being hysterical. I bet this visit isn't going how she imagined. I wonder if her husband Douglas or my parents know she's here. Probably. They no doubt discussed it over dinner last night, then spent the evening praying on it. She probably thought she would come in here, see me crying and struggling, wanting to give her my baby because life got too hard.

But I don't cower at hard. I thrive in it.

I step forward, pulse thudding. "You want scripture?" My voice is steadier than I expect. "Try *John 8:7*: 'Let any one of you who is without sin be the first to throw a stone at her.'"

She scoffs. "Don't twist the Word to justify your shame."

"I'm not twisting anything. I'm reminding you that grace exists. That God doesn't abandon people because they fall. He meets them there."

Eden's mouth opens, but Griffin cuts in. "And *James 1:17* says, 'Every good and perfect gift is from above, coming down from the Father of the heavenly lights, who does not change like shifting shadows.' That includes this baby. Doesn't matter how it got here. It's here. It's loved."

Eden's face flushes red, but she doesn't speak. Her silence hangs in the air.

I rest my hand on my belly again, not to shield, but to claim. "You don't get to decide what God forgives. And you don't get to decide anything about *my* baby."

Eden's eyes flicker. For a second, I see raw rage swirling. But it's gone as fast as it came.

She turns toward the door. "You'll regret this."

Griffin's hand tightens in mine. "Not today."

She pushes out the door so fast it bangs against the frame, and I blow out a breath.

"You alright?" Griffin faces me, his eyes moving quickly over my bump and back again.

"Yeah..." My shoulders sag as I rub my belly, ensuring the baby knows it's loved regardless of what their aunt says.

Griffin's hand rests on mine, and I look up at him. His large, warm hand encases my own, placing a caring touch to the bump like he knows we both need it. If anyone was walking past, they would assume he's the father, touching me like he is. It's intimate, yet I feel entirely comfortable in his embrace.

"Your sister?"

"The one and only." I take a deep breath, trying to fill my lungs, but this baby has everything squished so tight it's almost impossible.

"I'm proud of you. Sticking up for yourself. Sticking up for your baby." His thumb brushes across my belly before his hand glides around my back and he pulls me tight. I feel his lips on the top of my head, him breathing in my hair, and I close my eyes as my head hits his chest and I hug him close.

Feeling safe. Protected. Maybe even loved. It's been a long time since I let go and leaned on someone like this. Both physically and emotionally. My grandparents are probably the last time I truly trusted someone and knew they were on my side.

"So you remember some verses?" I speak into his shirt as I think about our conversation about religion we had after the baby shower.

"I may be old, but my memory is still strong. I found a bit of solace in the Bible when I was in juvie and have a few that I remember well." His hold on me remains. Like he knows I need it. For just a moment longer.

"You were in juvie?" I pull back and look up at him, and his face darkens a little.

"For a time." He nods. I shouldn't pry, but curiosity gets the better of me.

"What for?" My words are quiet, and I watch him swallow before he takes a breath.

"Assault with intention to harm."

I frown, not seeing that from Griffin at all. Sure, he's big, burly, a little guarded. But with intention to harm?

"Who was it?" I prod some more, fully expecting him to walk away, but he takes another steadying breath and tells me.

"Former foster father who was assaulting younger kids in his care. He didn't give a shit about me. I was almost aged out of the system by that point. But the younger kids, they were going to have to stay with him a lot longer. They wouldn't have survived so someone had to do something."

My heart clenches as I nod in understanding. While I don't condone violence, I can see how Griffin would protect those who couldn't protect themselves.

"To protect the innocent is a righteous duty."

His shoulders lower at my words. Like a load has been lifted.

"I'm no saint. But if you need shelter, I'll be the wings."

I smile a little. *Psalm 91:4* is one of my favorites. I like understanding him a little more. He's always been a good man. He needed to be stronger to survive than most. That's admirable.

"Why did you come through the back door of the bakery today?" I pull my head back farther to meet his eyes. It's almost comical how short I am next to him. And while I have a big belly, his chest is almost as wide. But I do love a dad bod.

"Ahhh..." He scratches the back of his head, his cheeks tinting a little. "I had a big delivery."

"Delivery?" I ask, not understanding why he seems so nervous.

He glides his hands down my arms and takes my hand.

"Come on. Let me show you."

We walk out the back to the kitchen, and I stop short, seeing bags and boxes and a whole mountain of things.

"What's all this?"

"Well, I'm going to build the baby nook for you here in the kitchen, and I figured you probably needed a few things..." He watches me closely as I take it all in.

"A few things? Griffin, this looks like you've purchased an entire baby store!" My eyes widen, taking it all in. There's a rocker, bassinet, high chair, car seat, and what looks to be bags of bottles, pacifiers, bibs, blankets, sheets, clothes, and so much more.

"I thought we can keep some things here, and I can have some things at my place..." He runs his hand through his hair, looking unsure.

My attention snaps back to him, in slight awe and confusion.

"This must have cost a fortune. I can't afford all this."

He's already shaking his head. "It's a gift."

"A gift?" My throat feels thick. I haven't cried for a few weeks. That emotional part of me regressed a little, but now it's coming back with a vengeance.

"I wanted to get some things for you. So we're prepared." He steps toward me, holding my hand. Watching me and searching my face.

"We're?" I'm hopeful, but I don't want to wish for it in case it doesn't come true.

"You're not doing this alone. I'm here to help. I told you that." He lifts his hand to cup my cheek, and I pull in a deep breath as reality settles in. A new reality. One where I'm not alone and Griffin is beside me.

I lean up on my tiptoes to kiss him, letting him know wordlessly how much he means to me. When our lips part, he holds me against his chest, and we stand in silence for a few minutes, listening to each other's soft breaths.

His phone buzzing makes me pull back, because he doesn't seem to care about answering it.

"Do you need to get that?" I ask.

"I usually meet Tanner and the crew at the bar tonight. I think they're probably reminding me since I never responded to their group text earlier while I was running around." He brushes some hair away from my face, something in his eyes telling me he'd much rather stay right here than go out with his friends. "You want to come? Maybe getting out and about will be good? I'll have them bring the girls too."

I'm tired, have lots to do, and need to rest. But hanging

out with friends at a bar where I can relax and talk might be good.

"I'd really like that." I give him a small smile.

"Good. Let's unpack some of this, and then we can get going." He walks over to the pile of things and pulls out a cream blanket from a bag, lifting it to show me.

And as I look at this man, tall, strong, grumpy, holding this soft, delicate blanket, my body reacts. Reaching for him like it knows something I don't, my heart thuds harder.

He says he wants to be here for me. He dances with me. Kisses me. Holds my hand, holds me. But as much as I want him, I still can't help but feel like I'm a burden... like I'm asking too much by existing in his orbit. But then he looks at me, really looks, and I swear the ache in my chest shifts. Not from pain, but from the terrifying hope that maybe, just maybe, there's a slight possibility that Griffin could be the one.

And that thought... It's almost enough to make me believe I deserve this. Deserve him.

Almost.

21

GRIFFIN

As we walk into Whiteman's Bar at the top of Main Street, I hold her hand tight. There's a lot of people here tonight. Usually, I slink in, find Tanner, and sit in a booth down by the back, paying no attention to anyone.

But tonight is different. I feel different.

"Wow, this really is the place to be. Is this what the locals get up to while I'm mixing icing and proofing sourdough?"

I look down at Savannah and see her glancing around at everyone and everything. The bar is packed. Tables full, the dance floor getting good use.

"I see the guys." I spot Tanner, Connor, Hudson, Sawyer, and Sutton all over near the pool tables. Their significant others are right by their sides. Tanner looks up and spots me first, and I see when it registers that I've brought Savannah with me tonight as his eyes widen before he has a chance to school them.

"I feel like I'm waddling... Do I look like a duck?"

"You look beautiful," I say like it's as natural as breathing. With her skin glowing, her face and body round and soft, her hair out tonight, falling down her back past her shoulders, she looks like my every dream rolled into one. Her cheeks pinken at the compliment, only making her more stunning.

"Not sure I believe you, but I'll take it. This baby is really pushing against my rib cage today," she teases, and my lips quirk, but it's replaced with my frown quickly as her hand rubs the side of her tummy and she winces.

"Maybe we could dance?" I've never danced in public. Never hardly danced in private aside from our bakery nights. But if she needs to dance, I'll do it.

"No, it's okay... maybe a fizzy drink might help..."

I nod to her, my mission now known.

"You made it. Hey, Savannah," Tanner greets us, and Victoria and Savannah hug hello.

"I need a sprite and a whiskey," I tell the bartender, who immediately gets to work.

"So how's the bakery going?" Tanner asks Savannah, and her grin is instant.

"So good. The town has been really welcoming."

I love seeing the joy in her face when she talks about her business.

"Oh, we're not talking about business tonight. Come. We need girl time." Victoria pulls Savannah away from me, over to the group of women on the side. My jaw tightens a little at having her removed from my side, but Savannah laughs.

"I'll be back later," she tells me quietly, dropping my hand and walking off.

"You need anything, you come to me."

Her grin widens as she nods, and I watch her until she gets to the group of girls and is settled before I can relax.

"Sooo, this is new?" Tanner asks, taking a swig of his whiskey to hide the grin he has.

"What is?" I mumble, looking around to not feel so on the spot. I notice a guy over by the other side of the bar. I haven't seen him around before. He's on his own, watching everyone and everything. He sticks out because his shirt is buttoned up tight, crisp, clean. Not the usual country vibe for this area. More uppity.

"That small grin on your face..."

My eyes flick back to Tanner, seeing him smirking at me like he knows something I don't.

"Don't know what you're talking about." I grab my whiskey from the bar and take a sip, needing the burn but knowing I need to be sober tonight to drive Savannah and the baby home safely.

"How long have we known each other, Griff?"

"Too fucking long."

Tanner huffs. "Did you know tonight was the first night in the twenty or so years I've known you that I've ever seen you hold hands with a woman?"

"Don't be ridiculous." I try to make nothing of it. But he's right. It is. I meet women. Lots of them. It's always been transactional, though. I've never had anything serious. Never anything loving. Some girls have tried. I've had friends with benefits before that lasted a while, but they become attached, even though they say they never will, and I've moved on from those quicker than a firecracker going off on the Fourth of July.

I don't hold hands. I don't touch softly. I don't place sweet kisses on girls' heads. I don't dance in bakeries or bars. Yet I'm finding that's exactly what I want to do with Savannah.

"Hey, Griff." Connor walks up, Sawyer on his heels.

"Gents." I nod in greeting.

"How's the build at Stonemore going?" Connor's straight

to business. Just like his dad, he wants to know all about what's happening over in wine country. God, if they only knew what's happening over at Stonemore. Hell, that family over in Sundown Valley gives these guys a run for their money.

"Going well. The build is big. Beautiful. It's a nice part of the world."

"Are you talking about Sundown Valley?" Hudson asks as he and Sutton walk up, the gang all here after finishing their game of pool.

"Yeah, I can't remember the last time I went there," Sawyer says.

"Remember that weekend wine tasting we did there years ago?" Sutton asks Hudson, the two of them hailing from LA first before landing here in Whispers, where they found their girls and never left. Sundown Valley gets lots of LA celebrities and locals.

"The one where the paparazzi stalked us all day, and we had to fly in and out of wineries in a helicopter like fucking royalty." I roll my eyes at Hudson's version of events. We're all rich men. All six of us have worked hard, made good money, and we're now at the stage of life where we can settle down a little, relax, and use our wealth how we want.

But Sutton Silvers, former Hollywood movie star, probably has the best stories. Now he's a local apiarist who comes out of showbiz retirement a few times a year to lead one of Tanner and Connor's whiskey commercials since he's the face of the Whiteman brand.

Sutton starts telling everyone another one of his stories, and I tune him out. I've heard them all before, and I'm not really into it all. Instead, my eyes wander over to the women, seeing Savannah sitting, nursing her Sprite, the women around her laughing and throwing questions, talking kids and babies.

"Is she resting?" Hudson murmurs to me.

"No. Stubborn."

"She still hasn't dropped."

I frown, looking at him. "Is that a problem?"

Hudson's eyebrows rise. "Could be. By now, I'd prefer the baby to be down a little more and in position. It's not a big issue, but if the baby doesn't drop in the next day or two, then things have an added layer of complexity."

"She's dancing, eating all the spicy food. Taking her vitamins. What else can she do?"

"Medically, I'll monitor her closely. Sometimes, women don't drop until they are in labor. But at that point, the progression is slow and things can escalate quickly. We might have to have the birth in Williamstown instead of Whispers."

I swallow roughly, not liking that option. Especially because I know she wants to give birth here in Whispers and also because I know her family is in Williamstown. And if her parents are anything like her sister, that isn't going to go well. I make a mental note to plan for that.

"Is there anything else we could be doing to help?" I'll get her anything. If she needs more spicy food straight from India, I'll ship that in for her.

"There are the old wives' tales..." he says quietly, being more than a little elusive.

My eyebrows pinch as I look at him. "What are they?"

"The spicy food, the movement and dancing were all on the list..."

I feel like he's trying to say something yet not.

"What else?" I almost bark at him, not liking how he's not getting to the point.

"Sex," he blurts, like it should be obvious, and I still.

"Sex? Doesn't that hurt the baby?" She already has a human inside of her, so I can't imagine that having another one would be beneficial. Regardless of how much my own dick would love it. I try to push down the thoughts now swirling. Her naked pregnant body moving on mine. Fuck, I'm getting hard just thinking about it.

"Well, yes, you'll need to go slow... let her lead... but no harm will come to the baby. Believe me, that kid is so cozy in there they won't feel a thing. Medically speaking, orgasms cause mild uterine contractions, which may help nudge the baby downward. That, combined with the fact that semen contains prostaglandins, which are hormones that can help soften and ripen the cervix, means having sex can potentially ease the baby into position or bring on labor."

I blink at him a few times, taking it all in, yet I've never felt so raw in a bar before. I look around, seeing if anyone can hear our conversation, but the music is loud and the boys are laughing at something Sutton's telling them.

"So no condom, then. Bare?" I clear my throat, feeling myself getting a little hot. I've never gone bare. Not since I was a teen and didn't know anything different. Since then, I've wrapped it every single time without fail.

"That's better for this particular outcome." Hudson's trying to be professional, but I know he's having too much fun with this.

I blow out a breath. "Fuck."

"Hmm, something for you to mull over for the evening..." His grin wraps around his whiskey glass as he sips, and I shake my head, trying to get my thoughts on other things, yet failing. Because now, all I want is Savannah, naked, moving on me, swaying her hips like she does when she dances.

"Hey, Griff, did you talk with Mother Maven?" Sawyer asks out of the blue, and all of the guys look at me, teasing grins pulling at their lips.

I blink at him a few times, my mind scrambling, trying to catch on to the conversation.

"Mother Maven?" Tanner asks.

"Yeah, Griffin wanted to help Savannah with a few things, so he called the experts." Sawyer lifts his eyebrows, and Tanner looks at me pointedly.

"I spoke with her. Organized a few things. She's on call for whatever Savannah needs," I tell them, because I have. I practically bought a whole store of things. I have no fucking idea what to get her and what she needs. Hell, I don't even know how to change a diaper, and with her mom and sister not in her life, I guess she'll be winging it too.

"Sounds like you've got it all organized," Tanner says, seemingly amused, and I nod.

"I got it handled." My eyes find the man again over Tanner's shoulder on the other side of the bar. I don't know what it is about him that has my attention. Maybe because he looks so out of place. I follow his gaze as he stares at something nearby, and my frown is instant.

"What is it?" Tanner notices immediately, his voice leaning into a warning tone, making the other guys fall quiet and watch us.

My eyes trail his line of sight until they rest on the group of women. Our women.

"Who's that guy?" I nod toward the man at the bar, not wanting to jump to conclusions, when he could be the local gardener around Whispers, for all I know.

"No idea... Connor?" Tanner barks at his son, and Connor takes a hard look at the man.

"I don't know him."

"Me neither," Hudson says, and Sawyer takes a look.

"Never seen him before," Sawyer says as Sutton shakes his head.

"Do you see what he's looking at?" Tanner's eyes are glued on him. This guy is so focused on the girls he can't even feel our gazes burning into him.

I put my glass down, thinking I might go have a word with him. But he stands, pushing his empty beer glass across the bar, and walks out. Alone.

I look back at Savannah, her and the girls completely oblivious to the man who was watching them so closely. But they remain smiling and laughing, sounding like a gaggle of geese.

She must feel me watching her, because she looks over, her face relaxed and happy, her eyes glistening in delight, and she gives me her sunshine smile. The one that thaws me from the inside out.

She thinks I feel obligated. But if she only knew what her smile does to me. How it melts every restraint I've built. Crumbles every wall I've erected over decades. She'd understand this isn't duty. It's desire. It's longing. And I'm one breath away from showing her exactly how much.

22

SAVANNAH

"Let's go." Griffin helps me out of his truck, his hands wrapping around my enormous belly as I slide to the ground in front of him. The move is now a familiar one between us, yet my heart races every time he touches me.

"Tonight was nice." I look up at him, grateful for his suggestion of going to the bar. We weren't there for long, but it was long enough for me to chat to the girls, get to know them all a little more. Solidify those relationships to the point where they're now inviting me to places and offering to help in the bakery or with the baby when it arrives.

"You looked like you had a good time." Griffin walks us into the bakery, the space dark and quiet, a little spooky without the lights on. His hand slips into mine, where it feels like it's right where it's meant to be.

"They're nice people. I'm so glad you introduced me. I haven't had a lot of genuine friends before."

"What do you mean?" He frowns as we step inside.

"Well... I worked, went to church, helped with the young adult group. I didn't have many friends, and none outside of church." I tell him as he locks the door, his eyes doing a sweep of the space as we make our way through to the kitchen.

"Your last boyfriend never took you out?"

"No. At the time, I thought it was nice him wanting to talk with me. Take me to secluded places in the car to chat. But I was naive. He was keeping me hidden. Keeping us hidden. I can't believe I thought he was a decent man." I shake my head at my stupidity. I look down at my belly, feeling a little remorse from my actions of nine months ago. Having sex in the back of a car without protection. Wanting to please him after he was really pushing for it. Acting like a silly fifteen-year-old, not the grown woman I am. I thought it was love.

"You deserve better," he grumbles, pulling me along to the stairs, the familiar journey to my apartment one we're taking together tonight.

"I know that now," I admit, because even though I'm pregnant with a very real outcome from that time in my life, I've grown so much in this past year that I don't recognize myself anymore.

"I was thinking I would start your baby nook tomorrow." He turns to look at me, where we now stand in my small apartment. Toe to toe, he gazes down on me.

"Do you have time?" The baby's foot thumps into what feels like my spleen, and I wince again.

"I have time. You alright?" Griffin's concern is immediate. He steps forward, looking too large and looming in my small apartment as his hand connects with my stomach, trying to ease my pain.

"Yeah. Just the little one pushing about. Daisy offered to teach me some yoga poses tomorrow, to help give the baby more room and to ease the pressure on my internal organs.

She thinks it could help put the baby into position, maybe help bring on labor." I look at Griffin and give him a small smile, and I swear I physically see his shoulders lower.

"Hudson suggested something else to me tonight."

"Oh? What?" My curiosity is genuine, considering I thought Hudson already told me everything I could do.

"He said sex could help..." Griffin swallows as his hand runs around my side and rests on my lower back. I still as a shiver travels through me. My mouth dries and my heart thuds.

We do this—touch, hug, kiss. It feels nice, but I'd be lying if I said I didn't want more. I tilt my head and look at Griffin, wondering for a moment if he's teasing or serious. My cheeks flame as I understand he's serious.

"You want to have sex?" I blurt out, surprised. "With this?" I'm looking at him like he's crazy as I make a show of moving my hands up and down my body so he can see exactly what I look like. I'm big, clearly not in my peak physical condition. My ex told me how my flabby bits weren't to his liking and that was before I was even pregnant. Now, I can't even tell what I look like from behind, but I'm sure it isn't sexy.

"Yeah, sweetness... I do..." His voice is a low rumble that has my smile wiped as he steps even closer to me, like he's daring me. His eyes are blazing with a hunger I haven't seen from him before.

"You do?" I whisper, already breathless at the mere thought. My skin tingles in anticipation.

"Yeah... I want you on top of me, showing me what you need... and letting me be the man who gives it to you." He leans down, his lips claiming mine, and I'm a goner. I'm falling, falling hard for this man, who's there for me even when he's physically on the other side of the country. All these kind words, soft touches, this mammoth of a man walking around my bakery, eating my food, dancing with me, building and buying me baby things. It's been like slow-building foreplay that's lasted months now, and like a pot boiling on the stove, I'm overflowing.

"Yes..." I say on an exhale so he knows I'm all in, but my words are muffled as our kiss deepens. I can't help it. I haven't felt the touch of a man like this in a long time. I haven't wanted a touch from a man like this ever. Any man I've known before felt simply like an obligation. *Is this what it feels like to be truly wanted?*

His hands wrap around me, pulling me to him tight. He's so wide and my belly so big that I can barely get my hands around him, but I feel his palms lower, slowly moving over the curve of my lower back, grabbing on to my ass and squeezing. I almost buckle.

My hormones are raging. His touch feels so warm, his hands so big they feel like they cover all of me.

"You tell me if anything's too much," he says between kisses.

"I will," I pant as my hands fall to his chest, and I unbutton his shirt. "You tell me if you... don't like it..." My self-doubt kicks in again, and he pauses.

"I'm telling you right now, I can't wait to get you naked, kiss your beautiful body, and have you rocking on me, using me how you need. Fuck, I'm so hard just thinking about it." He growls the last bit, and I can barely swallow as my hands glide down his torso, feeling the small bumps of his abs, the softness of his tanned skin with the sprinkle of salt-and-pepper hair scattered down his chest. He looks even better than I imagined. One hundred percent man.

Our eyes remain on each other as my hands hit his belt. He's waiting, watching, letting me lead us into our deep swirl of desire. I lick my lips as I pull at his belt, opening it quickly before I undo his button and lower his zipper. He wasn't lying. I can feel how tight his jeans are on his body. He throws his shirt off and stands before me, half-naked, his jeans open. His body is incredible, so strong and sexy.

"You alright?" he asks, and my eyes flick back to his.

"Just taking it all in…" I'm honest, because he's a lot. I've never seen a man like him. He's the kind of guy if you came across him in a dark alley, you would probably turn and run away. Solid, tall, grumpy, and angry-looking. Yet as his hand comes to my jaw, and he cups my cheek, he guides my face to meet his and kisses me in equal parts sweet and demanding. It's a complete contradiction, one I can't get enough of.

"My turn, sweetness…" he mumbles across my lips as I feel his fingers grab the straps of my dress and pull them off my shoulders and down my arms. I move them out, allowing the dress to fall, my breasts now on show as he pulls the dress lower, over my bump, and it flutters to the floor. I'm not wearing a bra. My breasts are so big it's more comfortable without one most days, as my dresses have supporting fabrics to hold everything in place. I swallow, feeling exposed as Griffin kisses down my cheek and across my jaw while his fingers trail up my arm and across my chest.

My skin prickles in the wake of his touch, my nipples hardening, and I wait breathlessly as his featherlight touch skirts across my hardened nipple, making me shudder.

"Mmmmmm." I moan a little, which makes him kiss back up my neck.

"Let's get you lying down…" He holds me tight, walking me to the bed, where I lie on the mattress and he pulls his jeans off.

"Wow." I didn't mean to say that out loud. He looks like any girl's dream man. His eyes hook on mine as his thumbs grip on to the waistband of his boxers and he lowers them until he's completely naked. Standing tall and proud right in front of me. And my Lord, he should be. I swallow, my eyes wide, as I look him up and down. My mouth is watering, and I'm a hot mess already.

"Are you real?" I whisper as he steps toward me, his hand palming his cock, which is what he said, hard and ready and looking bigger than I've ever seen.

"I am, sweetness. Are you?" He looks at me in awe, like I'm Aphrodite or something. I mean, I'm plump and round, naked, with my hair draped over my shoulders, lying before him like I'm offering myself up to him for a meal. But that's probably where the similarities end.

He kneels on the bed, the mattress dipping with his weight as his hands come to my underwear.

"Can I?" Oh my... he's asking me. He could rip them right off, and I wouldn't care.

"Yes." I nod eagerly and swallow as he pulls them down, leaving us both naked now. His hand rubs my ankles, massaging my calves, his touch feeling so good, before he glides them upward.

"Relax," he says, voice deep and soothing, and I close my eyes. "Let me take care of you..."

My breath hitches as I feel him spread my legs wider. Then I feel it. His lips touch my thigh, and I almost sag with relief. Relief to have his touch, relief to have my desires met, relief that a man like Griffin is manhandling me so delicately yet is so completely in control. It has me dizzy.

"Yes..." I breathe out as I feel his soft kisses move up my legs, my knees now falling wider as I settle into his touch. My heart thuds in my ears, my mind moving rapidly from this being the most amazing experience of my life, to a little guilt. Guilt for being with another man without being married. Guilt for being with a man who's not the father of the baby I'm carrying. Guilt for it all. It's something I'm continuously cloaked in. Yet I can't stop it. I don't want to. I want him. I want Griffin.

"Mmmm, your skin is so soft," he murmurs, his breath skirting across my sensitive skin, his stubble brushing my inner thighs. "Look at me..." he growls, and my eyes ping open, staring at him as he lowers, his gaze moving below my bump. He hits my center, and I gasp in air at the sensation. "That's it. Feel me lick you, kiss you, fuck you, and tease you with my tongue."

Oh my... Instead of a baby, I might have a heart attack. His words are filthy, but in the best possible way. I've never been spoken to like this before. My history with men is not extensive. I was courted by a few from church. The rules I had to follow became so suffocating that when I met my previous boyfriend, I was smitten. He didn't seem as strict or controlling, hence why it resulted in this pregnancy. He pressured me for months until I caved. It was never like this.

I breathe heavily as I lie here with all my wobbly bits on display, yet Griffin has his head buried in me like I'm his last meal. His hot tongue flicks out, swiping up my center, and I think my eyes roll back into my head.

"That feels sooo..." I can't finish the sentence as his lips latch on to me, and he sucks my clit until my legs start to shake. "Oh!" I lift my hands from where they grip the sheets beside me, and I mold my breasts, massaging them. They're large, heavy, and more than a handful for me.

"Fuck. That's it, sweetness... so fucking beautiful." Griffin's large hands feel hot underneath my ass as he buries into me farther, his tongue swirling before his lips attach to my clit again, and I almost see stars.

I whimper his name, writhing against him. Is this real?

Am I dreaming? I've never had a man go down on me. Never something I gave a lot of thought to. But if I knew I'd feel like this, so deliberate, so hungry, so perfect.

"Play with your perfect tits. They will get my attention soon enough," he warns, and I shiver as my hips rock harder against his face. I dig my fingers into his hair, and he growls against my skin as I scratch his scalp, pulling him against me a little more.

"I'm so fucking hard for you," he admits, and I almost choke all over again. Hard for me. I'm almost coming, his words, each and every one of them meaning so much to me and turning me on more than ever.

"Griff," I pant out, my body feeling every swipe of his tongue and every grip of his palm as tension builds inside me.

"That's it... Move against my mouth and take what you need. Let me suck your pretty clit while you come..." He latches on again, and I can't help the orgasm as it starts to flood through me.

"Oh... Oh, Griffin... *Griffin!*" I cry out his name, over and over, my body shaking. The heaviness of my belly, my life, my situation, all dissipate as Griffin grabs me tighter, and I grip on to his hair as I roll my hips over his face and fully let go.

Shock waves roll through me from head to toe and back again. My eyes sting and my limbs tremble. I collapse against the mattress, my body liquid as he pulls back to look at me. His hair is a little messy from where I grabbed it, his lips trailing sweet kisses over my belly. Whispering sweet nothings to the child I hold as he makes his way up to my face.

Is this real? Did that just happen? As my body turns to mush, my mind races. I can't believe we just did that. I can't believe how perfect it was. I can't believe how perfect he is. He hovers above me, the two of us staring into each other's eyes.

"That's number one..."

Still floating on a cloud, I frown, not understanding.

"Number one what?"

"Hudson said *orgasms* will help contract the belly to help the baby into position. So I figure we need to try for three or four... just to make sure..." The side of his mouth lifts a little, the smirk new and so incredibly hot.

"Three... or... four...?" I'm in disbelief. I've never come before. I mean my experience with sex was ok, it was nice enough. But it was never like this.

"Hmmmm, I'll need you up and bouncing on me this time, sweetness. I want to have your tits in my face and your pussy clenching my cock."

Those filthy words are already making me pulse again.

"I, ahh... I mean, yes, I want that." I swallow, my cheeks pinkening even more, but as his hand runs up and down over my skin, his eyes looking right into mine, I know. This man is even more than I expected. Caressing my bump, he looks over me as though I'm the most magnificent woman he's ever laid eyes on. Then his hand continues to lower, down between my legs where his mouth just was. My legs are already quivering, so sensitive.

"Oh my g—" My words get caught, the feeling immediate as I draw in a breath, feeling his finger circle my clit. The build is instant. Not sure how, but I'm already on edge, wanting, yearning for more.

"I can't stop touching you even if I tried," he admits. "You're so fucking responsive... so fucking delicious..."

"Don't stop... I don't want you to stop," I answer him, so self-assured, because right now, there's nothing I want more.

"So fucking wet," he teases as he slips a finger inside, and if I could move, I would buckle, but my body is mush, already pinned underneath him on this bed.

"Griffin..." I hiccup, my plea for more turning into a whimper.

"Hmmmm, sweetness?" He watches me, my eyes locked on his.

"That feels... so good," I whisper as I lower my hand, gripping on to his forearm, his fingers remaining focused on my clit as he slips another one inside.

"Take what you need. Use me how you want," he growls, his eyes not leaving me, and I reach down with my other hand, grabbing on to him. His hard, heavy cock now in my palm.

"I want this... I want you..." I pant, my orgasm building, his movement consistent, steady, strong. Touching me like he knows exactly what I need.

"Fuck," he hisses as I start to pump him. He's rock solid and hot in my hand, but I go slow. Teasingly so.

"I'm going to come," I warn him as we both pleasure the other.

"That's the plan, sweetness..." Deep and low, like a beast from the forest, the vibrations of his voice are felt around the room. "You come for me, sweet thing... Come on my hand and let me feel your pussy quiver for me."

His will makes it so, and like he commanded, I break.

"Oooooh... Oh my... OH..." I pant as I drop my hand from him, grip on to the sheets beside me, and with his hand pinching my clit, I come again. "Griff!" I scream and shudder, this release coming faster and fuller than the last.

My body almost spent, I melt into the mattress as his finger draws lazily over me, before running back up my side. We stay like that as I catch my breath and come back down to earth. When my eyes ping open, and I look at him, ready for more, his grin is wicked.

"Now I need you to move, sweetness."

I'll do whatever he says, whatever he wants, if I get to feel like that with him again.

23

GRIFFIN

The way she responds to me, the way her beautiful naked body moves, I've never seen or had a woman like her. And if I wasn't already addicted to her, I am now. I can't stop touching her. I want to kiss her body, suck on her clit, play with her tits. I want to lie here with her naked, all night long, and touch every inch of her, trail over every dip and curve with my tongue.

"All this action surely has to be helping..." She giggles as I help her move, lifting her up onto her knees, and I sit on her bed, leaning back on the headboard before helping her straddle me.

"I can do this all night... You can lie down and let me take care of it all," I tell her the truth. She must be tired, but as she straddles me with more ease than I was expecting, her eyes have as much fire in them as I'm sure my own do. This woman wants me. And that's a damn good thing, because now that I've had a taste, I'm going to find it difficult to remove myself from her.

"I think I'd like to try and take care of you now for a little bit..." She's breathy, sitting on my lap, looking perfect. I run my hand up and down her side, feeling her soft, supple skin. Nervous, not wanting to hurt her. Wanting to do right by her.

It's a feeling I haven't experienced too often in this situation. The whole activity of sex has always been one of necessity for me, not one of feeling or emotion or tender touches. This is already different from any that have come before, not because of her baby and our situation, but it's also different for me. Our connection is deeper. Our affection for each other is clear. I haven't allowed myself to get connected in the past. I have no idea what it is about her that has me feeling a certain way. But I do.

"Hudson said that my semen can soften your cervix, so it's good for bringing on the baby. I'm clean, but I can wear a condom if you prefer." I look at her, my eyes traveling the length of her body and back again. She's so fucking beautiful. Round, soft, carrying life. Her tits are massive, her ass a handful, her belly tight and round. She looks like Mother Earth herself, or a divine feminine life force that has pinned me for good.

"It's okay... It's not like I can baby trap you..." she jokes, and I grin as she lowers to me, and I run my hands up her back.

"Take your time. Take it easy. You lead... You tell me what you want, what you need, and I'll do it, sweetness," I warn her through gritted teeth because having her naked on me like this is going to be a core memory I'll never forget. One I will remember the day I take my last breath, I'm sure of it.

My dick is already weeping. The strength it's taking me not to pin her to the bed, pull her fantastic ass up, and fuck her like I want to almost overwhelming for me. But that time will come. I still taste her on my lips, feel her soft curves under my rough hands, and now as she lowers onto me, I hope I don't come too soon.

"I can't see. Tell me if..." she starts to say, doubt seeping in.

"You're perfect," I tell her, positioning myself, feeling her center touch mine. I hold her around her back, pulling her down onto me, guiding her as her belly hits my own, and we join. I pull in a breath as she sinks down, gliding onto me so well. She moves slowly, her mouth opening on a gasp, her full weight dropping onto me until I'm deeply seated inside her.

"Fuck... sweetness..." It feels too good. Having not been bare with a woman in forever, the feeling of her is different. Warm. Wet. Welcoming. I throb, having never taken things this slow before. My hands explore, roaming her body, unable to stop. I'm going to come too soon, I know it.

She whimpers as her hands move to the headboard behind my shoulders to find support, her tits now situated right near my face, and my mouth waters.

"You feel so fucking good, sweetness..." I grip on to her waist, my hands sinking into her ass cheeks as I start to help her move. Just the touch of her, her body joined with mine, is almost too much. Her sweet sugar smell, her soft skin, I'm not sure anything else has ever felt this right. Face-to-face like this with nowhere to hide, nowhere to look other than upon her.

"Sooooo good," she moans as her clit sweeps over my pelvic bone. Her head falls back, her breasts at my eye level as her round body grinds against my own in a teasingly slow rhythm I've never had before. "I'm so full."

I run my hands up her back, pulling her forward as my lips find her nipple. I wrap my lips around it, pulling it into my mouth and sucking.

"Oh my God..." I hear her whisper at the same time, feeling her pussy clench, and I know her nipples are sensitive. The app told me that. It also told me that nipple stimulation can bring on the baby, and since I'm a boobs man, I plan to give her a lot of stimulation. "Is this alright?" I move my hands lower, pulling and pushing her ass over and over my dick as my mouth stays on her nipples, and I swear I feel myself thicken even more.

"Perfect. I love it," she pants, and I grin around her nipple, biting it a little with my teeth, causing her hips to move a little faster.

"Fuck, you're moving so well, baby. Your pussy is clenching my cock so good..." I grit my teeth, my hands palming her ass, gripping on to her flesh and hoping she comes before I do.

A whimper crawls up her throat. "So good, so good, so good..." she repeats over and over again, lost to the pleasure, and I look up at her, basking in her beauty, my lips brandishing her skin, caressing her, touching her, not wanting this moment to end. I leave little love bites, wanting to mark her, mark my territory. God, I could drown in her.

"Sweet thing... so fucking sweet... Fuck me, sweetness. I need you, I need you so bad..." I'm making no sense. I'm completely gone. Almost to the point of begging, I need her so much. The feeling too raw and real, my chest burning in a way it hasn't before. Her hand wraps around my head, pulling me to her tighter. Holding me close, like she can't let go. Like she got me.

"Griff..." Her warning tone is now one I recognize, and I try not to grin, knowing she's close.

"Mmmmm... Sweetness, keep going... Rock on my cock and take what you need." I moan when she starts bouncing, my head falling back in disbelief, in awe of her and this, feeling her hips move a touch quicker. I start to buckle a little underneath her. I'm going to come. I'm going to come so fucking hard.

Moans and whimpers leave her wantonly as she grips on to my shoulders for leverage, her hips never stopping, chasing her release that's on the horizon.

"Ride me, baby... Give me one more... I need it. I need you," I tell her, our eyes meeting in time to see her mouth open on a silent scream as her body starts to quiver.

"Fuck... yes..." I let go then with a guttural groan. My movements become a little jerky as I thrust up into her, again and again, prolonging her pleasure before I come. "Sweetness, yessssss."

"Griffin!" Her high-pitched moan skirts across the small room as she trembles above me. I grip on to her hard, my fingers digging into her soft hips, pulling her tight, keeping her with me. My body slackens, feeling my stress and worries completely leave me.

Panting. Completely spent. Her skin and mine coated in a light sheen of sweat.

"Wow," she says, her head buried in my shoulder. I blink a few times. Feeling a little lightheaded, out of sorts. Are my eyes watering? I rub them quickly, wondering what the fuck is wrong with me before I swallow and come back to myself. "You alright?" She starts to move, and I help her get up and slowly lower her back onto the mattress, letting her lie down and get comfortable. She looks even better with that just-fucked flush on her face.

"I think so..." I tell her, still breathless.

She smiles, although her eyes are closed.

I watch her for a beat before I go to her bathroom. Cleaning up a little, I grab a fresh washcloth, taking it back to the bed.

"It's okay." She sits up, startled, as I brush the cool cloth against her.

"Relax. I'll clean the mess I made..." I tell her, and she's in no position to argue because she can barely lift her head right now. I pull the blankets over her, turn off all the lights, and crawl into her bed next to her, the two of us quiet for a moment.

"I've never had sex like that before," she whispers, like she's telling me a secret.

I look over at her, my hand coming to her bump, and I strum my fingers against her skin.

"Me neither," I admit, feeling vulnerable. It's true. That was a first for me, in almost every way.

"I'm grateful I don't have neighbors..."

I huff a laugh, and in the thin strip of moonlight that's sneaking through her curtains, I see her grin.

"I wouldn't care if they heard you like that. Means I'm doing something right."

"You do a lot of things right, Griffin."

"Yeah, well... not everyone would agree with you." I feel the familiar weight settle back on my chest. It's been absent for most of the night, but now as my reality seeps back in, ending this fairy tale, the real Griffin starts to surface.

She shifts, turning herself onto her side and facing me. "Not sure if you've noticed, but I'm not someone who follows the crowd or does what everyone thinks I should."

I huff a breath, almost a laugh, but not quite. "Lucky for me. I didn't exactly grow up with gold stars as a kid."

She waits, doesn't push. Just lets the silence stretch between us like a held breath.

"I was... a mess. Angry. Always in trouble. Didn't have much of a shot at life, really. Not after..." My voice catches, and I shake my head. "Forget it."

She reaches for my hand under the blankets and threads her fingers through mine. The move is a familiar one. One that brings comfort. "You can tell me. You don't have to, but... I'm here."

I swallow hard. I haven't told anyone. No one other than Tanner knows my past. Even then, he doesn't know all of it. It's been something I carried all my life, never wanting anyone to know exactly how low of a man I am. But then her hand moves, face cupping my cheek. Her thumb strums my skin, keeping me grounded.

"My little brother... I was supposed to be watching him."

I pause, trying to work out what to say. How to say it. Wondering if she'll look at me the same way. Wondering if she'll want me after I tell her. But after what we just did, I need to.

"I don't talk about this." My voice is rough now. The room is silent. She's silent. You could hear a pin drop. But she waits, like she knows I need to gather my thoughts. Gather my courage.

"He was ten," I rush out, and I feel her. Her hand still on my cheek, her belly pushing against mine. I can make out her glassy eyes as they look right into mine.

"What was his name?" Her voice is a mere whisper.

"Tommy." I almost choke on his name; I can barely say it. I haven't said his name in decades. The guilt. The remorse. The pain, it's always been too much. But not tonight. Tonight, I can do it. For her.

"What was he like?" she asks softly.

I feel myself remembering. Remembering the good bits, not the bad.

"He was... smart. Loved to read. He was quiet, you know. Like a little introverted, maybe..." I frown, trying to remember. It's been decades, but I can still visualize his face. I have a photo. One. But I haven't looked at it in years.

"How old were you?" I look at her, my nerves easing slightly with her complete attention locked on me.

"Twelve. I was running errands. Mom sent me out to get milk. I was on my way home but got caught with a flat tire on my bike so I was late..." Her hand moves, her fingers featherlight as they trace small patterns across my jaw as I clench it. Her breath is warm against my chest, tethering me to her.

"I told him I'd be home before Dad got home. I wasn't." The words slip out before I can stop them. "Dad always got home drunk. That day was no different..."

I pause, my memories swirling. I can see our house. I can hear the yelling. The familiar feeling of anxiety and unease that ran through my body when I pulled up on my bike and heard things crashing and Mom screaming for help.

"I heard it as soon as I rode up the drive. Dad yelling... Things inside smashing..."

Her fingers strum in a soft pattern, repeating up and down and around, keeping me grounded. Keeping me tethered to her.

"I ran up the porch steps and heard Tommy." My breath gets caught as the image of my younger brother pops into my mind. "He was there. He should've been hiding. I used to make sure he hid under his bed. Covered his ears and didn't come out until I got to him. But I wasn't there to tell him to hide... He was trying to help Mom... That was my job. He should've hidden. I should've been there..." My muscles feel tight as the visual of Mom with a bloody lip fills my head, her pleading eyes landing on me when I walked through the door. Still a kid myself, but in that situation, her only hope.

I push through and continue. "I walked in as Dad took a

swing at Mom. She hit the floor hard..." I swallow, still hearing the thud of her head hitting the countertop as she went down, the light leaving her eyes instantly. "Tommy ran toward him, pushed him." I huff, seeing this small kid trying to push a grown man who's filled with anger, alcohol, and a lifetime of demons. "Dad swung around, not looking, not paying attention. Tommy took the brunt of his backhand. I just..." I need to pull in a long breath. "I just stood there." I frown, still in disbelief at my own actions. "I should've run in, I should've screamed, I should've grabbed a weapon and fought... I should've..."

"You were twelve..." Her voice is what stops me. The pain I hear in it. My eyes meet hers in the dim moonlight, seeing them glassy. This beautiful woman, whom I just made sweet love to, and now I'm bringing her down.

I clear my throat, pulling myself out of the memories. "They both... That night... they didn't make it." Jaw clenched, I blink hard.

She presses her forehead to mine. "You were a kid."

I let out a breath that feels like it's been trapped for years. "Doesn't change it."

"Is that what your nightmares are about? That night?"

I nod. Not trusting my voice.

"I have something..." She moves, turning to her small bedside table and opening the drawer. I hear her rustling before she comes back to me. "Here."

She hands something to me. "What is it?"

"It's my grandma's little Bible. The one she gave me when I was a girl. Put it under your pillow, Griff."

I feel like my chest rips wide open. I stare at the book, moving my fingers across the cover, the red color bright against my skin.

"I can't..."

"You can. It helped me. Maybe it will help you too?" Her voice is full of tender care that a man like me doesn't deserve.

"I'm beyond help."

She gives me a small smile, shaking her head. "No, you're not. It's just, some things are harder to get through than others."

I pause, swallowing roughly. "I've been trying to outrun that night ever since."

"So maybe it's time to stop running?"

"I'm not sure I can... but with you, I sure want to try," I tell her honestly as I pull her tight against my chest, gripping the book in my hand with a silent promise to put it under my pillow. For her. For me. For us. She remains quiet, leaving me with my thoughts. Not offering to fix it. Doesn't offer platitudes. Just holds me like I'm still worth holding.

And for the first time in a long time, I let her.

24

SAVANNAH

I rub my eyes, wondering why it's so bright.

"Ahhhh... morning, baby..." I tell my bump as I rub it, yet it feels different. My mind connects, memories from last night swirl, and I open my eyes, looking at my side and seeing my bed empty.

No Griffin. I can't say I'm surprised. Last night was raw, in more ways than one. The sex was amazing. He was caring, supportive, and manhandled me in a way I've never been touched before. Even remembering him naked now makes me blush.

But also, our conversation afterward. How he shared a little more of his past. I knew he had demons. I knew he had a past he was not fond of. But when I heard some of his story last night, my heart broke for him. For him now, but also for the little boy he was.

I'm not surprised my bed is empty. He's a runner by habit. Not trying to run from me or anything like that, but run from his mind. Something he'll never be able to outrun. His memories will always follow him. The fact is that he's here. He stayed, we connected. I hope that even though he's a man who will always need his space, that he'll run to me a little more. Find solace with me instead of leaving town as often as he does.

I roll over and sit up before panic slithers through my body. It's full sun outside. My eyes flick to the clock, seeing it's past nine.

"Nine!" I yell to myself. I should've been awake hours ago. Hell, the bakery should already be open with the smell of fresh goods. I've never slept in this late. I jump up and waddle around as fast as I can, taking a quick shower and pulling my hair back, and although I'm stressed, I'm smiling. I feel at ease. Not as tightly wound as yesterday.

I look at myself in the mirror, admiring my body, my bump, not feeling fat and exhausted, but sexy and confident. I notice a few little love marks on my chest, making it obvious Griffin is a breast man. Good thing, considering mine are massive and are going to be out a bit with breast-feeding.

That man. He's a total contradiction and yet exactly what he's meant to be. And I'm falling for him more every day. My eyes rest on my bump for a moment, and I frown as I pull my dress over myself.

I tilt my head, trying to work out what's different before my eyes widen. I've dropped.

Does it happen that quickly? Was sex all it took to get this baby down? The heavy feeling I'm now experiencing on my pelvic bone tells me this baby is now using gravity to its full capability.

I pull in a breath, feeling my lungs expand a little more than they have in months, and I smile before I become instantly terrified. Oh shit, the baby is going to come soon. It's locked and loaded and ready.

I have so much to do and I'm already late. I wonder if people are banging on the front door.

As I walk downstairs, I'm careful on each step, surprised to see the lights on down here already. Griffin must have left them on when he headed out this morning. I wonder why he didn't wake me.

I pause at the bottom step, and my eyes widen. The bakery is open. I step tentatively into my kitchen, seeing it all with new eyes and surprise.

"Uhmm?" I'm confused as I spot Griffin, surrounded by tools, a fully built nook now almost complete.

His head whips around at my voice, and he stands quickly. "You're up? You feel okay?" He looks worried as he stalks toward me.

"What's happening?" My belly may have dropped, but my brain isn't firing.

"I opened the bakery. Got Melissa out in front serving. Just your cold stuff, since I wasn't sure I trusted myself to turn on the ovens. Then I got busy here..."

I blink up at him a few times, then I look at the baby nook. It's beautiful. All natural timber shelves and a small white feeding chair. A little table already full of diapers, clothes, wipes, bibs. There's the soft white blanket laid across the chair, looking so inviting I want to sit in it immediately.

"You did all this? This morning?" How did I not hear all this noise?

"I did. Oh what's a five-letter word for butting heads?" He rubs the back of his head, and I look at him curiously. He has a pen in one hand and the morning paper in the other.

"Argue."

"Nope, that doesn't fit."

"Clash." I serve back to him quickly, and his eyebrows rise.

"Why didn't I think of that?" He writes his answer, and I wonder what universe I've woken up in.

"Hey, Savannah! Good morning! Do you have any more of those frozen curry pies? Tim from the toy store and Bob are both after one each. Apparently, it's their night to cook dinner, so..." Melissa walks into the kitchen with a full smile. She's a lifesaver. I grin, my shoulders lowering before my head finally kicks into gear.

"Yes, sure, of course." I quickly move to my freezer and pulling out pies I baked last week. "Cooking instructions are on the front. I'll come out, and..."

"No need. Rest up. We got it." Melissa nods to me, and I pause as I peek around the door and watch her go back out with the pies. Melissa's serving and doing a little icing of cupcakes at the side, ready for the after-school rush. She's selling all the goods that I had previously prepared, and by the looks of it, a few of the frozen items as well. As was my strategy.

"Why didn't you wake me?" I frown at Griffin. I feel bad, with him here helping me when he has his own work to do.

"You needed your sleep. Here." Griffin passes me a glass of yellow liquid that looks like pee.

"What is it?"

"Pineapple juice. It's meant to help bring on the baby."

My eyebrows shoot up, and I immediately drink the juice, feeling dry and parched.

"Oh, wow. This is delicious." I look around for the bottle to see what brand it is.

"It should be. I flew it in from my Hawaii property this morning."

I splutter on the juice, my eyes watering from almost choking.

"You what?" I wipe my mouth, as a small pain laces through my side, and I rub my belly subconsciously.

"I also thought we could go for a drive later," he offers, not really answering me.

"A drive?" What in the world is he talking about?

"Yeah, drive over some speed humps and hills. Apparently, that may help as well." My brain finally catches up.

"You've been on your app all morning, haven't you?" My chest warms that he's researching all these things for me. But his gaze remains serious.

"Listen, about last night..." he starts, and my heart stalls. Is this where he says it was a mistake? Is this where he says it can't happen again? I steel myself. Was he just being a friend, helping me bring on labor by having one night of passion? It meant more to me. It felt like more to me. Self-preservation circuits through me, and I interrupt him before he can say anything more.

"You don't have to... I know you were just trying to... It's not your responsibility. I mean, the baby's father already told me he wasn't interested in being any part of this." I'm rambling as I indicate my bump, and Griffin's frown deepens to a shockingly new depth, so I continue.

"You have work and important things... dating, maybe... I don't know... I'm pretty sure once this thing comes out, it isn't going back in. Like it's a fixture in my life that's not going to be going anywhere for a good few decades, at least. I can't let you step in and fix everything with juice from Hawaii and sex... incredible sex... mind-blowing... amazing... I can't let you ruin your life for me, Griffin. You have so much, and I can't do that to you..."

His jaw looks like it's clenched so hard he's about to break a tooth as he steps closer.

"Do you see which way my boots are pointing?" he asks sharply. I look down, not able to see anything past my bump, but I have a reasonably good idea of which way they are pointing.

"Toward me?" I hazard a guess.

"There's only one direction they're walking in..." he growls, low and deep, looking me dead in the eye.

My heart skips.

"Toward you. I told you, I'm all in, and I meant it." He watches me intently, and I take a big breath and nod, relieved. Something about the way he looks at me, the way he speaks so sincerely, I believe him.

"How are you feeling? After..." he asks, and I feel my cheeks heat.

"Great. I think it worked..."

His eyes widen as he looks down at me, his hand coming to touch my belly as his brow furrows.

"Hmmmm... I think so..." He nods.

"How are you feeling? After...?" I ask him the same question and watch his Adam's apple bob as he swallows. He goes to move his hand from my belly, to step away from me, but I grab it. I need him to know I've got him.

"I'm sorry I unloaded. You didn't need that."

Now it's my turn to frown. "That's what friends do, Griffin. We listen. We don't judge..." I tell him, watching him carefully.

"Is that what we are? Friends?" he asks, and my chest hurts at the thought.

"I mean, last night was..." I blow out a breath because last night was amazing.

"It was... mind-blowing, I think you said?" A smirk tugs

at his lips as he takes another step closer to me, his hand moving back around my belly, and I almost melt into him.

"Are we more than friends, Griffin?" I ask tentatively. I don't even know how this is ever going to work.

"I can tell you right now that you better not have any other friends who fuck you like I did last night because that isn't going to end well for anyone." His voice is gruff but laced with a little humor, although I have no doubt he's speaking the truth.

"I mean, if that's us as friends, what does us as more than friends look like?" I can barely breathe as I wait for his answer.

"That's new territory for me," he says, looking a little apprehensive.

"For me too," I admit, because while I had a boyfriend, he never treated me like a woman he wanted to keep around, the benefit of hindsight showing me exactly what I didn't have, now that I do.

"So I guess we'll figure it all out as we go along. None of what we've done so far could be classed as conventional. No point changing it now."

"Don't go promising things you can't handle." It's almost a warning. Like if he's in, he can't be running off in a week's time when things get real.

"Let me be clear, sweetness... I thought I showed you last night exactly how well I can handle you. But if you need reminding, I'll pick you up and take you back upstairs and let this whole town hear how I take care of my business."

I think I sway on my feet. I feel my pussy flutter, my legs weakening. He's not committing, but he's not letting me go. I mean, he can't. None of us know what's going to happen when this baby comes. Will he run? Will I change? Will I be so overwhelmed that I can't handle it and end up going home, like my parents expect? That feels like it would be the worst decision I could make, but babies make you do weird things.

"I better get baking. Looks like I need to replenish the freezer."

Griffin's eyes search mine. Like he's looking for an answer he can't find yet, before he nods.

"I'll finish your baby nook." He kisses my forehead before he steps away and grabs the newspaper and pen on the way past.

"Hey, what's a five-letter word for devour with gusto?" he yells out to me, and I grin.

"Inhale?"

"No..."

"Scarf?"

"No... Isn't that something you put around your neck?"

I giggle at his confused frown.

"What about..."

"Gorge," we both say in unison before we laugh.

"It works..." He smiles.

And that's how our day continues as Melissa sells out and the bakery has one of its most profitable days yet.

Which is good, because that night everything changes.

25

———

GRIFFIN

"Should I be concerned?" I glance at Tanner quickly before grabbing the jar of sweet pickles I know he keeps here at the distillery restaurant.

"Nothing to be concerned about."

I wonder if I should grab two. Nowhere else in Whispers is open at this time of night, and when Savannah said she had a craving, I knew Tanner was the only one who could help. So I called him and made him meet me at the distillery. I swipe a jar of Sutton's honey while here, knowing that might be nice for Savannah too. Something sweet to balance the sharp.

"It's ten p.m. You're rifling through my cupboards like a poor man on a hunt for food."

"Savannah had a craving. I didn't have anything at home." I shrug, not wanting to make a big deal out of it. Even though it is. Even though it means something.

"'Bout time you sorted that out, then, isn't it?"

I pause and look back at him. "Sorted what out?"

"Your place. There's a baby on the way. You're running

around in the middle of the night, getting her pickles, for fuck's sake. Clearly, this isn't a onetime thing. Savannah and you, you get each other. I see it. So, get your place stocked, sorted, fucking furnished. Make it a home. For you, her, and the baby."

Tanner's eyes narrow on me.

A home. I've never had one. Not a warm, welcoming, safe one. I swallow hard, the anxiety of creating one filtering through my body like acid. It burns. Makes me feel like I might puke.

"What are you distilling here anyway?" I change the subject, eyes scanning the busy rooms. A small night crew hums around us, quiet and focused. Tanner always has something brewing.

"I got a new batch on," he admits.

"You gonna let me buy in yet or not?" I've been asking for years. Tanner keeps his whiskey close to his chest. How he distills it, what he and Connor own, the brand deals.

"Maybe?" He watches me carefully. I try to school my features. He usually shrugs me off. I'm shocked at the shift.

"Seriously?"

"Why not? You pretty much built this entire distillery with me. New spa, and now the accommodations are almost done. You remodeled Marie's Place next door. You built my new ranch, where I now live with my family. You built Connor's place. Hell, you built all the homes on Billionaire Boulevard."

I look at him, silent. Not refuting a word. I've built it all. I've constructed Whispers with him. Brick by brick. But I never let myself live in it.

"Now your place is finished, are you going to call Whispers home?" He brings the conversation back to me. My home. My place in the world.

I've spent decades hiding, running, not committing, not settling down. Not building a life where I can just be. Because I can't just be. The memories swirl too much. But I want it. I'm getting old. I want to settle. Have roots. I just have no idea how to do it. Not sure anything will work.

"Maybe." My jaw is tight. My chest tighter.

"Then maybe I'll let you buy in on this next batch."

I tilt my head, studying him. "What are you thinking?" My interest is piqued.

"It's small. Boutique. I'll sell it through our hospitality arm, the one we run out of New York with Valerie Van Cleef. High end. Luxurious. Unavailable to the masses. Something people keep. Something people cherish. Something people have in their *homes*."

"What return are we looking at?" I want to talk numbers. Not because I need the money. If I buy in, it isn't about the returns. It's about something else. Something that tethers me to this town. To my friends. To the idea that maybe I belong.

"I'm thinking fifteen to twenty percent on this one. It's almost ready for bottling. Lacy's done a good job of marketing it." He nods to himself, clearly proud of his team. He should be.

"What's it called?"

"The Builder's Arms." He looks at me seriously for a moment, and it registers. I stand there, stunned. He's had this planned all along.

"I've had this whiskey aging in old oak barrels since we turned the first soil on the distillery over twenty years ago." He continues, and I feel my throat tighten. "You made a comment back then. Something about the soil being black and the old oak trees on the perimeter of the land being so brown."

"The soil so black and rich, like it's been feeding generations, and the oak trees looked like old leather and memories. It was like the land had been holding its breath, waiting for something sacred to grow," I whisper. The recollection is clear. Sharp. Still alive in me.

"I remember."

"You're still holding your breath, Griff." Tanner's voice is low. Like he's handing me something fragile. "Probably about time you started to put down roots of your own and grow."

He reaches out his hand for me to shake. A gentlemen's deal. Letting me buy in on what will no doubt become one of his most profitable and most personal whiskeys ever made here at Whiteman's.

I shake his hand, firm and strong. My eyes go a little glassy. I don't know exactly when things started to feel different for me around here. But a few months ago, walking into that bakery, I think that was the first step. The first inhale. The first crack in my armor.

"Better get those pickles back to her. A hungry pregnant woman is not one you should battle with. Believe me, I know." I huff a laugh and nod in agreement, knowing that Victoria and his little girl Amber are both probably at home, where he wants to be.

Walking out of his distillery, the night sky is clear, still. There's no wind, and I take a deep breath, filling my lungs. First a house, now the whiskey... Looks like my roots are already established here in Whispers. And I'm holding a jar of pickles for a woman who might be the start of something sacred.

MY MIND WAS busy the entire drive back to the bakery. Thinking about Tanner's offer, his words, and the memories of when we started building the distillery. Of when I first arrived in Whispers. Feels like yesterday but also feels like a lifetime ago.

I slowly step up the stairs, lost in my thoughts, my body so wide I almost have to sidestep each one. I think about Savannah walking up and down these stairs every day with the baby. The trip hazards here, the baby proofing that still needs to happen. There's a lot to consider.

"Why are you frowning?" she asks as soon as I breach the doorway.

I look up, seeing her sitting in bed with her baby book.

"I think you should come and live with me," I say without hesitation.

Her eyes widen. "Live with you?" she confirms.

"At least for a while, just when the baby arrives..." My brain scrambles to think of a reason she might agree with. Anything other than *I want you with me all the time.* "The stairs, they're not good for you or the baby." Clearing my throat, I open the jar of pickles and grab a fork from her kitchenette.

"Not good?" She watches me with curious eyes as I walk over and sit in the chair beside her bed, passing her the opened jar.

"Tripping hazard for you now, and when the baby's older, they might fall down them."

"I'll put up baby gates," she reassures me, but it doesn't have the desired effect.

"But how about you having to lug a baby carrier and groceries up and down. And, uh, my bed is bigger. I... have a big bath for you to enjoy after a long day, but also to make it easier to clean up the baby..." I tell her all the things that are now swirling in my mind. Where the hell is she planning on bathing the baby? Her little shower isn't going to work.

"Where's your head at tonight, Griff?" she asks, watching me with nothing but kindness and love.

"On you. It's always on you," I admit as I look over her apartment. It's small, with no extra space, nowhere a baby can play. A baby can barely take its first steps in this small space.

Her cheeks flush at my response. She swallows audibly before asking, "Did something happen when you were out?"

"Tanner offered me to buy in," I tell her as I take a seat on the small armchair next to her bed.

"Buy in?"

"On the whiskey. A new release called The Builder's Arms. It's something I've been asking him for years for. He's never given me any indication that he would. Almost became a running joke." I rub my face, still not believing it.

"Well, that sounds nice? I mean, you do have nice arms." She bites into the pickle, looking at me adorningly. "Oh... so good..." She talks with her mouth full, and I grin at being able to satisfy her craving.

"He thinks I should be settling down. Putting down roots."

She nods, pausing mid-bite. "What do you think?"

"I'd like to. Just not sure how. Not sure if I..." I take a deep breath, my heart rate escalating, fear creeping in on all sides.

"If you deserve it?" She finishes off exactly what I was thinking.

I lower my head. I can't look at her. I feel so ashamed. Ashamed that I couldn't save my brother. Ashamed that I couldn't save my mother. Ashamed that I never was the man they needed me to be. Worried that I can't be that man for her. "Yeah..." is all I can say.

"How did you become a builder?" She puts the jar and fork down on the nightstand and turns to fully face me.

I look up, not expecting that question. "I was a kid traveling through Whispers. Caught the bus here, trying to find something new. Running from the heat I had on me back home. I had some experience in construction, did a shop class every day in juvie, and had an eye for detail. Spent a few years working with a crew in Northern Missouri, where I learned to hammer a nail before I learned to read properly. At least my dad was good for something. Drunk most of the time, but his laboring work meant he passed down some skills to me. When I bounced around foster homes, I always had a pencil in my hand and was drawing. Not art or anything like that, but plans, designs. I liked the idea of designing and building houses for people. Especially since I didn't really have one. Ended up here at a small bar on Main Street, which has now turned into the Whiteman's Bar, and that's where I met Tanner."

"And all these years later, what do you think makes a house a home?"

Blinking wordlessly, I stare into her beautiful eyes. I build the walls, the ceilings, the gardens, the floors. I build pools, spas, hotels, bakeries...

"The one thing I've been waiting my whole life for... but never felt good enough to have," I tell her, then almost hold my breath.

"What have you been waiting for, Griff?" she whispers, undeniable hope shining in her gaze.

"Someone like you," I whisper back, and unable to wait

a second longer, I reach out, cupping her face and bringing her lips to meet mine. I kiss her. Languidly. Wanting to savor this moment. As her soft lips touch mine, it feels like we're suspended in time. Half of me can't believe it. Can't believe I've found a woman who matches me. That accepts me for who I am. The other half is scared. Scared I'll mess this up. That my past will make it too hard for me to move forward, to accept that I'm worthy. But I know the truth. I'll never feel worthy of this woman. And I also know I'll never let her go. As I pull back slowly, I look at her, her eyes searching mine, and I grab her hand, our fingers entwining so effortlessly. Knowing it's the truth. Knowing she's what will help make my house a home. She and the baby.

"Well then…" She clears her throat. "We better go." She starts to get up, breaking our moment, pulling the blanket off her as she shimmies to the edge of the bed.

I frown, totally confused as I look up at her. "Go? Go where?"

"The hospital. My water just broke."

My heart stops beating before picking up speed.

"Your what?" I stand abruptly, panic making my insides curl.

"It appears this baby thought making a home with you, Griffin, was all it needed. Now it's coming."

"Oh shit." I help her out of bed, feeling warm all over. "Sweetness?" My voice doesn't sound like my own. My heart is thumping in my chest like it never has before. Fear. Excitement. *Love.* All overwhelming me yet fulfilling me in equal measures.

"It's alright. We've got this," she tells me, squeezing my hand tight. Giving me her strength. Her water just broke, she's about to have a baby, and she's comforting me?

I take a breath and settle myself. I need to step up. I have to be the man she needs. I couldn't be one before, for my mom or my brother, but I'm not going to let her down.

"I've got you." Kissing her head, I grab her bag and help her down the stairs before breaking every speed limit known to man on the way to Whispers Hospital.

26

SAVANNAH

I didn't know what to expect. But this is worse. Far worse. It's not just pain; it's pressure, heat, and I feel like I'm unraveling from the inside out.

"Okay, Savannah, the baby's heartbeat is a little low." Hudson's voice is calm, but it has a hint of firmness to it I haven't heard before. "It could just be a little sleepy, but you're also not dilating how I expected either, so we're going to transfer you to Williamstown. They're better equipped for births that might need intervention."

"No. Please..." I beg, resistance filtering through my body. I hear the heart rate monitors connected to me beep a little faster. I don't want to go to Williamstown. I never want to go back there.

"Williamstown?" Griffin barks, already pacing. His boots echo against the linoleum in the room like a warning bell. He hasn't left my side. Not once. The first glow of morning is beginning to bleed through the blinds, casting long shadows across the floor. We've been here all night, and nothing is happening, other than pain lacing through me constantly.

I blink hard, trying to sit upright. The room tilts slightly, my body swaying with exhaustion.

"There's no other option. The baby's heart rate is too low for my liking, and the Williamstown Hospital is better equipped for neonatal care. I know you wanted to deliver here in Whispers, but it's safest if we get you to Williamstown," Hudson confirms as he and the nurses here all run around, gathering things, preparing me to leave already.

"Griff?" His name is barely formed before another contraction slams into me like a tidal wave. "Ahhhhhhh..." I double over, gripping my belly.

Griffin is at my side in the next second, his hand catching mine, his other arm bracing my back. His face is close, eyes wild, but voice steady. "You got this... Breathe, sweetness. Just breathe."

"I'm breathing... I'm breathing..." I pant, eyes squeezed shut, trying to ride it out.

"I've got an ambulance ready." Hudson's voice fades behind the rush of people in the room who are unhooking my bed, and then they start to wheel me down the hallway.

"What's happening?" I say through a gasp, my eyes finding Griffin's. I need him to anchor me.

"The baby's just as stubborn as its mom." His jaw is tight. "We're going to Williamstown so they can help encourage the little one to come out."

"I'm scared... Don't leave me, Griff," I whisper as the lights on the ceiling whizz past my line of sight, one after the other, almost rhythmically.

"Never, I'll never leave. I'm right here." He walks quickly beside me, his hand still in mine. And I believe him.

As panicked as I am, the fact that Griffin holds my hand

and never lets go while my bed is pushed down the hallway, then outside and into the ambulance, gives me the support I need and the support I've lacked my entire life.

"I'll meet you there!" Hudson yells out as the doors close us in and we start to move instantly. Griffin is at my side, still holding my hand. He looks comically large, squished into the back of the ambulance next to me, watching me closely before looking at the paramedic with a gaze that would make any grown man tremble.

I feel another contraction, and I squeeze my eyes shut and groan, gripping his hand tight again, squashing his fingers together, but he never once complains or winces.

"You're doing good, Savannah. So fucking good. I'm here, I'm right here... Breathe, sweetness. Keep breathing..." I flop back onto the bed as the pain subsides, the vehicle moving rapidly through the roads to Williamstown.

"Can't you drive any faster?" he grits out to the paramedic. I have no idea how quickly we're moving, but it feels fast.

"We'll get you there as fast as we can." The female paramedic doesn't offer him anything else as she watches the heart rate monitor and ensures the drip in my arm is still connected.

"I bet a few months ago you never ever thought you'd be in this situation." I look up at him through teary eyes, trying to lighten the mood. His gaze is laced with a mixture of fear, protectiveness, stress.

"The app didn't really prepare me for this bit."

I smile, my head lolling around a little with the movement of the vehicle, my body spent. I'm almost at total exhaustion and the baby isn't even here yet.

"I meant what I said. I want you to live with me. I want to take care of you... and the baby..."

My heart skips a beat, feeling the most secure in my life with this man by my side.

"You're taking pretty good care of me now." I give him another small smile, knowing he feels a little out of his depth. We both do.

Griffin leans closer, brushing a damp strand of hair from my cheek with a touch so gentle it almost undoes me. "Savannah... look at me, baby."

I force my eyes to meet his.

"You're not doing this alone. Not now. Not ever."

Another contraction curls through me, sharp and hot, and I gasp, fingers clawing at his as I tense. He squeezes back instantly.

"I've got you. I'm right here. You hear me? They can move us, they can poke you, prod you, wheel you through every damn hospital hallway in this state"—his voice cracks, just barely—"but I'm not letting go."

A tear slips down my cheek, my emotions, the pain, my whole body feeling out of control. "Promise?"

He leans his forehead on mine, breath shaking. "Sweetness... you're the only thing I've ever been sure of. I'm not going anywhere."

The ambulance hits a bump, and the monitor beeps again; it's too slow, too soft, and I'm scared, but I feel Griffin's hand wrapped around mine, steady and unbreakable.

"Just hold on," he whispers, thumb stroking my knuckles. "Hold on to me. We're getting your baby out safe. Together."

～

"AND I SEE THE HEAD... Get ready to push!" The doctor's voice cuts through the haze. It's a new doctor. Someone apparently specialized in obstetrics who took over my care as soon as I arrived. It should feel unsettling to have yet another man all up in my business, but it's all a blur.

I turn to Griffin, searching his face. "I can't do it... I can't..." I'm sweating, my hair is wet and stuck to the back of my neck. My body hurts from my head to my toes. I feel exhaustion like I've never felt before, deep down to my bones.

"You can... One more, sweetness. Just one more push, and it's done..." His forehead presses to mine, his hands gripping mine like a lifeline. "You've got this, I know you do. You're amazing, a fucking warrior. One more, sweet thing, just one more push..."

"Okay..." I whisper, though nothing feels okay. My body is a battlefield—limbs numb, belly taut, my core a burning ring of fire.

"Push!" the doctor orders, giving me an encouraging look.

I scream, the sound primal, raw. I squeeze Griffin's hands so tight, I expect to feel his fingers crack, but he doesn't flinch. He holds on, steady, as he has been all this time. My calm river through the storm, grounding me. Giving me his strength. I push with everything I've got, which admittedly isn't much. And it's then I hear it. A cry. A beautiful, furious cry.

I freeze. The world stills.

"You did it! You did it!" Griffin kisses my head over and over, and tears spill down my cheeks as I choke out my emotions. Pulling me close, he cups my face, kissing my cheeks next like he's trying to memorize me.

"I did it... I did it..." I barely exhale the words, in disbelief. I did it. I delivered my baby.

"Good work, sweetness... I'm so proud of you," Griffin murmurs, looking a little in shock himself.

"We did it," I whisper, because we did. We've been in this together for hours. For months. For a lifetime, it feels like.

"And it's a boy!" the doctor announces.

"A boy?" I echo, stunned. I look at Griffin, wide-eyed, and then around the room, trying to see. The doctor lifts him, tiny, wrinkled, perfect, and places him on my bare chest.

"Oh my..." My hands tremble as I cradle him. I don't feel like I have enough strength to hold him, but Griffin's large hand is there, helping me, guiding my son to me. My baby's skin is warm, damp, impossibly soft and pink. He has a sprinkle of dark hair crowning his head.

"A boy," Griffin says again. His voice is reverent and full of wonder. He hasn't let go of me. One hand brushes my hair back from my face, the other resting lightly on my son's back. The three of us are tangled together in this moment, a fragile, sacred bubble.

"Let us take him quickly and wrap him so he remains warm. Does Dad want to cut the cord?" a nurse asks innocently.

"Oh, I'm..." Griffin starts, looking a little lost now in this busy hospital room. The shock of what he witnessed is obvious.

"Do it," I tell him quickly, wanting him to be part of all of this.

"You want me to?" His eyebrows pinch, like he's not sure he's allowed.

"Yeah. I want you to." If my son can be half the man Griffin is, then I know he'll be amazing.

He swallows hard. I see it. The emotion he's trying to

keep down. He hasn't slept. Not a second. He's been with me every step. Feeding me ice chips. Holding my hair back. Lifting me when I couldn't stand. Walking me through contractions. Dancing with me in the hallway when I needed to move. He's been on the phone, barking orders, ensuring I'm looked after. He's been my anchor, my strength.

He deserves this moment.

Griffin cups my face, kisses me once, but it's enough to have my stomach flipping, and then follows the doctor to the side.

I hear the baby's soft cries as the nurses tend to me, adjusting the bed, checking vitals, cleaning me up, but I'm oblivious to it all as I watch Griffin, the biggest man in the room, standing protectively over the smallest. His shoulders are squared, but I see him swipe at his eyes before he turns back to me.

"Here, Mom," the nurse says gently. "Place him on your chest. He may start to suckle."

I do as she says, and sure enough, the baby latches on, instinctive and determined.

"He won't drink much, but it's great to get him started. Skin-to-skin with Dad is important too."

She smiles and leaves us be. We don't correct them. We don't feel the need.

"Everything went well. You'll be in recovery for an hour or so, then we'll move you to the ward. I hear there's quite the audience waiting."

I glance at Griffin, eyebrows raised. "My family?" My heart starts to race, not wanting to see them. Not wanting them near my son at all. If I felt protective before, the feeling welling inside my chest right now is enough to burn down the hospital. Being a mama bear is a real thing.

"No," he says gently, already knowing what I'm thinking. His hand brushes mine soothingly.

"Who then?" I ask.

"Tanner. Victoria. The others. Hudson called them for me. They've been here for a while."

"Really?" I blink, swallowing the lump in my throat. I didn't think anyone would come. I thought I'd be alone. Months ago, I assumed I would be a lonely single mom with no support, going through all of this solo. But I'm not.

"I also arranged security," Griffin adds. "No one gets to you without your say-so."

"Security?" I frown, confused.

"I want you to be calm. Rest. Recover. Anxiety about being in the same town as your family I know isn't going to help you. So I got a few guards in the hallway, watching things. It's a public hospital, so they can't stop people from coming or going, but they sure as hell can stop someone from coming into your room. So you can rest easy."

Relief floods me. The anxiety of being back in Williamstown has been a weight on my chest for hours, although I had pushed it to the back of my mind until now.

"Thank you for doing that," I breathe out and smile up at him. He nods, his fingers lightly caressing my hair back.

"So... a little man, huh?" Griffin grins.

"Look at his hair." I run my finger over the soft fuzz. "And his little nose..." I bop it gently.

"Look at his little hands..." Griffin's voice is thick. The baby's fingers curl around one of his, the contrast almost laughable.

"You did good, sweetness. Real good." He brushes my cheek with the back of his hand.

"Thank you, Griffin. For everything." My voice wobbles.

I'm trying not to cry again, but I've never been more grateful for anyone in my life.

He clears his throat, his eyes looking deeply into mine. "That was the most amazing thing I think I'll ever experience. So, thank you."

And I believe him. Because it was.

27

GRIFFIN

I walk out of her room and almost stumble before I lean against the wall, my back sliding down along it until I hit the floor. My legs feel like they've been hollowed out. They're jelly. The shock and adrenaline of what I experienced now pulsing through me.

I thought I'd seen it all. I've seen and experienced more in my lifetime than most. Violence, greed, neglect, scarcity. But I've never experienced the complete and utter helplessness, fear, and shock I just went through, followed by complete devotion and the overwhelming feeling of love that I do right now.

There was no way I was letting her go through that on her own. I wanted to ensure she had support, that she knew I had her back. I have no idea how women do it. I feel insignificant. It was the most insane and unforgettable thing I'll ever witness.

I haven't fallen for her; I crashed straight through whatever walls I had left. I love her. God help me, I love her so much, it scares the hell out of me.

"Griff."

I look up at the familiar voice, seeing Tanner striding toward me.

"It's a boy," I tell him, sounding hoarse, as ten pairs of eyes blink at me in stunned silence before the hallway erupts.

"That's brilliant!" Hudson grins. Tanner slaps me on the back, firm and proud, then extends his hand and pulls me up from where I've indeed fallen to my knees.

I know it's not my baby. Hell, Savannah and I are just starting whatever it is we're doing. But after what I just witnessed, I couldn't even tell you what day it is.

The girls do that high-pitched squeal thing, and my head spins. A fucking baby. Savannah had her baby.

"She was a queen. She's amazing. And the kid, he's got ten fingers and ten toes and dark hair, and I cut his cord..." I almost tear up. I cut that cord with precision. The most precise cut I've done in my entire career.

But I'm barely surviving. Two days without sleep, without a moment to breathe. I have no idea how Savannah's still awake, still functioning, after what she just went through. I had no idea labor lasted that long.

"It's a memorable event. How do you feel?" Tanner asks.

"Insignificant." It's the truth. What that woman did, what her body endured, I'm in awe. I've built empires, ranches, homes, but she built a human.

"Just wait until he grows up and becomes a little asshole..." Sutton nods toward his nephew Noah, who sits on a chair over to the side, currently knotting one of Sawyer's spare ties around his neck like he's prepping for a board meeting.

"Thanks for coming. Savannah couldn't believe that you all showed up when I told her." I nod to them all, seeing their happy faces, amazed by the woman I'm in complete awe of.

"Of course. Just glad it all went well." Connor slaps my shoulder, his grin wide.

"What do you need us to do? Does Savannah need anything? Do you need anything?" Sawyer's already in logistics mode.

"I've got no idea." I shake my head and rub my eyes. The app doesn't tell you what to do after the baby's born. There's no blueprint for this. I need to research, find out what I can do, what Savannah might need and get it organized for her.

"Mom and baby will probably stay a night or two here and rest." Hudson is the voice of reason I need right now. "After that, if she needs to, she can come back to Whispers Hospital or go straight home, depending on how they both are and what support she has in place."

I frown. I told Savannah she could live with me, but I never got a clear answer. Now, after what I saw, what she went through, I need to do more. Hire a nurse. Hire a chef. Stock the pantry. Get bath salts. Maybe one of those beds that elevates her up and down like they have here. I need to call Mother Maven again. I need to make it easy for her to heal. I also want to ensure the baby has everything he needs. Diapers, clothes, a warm safe home. Home... There's that word again...

"Alright, well, we'll all go and let you guys have your time. You call if you need anything." Tanner starts to round up the troops.

"I will." I nod, shaking his hand.

"Do you want to open the bakery tomorrow or...?" Victoria offers as she gives me a hug, and I feel grateful.

Fuck the bakery. I haven't spoken to Savannah about what to do with the bakery.

"I'll call her helper Melissa. See if she's available." I know Savannah is prepared with readymade pies and things. Melissa is more than equipped to handle the sale of items.

"Thank you all. Really... I feel a little numb... but I know Savannah appreciates you all."

Hudson gives me a grin. "You'll learn to survive on no sleep," he says jokingly. If only he knew I slept very little anyway.

"Daisy and I can babysit anytime." Connor grins, punching my arm before he and Daisy slink off.

"I'll keep an eye on your place. I assume you're staying here with Savannah?" Sutton comes to shake my hand, Charlotte right by his side.

"Yeah, I need to get some things at some point. I need to organize my place." I make the mistake of looking at Tanner, who has a big grin on his face and an *I told you so* smirk.

"You'll figure it out, Griff." I glance at Sawyer, who's watching me. "You will. Might take a bit, but if I can work out monster spray and farm life, you can work out dirty diapers and pacifiers." He gives me a knowing look, and I pull in a deep breath.

"Thanks, Sawyer." I shake his hand. "I might need a hand. I need to draw up some paperwork."

"Whenever you're ready." He grins like he already knows. Maybe he does. He's a father to two kids who aren't his blood. He gets it.

I stand there, watching everyone leave. I have no idea what time it is. But the hallway is quiet. The weight of responsibility sits on my shoulders. Wanting to provide. Wanting to be a safe space for her and the little one. Wanting to protect.

I look up and spot my two guards at the end of the corridor, grabbing coffee from the vending machine. I nod to them. They stick out like sore thumbs, but I don't care. No one's getting into Savannah's room, and after her sister walked into the bakery, acting like she owned it, I wouldn't be surprised if her family tried something. Thank God, they don't know she's here.

After what Savannah went through, she needs to relax and heal, not be scared or anxious about her fucked-up family. I'm thankful Hudson helped me clear the security requirements with the hospital staff and strategically placed Savannah in the room tucked away, down the end of the hall, out of sight.

I want it quiet. Safe. Special. For her.

Before I go back in, I take a seat in the hallway to gather my thoughts. The small hard plastic chair groans under my weight, but I sit anyway, hang my head, and stare at the floor.

My life just did a full circle. A few decades ago, I watched life leave my mother's and brother's eyes. Today, I watched life enter the world. I never thought I'd see something so significant. Never thought it would happen to me.

The fact that the baby isn't my blood? Means nothing. He's mine. Because she's mine. Because I choose them. And they choose me.

I exhale, slow and shaky. I'm not ready. I'm scared. I'm scared I'm going to fuck it up. I'm scared I'm going to let her down. But for the first time, I'm willing to try. And maybe that's enough.

I sit for a moment longer, elbows on knees, head bowed, catching my breath, trying to gather my thoughts.

When I finally stand, I glance toward the nurses' station at the far end of the corridor. There's a man there.

Button-down shirt, pressed pants, hair combed to within

an inch of its life. He's talking to the nurses, but something about him feels familiar. Not in a friendly way. Like a name I forgot or a face I saw once in a place I shouldn't have been.

He catches my eye and nods, polite, distant. I nod back, slowly. But the unease lingers. I'm clearly exhausted. Thinking I'm seeing things I'm not. Shaking my head, I rub my eyes and then turn and walk back toward Savannah's room.

I pause at the doorway. It's open, a small crack showing me the vision inside. I push the door a little more, and I step inside quietly, not wanting to disturb her.

She's sitting in bed, cradling the baby against her chest.

He's suckling, slow and steady, his tiny hand resting against her skin.

Her head is tilted down, watching him, eyes half-closed, one hand stroking his back in lazy circles and whispering sweet nothings to him.

She looks... Holy. Beautiful. I freeze, watching her in total awe.

There's something about seeing her like this. Feeding her son, giving him more of her like she didn't just give him life. Her body still trembling from everything it endured. It makes my chest ache.

I've never seen anything so powerful. So gentle. So damn breathtaking.

She looks up and sees me standing there like a stalker and her smile widens. Like she has enough love and life to give me, even though she gave all of what she had to the bundle of joy in her arms. I feel privileged.

"Hey." Her voice is soft, medicine for my soul. Welcoming me to her space. I walk over to her and take a seat on the edge of the bed, brushing a strand of hair from her face. Even now, exhausted, no makeup, hair pulled back haphazardly, she's still the most beautiful woman I've ever seen.

"He's hungry." She gives me a tired smile.

"Smart kid," I murmur, eyes locked on the tiny miracle in her arms.

I rest my hand on her thigh, grounding myself.

"I didn't know it would feel like this," I admit.

She doesn't answer. She doesn't need to.

Her hand finds mine. And for a while, we sit there. The three of us. Quiet. Safe.

Home.

28

SAVANNAH

It's been a day, and my body is now fully aware I gave birth. Everything aches. My feet, my back, my breasts. But I feel nothing but joy. Okay, and tired.

Griffin has barely left my side. He slept here with me last night and showered here this morning. Apart from taking a few calls in the hallway and going to grab us coffee, he hasn't left.

"So have you thought of a name yet?" the nurse asks as she takes my vitals and records it.

Griffin looks up at me, waiting.

"I have a few ideas."

"I'm sure whatever you decide will be perfect. I think you'll be able to go home tomorrow. One more night to recover, and then as long as you have someone at home to help you, then there should be no need to go into Whispers Hospital."

"Oh, I..." I start to say.

"I'll be there." Griffin's answer is instant. And while I should feel bad, want independence, not to be a burden, there's more than just me to think about now. And he just saw me give birth. There's literally nothing else to hide from him, and he's still here.

"Good. Well, we'll be back later with supper." She smiles and walks out as the baby starts to fuss.

"Can you grab him?" I ask Griffin as I sit up in bed, trying not to cringe at the aches in my body.

Griffin stands, walking to the bassinet, and scoops up the baby like he's a mere football.

"You want him?" Griffin asks, but the moment he has him in his arms, the baby settles immediately.

"Why don't you cuddle him for a bit?" I offer, laying my head back down, barely having the energy to lift it a moment longer than necessary. Griffin helped all night; he brought the baby to me for feeding and helped me with everything so I didn't have to move too much. But he hasn't really sat with the baby. Facilitated yes but not cuddled yet.

I watch as Griffin swallows, the reality of his situation now apparent. He slowly takes a seat, the baby looking comically small in his arms and all too well protected. Griffin maneuvers the baby so he's lying on his broad chest, his movements slow and steady, like he's holding a thousand-year-old vase that he doesn't want to drop. He rests the baby's head on his chest, near where I think Griffin's heart is. And watch in awe as this big, gruff, grumpy man places his large hand on my son's small back.

Watching in silence, I hold my breath. Griffin's shoulders lower a little, my son snuggled and warm and now quiet and content. My eyes sting, my chest feels heavy. My life has never been perfect, but at this moment, I feel like it comes close.

"So you got some names?" Griffin's voice is a soft rumble.

"I've got one," I admit, feeling nervous. My palms are

sweating. I love the name I've chosen, not sure the man holding my baby will, though.

"Oh yeah?" Griffin's looking at my son closely, memorizing his little features. Taking in his little nose, his soft little breaths, and his long lashes.

"I thought maybe we could call him Tommy." Griffin's hand pauses, and his facial features still.

"But I wanted to ask you first, what you thought of that." I continue quickly as my mouth dries and my heart thuds heavily in my chest. Thomas is a nice name. Strong, meaningful. Sentimental to the man who has already given me so much.

I remain quiet, waiting. Griffin leans his head down, putting his lips to my son's head, so softly I almost shed a tear.

"I think that's a beautiful name for a beautiful boy." He looks at me for the first time, his eyes glassy.

"Thomas Griffin Sullivan," I tell him, and his face stills, his eyes searching mine.

"You don't need to…"

"I want to." I swallow. "My son is going to need a strong man to look up to. A man to show him how the world works. A man who knows you don't always need to be hard to be strong. That softness and kindness are just as important. I think he should be named after such a man as well."

"Oh, sweetness. Don't go putting a halo around my head now… I'm no guardian angel," he murmurs.

"Hmmmm, maybe, maybe not. Who knows, you might walk out of this hospital room now and never look back." I swallow hard, hating the fact that my words do have some truth to them. "But in the time of my life when I needed someone, you were there," I tell him as his gaze remains on me.

"I'm not going anywhere... You should get some sleep, sweetness. Your body has been through a lot," he tells me, not acknowledging the name, not refuting or replying.

I lie back down and get comfortable, pulling the blankets around my chin, watching Griffin holding Tommy until my eyes get heavy.

Feeling content, not knowing exactly what awaits me when I wake.

~

Hearing the baby fuss, I sit up. I'm alone, and the afternoon sun sits high.

"Oh, you're awake," a kind nurse says as she walks into my room. She takes a quick look at the baby and then comes over to me.

"How are you feeling? Did you get a little sleep?" She pours me a small glass of water.

"An hour, maybe... I think." The nurse hands me the glass, and I see her eyes look down at my chest and then back to me.

"He'll need feeding soon, but I noticed your necklace. Would you like the hospital chaplain to come in? Perhaps say a blessing for you and the baby?" she asks, and my fingers find the cross hanging from my necklace, and I thumb it a little. It's a necklace my parents gave me when I was younger, and I've worn it every day since. So much so, I forget I'm even wearing it.

My eyes dart to my son. A blessing would be nice. He's only a day old. I'm not sure what awaits him in his life. I'm not sure if I'll even take him to church or raise him with religion being a big part of our lives after what the community did to me, but a kind blessing couldn't harm.

"Sure. If he has the time."

The nurse smiles. "Of course. I'll ensure he knows to stop by."

She nods and then starts to move.

"Um, my ahhhh... Griffin? Do you know where he went?" I wonder where he is.

"He went to make some calls, and then he was going to the cafeteria to grab a coffee. He said he won't be long."

I nod as she walks out. It makes sense. He's lacking sleep as much as I am. I feel bad that he's by my side, at a time when he has so much work going on and clients to meet. I think about the bakery then. Griffin mentioned that he'd call Melissa to go in with reduced hours and to sell a few things to keep the locals happy. I'm grateful, because I know this hospital visit isn't going to be cheap. I swallow harshly because I haven't thought about that too much. I mean, I saved my money. I knew it would cost something, but Hudson mentioned the new mothers program at Whispers, so I thought most of the fees would be covered. Now that I'm in Williamstown, a different hospital with a different doctor, I suspect that won't be the case.

The new ovens and mixers I'd planned to purchase in another month or so will have to wait a little longer.

"My dear. Congratulations..." I look at the door to a man walking in and my stomach curls.

"Pastor Greg... what are you doing here?" My heart rate escalates as I try to sit up straighter without wincing too much.

He has a scarily soft smile on his lips as he walks straight over to Tommy and peers into his bassinet.

"A boy?"

"That's right." I swallow, feeling uncomfortable. Fear itching my skin.

"What are you doing here?" I try to reach for the call button, but it's out of reach. It must have slipped off the bed when I slept.

"The nurse said you wanted a blessing for the baby." Shit, he's the hospital chaplain. How did I not realize that?

"Oh..." I regret my decision now. I didn't want anyone from my past to see Tommy. I don't want anyone near him.

"It's okay. I know you're busy," I say because now that he's here, I just want him to go. I know he'll immediately tell my family. Tell them all about his name, his birth information, all things I don't want them to know.

"Dear Lord, I come to you now and ask you to bless your poor child, Thomas. Lord, bless him and protect him. Protect him from sinfulness and from the ways of this world. Smile on him, Lord, and be gracious with him. Let him be like your Son, Jesus, and grow in true wisdom and stature, and let him always seek Your favor. Lord, we pray that his life will be like a light in this fallen world. Let him know he is deeply loved by his family, by his Church, and by you, his Father in Heaven. In Jesus' name we pray, Amen."

I swallow as Pastor Greg stays, looking at Tommy for a moment.

"You know God delivers what we most need in the world." He turns to look at me. His eyes run from my face down the bed and back, like he's assessing me. For illness, for clarification, for what, I don't know.

I shiver, feeling cold. "He does."

"This child of God. Thomas. He needs to be in a home with God-fearing parents. Two parents, a husband and a wife."

My heart thuds faster. I want to move. I want to grab Tommy and hold him. Seal him to my chest so no harm can come to him. But I don't think I can move. I'm scared still.

"A child of God needs to be with its mother," I state clearly.

Pastor Greg knows my parents well. They all grew up together. He and my father spend so much time together, praying and working for the church. I know what he's thinking. It's what he's always thought. Along with my parents. This baby should go to Eden. He smiles at me. Like I'm some young, silly girl who doesn't know how the world works. Like I'm stupid and he's superior. I hate it.

"The Lord sees all things, and sin does not hide behind innocence. This child was already born into your unrepented shame. Don't let him grow up with sinfulness."

"You must have the wrong room."

I gasp as my gaze flicks to the door to see Griffin standing there with two coffees in hand. He walks in calmly as Pastor Greg finally steps back from Tommy. His eyes widen, taking in all that Griffin is. Which is a lot. Especially today, with his hair ruffled and his eyes darker due to lack of sleep.

Griffin remains calm as he places the two cups down on the side table, but I see his shoulders tight as he walks straight over to Tommy, almost hip-checking Pastor Greg as he moves past him. Griffin picks up my son and walks him to me, passing him over, and I grab him, holding him to my chest tightly. Relief so instant from having him in my arms, I almost cry.

I don't say a word, but Griffin turns, putting his body between me and Pastor Greg, and they face off. It's almost comical, though, because Pastor Greg only comes to Griffin's shoulders.

"I said, you're in the wrong room," Griffin repeats, this time his voice lower, his eyes narrow.

"I was invited to give the baby a blessing."

"The blessing has been done," I say quickly, as Tommy starts to fuss.

"There's the door." Griffin isn't in the mood to make friends, and I see Pastor Greg's lips purse like he sucked on a sour lemon. But he takes the hint and turns, walking to the door. He pauses as his hand grabs the door handle and looks back at me.

"You may cradle him now, but the Lord scorns those who suppress the truth with their wickedness."

I suck in a quick breath at his threat. Griffin takes a step forward, his fists clenched, but Pastor Greg is already out the door. Moving swiftly.

"Someone you know?" Griffin looks at me, scowling.

"The nurse saw my necklace and offered to get the hospital chaplain for a blessing. I thought it would be nice. I didn't know the hospital chaplain was Pastor Greg from my old church. Best friends with my dad and the leader of the church community who betrayed me. How could they claim to *love* me if all they did was admonish me and prayed for me to abandon my baby?" I swallow, bitterness coating me, feeling bad that I put Tommy in this situation already. What kind of mother am I? Remorse eats at me as I look down at my son, who's rooting for my breast, hungry.

"My security guys shouldn't have let him in."

"The nurse got him. I suspect they thought it was all okay, as it was someone from the hospital. I thought it was. I didn't think..." As Tommy nurses, I feel a tear drop down my cheek. I need to be more careful. I have a child to protect now. I can't be letting anyone in. I'll pray for him in my own way. Or not. The religion I grew up in is starting to feel more like a vise around my neck than hope in my heart.

"Does this mean your family will now know?" I sigh and

nod slowly as his hand comes to my cheek and he wipes my tears.

"Yes," I whisper before I swallow. Wanting to leave. Wanting to get out of here and far, far away.

"You never answered my question the other day."

I look up at him with glassy eyes. "Which one?"

"I want you and Tommy to live with me. Given you need someone around at least for the first few weeks, I think it's the best solution."

"Don't you have work? Sundown Valley and Colorado. Two big projects." I shake my head, still feeling like a burden.

"I do. But I can work around it all. At least for a while. There might be a few quick trips I need to make, but I've spoken to Melissa, and she's ready to help with the baby or the bakery, whatever you need."

"It's a lot. It's a lot for you to take on. Two people in your home, in your space..." I want to. I want to be with Griffin all the time.

"Maybe. But I want you with me. Both of you. And your family won't be able to get into my house. They don't even know where I live."

It's true. Tommy and I will be safe there. I swallow and look at my son. I need to keep him safe and given that my family knows the bakery and knows I live there, it may not be the best option.

"But your sleep will be interrupted. Your work may be impacted. I'll probably be all hormonal and teary..." I'm giving him every opportunity to renege his offer.

"You and I both know I don't sleep well. Besides, Tommy might become my midnight companion..." Griffin's eyes haven't moved from mine. He looks at me so intently, so firmly, like nothing else in the world matters.

"Your place? Is it ready? For a postpartum woman and a newborn? The number of dirty diapers alone is probably enough to have you running." I try to make light. In truth, staying with Griffin would be amazing. My feelings for him are growing by the second. I thought for sure that as soon as the baby came, he would run. It all being too much. Too real. The responsibility overwhelming. But he's hardly left my side. He hasn't wavered. I feel his protectiveness. I feel his desire and care for me. There's nowhere else I want to be than with him.

"It's ready." Griffin nods. So self-assured.

"What about Tommy..."

"I got a crib." He nods, and my eyebrows rise in surprise.

"You do?" I'm going to cry all over again.

"And a change mat, baby bath, bottles, blankets. I got it all. The house is ready for you both. Plus, I organized a chef to prepare healthy meals for your recovery. Hudson is literally down the road if we need him..."

My heart lurches. I have no words. He doesn't have to do any of this.

"That was quick..." I smile a little, and his face softens.

"Been making a lot of calls while you've been sleeping," he admits, and his cheeks seem to flush a bit.

"Tommy's lucky to have you. We both are."

"I'm the lucky one."

I look up at Griffin and nod, accepting his offer and his obvious feelings for me. Pushing away my insecurities.

"Okay. We'll come home with you," I tell him, and he leans forward, kissing my forehead, staying close and not leaving my side at the hospital again.

29

———

GRIFFIN

I don't think I've ever driven these roads so slowly. Although I've never had the precious cargo that I do now.

"We're here." I keep my eyes on the road, but I notice Savannah sitting forward and looking out the window.

"You weren't kidding about the privacy..." she murmurs, seeing my house surrounded by high stone fences. As the solid timber gates open, I roll past, making our way down the long driveway lined with large oak trees on each side.

"I like to remain unseen," I tell her, and her gaze swings to me.

"But you're so pretty to look at." She grins, and I huff a laugh.

"Hmmm... pretty isn't something I've been called before."

"Well, there's a first time for everything," she quips as I pull up to the front of my place. She's still tired, but I'm starting to see her confidence shining through. I witnessed it before Tommy arrived, but it's almost like the baby has given her an extra boost. Like she knows her place in the world and is stepping into it.

I haven't been here at home for days. Either at the bakery or in the hospital with Savannah, but I've had people here, setting up the nursery, stocking the fridge and pantry, and Mother Maven delivered so many baby things, I could probably open my own store and become one of her new franchisees.

"It's so pretty here," she says as she starts to open her door.

"Wait," I whisper-bark, then jump out and run around to her side. She's getting around okay, but my truck is big, and her body went through one of the most traumatic things it probably can. I don't want her falling on my watch.

"I'm fine." She might want to deny my help, but she's smiling anyway. Looking at the car seat, I notice Tommy stirring. My voice obviously wasn't quiet enough.

"He woke up?" I place her on her feet in front of me, my hands not wanting to leave her.

She pats my chest, leaning up to kiss my cheek. "Babies tend to do that..." She's relaxed. Her eyes shine, and her smile is warm. I move my hands around her waist, wanting to hold her for a moment. The past couple of days have been a whirlwind.

"Are you feeling alright... after the drive?" I look over her. Beautiful, as always.

"I'm feeling good. Not one hundred percent, but good. Being with you makes me happy," she says, humming against my chest, and I defrost a little before we hear Tommy again. "Are you ready for this?" Pulling back, she looks up at me expectantly.

"For what?" I rub my hand up and down her back, keeping her close.

"For Tommy and me to be here. In your space..."

"I can handle it." I nod, my lips quirking a little, and her grin widens. "I want it. I want you."

Her hands run up my arms, and her fingers curl slightly around my shoulders, like she's anchoring herself. Or maybe anchoring me.

"You sure?" Her voice is softer now. "It's not just about the nursery or the fridge being full."

"I know." I meet her gaze. "It's about you. Him. Us. I'm ready. I want it."

Her breath catches, just a flicker, and I feel it like a punch to the chest.

I cup her face. "I know the minute you walk in, the walls will stop echoing."

She swallows, eyes glinting with something I can't name. "That's dangerously poetic for a man who claims he likes to remain unseen."

"Hmmm, don't get used to it," I murmur, which makes her giggle. Leaning down, I place my lips on hers and almost groan at the contact. While I've held her, rubbed her back, placed kisses on her forehead and tried to bring her comfort through her labor and the time after, days between kissing her like this have felt far too long.

Tommy's fussing has us stopping before we can get carried away, and we both turn and look at the back seat, where he looks comically small for the luxury car seat I had professionally fitted yesterday. It's one of the things that kept me from her for a longer time than it should've when that so-called pastor walked into her room and made the birth of a beautiful boy all about him and his beliefs. My jaw tightens thinking about it now.

"Time for a feed, I think..." I reluctantly let her go and move to open the back door. Leaning in, I see him as snuggled as he was when we left the hospital. Earlier than what the doctors wanted, but after the visit from the pastor, who looked more like a serial killer, I didn't want to stay another night.

I unclip the seat belt as Savannah stands nearby, looking over my vast green lawns and my Whispers house.

"So you designed and built this? From scratch?" she questions, and I hug Tommy to my chest.

"I did." I nod as I steer her inside, my hand at the small of her back, Tommy held tightly in my other. She's moving slowly, but she's in perfect health. Tommy's restlessness has stopped now that he's in my arms. The kid is cute. He has Savannah's big eyes and button nose.

I look at my place and try to imagine it from her eyes. Two stories, stonework, and timber. Large windows allow a lot of natural light inside and a picturesque image of the outside. It's a little cold. Certainly no color, no flowers or decorations of any kind. I open the front door, and we step inside.

"Wow." She stops suddenly, taking it all in. I stand a little taller at her reaction. "You have a chandelier!"

Glancing up, I spot the large crystal light Victoria said *I just had to have*. The one I forget is even there.

"Oh my God, your sofa is white!" She whips around to face me, her expression alone telling me that I'm crazy. I can only nod, because it is. It's yet another thing Victoria said *I just had to have*. "Griffin!" she whisper-yells at me this time, and I frown in confusion as Tommy starts to fuss again.

"What?" Brow furrowed, I watch her take a few tentative steps, like she's too scared to step inside.

"Have you lost your mind?" she asks me seriously, hand on her hip.

My eyebrows shoot to my hairline. "What? Why?"

"This is the most amazing, luxurious place I've ever stepped into. And you brought a new baby in here!"

I shake my head. "I'm not following...?"

"You have floors so clean I can literally see my face in them..." She walks around, looking down at her feet as she moves across my polished timber floors, seeing her reflection.

"That's good. No germs," I tell her simply. I called in a cleaning crew while we were at the hospital. They were tasked with removing every speck of dust they could find.

"That rug in your living room... it looks expensive..." She swallows, looking at the living room like there's a barricade between her and that open space and she can't walk in.

"It's soft. Soft enough for Tommy to lie on when he needs tummy time." I'm pretty sure Victoria sourced that Persian Rug exclusively for this space.

"Lie on?!" Her eyebrows find her hairline. "Oh my God." She slaps her face, and if I wasn't so confused, I'd grin. She's so damn cute. "Griffin, we're going to ruin your beautiful house. Babies puke, spill things, throw food. Not to mention, diaper explosions... and then, there's me... Have you seen me bake? I literally spill flour everywhere... *all the time!*"

I shake my head, not concerned with my material things being ruined. "Let me show you his room." Taking her hand, I lead her up the stairs, going slow, ensuring she's not in pain and moves slowly. "In here," I tell her, opening the door and stepping inside. I hear her gasp behind me, and I turn to look at her. Her eyes are glassy and open wide as she looks around.

"This room is bigger than the whole apartment at the bakery..."

Decorated in whites and soft blues, the windows are large and let in a lot of daylight. I didn't know what she would like, so I have a few basic furniture items. I'll get her more, though. Whatever she wants.

She moves straight to the crib and looks over it.

"This is beautiful..." she murmurs, her hands running over the curve of the timber.

I swallow roughly. "I made it."

Her head whips around so quickly she almost stumbles. "You made this?" Seeing her in awe like this makes my chest expand. Fuck, now I want to make her more things.

"I did." I nod. "I started a few weeks ago. Before I left..." I don't need to explain myself; she remembers me leaving for a week or so. Running. Like I always do. Like I always *used* to.

"It's amazing..." Her voice drifts off as she takes another look around the room. I have a changing table set up, fully stocked. There's a walk-in closet, full of baby clothes, blankets, and other items. Off to the side is an en suite. I got baby shampoo and soaps and those little bamboo washcloths. Inside the enormous tub, I have a baby bath ready to go.

"If there's anything missing, anything you need..."

"It's all here. I mean, there's literally everything here..." She huffs a laugh, and Tommy fusses a little. I hold him close, not believing that I have this little human in my arms. I haven't held a baby before, not really. The kids of my friends climb all over me, but a newborn. A baby only days old. This is new. Completely frightening, yet it feels so natural.

"I need to feed him." Hearing his little whine, she walks over to us.

"Take a seat. Put your feet up," I tell her and she sits down in the new rocker I got her, and I pass her Tommy.

"Oh gosh, this seat feels like a cloud..." she moans as she gets comfortable.

"I'll go get your bags and things. I'll be back." I start to walk out, feeling good. Feeling like I've finally got my shit together and I'm doing something right.

"Griffin," she says, and I pause at the door and look back.

"I can't..." She stops and swallows. "I don't think..." Pausing again, she takes a deep breath as Tommy settles on her breast. "I'm never going to be able to repay you. I'll never be able to replace something if it gets broken. I'm going to have to go on a payment plan to pay the hospital fees..." She rubs her weary eyes.

"You don't need a payment plan. I paid," I tell her, and she looks up before she frowns, thinking about it.

"Is that what you did when I saw you at the nurses' station?" She pieces our morning together.

"I paid it all." I nod, not wanting her to worry. I've got the money. I've got more than enough money for me to live a hundred times over.

"You didn't need to do that. I had it handled..." I can see her shoulders tighten, clearly not happy about it.

"Yeah, well, when you get back to work, you can make me some of those cinnamon buns I love so much."

"That's not... I can't..."

"Savannah," I say abruptly as I slowly walk back to her. Her eyes widen as I get closer and lower down to her level, making us face-to-face.

"I haven't always believed in God after everything I've been through. I prayed often, hoped that something bigger than me could put me on a path that was paved with gold instead of the one I was dealt. For the most part, prayer worked. I have money. I have a skill. I enjoy my work, and I have good friends. But finding a good woman who understands me, having a family, a safe haven with someone else, was never something in the cards for me. But I know God brought you right to me. He's been listening. Knowing what

I need. You're the most amazing woman I've ever met. Let me take care of you. I want you with me. I want Tommy too. I want you here, to live here together. Be... together." I inhale a deep breath and watch it all finally sink in exactly what I mean.

"I think God brought me to you too. I've never been more grateful to Him than I am right now." Her eyes are glassy as she watches me. It's a lot. She's tired, her body sore. Kissing her forehead, I brush my thumb across her cheek before I stand, taking in another full breath to calm my surfacing emotions and settling into myself again.

"I'll go get the bags," I start to step out before I say anything more.

"Do you have sweet pickles in your kitchen?" She rolls her lips like she's trying to tame a smile while my lips curve.

"You still got a craving?" I don't tell her that I had a carton of them delivered here while we were at the hospital. I wasn't sure if her cravings would continue or not. That wasn't something the app or any internet sleuthing could tell me for sure.

She nods, and I huff a laugh. "That and ice cream."

"Good thing I have both. I'll get the bags, and then the two of you can rest. I'll bring you up a little snack on my way back."

"Griffin..."

"Yeah, sweetness?" I look at her adorningly, stepping closer to her again.

"I'm so glad you walked into my bakery all those months ago." Her voice is a mere whisper.

"Walking into that bakery was the best damn decision of my life."

30

SAVANNAH

I feel like a stalker. Standing here, barely awake, yet totally captivated by the sight in front of me. Leaning against the doorframe, I feel content for the first time in a long time.

"This here are the plans. See that?" Griffin points to something on his laptop screen.

"That's where the pool will go, right up against that giant rock. It's called a boulder." He continues, talking to my son like he's a grown boy, not the mere baby that's cuddled on his naked chest.

"Now, boulders in that area are common. So we're going to incorporate it into the build and utilize it as a waterfall feature. Pretty cool, huh?" Griffin smiles as he kisses the top of Tommy's head, my son clearly fed by the look of the empty bottle on the countertop nearby.

Seeing Griffin like this does something to my chest. Warmth spreads through me at how much love my son has and how much this man does for me. We've fallen into a routine of sorts. Griffin lets me sleep a little longer in the mornings, and he gets up, grabs Tommy, and feeds him a bottle. The morning routine we now have is one that works for all of us.

Griffin's a natural. His large hand holds Tommy securely to him. Tommy is content, warm, and safe. Seeing the two of them together makes me think of how far we've all come. Griffin's parenting skills are getting better with every passing day. Mine too.

"Good morning..." I walk into the room, pretending I didn't watch their entire conversation.

"Mornin', sweetness."

I step over to him, kissing my son before I kiss Griffin. His free hand wraps around my middle, the t-shirt I'm wearing lifting a little as his palm settles on my ass and he pulls me close.

"You teaching Tommy how to build?" I grin, and Griffin's eyes sparkle.

"You creeping up on us again?"

I blush a little a being caught. "I wasn't creeping..." I tease as his hand squeezes my butt cheek.

"Don't think I don't see you standing over there at the doorway, watching us each morning."

"You knew I was there?" I pull back, shocked. "I thought I was so quiet." I roll my lips as I step away from them, wanting to start breakfast.

"I always know where you are." He looks at me over the top of the coffee mug as he takes a sip.

"Eggs today?" I grab a pan and the eggs, ready to start a scramble.

"You know you don't need to make me breakfast."

"I know, but I like to." I like to be kept busy, otherwise my mind wanders too much. I haven't heard from my family, which unsettles me. They would all know about Tommy by now, that I'm one hundred percent sure of. But since I haven't seen or heard from them, I feel like something is brewing.

"I left you the crossword today."

I look over at him and smile as he pushes the newspaper my way. We've been taking turns to do the daily crossword, and on the weekends, we do it together.

"A man after my own heart."

"Mmmmm, you in that t-shirt is killing mine," he mumbles, and I look down at myself.

"My hair is a mess, I barely slept, and I'm pretty sure my breasts leaked milk on this t-shirt of yours at some point last night," I scoff playfully as I plate our eggs.

"Your breasts are..." He raises his eyebrows and looks right at my chest.

"Out of control. I had no idea this was going to happen when my milk came in, but here we are. About three sizes bigger than normal." I throw up my hands in mock exasperation.

"Three sizes bigger, huh?" He smirks. "Tragedy." Then he taps the counter beside him. "Come eat, sweetness. Before you run off to feed the whole town."

"Melissa is opening again today, so that helps." She's been a godsend, helping with not only the bakery, but with Tommy as well, nearly every day. I was surprised she doesn't have children with how wonderful she is with him.

I take a seat on the stool next to Griffin and look at the wall clock, knowing the bakery will already be open and some of the pastries I made late last night will sell this morning before I get there and make fresh products.

"Go easy. Tommy is only a few weeks old, and you're still healing too." Griffin watches me carefully, concern pinching his brow.

"I know. I feel good, though, and I want to take advantage of that. Besides the lack of sleep and the outrageous breasts." I grab my chest, knowing I need to express soon. They're feeling fuller and heavier than ever this morning.

"Again... such a tragedy..." Griffin clicks his tongue in jest, and I laugh.

"Stop it." I throw a piece of toast at him. "Here, let's look at this." Grabbing the newspaper, I scan the crossword.

"Four-letter word for cereal's usual companion..."

"Milk," Griffin says quickly, beating me to the answer. I write the word down and move to the next one as he takes another sip of his coffee.

"Parts of a chest that aren't drawers..." I murmur, frowning. Thinking of the chest of drawers in the room upstairs, wondering what it could be.

"Breasts," Griffin says immediately, and I sit up.

"Oh, you can't be serious..." I look back at the crossword, and sure enough, it fits.

"Is the universe trying to tell me something today?" I write down his answer, grinning, a giggle fluttering past my lips.

"That you're perfect... and you have fantastic breasts."

I pause and look at Griffin, who watches me intently, my son peacefully resting on his chest.

"You're full of compliments this morning," I tease, shaking my head as I bite my lip.

He nods, leaning back a little and sighing contentedly. "I like it."

"Like it?"

"Like you in my home. Like you in my bed. Like you in my life. I like it all... a lot."

"I like it a lot too..." I tell him honestly, wanting to say so much more but hesitating.

"Probably should've taken you out on a few dates before

I brought you home and made you mine..." He looks a little remorseful.

"I don't need fancy dinners or flowers. I think what we have together is perfect."

Swallowing roughly, he looks down at Tommy before bringing his gaze back to mine. "I don't want it to change. You. Me. Tommy. Together."

"Well, by the look of Tommy, he isn't going anywhere..."

He smiles, his big hand gently rubbing Tommy's back as he sleeps.

"Is Tommy preventing you from starting your day today?" I ask, wondering what he's up to.

"I'll take you both to the bakery this morning, then work from my home office for the rest of the day. I have a few things to iron out on the Colorado project."

"The boulder?" I ask, and he chuckles.

"See, you were creeping..." His grin widens, and I love the look of it.

"Fine. I was creeping. Happy now?" I slip off the stool where I was sitting to start packing up from breakfast.

"The happiest I've been in a long time, sweetness. Maybe even ever," he says, pulling me close, the three of us cuddling before Tommy starts to squirm.

Griffin presses a kiss to Tommy's head, and something in my chest aches with how badly I want this life to stay untouched.

❁

I SIT IN THE DARKNESS, the little nightlight my only light, feeding Tommy. I'm tired. I had a big day at the bakery, and my nights of broken sleep are wearing me a little thin. It's almost hard to keep my eyes open in this soft cozy rocker Griffin got me.

"Hey, sweetness…" Griffin says softly as he walks in. He does most nights. It doesn't matter if it's two a.m. or four a.m., he's always here. He steps up to me, kissing me quickly, and places a glass of water on my side table before he sits on the footstool and grabs my feet.

"You don't have to get up for every feed, you know." I grin, secretly loving these quiet nights we have together. We've grown closer because of it. Shared more together than I think either of us have ever before.

Griffin hasn't left our side. He works from home but had one day last week when he flew from Whispers to Colorado and back in less than twelve hours. Spending more time in the air than he did on the ground, but he was adamant he was checking on his crew and signing off on a few things, then would be back in time to pick us up from the bakery. Which he was.

My feelings for him have expanded. Our story isn't one that's followed a traditional path. In fact, we're so far off from tradition it's almost comical. Young pregnant woman, grumpy older builder. Friends before we became friends with benefits to help the baby along, and then a birthing partner. To now acting like new parents and living together.

"Hmmm, you do, so I will too." He's so matter-of-fact; I know there's no way to stop him.

"Did you sleep much?" Griffin's night terrors don't seem to happen that often anymore. Perhaps because we're being woken almost every three hours, or maybe it's not being in his bed alone anymore, or maybe because he sleeps with my gran's Bible under his pillow. Either way, something has helped him.

"A little." He rubs my feet, the feeling of his large, warm

hands relaxing me more than I ever thought it could. I'm so not used to treatment like this. He spoils me daily with his affection, and I'll never tire of it.

"That feels so good..." I moan, feeling the release of any stress and anxiety.

"I love your little moans, sweetness." The hungry way he says it has my eyes opening to look at him. We haven't had sex since the night we brought on labor. But right now, there's heat in his gaze that I feel wash over me like I haven't felt since then. My body isn't recovered yet, though. There's nothing we can do without the approval from the doctor. But we both want to. I feel it in the way he caresses me in bed at night before we fall asleep. How he kisses me first thing in the morning. I feel it in the way his hands linger on me when he drops Tommy and me off at the bakery, like he doesn't want to leave. How he looks at me like I'm the most beautiful woman he's ever seen, even when I'm a complete mess most of the time lately.

"You do?" I offer a soft smile as my body continues to melt at his touch.

"Oh, yes, baby, I do..." His voice is a rumble, one that vibrates around the room. Griffin's hands slow their movements on my feet, his thumbs pressing just enough to make me sigh again.

"You keep making those sounds," he murmurs, quirking his eyebrow at me "and I'm gonna forget we're on doctor's orders."

I glance down at Tommy, still latched to my breast, blissfully unaware. "You wouldn't dare."

His eyes flick to mine, dark and amused by my teasing. "Sweetness, I've been daring since the day I met you."

I shift slightly in the rocker, tired yet unbelievably

turned on, the movement subtle, but his gaze tracks it like it's seismic. He knows me all too well.

"You need sleep," I mock, in disbelief that he's wanting me now with the way I look.

He leans in, voice low. "I need you."

My breath catches. The air between us thickens. His hand slides up my calf, slow and deliberate, massaging my muscles and stopping just below my knee.

"A few more weeks..." I tell him, trying to tamp down the way my core aches for him. Knowing that I have a follow-up visit with Hudson at the six-week mark. Hopefully, we'll get the all-clear.

"I would wait a lifetime..." he whispers, as Tommy cries a little, and our moment is broken.

For now.

31

GRIFFIN

It's a Friday night, and I opened my front door to the gaggle of geese and all their gifts. Once Savannah and Tommy were settled, I grabbed my keys and left the ladies to do whatever it is that they do. Giggling and cooing at the baby seemed to be what was on their agenda, but the way Savannah was smiling, I didn't mind one bit.

Now as I sit with Tanner at the Whiteman's Bar, I'm enjoying a whiskey and feeling better than I have in a long time.

"You've been quiet," Tanner comments as we relax in the booth, music playing around us, people milling about. Everything feels clearer to me now. Sound has less static. My eyes seem more focused and notice the little things. Which is ironic, because I'm fucking tired. But with how things are going, no matter how tired I am, I couldn't be happier.

"Got a lot going on." I shrug as I take a sip.

"How's she going?" he asks, looking at me like he knows I'm holding out on him. I give in, my words falling from my mouth in a rush.

"She's amazing. What she went through... she's a powerhouse. I can't live up to her."

Tanner's eyebrows rise a little. A knowing smile spreads across his face. "Sometimes all it takes is a good woman to put us on our ass." He huffs a laugh before he takes a sip of his liquor.

"How did you know?" I frown, looking at him, feeling vulnerable. I don't talk about my feelings; I don't talk about myself much. Must be the lack of sleep that's making me share more than usual.

"Know what?"

"That Victoria was the one?" I ask him, and he takes a deep breath, leaning back in the booth.

"Truth be told, I think I knew the moment I saw her. Up on the porch at Marie's Place, shoulders back, hair blowing in the breeze..."

My chest constricts as Tanner gets lost in his memories. I remember the moment I walked into that bakery, annoyed that I had to help fix the place when I had a million other things to do. I was even more annoyed that I could just walk in, the door unlocked, and I remember striding to the kitchen, ready to yell at whomever was in charge about their lack of security and preparedness with opening a new business. But the moment I saw her, I stopped, watching her in the kitchen from the doorway, completely mesmerized. Then she burned her hand on the hot tray, and my legs moved, and I was on her in an instant.

"She thinks she's a burden. That a man like me couldn't possibly want a woman like her," I tell him, and while she hasn't fully said the words, I know that's what she thinks. If only she could understand that I don't feel worthy of her.

"So you haven't told her you love her, then?" Tanner

pushes, and my jaw clenches. I won't bother denying that's exactly how I feel.

"Doesn't seem to be the right time…" I grip the glass and lift it to my mouth, the burn of his whiskey needed. Love. It's a funny feeling. It squeezes everything out of you before it fills you up so quickly it's like you never knew you needed it until you got it. I've spent my life running from that feeling. Spent my life hiding, not wanting to experience the pain that comes with it. Losing my mom and my brother almost killed me, and I swore that night to never feel that kind of pain again. With Savannah, and now little Tommy, I'm running too close to that flame once more.

But this baker of mine. Hell, she was unexpected. But she just had a baby. She needs to heal. Needs to give all her energy to that little boy. Not me. But I'll be right there with them. Ensuring they have everything they need. I'm too scared to say the words out loud. Too scared that once I put that out in the universe, they'll get taken away, just like before.

"There's never a right time," Tanner says, and I nod, knowing he's probably right. My cell chimes, and I pull it out, thinking it might be Savannah, but it's not. It's a message from an unknown number, and as I open it, reality hits me in the face.

> I'd like to see you

My vision clouds, the noise around me dulls, and I feel my chest tightening so viciously it's hard to take a breath.

"It's not the right time." I look back at Tanner, who watches me carefully as I pocket my phone and grab my drink, throwing the rest of it back.

I'm no good for her. She deserves better. I need to be

better.

~

SWALLOWING ROUGHLY, I walk into Sawyer's office on Main Street. I have no idea what I'm doing, but he always seems to have answers, so here I fucking am.

"Griff? Hey, good to see you. How's little Tommy?" He greets me with a smile and a backslap, asking about the kid like he's mine.

"He's doing good," is all I can muster.

After I left the bar last night, I drove around almost all night, not wanting to go home, my thoughts muddled. I walked into the house once it was dark and quiet and slept in the spare room, although sleeping is an understatement. I lay on the bed, staring at the ceiling until the sun came up. I didn't even help Savannah feed Tommy like I usually do. I couldn't move. I was paralyzed.

The old me would have my bags packed and jet fueled and been out of Whispers faster than you can say "Whiteman's Whiskey." But the new me, the one who's undeniably in love, with a young baby boy whom I want to make my own, with a house that's starting to feel like a home, and a life that's starting to build... I knew I couldn't run. Not anymore.

But I did need space. I needed to drown in my thoughts, process them. Think of a plan of what I need to do to fix my mental state, to help me move on, to make me the man I need to be. I can't be the man she deserves without dealing with all this shit, and I can't look her in the eye until I get it all sorted. All that thinking has led me here.

I have thoughts on how I want my life to be now. I look at the future, and all I see is her in it. I want to make us permanent. I want a ring on her finger and a shared life together. But that can't happen until I clean out my skeletons, sort out the legal ramifications of the baby, and get rid of my history that has a way of hanging around.

"Good. What's going on?" He frowns at me, obviously sensing something.

"I've got a few things I'd like advice on."

"Sure, let's go down to my office." He leads the way down the hall, and I step inside, taking a seat, my knee bouncing, my anxiety swirling. I handle my business. Sure, I've had Sawyer help with other legal things, business management, new build contracts and the sort. But I've never asked or wanted help with my private life. I've kept that firmly locked. But there's more than me to think about now. I need to try and move past my demons, share the load, and ask for help. It's one of the hardest things I've ever done.

But I will do it. For her.

"Everything alright?" he asks.

I swallow as he closes his door and walks around to his desk. My chest is pounding and my hands are sweating.

"Not really," I tell him honestly.

"Okay. Start at the beginning." Sawyer nods, like he's ready to solve an unsolvable problem.

"How much time have you got?" I huff a laugh, but I don't feel humorous. I feel sick. Weak. Like I can't handle my own shit.

"I've got all day, Griff. A problem shared is a problem halved. None of us are superheroes; we've all got shit, believe me. I handle everybody's." He sits back and waits, and if I didn't know any better, I would say this is a counseling session, not a legal meeting.

So I do as he says. I take a deep breath, and I start at the beginning.

32

SAVANNAH

My business is booming. My baby is growing. Life should be good. But something is up with Griffin, and I don't know what.

I had a great night with the girls a few nights back, and he left smiling, but when he came home, he slept in the spare room. He missed the night feed, and he feels distant. It's been days now, and even though he still wakes in the morning and brings us to the bakery, then picks us up in the afternoon, he hasn't truly come back to me. He's so quiet and seems to be mentally preoccupied. It could be work, but I don't think so.

Now, as I try to be quiet in the dark, early hours, which is idiotic, because Tommy is screaming the house down, I get out of bed and grab my son, hoping to soothe him.

"Shhhhh, it's alright, honey..." I pick him up, wondering why he's so fussy tonight. As I pull him to my chest, his cries intensify, so I rub his back and start to bounce a little. "I got you... Everything's okay," I murmur, but my voice is drowned from his cries. I swallow hard, knowing that he's sure to wake up Griffin. "Ohhh, baby... what's wrong?" I pat his back a little.

"Everything alright?" Griffin's gruff voice has me gasping.

Looking at the door, I see him standing there, his eyes dark like he hasn't slept for days, dressed in nothing but his tight boxers, his hair looking like he's run his hand through it all night. He slept in the spare room again.

"Sorry, I didn't want to wake you," I rush out as Tommy's screams intensify.

He shakes his head. "Want me to try?" Stepping into the nursery, he looks too tall for the space as he walks toward us.

"It's okay, you don't have to..." I tell him, yet I'm excited to see him. To talk with him.

"Let me try, sweetness." The use of my nickname has relief pouring from my body as he puts his arms out, and I pass Tommy to him. He sounds better, like the man I know. Tommy's still crying, but Griffin puts him onto his bare chest and rubs his back softly, kissing the top of my son's head before his eyes meet mine. "Come here." He reaches out for me, stepping forward, his hand circling my waist. I fall into his side, and he kisses my forehead as I hug him.

"Sorry I've been a bit MIA," he mumbles as Tommy continues to wail.

"It's okay..." I start to say, melting into his hold.

"It's not."

"We're a lot, I get it," I tell him, knowing that Tommy and I are a lot for a man like Griffin. Someone who's never had anyone in their space and occupying so much of his time.

He presses another kiss to my head. "It's not you. It's not Tommy—"

Before I can finish, Tommy vomits, his reflux clearly what was bothering him, the milky sickness going all over Griffin's bare chest and Tommy's clothes.

"Oh nooo." I wince at the sight of the mess.

"It's alright." Griffin is the calm to my panic as I grab Tommy and start to undress him, his wails continuing.

"His reflux. He must have an upset tummy." I quickly take off his soiled sleepwear.

"He needs a wash. Bring him in here." Griffin heads into the bathroom, turning on the shower. I pick up Tommy as Griffin dims the bathroom light and steps into the spray of warm water.

"I did some research. He might like the comfort of the water," he tells me, and my eyebrows rise.

"Another app?" I ask as I pass my screaming child to the sweet man in the shower.

"Yeah. Another app." He's sheepish, a small grin pulling at the side of his lips, and I smile, standing and watching them. Tommy snuggles into Griffin's chest as the warm water streams down on them both and Tommy's cries soften.

"It's working!" I'm overjoyed that my son is no longer screaming the house down at two in the morning and things are quiet again.

"He likes the water. We should take him to the mineral springs when he's older."

I tilt my head. "Mineral springs?" I have no idea what he's talking about.

"Natural mineral springs. It's on Tanner's land. It's warm, so we might need to gauge the temperature, but I'm guessing he would like it."

"I'm guessing you're right." I nod, looking at my son now content on Griffin's chest, the warm embrace something I envy and have missed.

"We'll have to teach him to swim in the pool," Griffin adds, and I swallow, because Griffin's pool is massive, and as a new mother, I'm already worried about water safety for Tommy.

"Swimming lessons will be a must."

Tommy's face settles, his eyes closing as Griffin sways with him under the water stream. Griffin is completely wet. Water drips down his body like he's in a swimwear commercial. I swallow as I look him over. The salt-and-pepper hair on his chest is sticking to his body, Tommy grabbing a fist full of it. His broad shoulders, his muscles all glistening. Griffin's boxers are still on, but now they're see-through, and I feel my cheeks heat.

It's been weeks. My visit with Hudson is next week. I feel ready and seeing him soothing my son makes me want him even more.

"He's missed you." When I look back at Griffin's eyes, I see he's already watching me.

There's emotion in his gaze before he says deeply, "I missed you both."

"What happened?" I ask, knowing something did.

"Old scars have a way of resurfacing. Just needed to deal with it. Didn't want to put any of that on you."

I nod, understanding but also wishing he felt comfortable coming to me. "You can talk to me, you know. I can be there for you."

I see him swallow. "I don't want you to get remotely close to what I'm dealing with. I don't want to tarnish you with my demons."

"I used to watch *Buffy the Vampire Slayer*; I kinda have a few tricks up my sleeve." I try to keep it light, hoping to ease the tension.

"I don't doubt it, sweetness. But I would never forgive myself if anything happened to you or Tommy because of me."

I frown. I thought he meant his nightmares and dark thoughts, but it sounds like it's something more.

"I might buy some extra garlic and hang it in the kitchen... you know... just in case," I add, my mind now a whirl, but I don't prod. We're safe here with him. Griffin would never let anyone hurt us. Not my family, not the pastor. No one.

He nods, his smile small but there, and I watch my son finally fall asleep as Griffin holds him. Knowing that this is everything I never thought I could have and praying it will last.

33

SAVANNAH

I'm nervous.

I've had a shower, shaved everything, washed my hair, and now blow-dried it, and while the body I see in the mirror is not one I'm overly familiar with, it's the one that I've got and the one that bought me Tommy, so I'm grateful.

Now as I pace the bedroom with my robe on, I feel flutters in my stomach like I haven't in a long time.

"Well, he's down. Out like a light and no fussing." Griffin walks into the bedroom absentmindedly, and I pull in a breath. "He's so cute when he—" He stops short when he sees me, his feet glued to the floor, halfway turned from the door, looking to where I'm standing.

I can't help smiling at his reaction. "Hi..."

I watch his gaze widen in surprise, then heat as he looks at me from my head to my toes and back. He swallows before his eyes meet mine again.

"What are you doing, sweetness?" He tilts his head a little, his face softening as he tentatively takes another step toward me.

"Well... I had my doctor's appointment today. I'm officially healed..." I tell him, my heart beating faster. It's not unusual for Griffin to see me in my robe, but this is different. This robe is satin and lace and barely covers my body. One Victoria helped me pick out. My hair is usually up in a messy bun, but it's now in soft waves around my shoulders. I grab the collar, widening it a little, showcasing a little peek-a-boo of what's underneath. Which is absolutely nothing.

"Are you telling me I can touch you..." Hungry eyes search mine as he takes another step. "That I can taste you? Feel you...?" He continues, all the while taking frustratingly small and slow steps to me.

I nod as my core clenches. "Yes." It's barely a whisper. "We have to go slow... careful... but yes..." I'm already panting. It should be embarrassing. But it's not. It never is with him. He makes me feel so safe, secure, and assured.

"I'm guessing we have about three hours?" I tell him, because Tommy will wake for a feed at some point. Griffin steps right up to me, our toes almost touching. I lean my head back, looking up at him as his hand runs down the soft satin lapel of my robe until it hits the flimsy belt half tied at my waist.

"Hmmm, and I'm planning to use every single second of them making you mine," his lips hit mine, and I almost stumble. But I don't, because his warm hand is at my back, pulling me to him as his other opens my robe.

The cool air hits my skin, my nipples pebbling as my body alights. I didn't want to get flashy underwear or fancy panties. With time not on our side, I didn't want to waste a moment. His lips are warm, and as his tongue swipes against my own, I lean into him instantly. His hands wrap around me, making me feel like they go around twice as he lifts me from the floor, my feet dangling before he places me on the bed.

"Look at you..." He stands at the side of the bed, looking down on where I lie on my back. My robe is completely open, my entire body on display.

"You're the most beautiful woman in the world..." He admires me, and I take a small breath and swallow.

"I mean, my breasts are—"

"I fucking love your breasts," he cuts me off immediately as he leans over, his fingers featherlight, touching my shoulders, before he slowly trails them down to my breast. He circles my nipple, his touch so soft it's almost excruciating. I'm a little touched out, my breasts tender due to breastfeeding, but with his careful caress, I feel taken care of instead of giving any more of myself away.

"I'm not exactly—" I touch my belly, fingers grazing the softness that wasn't there before, but I don't get to finish the sentence before Griffin's hand covers mine.

"You're *exactly* mine."

I blink, heart stuttering at his rumbling claim.

Eyes on mine, he kneels on the mattress and leans in, his lips brushing my temple. "This body made Tommy. It held him, fed him, kept him safe. You think I'm gonna look at it and want less?"

I let out a shaky breath, eyes stinging.

"I want more," he murmurs. "More of you. More of this. Every curve, every mark. You're beautiful," he says as his hand on my belly lowers, and he lies beside me. "Precious. I want to cherish every inch of you." His fingers drag down my naked body, from my stomach to my hips, moving across my hip bone. My breath quickens, my chest moving up and down as anticipation builds. "Would you like that, baby?"

I nod eagerly, as his fingers hit my core, and I gasp at the contact.

He watches me carefully, going slow, being gentle as my eyes close and my body softens at his touch.

"Spread your legs, sweetness. Let me feel your perfect pussy..." he growls in my ear, kissing my neck, and I heat all over. But I do as he asks, relaxing my hips, moving my legs wider as Griffin's hand settles between them. I'm not going to lie; I'm a little anxious. Giving birth was a big deal. I don't even know what sex is going to feel like now. Is it going to be painful? Is it going to feel normal? I mean, whatever normal is. Griffin and I have only been together once. I have so much more to explore with him.

"Good girl." His words ghost over the sensitive skin of my neck as he continues kissing and sucking, his fingers rubbing my clit lazily yet purposefully.

"Mmmm." I bite my bottom lip as I move my hips, wanting more, my eyes closed, confidence building.

He moves his hand then, his thumb replacing his finger as he glides lower and pushes inside.

"Yesss..." I whimper, the sensation pure pleasure. I feel him grin where he kisses my neck, and my back arches a little, wanting more. Needing more. He moves his finger in and out, slowly at first, starting languidly before moving a little faster. "Griff," I pant, my voice a little pitched, my mind almost mush as I start to tremble.

"Your beautiful body is so fucking responsive... so perfect..." he growls again as his hand quickens, and I grind against him.

"Yes... more... more..." I beg, my hand moving and gripping onto his wrist, keeping him right there as my hips start to buck against him.

Leaning up, he watches me, eyes full of desire. "Take what you need. Use me how you want. I'm all yours, sweetness..."

I can barely understand his words. I'm out of breath, my chest heaving, needing this, needing him, needing a release and this man's touch like I need air.

I moan his name, my body starting to shudder. "Griffin... Griffin..." I pant repeatedly, eyes closing as my orgasm crests.

"Open your eyes, sweetness. Look at me when I fuck you... Look at me when you come with my name on your sweet lips..."

My eyes flick open, and I stare right at him as I come so powerfully, the world dissolves around us. My back arches, my toes curl, and I push my head back into the pillow and call for him.

"Griffin!" I should be quiet; I might wake Tommy. But I can't help it. I can't stop.

I come hard. Fully. Completely. Then my body liquifies and I sink into the bed a panting mess.

I had no idea I was holding on to so much tension.

"Fucking beautiful." Griffin kisses my chest, shoulders, and neck. I grip the back of his head and pull his lips to mine.

We kiss with slow passion, sharing moans, gripping on to each other, not an inch left between us. We haven't kissed like this in weeks. Even then, it didn't feel like this. His lips brand mine with so much force there's no question what I mean to him. I give him back everything he gives and more.

It feels like love. Yet I'm too frightened to say it. Not wanting to tell him and then have him run. So I show him with this kiss.

I give him everything I have and hope he understands the unspoken truth.

I'm totally and utterly in love with my builder.

34

GRIFFIN

I kiss her like I've never kissed anyone else in my life. My lips are glued to hers, my hands pulling her close, and if I could make us one, I would. There's no doubt she's my other half. The other half of my heart, but also my soul. I'm not only connected to her, but I'm one hundred percent tethered. Tethered to something for the first time in my life.

She sticks with me. Her hands delving into my hair, pulling my head to hers, like she's scared to let me go too. So together we lie here, kissing like we need each other more than the air we breathe. We kiss like it's our last moments on earth. I'm hungry. Hungry for her, although I know even if we have the green light from the doctor, we still need to go easy, be gentle. I've been researching. I've learned all the ins and outs of the situation post birth. How she'll feel physically, but also emotionally. So I move my lips to her jaw, then her neck, wanting to cover her entire body with my kisses. I want to let her know she's wanted, she's beautiful, and I meant what I told her earlier—she is mine.

"Griffin..." She moans my name in a way that makes me

feel seen. No other woman I've been with sounds like this. Like she's calling just for me and what only I can do for her.

"Yeah, sweetness," I murmur against her chest. Her breasts are phenomenal, but Tommy has the rights to them at the moment, so I move over them quickly, happy to wait until they're all mine again.

"This feels..." She doesn't finish, but I hear her heart pounding. Matching my own. She feels it. I know she does.

"I know," I tell her, wanting to comfort her as she threads her fingers through my hair. The tug against my scalp feels heavenly as I kiss across her torso. I cover every inch, my tongue tracing patterns, my lips stamping their ownership. I move down her hip, across her hip bone, down to her core. I kiss across her upper thigh, right down her knees, to her toes before I move to the other leg and kiss back up.

"Are you kissing all of me?" She grins, a giggle popping from her lips, delight in her eyes.

"Every fucking inch..." I murmur, my lips not leaving her for a second before I come back up to her face.

She cups my face, looking at me, something in her gaze that speaks for her matching hunger. "I think it's my turn," she says as she sits up, and I sit up with her.

"No, tonight is about you," I tell her, adamant that I want her looked after, nourished. Giving so much of herself to Tommy, to the bakery, she needs someone to give her the world. That's a role I firmly put my hand up for. In the bedroom and outside of it.

"Tonight is about us," she replies firmly. "Besides, what I want is to kiss you."

I wait for a beat, but then she moves off the bed and I swing my feet over the side, ready to stand. Wondering what she's doing.

"Where are you going?" I frown.

"Nowhere." She slowly lowers to her knees in front of me. My hands grip the blankets on either side of where I sit on the edge of the mattress.

"Sweetness... You don't—"

"Don't go telling me what I can and can't do," she bites back, sassy as can be, as her hands grab the sides of my boxers and she pulls them down. I do little to stop her. How could I? This beautiful woman of my dreams, naked and on her knees in front of me, wants to touch me. I shimmy them off and sit back on the edge of the mattress, completely naked, awaiting her next move.

"I wouldn't dream of it," I say as her hands fall onto my knees before she runs them up my inner thighs. I lean back on my hands, watching her, holding my breath, my cock rock hard, throbbing for her touch.

I don't have to wait long. Her small, soft hands curve up my thighs, and with a double grip, she palms me.

"Fuck," I grit out at the contact, not able to help it. My dreams are coming alive.

I'm a big man, I know I am. Women have commented all my life, some even decide they don't want me because of it. But Savannah leans in, moving her hands up and down, getting a feel of me, while my grip on the sheets underneath me turns white-knuckled, not wanting to come too soon. Which is a constant threat around this woman.

It feels good. Being open with her like this, having her on her knees for me. I can't believe how lucky I am.

"This okay?" she asks sweetly, looking up at me.

"It's more than okay ... It's fucking phenomenal." My breathing quickens as my gaze roams her naked body, her curves, her tits that I love so much.

"How about this?" she leans in and takes the tip of me

into her mouth. I'm speechless for a beat. The air completely leaves my lungs.

"Fuck," I choke out, my fingers digging into the blankets more, squeezing the fabric. My head drops back, and I look at the ceiling as I feel her warm, wet lips on my cock. Sucking, licking, keeping me at her mercy.

She moans as she takes me in again, and when I look back down at her, I swear I see stars. She's teasingly slow, almost playing with me, smiling around my length and getting a feel for how we are together like this.

"Baby, please," I beg, my chest now heaving as I try to hold on. I never fucking beg. Never begged for a thing in my entire life. But I'm begging for her. I need her, want her, my legs are almost trembling with how much.

"So good," she murmurs against the tip, swirling her tongue around it before taking me in again. A little deeper this time. I look so fucking good in her mouth, her pretty pink lips stretching to fit me. The visual is spectacular.

My teeth are gritted tight, body tense, trying to hold on when she sucks me in even deeper, then starts bobbing slowly up and down, up and down. "Fuck!" I almost buck off the bed as she picks up speed, her tongue massaging me as she goes. I want to fuck her face. I want to grip her head and thrust into her mouth over and over. But I sit as still as I can, letting her manhandle me. Letting her tease and lick and suck, and I've never felt such intense pleasure and pain at the same time.

With my cock settled against her throat, she moans again, the vibration making my eyes roll into the back of my head.

"Yes... Fuck yes... Don't stop, baby." I'm nearly whimpering, not even recognizing the sounds leaving me, before she pops off and smiles coyly at me. Then I feel it, one of her soft hands lowering to cup my balls, squeezing and tugging lightly, like she knows exactly how to make me lose my mind. She has a gleam in her eyes, thoroughly enjoying herself.

"Get your mouth back on it, sweetness... Suck me, fuck me with that pretty mouth of yours... I need it, baby," I tell her, my panting increasing, my limit almost reached.

"You want more?" Biting her bottom lip, her other hand palms my length, gripping me firmly and stroking slowly, keeping me right on the edge, but never letting me fall over. Her hair flows in waves in front of her shoulders, her large breasts playing my favorite game of peek-a-boo from beneath the strands. I'm so wired and needy for her it's almost embarrassing.

"Please, baby... I'm aching for you."

She leans forward, her eyes glued to mine, and licks my tip.

"Please... please... please... I can't. Give me that perfect mouth, sweetness... please..." I'm making no sense. I swear, one more little lick like that, and I'll come. I need her mouth on me one more time.

She takes me in again, this time deeper.

"Fuuuuccckkkkk..." I groan, wanting to buck, but as she pulls off, she comes back immediately. Bobbing on me once again, like she knows I need it.

"Yesss... like that... Fuck, sweetness... yes." I start to chant before I can't take it anymore. "I'm going to come, baby. You ready for me?"

"Mmmm..." Her hands grip on to my thighs, her nails digging in a little as she takes me in until she gags, which becomes my undoing.

I come so hard I see stars. Releasing with a roar down her throat, and she doesn't move, she doesn't pull off, she swallows all of me, and if I wasn't already sitting, she'd have me on my ass.

My fingers thread through her hair, gripping it tight, keeping her close, and I feel her hands relax, massaging my thighs as my orgasm ends and she sits back on her heels as I take a deep breath, feeling dizzy.

"Sweetness. Holy fuck."

It's then we hear it. Tommy on the baby monitor, starting to fuss. Our moment is over too soon, but she looks up at me and grins. She stands before me as I swallow down air, her perfect naked body between my legs. Kissing me quickly, my hands find her ass, and I squeeze it. I want to pull her close, have her straddle me, make her come over and over again.

With her eyes alight, her cheeks tinted, the most relaxed and happy I think I've ever seen her, she cups my face.

"You alright?" I move my hands, running them up and down her curves, unable to stop touching her. I still can't believe this woman made a human. She's so fucking amazing.

"I'm better than alright," she breathes out against my lips, kissing me again, and I smirk as she pulls away. "I'll go see to Tommy."

"I'll be there in a minute..." I tell her as she pulls away, not wanting her to be up at night feeding on her own. It's too quiet. Too lonely. I take pleasure in sitting with her, whispering together and massaging her feet. "I'll just catch my breath," I tell her honestly, and her smile widens.

I watch her put on her robe and walk out of the room, completely transfixed.

My life has never been perfect. I've never been so lucky. But right now, it feels really fucking close.

35

SAVANNAH

I slowly open my eyes and wake. My body is liquid. I feel like I've slept for days, which is amazing, considering I haven't had a full night's sleep in what seems like forever. The bed is soft and soothing against my skin, my body sinking into the blankets, and I stretch out, feeling the kinks in my shoulders relax.

But I then pause. Because it's still dark. The house is too quiet. I roll over and grab my cell from the bedside table and then bolt up.

"Oh my God." Panic fills me. It's four a.m., and I haven't heard a peep from Tommy since late last night.

"Tommy!" I scramble to get out of bed, moving so fast my feet get caught in the sheets, and I nearly fall face-first onto the floor. I jump up, the pain in my knee from carpet burn not registering as I grab Griffin's shirt that's lying on the armchair, my heart beating out of its chest.

He never sleeps this long. Did he scream for me and I slept so deeply I didn't hear it? Did something happen to him in the middle of the night? *Oh my God, is he breathing!* Terror barrels through me like I've never felt before.

Running down the hallway, I push open the door to the nursery and stop abruptly.

"Hey, sweetness," Griffin croons, and I blink a few times, taking in the scene.

I'm a panting mess. The shirt is half-on, my hair flying everywhere, and yet here in the nursery, it's a perfect picture. Griffin's in his boxers and sitting in the armchair. His hair is everywhere, his jaw covered with stubble that's sexy as hell, and he looks so content, his facial features having softened.

Tommy is lying on Griffin's bare chest. Looking around the room, no doubt hearing my voice. There's an empty bottle on the side table, and I can see Tommy is changed into new sleepwear as he snuggles into the chest that calls to me every night as well.

"I slept through..." I'm still half-asleep. My brain is not firing, and I'm trying to work out what's going on and what I've missed.

"Tommy here slept through most of the night. Started fussing about an hour ago. I thought I'd let you sleep a bit more, so I changed him, then he and I went into the kitchen and grabbed the milk you pumped, put in it a bottle, warmed it up, and he had a feed."

My heart warms, and my tension fades. I pull the shirt across my chest so I at least look dressed properly and take in a breath. My breasts feel full, but they're not sore, which is a miracle in itself.

"He was a good boy and drank it all. Hungry little guy. Since then, we've been here talking."

"Oh, what have you guys been talking about?" I step toward them, smiling.

"Well, Tommy here is more of a listener than a talker. But he did make some gurgle sounds when I was telling him about Sutton's bees."

"Sutton's bees?" I arch an eyebrow as I sit on the arm of the chair and lean over, kissing my boy on the top of his soft, warm head.

"I told him all about the fresh honey he'll get to try when he's old enough... Do I get one of those?" His voice is low, and I look up, meeting his gaze, our noses an inch apart.

"Sure do." My stomach flutters as I lean in to kiss him. Our lips linger, our affection obvious.

"How are you feeling... after last night?" I'm always surprised by his constant care and attention to my needs. How Griffin hasn't had a wife by now, I have no idea. But I'm grateful he hasn't.

"I feel... good. Great. I had an incredible night." My smile isn't one that can be wiped. After getting interrupted by Tommy, we stayed awake talking for a little while before I fell asleep in his arms, both of us sated—at least for the time being.

As Griffin's hand trails up the back of my naked thigh, I'm starting to feel like we might need to pick back up where we left off.

"Hmmm, me too, sweetness. Me too." His gaze is full of heat, the molten look he gives me warming me from the inside out.

"Tommy's drifted off..." I whisper as I lean back, seeing my son's eyes closed, his bottom lip relaxed, knowing he needs to go down for his next sleep cycle. Clearly, he's full and happy.

"Why don't you put him down and come help me in the shower?" I offer, taking a few steps toward the door.

"You alright? Need help with the shower?" Griffin is gentle as he stands slowly, looking like he's walking with a live grenade, carefully putting a sleeping Tommy into his crib.

"Oh, you know... I can't reach all the spots..." I tease, and as his gaze flicks to mine, he understands my meaning.

"You better run, sweetness. Because if I catch you, we're not making it to the shower."

I bite my lower lip and turn quickly, bolting out the door and running down the hallway back to our room. I barely make it two steps inside before Griffin's hands are on me.

"Let's get you wet, baby," he whispers in my ear from behind as I feel the shirt I'm wearing fall from my shoulders. The cool air whips over my body as his hands circle my waist, his palms flat against my hips, pulling me to him. My bare back against his bare chest. His head lowers, kissing my neck, and I take a deep breath and rest my head back against his shoulder.

"How wet?" I groan as his hands run up my torso, cupping my breasts, massaging them in a way that's both relaxing and turning me on.

"Very fucking wet," he growls, and I grind my ass into his pelvis, feeling him already hard.

"I need this... I need you..." I tell him honestly as my fingers scratch the back of his neck, pulling him down to me. Earlier was amazing. Touching, kissing, and tasting him. But now, I'm ready for more. My body feels good, and my mind is clear. We've waited long enough.

"Look at you, all open and greedy," he murmurs against my skin as I stand completely naked with him at my back, his warm hands roaming all over me. "I'll go slow. You tell me if anything doesn't feel right..."

"I'll be fine. I just want you." I lower my hands, reaching around behind me, and start to pull down his boxers.

"Eager, sweetness?" He helps me undress him, his bare body hot against my own.

"Very..." That shower I mentioned earlier is still on our minds. I don't know how he does it. How his hands and lips roam over me so well that it feels like he's everywhere at once.

We stumble into the bathroom, but he doesn't take us to the shower; he stands us in front of the vanity, the full mirror giving our reflection back to us.

"Lean back on me." His voice is a command I follow willingly, my body weight leaning back against his chest as his hand lowers. Eyes closing, I bite my bottom lip as his fingers hit my core.

"Eyes open, sweetness."

My eyes ping open, and I meet his gaze in the reflection before I look over us. One of his hands is gripping my hip, pulling me to him tightly. The other is on my pussy, his fingers working me over and over, my skin becoming hot, my heart starting to thud.

"Yes..." I pant, watching us together in the mirror. His tall, broad frame towers over my smaller one. My body is full of new curves, and his is hard and solid. We're a contradiction, yet he makes me feel so alive, so beautiful, so wanted.

"You're already wet for me, sweetness... I know you love my fingers, but my cock really needs you." His lips haven't left my skin, and I nod into his kisses.

"Yes... yes, I want that... So bad..." I gulp, my mouth dry from panting so much. As his finger circles my clit, I feel myself getting close. My legs start to tremble before he moves his hand to my inner thigh, spreading me wider, his other hand doing the same on the other leg.

"Put your hands on the vanity." His voice is low, his

command clear, and I do as he says without question. My hands find the vanity as he widens my stance and grips on to my hips.

"Slow and steady, baby," he tells me, and I already feel him nudging my core. He goes slow. It's the smart thing to do after what I've been through, but my need for him increases with every touch. I push back a little, ensuring he slides in quicker, and he growls. There's no pain. I feel full, tight, but no pain at all. I love the stretch of him.

"Greedy girl..." I hear his restraint. His body is coiled tight, going slow for me. I feel him inch by inch, almost all the way inside me. "You good, baby?"

"I'm good... I'm sooo good..." I reassure him breathily, gripping the counter, and he starts to move.

"You're fucking amazing." His hold on my hips is claiming. The kind that leaves bruises, the glorious kind. He thrusts forward and pulls me to him, starting gently, his need increasing gradually until there's nothing for me to do but hold on so I don't topple.

"Yes, Griffin... yessss..." It feels amazing. Different than before, not harder, not painful, just a little different.

Our skin slaps as he goes a little harder. The pleasurable pain starts to rise. My body jiggles, my breasts large and heavy and moving in ways they haven't before. His eyes watch them in the reflection of the mirror.

"Fuck," he growls as his hands move, cupping my breasts, keeping me braced against him.

I whimper as one of his hands glides up my chest, to my throat, and he grips my neck, pulling my head to meet his. A brandishing kiss awaits. His lips move against mine, and everything in my mind is gone except for this moment.

We missed this stage of our relationship. The stage when you have sex everywhere, on every surface, whenever you can. The stage when you're so eager to be with one another that it's all you think about. All you want. The fun, flirty, dating phase. We moved straight to the baby makes three stage and are only now coming back to each other. Exploring, finding what works. How we feel together.

And this definitely works.

While I know my old church would see what I'm doing with Griffin as a sin. Sex before marriage. Sex like this at all. But I don't care. I've never experienced anything like this. The overwhelming desire to give this man everything he wants. Do anything he asks of me and give him all of me in return. He makes me feel alive. Wanted, cherished. I've never had that before. From anyone.

"Harder..." I beg of him, and as his gaze shoots down to meet mine, I nod.

So he does. He thrusts harder, his hands grip me tighter, and the sweat we're both working up is slick against our skin.

"You begging for me, sweetness?"

"Yes... pleassseee..." I moan, long and low.

"Fuck, I'll give you anything. I'll give you anything you want." His grip on my neck tightens, in a good way, and he pulls my face to meet his again, leaning down and kissing me as my body starts to shake.

"I'm coming!" I gasp.

"I'm going to come inside you..." It's a question I'm already nodding to.

"Yes... Oh God... I'm coming..." I lose it then. All awareness of time, of responsibilities, I'm lost in the sensation of being a wanted woman. My orgasm takes over, my toes curl, my body tenses, and my legs widen automatically, wanting all of him as deep as he'll go.

Griffin tenses, his thrusts powerful before he lets go with a guttural groan. "Fuuucckkkkk yessssss..."

The two of us are panting. My feet barely touch the ground, my back sealed to his front. His mouth is already on my shoulder, kissing me all over as we both come back to ourselves. Our movements turn to soothing touches as we catch our breath.

"Are you feeling alright?" he asks as he kisses my lips again.

"Never better... you?" I admit, not caring that he's taking my full weight, not having a lot of strength in my legs now anyway.

"Oh, sweetness... I want to do that over and over and over again..." he says with a smile, and I can't help but giggle. Because I would like to do it again too.

36

GRIFFIN

I sit in my home office, going through a million emails and overviewing project plans. Business has been good for many years and shows no signs of abating. I'm a wanted man. My designs, my building skills, my extremely knowledgeable teams, all in high demand. And I like it. It keeps me busy. Keeps me focused. Keeps my brain from sinking into thoughts and feelings that aren't worth remembering. It also keeps my bank balance growing to an obscene amount, so much so, I have no idea what to do with it all.

I have investments. I've got real estate. I've got my own jet. None of it matters, though. None of it has ever been my driving force.

But the woman who shares my bed and her son who rests down the hall have my full attention.

They got home from the bakery, her working hard to build something for herself and her son. The two of them are now well known in Whispers, the locals supporting her like I never knew they could.

Now they're part of my life, this is how I spend my days.

In my home office, on calls. Video conferences to review site plans with my team managers. I'll have to start flying out to sign off on plans and builds soon, but so far, I've managed it all okay.

Because the thought of being away from her makes me nauseous. Not sure how it happened. Not sure what magic voodoo that woman has over me, but she has cast her spell and left me entirely at her mercy, and I don't ever want to leave her side.

It's not a feeling I know well. But with her, it feels natural.

I rub my eyes, my vision blurring from all the computer work, and sigh when my cell rings.

"Sawyer." Sitting in his office for most of that day and telling him everything that's happened was both cathartic and overwhelming. I've never been to therapy. I spoke to a woman at child services once as a kid. I still remember her purple hair and dark eyeliner and the way she smelled of cigarettes so thickly I almost choked being next to her. She had a cackly voice to match her bad habit.

But after one session, I knew it wasn't for me. What good could come of talking about all the bad things in life? So instead, I ran. Got in trouble, ran again. Ran all the way to Whispers, where I'm still running. Until now.

"Hey, Griff. So I have some information." He's not jovial. Not making jokes. This is Sawyer in lawyer mode, and I feel the heaviness settle in my chest, knowing I'm not going to like what he's about to say.

"Go on."

"Well, your father was released early. Seems he had some notable good behavior while in jail, a model prisoner, by the looks of his record."

"Model fucking prisoner..." I mumble, my shoulders tensing and my stomach churning.

"So he served his time but had close to five years cut off his total sentence, which means he's now out."

"Fuck." I knew this day would come. He didn't get life, even though he took theirs. He was charged with second degree manslaughter. From what I understand from the records, his lawyer pushed that the incident wasn't premeditated. He was under the influence and his violence was uncharacteristic.

If you had asked me, it was very characteristic. Happened every fucking Friday night. And again on Sunday if his football team didn't win. But nobody asked me. As a twelve-year-old, I was whisked into foster care and never looked at again.

"Looks like he's living in a housing support service somewhere in Missouri."

I pull in a deep breath. I travel to a lot of places, but Missouri is one place I've never been back to. I left as a delinquent teen and never once returned.

"He has restrictions. Needs to check in weekly with his parole officer. Not allowed to travel out of state. He's working at the local supermarket, stocking shelves, but otherwise, so far, he's been pretty quiet. Sticking to his requirements."

"Piece of shit..." I'm not happy. Not happy that this is happening. Now or at all. I remember the phone call I got a month or so ago, along with that more recent text.

"When was he released?" I ask out of curiosity.

"Looks to be two months ago," Sawyer tells me, and I nod. The puzzle pieces fall into place. I never once visited him in prison. Never once wrote. He didn't either. Not sure why he'd be trying to contact me now. But I remember his voice like I spoke to him yesterday. I know it was him who called me that night.

I never changed my name or identity. One quick look online, and there's a variety of articles and media about me. Including my billionaire status. Even though I keep my life as low-key as possible, my business speaks for itself, and people like to brag to their friends and strangers on the internet when they move into their luxury mansions. My name is mentioned repeatedly in those posts.

"I had a look over everything. Given his parole conditions, I don't think you have anything to worry about."

"It'd be his death sentence if he came looking for me." I don't carry a gun, but maybe that's something I need to consider.

"As your lawyer, I'll pretend I didn't hear that. But when I spoke to his parole officer to clarify these things, he mentioned that your father was wanting to talk to you. Reach out to you."

"He tried. I don't want anything to do with him," I grit out, never wanting to think of that asshole again.

"I thought as much. I'll go back and reinstate a no contact and ensure he's aware and that should be the end of it. Now, on to the other things you needed. Adoption in this state is reasonably straight forward. In your case, given that there isn't a father on Tommy's birth certificate, and no one has claimed paternity, then if adoption is something you and Savannah want to look at, I could get the paperwork started without any delay. Did Savannah want to start that right away?"

I clench my jaw.

"She doesn't know about it yet." She will. I'm waiting for the right time.

"Ahhh, yeah, might be best to talk with her and see if

that's something she wants to do before we start anything." He has slight sarcasm in his tone, lightening the mood a little.

"Anything else I need to know?"

"I have the paperwork for the trust fund for Tommy all sorted, so I'll email that to you to review and sign. His schooling, college, his entire life will be all set up, thanks to you."

"Good." Not sure how Savannah will feel about that either, but it seems I'm on a roll with my lawyer now, no point stopping at criminal activities and whereabouts.

"Alright, if I find anything else, I'll let you know. You guys coming to the kids' baseball game on Saturday?" Sawyer's tone has moved into relaxed friend and father mode. Baseball is one of his loves, third to that of Annabelle and the boys.

"I'll speak to Savannah."

"Really? Shit, you are a changed man. I ask you every week and you never come. I guess it's true what they say..."

"What who says?" I bark.

"A leopard can change its spots." He laughs, and I hang up on him. But my lips quirk. *Asshole.*

I sit in silence for a moment, gathering my thoughts. The two items I gave Sawyer ran parallel in my head. I want to do right by Savannah. I want to provide, protect, and love. Tommy too. I don't know if I can be the father figure he needs. Thinking of my own father, I hope my skills in that department are better than what I grew up with. He doesn't even belong here. He shouldn't be allowed to live. He should've rotted in jail for the rest of his miserable life.

I lean over, opening the bottom drawer of my desk, and pull out the box. A wooden box I made two decades ago and the only thing I would grab if there was a fire. But I haven't opened it in years. Can't. Couldn't look at him. I couldn't deal.

Sucking in a breath, I unlock it, the click of the small lock echoing around my quiet office. I lift the lid slowly, like danger is lurking. My head pounds, my breathing labored, and I swallow past a sudden lump in my throat as I stare at the contents.

There he is. My brother. The only photo I have of him. His hair is ruffled, because no matter how many times Mom asked him to brush it, he never did. His grin is wide, full of teeth. He had big canines, and I always teased him for being a vampire. He's leaning over his bike. We were fixing the chains since they had come loose that day.

My eyes sting as my heart feels like it's breaking all over again. I remember him like he was here yesterday. He's forever ten years old to me.

I put the photo down and look at what else is in my box. One of the things not many people know about is when a kid goes into the system, they take nothing. They get driven away, placed with emergency foster parents, with nothing but the clothes on their backs. Our house was sold, bills were paid, no money, no assets, nothing. But that emergency foster carer I had for those first few nights ensured that I was brought some things from home. She could tell I was traumatized. She could tell I needed something. Anything to hang on to. I'm forever grateful to her for that. Hence why one of the first things I did when I came into some money was ensure she had some. Had my legal guy at the time deliver it to her anonymously.

Now as I pick up the small plastic green soldier, I turn it over in my palm. Tommy used to love playing soldiers. It's what we used to do under the bed when we hid from Dad's wrath. I would play and play and play with him, distracting him from the yelling downstairs. Couldn't hear the shattered glass as they broke against the wall. The slamming of the front door, the car as it screeched down the street. I did anything I could to make sure he wasn't affected by having a drunk as a father, but I failed him in every way when he paid the ultimate price.

That's something I'll never forgive myself for.

I look at the gold watch at the bottom of the box and gently pull it out. It hasn't been touched in years. I haven't picked it up, haven't wanted to. This watch rested around my mother's wrist. I turn it over, inspecting the back, seeing it etched with her initials. It feels smaller now, lighter, and I try to imagine it around her wrist, my mother a dainty woman. Her wrists were tiny, if this watch is anything to go by.

"What you doin'?"

I look up, startled, seeing Savannah leaning against the doorframe, watching me.

"You creeping again?" I blow out a breath, smiling at her.

"No... I wanted to see if you were ready for dinner, but I didn't want to interrupt. You looked... like you were concentrating pretty hard." She steps into my office tentatively. "What's that?" she asks, looking down at the gold watch in my hand, and my chest aches.

"It was my mother's." I admit, feeling lighter the minute the words leave me.

"Your mom's?"

"Yeah, the only thing I have left of hers." I lift it and pass it to her, and she takes it gently from my hand, looking at it, carefully handling one of the most precious things I own.

"It's beautiful," she says quietly, giving it back.

I reach back into the box. "This is my brother Tommy."

Clearing my throat, I lift the photo to her and watch her take it.

"He looks like you." She smiles sadly, looking at me, and my shoulders lower. The stress and heartache I usually feel when thinking about them dissipates the slightest bit, sharing this with her.

"I used to call him a vampire because of his teeth..." I shake my head, the images of us running around as kids vivid in my mind.

"You have the same eyes." She looks back at me, then the photo and back again. "We should frame it. Display it here somewhere?"

My heart thuds a little heavier. Could I do that? Could I look at my brother every day and see the love for him and not the self-loathing I usually feel?

"This is the only other thing I have from my childhood." I pull out the green army man, and her smile widens.

"Oh, I've seen these before..." She looks at it in wonder. I guess these kinds of toys are a little vintage. Probably not something she played with as a kid. "You taking a trip down memory lane?" She passes the toy back to me, and I blow out a breath, putting the things back.

"My father was released from jail recently." I've been needing to tell her. Needing to tell her everything. I didn't plan for it to be right now, like this.

"Oh?" Her eyes widen.

"He was incarcerated for twenty-five years. I haven't seen or spoken to him since that night he killed my family."

She steps forward, and I lean back in my chair, lifting my arms, wanting her close. I feel immediately at ease when she sits on my lap, and I wrap my arms around her.

"That must feel... Well, I don't know what that would feel like. How do you feel about that?"

"Angry," I say without hesitation. "A little melancholy... but mainly angry."

"That's understandable." She nods, not jumping from me. Not looking at me any differently.

"He called me."

I feel her body tense a little in my grip, and I rub my hand up and down her back instinctively.

"And what did he say?"

"He didn't get a chance to say anything, really. I told him not to call me. I've had Sawyer relay a message to his parole officer that I want nothing to do with him. He's dead to me."

Again, she nods slowly, taking in all the information so I continue.

"I don't want him here. I don't want him near me, near you, near Tommy..." I have to take a calming breath to try to regroup.

She cups my cheek. "Okay... whatever you want. I'll support whatever you need."

Fuck. I told her my deadbeat murderer of a father wants back in my life and half expected her to leave, grab Tommy, and rush out the door. But instead, she leans into my hold, giving me her support, her touch soft and sensitive. I don't deserve her. Not in the slightest.

"Have you talked to anyone? Looked into therapy or anything like that?"

I shake my head. "That's not really for me. But I've spoken in depth to Sawyer, and I feel lighter for talking to you. Now you know all my skeletons... There's nothing else about me that you need to know." I nod, a heavy sigh leaving me, liking the fact that there are no secrets.

"Thank you for sharing..." She presses a kiss to my head.

"I want us to be honest with each other. I want you to know everything about me and me about you."

"Well… since we're airing our skeletons…"

"What?" I ask too quickly, wondering what I don't know.

She blows out a breath, long and slow.

"Savannah isn't my real name. I mean, it is, but it's my middle name, not my first name."

I frown. "What's your name?"

"It's Faith. Faith Savannah Sullivan." She swallows, watching me carefully. "I decided to use my middle name when I moved to Whispers. I wanted to start fresh, to leave the past me behind, and it felt right. I've always felt more like a Savannah than a Faith anyway." She shrugs, and I smile, shaking my head.

"Faith. Savannah. It doesn't matter, because you will always be my sweetness…"

Smiling, she hums, cuddling against me.

"And you will always be my Grumpy Griff."

I huff a laugh and pull her close, feeling lighter than I have in years.

37

____

SAVANNAH

My feet are sore, my hips tight, but I wouldn't have it any other way.

"So, we're out of cupcakes, but we still have some gingerbread left, so that should cover us for the after-school rush." Melissa walks out to the kitchen, the two of us a little tired after a busy day.

"Great, what about the pastries?" I finish feeding Tommy and fix myself before putting him over my shoulder and tapping his back.

"We have a few left. They'll go after school too, though. It's crazy; no matter how much you make, we're never left with much at closing." She grins, walking to the coffee maker and putting on a pot.

"I know. It's great, but so hard to judge what quantities to make." I frown, thinking about it. I want to be efficient with my time and my ingredients. I could look at freezing more things, but I prefer to have my items sold fresh, straight from the oven that morning. But I already get up at four and I'm here early every day. There's not too many more hours I could put in to bake things for the shelves.

"I think you could make double and still not have enough. But that's good. It keeps people wanting more. Gives them the scarcity mindset. That's why there's always people here first thing in the morning. They want to be able to grab what they need."

I stand, placing Tommy down in his bassinet for a moment as I stretch out.

"I guess you're right." I ponder over her words. She's smart, such an asset to me and the business.

"Have you noticed any requests lately? Anything people are asking for that I could add to the daily production?"

Melissa grabs two cups automatically, making me a coffee, not needing to ask. She knows me well by now. She's like the friend I never knew I needed. Her husband works all day, and I can tell this job gives her a new lease on life. She's so energetic and genuinely happy to be here in the bakery, which makes my job so much easier.

"Nothing too specific. The older guys always come in wanting a pot pie for dinner on their nights they have to cook." She huffs a laugh and shakes her head. I've come to know Bob from the hardware store and Tim from the toy store well. Clearly, their wives are happy to have them produce a pie for dinner every Thursday night. It's cute.

"Maybe I need to change the filling. Keep them from having the same things each week." I grin as she passes me the cup, and we both look up at hearing the front door open.

"Oh, I'll go," she tells me, then puts down her cup and walks out the front. I do the same. I've been back in the kitchen all day. I miss interacting with people, especially the locals who have been so welcoming.

"Ahh, Savannah?" Melissa's voice sounds unsure, and I step through the door and look up with a smile, ready to greet our customer, but it falls from my face quickly.

"What are you doing here?" I look at my mother, seeing Eden right by her side. She's come back with reinforcements. It took her a while. I'm surprised she waited that long.

"You know why we're here." My mother's voice sounds cold and detached. No warmth, no love. Melissa looks between us, a frown on her face. I haven't had the time or the energy to explain to her about my family. She's unprepared for this.

"I'm afraid I don't? Did you need some pastries?" I fold my hands over my chest and try to stand tall.

"We're here for Joseph," Eden says, and my eyebrows pinch in confusion.

"Joseph? Who's Joseph?" Are they meant to be meeting someone?

"The baby. Eden has decided to name him Joseph."

"Decided to name...?" Melissa trails off, understandably bewildered. But my eyes remain on my mother and my sister. Watching their every move.

"*My* baby isn't here," I emphasize while praying that Tommy stays quiet in his bassinet.

My mother huffs. "Of course he is, we saw you walk in with him this morning. Stop with the lying."

I pull in a breath, my heart beating faster. "You've been watching me?" I feel angry and scared. Whispers is quiet in the early hours, Griffin driving me and Tommy every day, staying until Melissa gets here and the bakery opens before leaving us to it.

"We have been keeping an eye on the baby, and I have all the formula at home ready to go. Now give me the baby." Eden steps forward like she has any right to.

"Should I call Griffin?" Melissa looks at me, unsure. She tentatively takes small steps toward the kitchen, and I thank

God she's here, so at least we're equal numbers against them.

"There's no need. He's not family. He's not required, and this has nothing to do with him," my sister says, and my anger rises.

"He is family," I state clearly.

"Faith, you're being ridiculous." My mother takes a purposeful stride toward me, toward the kitchen, and I step forward to meet her. Her use of my real name has me on edge. I feel so far removed from that girl now. She halts, apparently surprised that I would stop her.

"Get out," I grit out, on the verge of tears.

"You're clearly unstable. Look at you standing in front of Mom like that." Eden tries to slide past me, and I see what they're trying to do. Trying to manipulate me with words, which is what usually would work on me. But not anymore. Simultaneously trying to move past me to get to Tommy.

"If you don't leave, I'll call the sheriff and have you removed and charged with trespassing."

They both stop and look at me in disbelief. "Oh, now I know you're mentally incapable. That baby needs to come with us. You're not suitable to be a mother," my own mother says as she pushes past me. I reach out to grab her arm, to pull her back, but as I do, Eden runs past me and into the kitchen.

"No!" I yell, letting go of Mom and rushing after my sister.

I see Eden looking wide-eyed at Melissa, who holds Tommy close to her chest and is backstepping slowly, away from her and toward the back door.

"I don't know who you are, or why you're here, but this is not your baby," Melissa says forcefully, and I couldn't be more grateful that she's here.

"Give me my baby! If I need Douglas to come back here, I will!" Eden's shrieks fill the bakery, and I'm relieved it's the afternoon slump and no customers are here. This would ruin my reputation, for sure.

I push past them and stand in front of Melissa. Tommy's looking at her in wonder, having no idea of the storm brewing around him.

"You both need to leave. If not, I'll call the sheriff," I threaten again. I don't want to. What daughter would ever want to call the police on their own mother? I've moved out of that community. I've started my own business, not needing their support or their money. I've built my own group of friends and have a new community here that I love. And I have Griffin. The man who stands by me every day when he could be anywhere doing anything else but. Why can't they leave me alone?

"I pray for your soul..." My mother's loose warning lingers before she snatches Eden's wrist and pulls her out of my kitchen. I follow them, ensuring they walk out of the bakery and that the door closes firmly behind them. I stand at the door, looking out the window, watching them get into a truck I don't recognize, and I don't move until the truck is gone.

"Are you alright?" Melissa asks, and I whip around, seeing her still holding my son. I rush over, needing him in my arms.

"I'm sorry. It's extremely unprofessional... They were my family..." I swallow down the hard lump that's formed. My hands are shaking, my heart pounding in my ears.

Melissa's visibly worried and upset. "I think we need to speak to the sheriff..." she says. I probably should. It's all getting frightening and well out of hand.

"Why do we need the sheriff?" Griffin's voice comes from

the back, and I see him step through the kitchen to the front of the bakery, looking at Melissa's concerned face. His eyes take in Tommy's content grin next, and then he looks at me, and his frown deepens.

"What happened?" He steps toward me, his arms circling my waist, pulling me and Tommy to him tightly.

"My sister came back with my mom..." I whisper, feeling helpless.

"They tried to take the baby. They called her Faith," Melissa informs him before looking at me questioningly.

"Faith is my first name. I go by Savannah now, which is my middle name," I explain quickly.

"I'm calling the sheriff. This stops now." He pulls out his cell and makes a call. And I don't stop him. Maybe that makes me a bad daughter. A horrible sister. But I hope that means I'm a good mom.

Because Tommy needs to be protected. Damn the consequences.

38

GRIFFIN

We closed the bakery for the afternoon, and the sheriff has been here for the better part of an hour, talking to Savannah and taking a statement from Melissa while Tommy and I stand guard, ready to intervene at a moment's notice.

I'm trying to keep my anger at bay. Trying to be supportive, helpful. Letting her lead, telling me what she needs. But fuck it. While she spoke to the sheriff, Tommy and I went upstairs, and I called my security team again. The same guys I had standing guard in the hospital. They'll be here by morning and will protect her and this bakery so fucking tight, no one will get to her.

"Well, I think that's all I need. But like I said, if you don't want to press charges, there's not a lot I can do. I'll make a report to have on file. But there's nothing stopping them from turning back up tomorrow," Tony, the local sheriff, says, and I clench my jaw. I'll fucking stop them. That's what will.

"Let me walk you out." I pass Tommy over to his mom and walk the sheriff out the front of the bakery as Savannah blows out a breath and Melissa potters around. I'm grateful for her. Not sure what would've happened had she not been here.

"There'll be three new people in town by morning," I tell him. Not asking for permission.

"Private security?" He raises his eyebrow at me but doesn't seem surprised. I nod.

"Thought as much. Tanner and his friends always take things into their own hands; not sure why I thought this would be any different." He puts on his hat and walks out the door, clearly trying to manage his town with a group of billionaires who don't give a fuck about his rules.

I turn and see both the women standing, talking in hushed tones, and Tommy snuggles into Savannah, clearly tired. It's been a big afternoon.

"Melissa. Would you mind taking Tommy up to the apartment for a while?"

Melissa nods, and Savannah looks at me.

"Why?"

I get it. She's protective, too. But she needs to breathe. She needs to have a small moment.

"Oh, I can take him for a little while. Give you guys a chance to talk. He's all fed, so he'll be happy for a bit." Melissa smiles, and Savannah mimics her, passing him over and watching her hold her son.

"Just bring him back down as soon as he starts fussing," Savannah tells her.

"No worries. I'll be back down if he starts to cry." She slowly walks up the stairs, and silence falls across the bakery as the small apartment door closes behind her.

"Talk to me." Moving closer, my hands cup her face, forcing her to look at me. Needing to touch her. Needing her in my arms.

"I feel... hopeless..." She swallows as a small tear trails down. I wipe it away with my thumb, caressing her cheeks.

"Why?" My chest tightens at seeing her so upset.

"Because if Melissa wasn't here, I wouldn't have been able to protect him." Her words are mere whispers as another tear falls. It's a feeling I know too well. She had a huge scare today. I'm sure her shock and adrenaline are still running through her body.

"I've organized some security. Three men will be here tomorrow."

She shakes her head immediately.

"No. I can't. It's a family-friendly bakery. I can't have suited security standing around here like it's a nightclub or something. It would ruin the entire feeling I'm trying hard to evoke." Still thinking of the business. Of building something. Trying to prove to everyone around her that she can do it. Of course she can. She's amazing. But she needs to know she can rely on me now. That there are people who can help her.

"I'll place them down the street. Have one sit out the back. One up in the apartment. They can be discreet."

She swallows, still looking uneasy, and I cup her jaw as she slowly nods in agreement.

"I was so scared they were going to take him, you know?" Her eyes are glassy as she looks up at me pleadingly.

"Yeah, sweetness, I do know."

Understanding washes across her face. My brother and mother were both taken from me, and I never saw them again. I know firsthand the pain she's feeling.

"How can they think it's okay to walk in here and kidnap my baby?" Her brow wrinkles, and I rub her cheek with my thumb again, trying to soothe her.

"I suspect that they're not really thinking at all." It's the truth. No person in their right mind would try anything like that. They are entitled, probably borderline mentally unstable, but I don't say it.

She takes a deep breath and blows it out, her shoulders relaxing with the movement. I drop my hands, lowering them to her waist. She's beautiful today, as always.

"Thank you," she whispers, her arms looping around my neck.

"What for?"

"For being here. For taking such good care of me and of Tommy."

"Always." I nod. Certain of it.

"Always?" Her facial features lighten, her frown now almost completely gone.

"Yeah, sweetness. Don't really know how we came to be. Hell, I think we're both still trying to work it all out. I certainly never thought I would ever commit to someone. Now here I am, with not only a beautiful woman, but a beautiful baby at home too."

"You're a lucky guy..." She's being sarcastic, but her words are true.

"Never thought I was until I met you."

"Don't go getting all soppy on me, Griffin," she teases, her smile widening, and I love to see it so much, I keep talking.

"You calling love soppy?"

She stills, her mouth opening a little in shock.

"Because that's what this is, sweetness."

"You love me?" She says it like it's the most unbelievable thing. Like no one could possibly love her.

"I do. I'm not worthy of it. Not worthy of you. It's foreign to me. I haven't been close to anyone in a long time. You know that. But hell, sweetness, I'd scorch the earth and everyone on it for you." I try not to get choked up, and I swallow hard. Fuck, I'm turning into a vulnerable asshole lately.

She looks at me, wide eyes blinking, like she's digesting everything I said.

"You... love me?" she says again, and if she needs to hear it a hundred times, I will tell her a hundred more.

"Yes, I love you, Savannah. More than I ever thought I could."

"I love you, too. I love you so much it scares me."

When those words pass her lips, I nearly crumple at her feet. I haven't heard those words in a long time. Not in the way she's saying them. Like she knows it right down to her bones. I pull in a breath, trying to steady myself. I'm in territory I haven't even been in before. There's responsibility now. There's commitment. There's love. And I want it. I want it all with her.

"Scares the hell out of me too, sweetness. And I promise to always look after you and Tommy. I promise to protect you, love you, be there for Tommy when he needs me..."

Her smile widens as my arms close around the small of her back. She leans away just enough to look at me, her fingers brushing the stubble along my jaw like she's memorizing every detail.

"What are you thinking about?" I ask her.

"I'm just thinking about our journey to get here." Her soft laugh catches in her throat.

I huff a breath. "Not exactly a straight line."

"More like a car crash. With detours. And a few explosions."

I grin, and it feels strange on my face, like my muscles forgot how to do it until she came along. "Still standing, though."

"Barely," she teases, but her voice is thick with emotion. "But yeah. Still standing."

She presses her forehead to my chest, and I rest my chin on her crown. Her hair smells like sugar and something warm, like home. We stay like that for a long moment, breathing in sync, hearts slowing. I could stand like this forever. Have her in my arms. Our baby safe and loved. I feel a little nervous thinking about it. About how I can make her mine. About how I can build this little family we have started. How I want her to be my forever.

She exhales, shaky and soft. "I used to think love was something other people got. People who didn't screw up. People who weren't... me."

I pull her tighter against me. "You didn't screw up. You survived. You fought. You kept going when most people would've folded."

Her eyes glisten, and she tries to blink it away. "I don't know what I did to deserve you."

She lifts onto her tiptoes and presses her lips to mine. It's gentle, reverent, like she's afraid I'll vanish if she moves too fast. "I don't want to lose this," she whispers.

"You won't," I say, too fast, too certain. "I plan to be here with you forever if you'll have me?"

She is my future. She's my everything.

She lifts her head back from my chest, eyes on mine.

"I'll have you today, tomorrow, and forever."

I release a breath I didn't know I was holding, then I lean down and kiss her until we're breathless all over again.

Cementing our words. Sealing our fate.

39

SAVANNAH

"He's getting so big now." Griffin lifts Tommy from the crib as I take my seat in the rocking chair. It's close to three a.m., and while tired, the exhaustion I was feeling after birth has left me, all three of us now getting more sleep as Tommy settles into his routine.

"He'll be gone off to college before we even realize," I joke as Griffin passes me my son, and I rest him on my chest. He's hungry tonight, nuzzling me within seconds. Sometimes I still can't believe this is my life. That this impossibly steady, impossibly gentle man chooses to sit on the floor at my feet every night like it's the most natural thing in the world. That he touches me like I'm something precious. That he looks at Tommy like he's a miracle instead of a complication.

"I wanted to talk to you about that, actually."

I look at Griffin curiously as he takes a seat at my feet, picking one up and starting his nightly massage. I live for these moments. They're so peaceful, all three of us together in the darkness of the early morning. While the world is asleep and quiet, Griffin pampers me as I feed my son. I know I'm lucky. I'm not sure what other partners get up for every nighttime feed to support new moms, but the percentage is undoubtably low.

"About what?"

"College," he says, and my eyebrows shoot up.

"What about it? We have a while to go, you know." I smile, teasing him.

"Well, you know I've been working with Sawyer on some things with my father and all, but one of the other things we've been working on is putting together a trust for Tommy. Something he can use when he's older. But I also put money away for a college education in case he wants one."

I stare at Griffin, eyes wide in disbelief. "A college fund?"

"Just putting things in place. Ensuring he's looked after. The money's locked away. No one and nothing can touch it." He nods, assured. Clearly, it's a done deal.

"I don't know what to say…" It's the truth, I don't. I'm happy, excited, relieved, grateful. Who knows if Tommy will want to go to college; he might be like Griffin and take to more of a trade. But saving for college would have been something I'd need to think about at some stage, hoping the bakery could be a roaring success to provide Tommy with that option. Now I don't need to work myself to the bone to ensure that happens.

"You don't have to say anything. I just wanted to let you know."

"You know that I'm not expecting that from you. I'm not expecting you to fund any type of lifestyle. I mean, I know you're wealthy. This house alone tells me that. You even have your own jet. But I'm not with you because of that. I want you to know… I'm not looking for handouts…" I know he knows, but I want to reiterate it. Because this is very generous, and for him to have it already set up with Tommy so young, I can only imagine what else he might do as time goes on.

"Oh, believe me, I know. You haven't taken a single cent from me that I haven't given you because I wanted to. You never ask for a thing. And I know you've been saving money to pay me back for the hospital costs for when Tommy was born, which you damn well know I won't be accepting."

I gulp. I should've known he'd catch on to that.

"I have money. Not a lot. The bakery is growing, though, so I can take care of myself and Tommy." I feel proud of that fact. Sure, I'm no millionaire, but Betty's is getting busier. It provides a strong, regular income now, and while I still have some big purchases to make, like new mixers and a new oven, the weekly revenue the bakery generates is more than I ever expected.

"I know you can. I also know that bakery of yours is doing well, going to continue to do well, and is going to be a fantastic and extremely profitable business for you. But you need to know that I have a lot of disposable income. And I would like to invest it in us. Our family."

I take a deep breath. This conversation is more serious and life-changing than our usual nightly chats.

"Okay... anything else you *just want me to know* about?" I ask tentatively, feeling like there's more.

Griffin shifts on the floor, and for the first time since I've known him, he looks... unsure. His thumb rubs the inside of my ankle, slow and distracted, like he's grounding himself. His jaw flexes once, twice. It hits me then that he's nervous. Griffin Patterson, who stares down million-dollar deals and construction disasters without blinking, is nervous.

"Well, I was thinking that Tommy should probably get a new name."

My heart clenches. He doesn't like calling my son after his brother? I feel like ever since our chat in his office, he's been a little more at ease with this. His shoulders not as tight, his face not as angry. But maybe I was wrong.

"You don't want him to be called Tommy anymore?" I frown, disappointed.

"I don't want him to have the last name Sullivan anymore. I think Patterson is better. I'd like him to have my last name if you agree?" He continues massaging my feet like he didn't drop a bomb on me.

"You want to adopt Tommy?" I can barely get the words out. In complete shock. Happily so.

"I do. While we're at it, I'm thinking we should change your name to Patterson too."

I'm glad I'm sitting down because had I been standing, my legs would've given way.

"I... I, um..." I can't talk. I'm excited, surprised. I look down at Tommy, tears in my eyes, and Griffin's hands leave my feet to reach up, brushing a loose strand of hair behind my ear. His fingers linger at my jaw, warm and steady, and my breath catches as I look up at him. There's something in his eyes I can't name, something soft, something certain, something that makes my heart stumble.

I'm about to agree, but then I watch Griffin lower down on bended knee beside me. At the sight, my stomach does backflips.

"Savannah. Sweetness. Nothing we've done has been what anyone could call traditional or in any usual pattern of how couples build relationships. But that seems to be our thing. I didn't think I was made for this. For a woman. For a child. A son. It doesn't matter that he isn't my blood. He's mine because you are mine. I knew the moment I met you there was something different about you. I couldn't put my finger on it at the start. Just had this natural pull. It was new, different, and scary as hell. But now that we've been doing life together for a while, I figured out what it is about you that has me completely transfixed."

I stay silent. I can't talk because I can't even breathe, the air leaving my lungs almost completely.

He clears his throat, eyes locked on mine like he's afraid I'll vanish if he looks away. "It's the way you walk into the room and I feel like I can breathe again. It's the way you fight for the people you love and for yourself, even when you're breaking inside. You make me want to be a better man, even when I don't know how the hell to do that. I've spent most of my life keeping people out. Easier that way. Cleaner. But you... you tore down every wall I built. And I didn't even see it happening until I realized I can't imagine a single day without you in it."

My lips part, but again, no words come, everything he's saying overwhelming me with the certainty of my love for this man.

He keeps going, voice rough, almost breaking. "I don't have fancy speeches. I don't have promises of perfection. What I've got is me, flawed, stubborn, grumpy as hell. But I'm yours. Every damn piece of me. And I want you to be mine. For the rest of whatever time we've got."

He pauses, swallowing hard, and the silence between us feels like it's holding its breath. "So I'm asking you, Savannah, here in the quiet morning hours, with our son in your arms, if you'll be my wife."

With that question lingering in the air, he pulls a small box out from under the rocking chair, clearly having had this planned for a while. My throat dries as he opens it and I see a sparkling diamond throwing patterns around the room from the reflection of the nightlight.

I look at the ring, then back to Griffin, feeling like I'm going to have a heart attack.

"Yes..." I whisper, my eyes steadily leaking tears as I pull in a breath, filling my empty lungs. "Yes, Griffin. Yes, I will marry you. I want to be your wife, want your last name, want you to be mine, officially."

He grabs my hand, sliding the ring on, and kisses me hard before he kisses the top of Tommy's head.

I lift my hand and look at the jewel that now adorns it. The diamond catches the faint nursery light, scattering tiny stars across the walls. It's simple, elegant, and heartbreakingly thoughtful. If I were to choose a ring to wear forever, this would be it.

I cup his jaw as he looks deep into my eyes from a mere inch away.

"I love you," I whisper again, my thumb brushing the rough line of his jaw. He looks more relaxed now. Happy.

Griffin's lips twitch into the smallest grin, the kind that only ever shows when he's caught off guard. "Guess that makes two of us, then."

He rises and presses his forehead to mine, his breath warm against my lips. Neither of us speaks. We don't need to. The room feels different now, fuller somehow, like the air itself has shifted to make space for this new version of us.

Tommy sighs in his sleep, his tiny body warm between us, and I swear I can feel the future settling around us like a blanket.

"See? Even Tommy's on board." He presses another kiss to Tommy's head.

I smile through my tears. "Team Patterson all the way."

40

SAVANNAH

I should feel safe. Secure. But every time the bakery door jingles, I'm on eggshells.

Waiting. Knowing my family is going to come back. Maybe with more reinforcements. They could be outside watching, waiting. But I have a feeling that the security Griffin hired would spot them. Which makes me think they're planning something big.

That thought leaves me unsettled. As much as I try to put it out of my mind, it's nearly impossible.

But now with the bakery closed for the day, and me baking into the late afternoon, I've tried to continue. The new ring on my finger is so large I can't really cook with it, yet I don't want to take it off. A new balancing act that I'm trying to get used to.

Tommy looks at me from his bassinet in the corner as I slide another tray of croissants into the oven.

"There. I'll set the timer for twenty minutes," I tell my son and get absolutely no reaction. I grin, loving having him here to talk with. Obviously not for conversation, but for company.

He yawns and rubs his eyes, and I jump into action, not wanting him to get overtired or overstimulated. I whisk him upstairs, the security man sitting at my small table.

"I'm going to put him down for his nap."

"I'll go across to the diner. The others are outside. Let me know when to come back." He nods as he stands, gathering his laptop and phone and walking down the stairs. A man of few words, he's sat upstairs here for most of the week. Quiet, looking at his laptop. Assessing different situations and talking to his team. But every time I need to put Tommy down for a nap, he leaves. Ensuring that the others are out front, the bakery protected, yet giving Tommy and me our space. I'm not sure where Griffin found these men, but they're all so professional. They look like they need to be finding fugitives, not babysitting a bakery.

I kiss my son on the forehead, snuggle him in tight, and put the baby camera on, knowing that I can watch him sleep from the small monitor downstairs in my kitchen.

As I walk back down, I run through my mental calculations; the croissants have twenty minutes, and Tommy should be down for at least two hours. I can get some dough ready for bread and maybe do some additional rolls for tomorrow.

"Hey, sweetness," Griffin croons, and I look up as I hit the final step and grin. He's holding a large bouquet of flowers, bright blooms that instantly bring more life to the bakery.

"Hey. What are you doing here? What are these?" I walk toward him, the stupid grin on my face one that I can't remove. He's usually here to pick us up in another few hours, so I'm surprised he's early.

"Just had to zip into town. Wanted to pop in and see you both. Bring you flowers to make you smile." I step into his arms as they wrap around my waist, and he pulls me to him tight. It's easy with him.

"I just put Tommy down," I tell him as he leans forward, nudging my nose with his.

"You did?" He doesn't let me answer before his lips touch mine. Soft, slow, sultry, our lips move against each other like we're cherishing every moment. I melt in his hold. This perfect man, strong, protective, ensuring that my every need is met. It feels so good to lean on someone. Rely on them and know they'll always have my back.

"Mmmm, he'll be asleep for at least a little while..." I murmur against his lips as his hand splays across my lower back before he glides it up, past my shoulder blades and cups the back of my head. He deepens the kiss, his fingers tangling in my hair, clearly aware no one else is here. The bakery is shut, and the front doors locked.

"How long do I have?" His kisses leave my mouth, and he peppers them down my jaw, pulling a moan from my chest.

"Tommy will be down for a while, but the croissants have about ten minutes..." I tease. I hate burning my pastries, but for Griffin, I'd burn them all. His lips hit the sensitive part of my neck, and my nipples pebble instantly. I release a little sigh as my head falls back into his grip. He has my body molten with his touch.

"Challenge accepted." His hands smooth down my body quickly, and he grips my waist, hoisting me on top of the cupboard at the back of the bakery in one fast movement.

"Whoa!" I almost squeal in surprise as my butt hits the ledge, and I hold on to it, scared I might fall as he opens his belt, the clink heard throughout the space. His jeans are open and boxers pushed down in the next few seconds, his cock hard and ready for me.

"I need you," he pleads, and butterflies start to swirl below, overtaking my core.

"You've got me," I whisper, following his lead, pulling up my long dress, my bare legs dangling off the edge as he steps in between them.

"What about the security guys?" My voice is breathy. I want this. I want him. But knowing there are guys walking around right outside...

"Let them hear exactly what we're up to. Let them know what I do to you, sweetness," he grits out, grabbing the back of my knees and pulling me closer to the edge as I lean back on my hands, hoping I don't fall.

"Come here... wife," he growls as his hands move around my waist, one hand gripping on to my ass as the other one slides my underwear to the side. My breath hitches. While technically not married, we will be. Sooner rather than later, I think. I love the sound of that.

But I can't reply, because he slides into me so quickly it steals my breath.

"Yessss," he groans, and my head falls back at being filled by him. I try to breathe, getting used to his size.

"Fuck, I've missed your pussy..." he says into my ear as both of his hands grab on to my ass, lifting me a little, my legs curving around his waist, and he starts to move. "Your pretty pussy is fucking beautiful taking me in."

His words have me moaning as I quickly adjust my dress, loosening the straps from my shoulders, letting my breasts bounce free. His eyes flare as his head leans down to kiss them.

"You saw her this morning..." I pant out, my hands wrapping around his neck, grabbing on for dear life as he lifts me from the cabinet and takes my entire body weight onto his.

"Too damn long." He's frantic, and my body heats as his

thrusts become quicker. My body bounces against his, my clit rubbing his pelvis with every movement. Meeting him with every push, I feel the sensations that only Griffin elicits from me. He's made me entirely comfortable in my skin.

The way his hands always roam. The way he looks at me like I'm his every wish. The way he traces all my curves, kisses my entire body, looks after my every need. I grew up being told I needed to hide. I had to cover up, I had to remain quiet, I had to do as I was told. But Griffin lets me do life how I want to do it. Who knew men like him existed? I just had to come to Whispers to find him.

"That's it, sweetness... Fuck... Bounce on me, baby. I can feel you fluttering, and you're so damn wet for me." I love how Griffin gets during sex. His dirty talk, the way he sounds so needy. Like he isn't chasing a high, but in a deep state of need for me.

"Griffin..." I warn, my body getting hot all over, panting, sweating, my cheeks no doubt red.

"I fucking love your breasts..." He groans, lowering his head again and burying himself between them, licking and sucking all over. My skin prickles, my orgasm closing in on me, his thrusts, his hands, his mouth, all doing me in.

"Yes, Griffin!" If the oven timers go off, if someone bangs on the door, none of it would stop us. Here in the bakery, the place where we first met. My dress bunched at my waist, Griffin's jeans around his ankles. Him holding me so tight as his every movement shows me exactly what I mean to him.

"Ohhh, sweetness... you're my fucking undoing... Come for me. Slide that pretty pussy over and over on my cock and let me fuck you a million times in our lifetime."

I start to shake, the thought of forever pushing me over the edge.

"Over and over... again and again. That's it... feel me, feel every inch wanting you..."

"Yessss, Griffin, please. Oh my g— YES!" I scream as I come, gripping on to him tight, my hands pulling at his hair as he looks at me, our lips smashing into each other as I shake and bounce like my life depends on it. The old me would feel shame. The old me would feel even a little bit dirty. But none of this is dirty. This is love. Hard, fast, deep-burning love.

"Yes, sweetness... Fuck, you're so perfect. You're every-thing..." Griffin grabs my ass tight and thrusts into me with one more powerful thrust before he lets go.

"Savannah!" He yells my name, his teeth grinding through his climax, his jaw tight before he starts to relax. Slowly putting me back on the cupboard, his hands run up and down my back as he kisses me softly.

"Well, that's a new way to get me through the afternoon slump..." I tell him with a laugh, and he grins.

"I'm at your service. I like seeing you like this during the day." He kisses me again. Taking his time. Like he isn't finished with me. He never is. The oven bell chimes, reminding me of my croissants and the work I need to be doing.

"Hmmm, my time's up, isn't it?" It's him biting his lip this time, and I smack him playfully on the chest.

"For now..." I tease as we sort ourselves out, and I race to pull the tray out of the oven.

"Ouch!" I burn myself in the rush, and in an instant, Griffin is at my back, moving my body to the sink, running the cold water, trapping me between his body and the bench.

"Déjà vu." I giggle through the pain as he kisses my neck from behind. It feels like so long ago since we were here at this moment when we first met. But it's been months now, our situation, our relationship all morphing into something so serious and sacred I've never felt so right in every step.

"I don't like you burning yourself, baby." He's cute when he's not so grumpy.

"Part of the job."

"Do you have a few spare minutes later? We need to pop over to Sawyer's office."

"Sure, what for?" I turn in his embrace as he turns off the tap.

"Sign the papers."

"Papers?" I ask, head tilting.

"Get married. Legally start our family."

A slow smile takes over my face. "Seriously?"

I never thought I'd have a big white wedding. Getting up in front of a lot of people and saying vows didn't really appeal to me. It was something that Eden did when she got married. I saw the stress of it all, I saw the requirements that my parents had and Pastor Greg. It wasn't something that I was overly keen to do.

"Well, I got you a bouquet. All our friends are going to meet us at the office this afternoon to witness... and I also got you this."

He hands me a small box, and I frown, confused, before I open it and gasp.

"Take a look at the inside," he prompts me, and I pull out the wedding band of solid diamonds and look on the inside.

I wait for the light to catch it, and then my breath hitches as I read the engraving: "My Home."

"So what do you say? Ready to make us official?" he asks, and I look at him with tears in my eyes.

"Really?" I'm in slight disbelief.

"Sure, nothing about us has ever been standard, and that's exactly why it works. We just consummated the marriage before we're actually married, right here in your bakery, so might as well have the marriage in a legal office."

He's right. But I see his eyebrows pinching.

"Unless you want a big wedding? Flowers, the dress, the whole thing? I can arrange that too. I can get designers out to fit you a dress, I can fly in any flowers you choose." My grin widens at how considerate he's being, that he would do all that for me, but I shake my head.

"No. Paperwork in Sawyer's office is fine with me. Normal couples might do things by the book, but we've been writing our own script since the day we met. I love our life and don't want anything to change."

Nodding, he sighs and presses a kiss to my lips.

"I also made a new batch of cupcakes. Maybe I can ice them in white. We can take them home as our wedding cake and cut them and feed each other later?" I suggest, loving all these quirky ideas that make us, us.

"I love you," he says firmly, and I swallow as more emotion surfaces.

"And I love you."

But things are never that easy. Not for me.

41

———

GRIFFIN

Looking at the woman next to me and holding my little man on my lap as he dribbles spittle on his new outfit, I think I've finally made it. I think I've broken through the hardest chains that were around my neck from my past.

While I still have a lot to process and a lot of work to do, Sawyer has helped with all the legal things. Tanner has been a man to confide in, and Hudson, who's sitting here with us now, provided some introductions to a therapist. He's good. Met him a few times already. No doubt I'll meet with him many more.

I always hated talking about things. I hate the whole *woe is me* mentality. But there's more than just me to think about now, and Savannah and Tommy deserve the best version of me. I'm going to give that to them.

"So little Tommy is doing well. Growing, all things indicating that he's happy and healthy. Congratulations on the engagement, by the way, and the marriage..." Hudson's eyes gleam at me.

"Thank you." Savannah gives him the brightest smile,

and I give him my standard nod. I did what I said and took Savannah and Tommy over to Sawyer's office and signed the paper with Sawyer and all our friends as our witnesses. Victoria cried, Tanner promptly served everyone a shot of our new Builder's Arms Whiskey, and the whole thing was done in about fifteen minutes. Enough time to ensure we did everything legally required and not too much that Tommy started fussing.

"We didn't want bells and whistles... Didn't want a long engagement," I tell him, and he nods, still smiling, looking at me in a way that tells me he knows something I don't.

"Hmmmm, we'll have to have another whiskey to celebrate at the bar this week. Your Builder's Arms was nice." Hudson stands, and Savannah grabs her bag. I pass her the little man as I take the baby bag from her. The thing weighs a ton. Who knew babies needed so much shit.

"You're right. It is. The best Whiteman's has ever made." I'm a little biased, but the whiskey Tanner made with me in mind is by far my favorite.

"How're things going with the therapist?" Hudson asks me, and Savannah looks up at me, pride shining on her face. It was something she mentioned to me that time in my office, and after some thought, I decided to listen to the woman I've made my wife.

"I'm going to take Tommy out into the sun while you finish up."

I watch her walk down the hall, giving me the space to talk to Hudson alone, not that she needs to. I'm not hiding anything from her. She knows I'm talking to a therapist about my past.

"It's going okay. Is it helping? I'm not sure yet, but it sure isn't harming any, so I'll continue to chat with him every week," I tell him honestly. The feeling of being stripped bare isn't as raw as it once was, but it's still present. I walk toward the exit, Hudson keeping pace beside me.

"It might not feel like anything changes, until one day things just shift a little. Trust the process."

I nod, knowing he's right. It's kind of like how Savannah and I came to be. Nothing changed until it did. She crept up on me while I stayed in denial until the point of no return hit me and then I was all in.

"I'm trying... taking my time..."

"Griffin!" Savannah screams, and my head whips to the front glass doors, my feet moving toward her instantly.

"What the heck's happening?" Hudson looks up, eyes wide with concern, and I see Savannah in the parking lot, two men approaching her.

"Fuck," I grit out, running to meet her.

"Call the sheriff!" Hudson yells to his staff and follows me.

"Who the fuck are you?" My shoulders are tight as I stand to full height and feel ready to rumble with them. One guy is older, tall, skinny, pale-looking. Sports or fitness is obviously not his hobby. The other guy is younger, late twenties, maybe early thirties, his shirt done up right to his collar, his hair brushed so precisely I'd think he sold insurance.

"We're here for the baby."

My stomach twists. Not again. Not this nightmare. Savannah deserves better than this.

"It's not your baby, Dad. It's mine." Savannah's voice is stern, but I see a flicker of self-loathing in her eyes. That flicker guts me.

"Give me that baby. It's my baby!" The young guy steps up to me, getting right in my face. I spot two women walking towards us with purpose, one looking familiar. Eden. Savannah's sister. I assume the older woman is her mother.

"Are you Savannah's father?" I look to the older man, completely ignoring this fucking idiot in front of me who thinks he has a chance getting past me to grab Tommy. *No one* is getting past me.

"The Lord commands obedience, and she has chosen nothing but rebellion and sin. That's not something I can accept." He strides toward me, thinking I'll let him past because he's spouting words from the Bible, but I step in front of him, halting his path. Savannah deserves better than a father who spits scripture like poison, better than a mother who cuts her down with every word.

I step forward, fury boiling. "You're not going near my wife." My voice is low, dangerous. He falters, shocked that I'd claim her so openly.

"We don't want her! We want our baby!" Eden screams, taking my attention. "Douglas, get him!"

The younger man lunges. I yank his collar, slam him back, forcing him to stumble, almost falling to the ground. My knuckles itch to break bone.

"Do not touch my son!" I shout at her, turning back in time to see Douglas reaching out to snatch Tommy from Savannah again. This asshole clearly didn't learn the first time. Hudson's next to her in a heartbeat, but I reach out and pull his collar again so hard he falls backward, this time stumbling on the ground.

"That baby is ours." He's angry now. Not because he loves Tommy. But because probably for the first time in his miserable life, they aren't getting what they want. What they feel entitled to. They probably prayed on it, thought that God would deliver whatever they wanted immediately regardless of who they step on to get it. Ignorant fools. Even I know God doesn't work that way.

"You need to get out of my way!" The young buck stands and takes a swing, hitting me in my gut. I hear Savannah gasp from behind me, but it barely registers. My body is stiff, so his hand practically bounces right off before I throw a punch, my fist landing on his cheek so solidly that it knocks him from his feet and he staggers back even farther.

"The sheriff is on his way. You need to leave," Hudson tells them, but the air of authority standing there in his white doctor's coat isn't something these people seem to care about.

"Faith. Please, please, give me my baby…" Eden's crying now, almost screeching, completely losing it, and the use of Savannah's real name trips me up a little.

"Oh, you horrible, horrible girl. You selfish, disgusting, sinful girl. How could you do this to your sister? How could you do this to your family?" Her mother starts to rant, and I see Savannah flinch, the light dimming in her eyes. Tommy wails in her arms, sensing her fear. My chest aches with anger, disgust, and heartbreak all at once. *She deserves better than this. We both do. We both had parents who failed us. But we will not fail our child.*

"Hudson, get them inside," I tell my friend. He grabs some nurses who all wrap around Savannah and the baby and pull them back into the hospital. They're safe, secure as Hudson falls in line next to me.

I turn back to face them, rage burning. "This stops now. Tommy isn't yours. He will *never* be yours. If you come near my wife or child again, you'll rot in a cell."

Douglas snarls and lunges at me again, his fist slamming into my ribs once more. Pain flashes hot across my side, but I barely flinch. I've taken worse. My own father used to whip me with a belt some days, so I can take anything this bastard gives me. Instead of a punch, I drive him back with a shove to his chest that rattles his teeth.

Savannah's father moves to stride past me, his eyes wild, word vomiting more scripture, as the women continue with their tantrum, screaming into the air.

"The Lord will strike down the wicked! The child is ours by divine right!" He spouts a twisted sermon, his steps determined, but I plant myself in his path, chest to chest, refusing to yield. I don't want to hit him. I don't want to hit the man who is my father-in-law. But I will if I have to.

Behind him, the women shriek. "The wages of sin is death!" Eden screams.

"The Lord will destroy the unfaithful!" Savannah's mother wails, sounding more out of control with every breath, their voices pitched in desperation and anger.

Douglas steps forward and swings again, wild and desperate. He's determined; I'll give him that. I catch his wrist midair, twist hard, and he yelps as I slam him back against the pavement.

I'm trying hard not to completely lose it with them. If I took a swing, I would knock teeth out. An assault charge is not something that's going to help in this situation even though they have now thrown multiple punches my way. Self-defense is one thing, but deliberate assault is another. Something I learned at a young age.

Then I hear it. Sirens. Blue and red lights flash across the white hospital exterior, and the sheriff and Sawyer stride towards us, voices cutting through the madness.

"Enough!" the sheriff bellows, and he and his team take stock of the situation.

Sawyer looks at me. "I was in his office when he got the call."

"Probably good that you're here. This is Savannah's family. They're here trying to take Tommy. *Again*," I emphasize, and he nods. Knowing everything about this situation, since I briefed him regularly as we worked on the adoption paperwork. "Sheriff, these people came into the hospital with the intention of kidnapping my son. Doing so by using physical force, harassment..." I say, and Sawyer steps forward.

"Kidnapping, assault, harassment, endangerment of a child..." Sawyer starts listing legal terms, taking over talking to the sheriff as the deputies move fast, cuffs snapping onto wrists.

Hudson talks to the sheriff, telling him what he saw, and the sheriff looks at me with narrowed eyes.

"I won't cuff you, but I'll need you and your wife to come to the station to be interviewed."

I nod, happy to oblige. "We will." We know each other. He isn't stupid; he's aware of the situation.

"I can get you the hospital security camera footage. It would've caught everything," Hudson adds. I've nothing to hide, and now that I know cameras are here, I'm glad I didn't start punching.

As the sheriff moves toward his deputies who are restraining the two men, Eden starts striding toward me, shrieking nonsense, her palms raised like she's calling down fire from Heaven.

She steps right up to me, lunges at me, and slaps my face with a shrill cry. I stand rigid, refusing to strike back, though every nerve screams to retaliate. The deputies seize her instantly, cuffs biting her wrists. She looks stunned, as if she truly believed she was untouchable. Her face laces with fear as she's thrown into the police car.

"Assault by the female perpetrator," Sawyer says, making

notes on his phone, and I take in a deep breath, refusing to feel the sting on my cheek.

One by one, they're dragged to the waiting police cars, still screaming, probably still praying I would submit to their will.

Not able to watch this anymore, I turn and walk into the hospital, needing to see her. I stride down the hall and find her hidden in Hudson's office with a nurse nearby, some water, and a cup of tea. Savannah's still shaking, tears in her eyes.

"What happened?" She looks at me as I enter the room. Thank God she didn't see it. Didn't see the craziness I just witnessed. "What happened to your face?" She's on her feet instantly, rushing toward me and cupping my cheek.

"Your sister slapped me."

Her eyebrows rise, and I see the anger swirl.

"She has gone too far," she grits out, looking like she's about to walk out to the parking lot herself to defend my honor. I grab her hand before she can leave.

"They're gone. The sheriff took them to the station. We'll be charging them with everything we can," Sawyer says, looking between us as he enters the room.

"I'll go down to the station now and make sure everything is handled. I'll be putting forth an AVO so they can't come to the bakery, to your house, or within a mile of it at any time. But I think after what I witnessed, they would be stupid to try."

I nod to Sawyer, knowing he has it handled. It's handy having a friend who's a lawyer. Things move at a much more rapid rate.

"Let's give them some space," Sawyer says to the nurse, and they both walk out, the door shutting behind them.

I look down at Tommy, now sleeping peacefully in his mom's embrace.

"It's over. It's all over. They won't bother you again. They won't bother us. Tommy is safe. You are safe," I reassure Savannah. She pulls in a deep breath and leans forward, her head pressing against my chest. I wrap my arms around her and pull them both to me tight. She doesn't say anything. She doesn't have to. I feel her body shaking. And when I feel my shirt get damp, I know she's crying. But I stand, holding her through it all.

Letting her get it out. Knowing her nightmare is now over. And we can finally move on.

42

SAVANNAH

I have one eye on my son and one eye on the cupcakes I'm icing. I don't exactly know when it happened, but he's started to roll. Well, he's attempting to. He's moving around more and more, and I have absolutely no thought as to how I'm going to work when he's a toddler. The kitchen isn't built with kids in mind. Baby, yes. Toddler, no.

I haven't heard anything about my family since the hospital incident a few weeks ago. I was interviewed, but the sheriff knew everything anyway. Sawyer and Griffin have handled most of the paperwork, and I gave my statement and decided to press full charges. They have a court hearing coming up, but their reputation has been tarnished in the community, in their church. Their behavior wasn't condoned by Paster Greg, at least that's what he has publicly declared. I'm sure as soon as his church's reputation was mentioned in all the news stories, he decided to part ways with my father.

So now we're back to what I hope is our normal. Whispers being the small town it is, the gossip was intense for the first week. Everyone now knows what happened at the hospital and now many people around here know more about my life than I ever was prepared to share. Yet instead of shunning me like I thought they would, my business has almost doubled. It's like Tanner always says: the people of Whispers support one another, and I'm seeing it firsthand. Betty's is busy, all day, every day. The town's support, the support of my friends, it means the world.

The chime on the front door rings out, and my shoulder stiffens; the instant anxiety I feel from that ringing bell is still something I'm working on.

"Hey, sweetness." Griffin's warm tone fills my kitchen, and I relax.

"Hey. What are you doing here this time of day?" I look at the clock on the wall, seeing it's early in the afternoon.

"Just in town, so thought I'd pop by. Tanner asked me to check in on Bob with something."

I nod, smiling. That sounds about right.

"Why don't you two go have a break at the diner?" Melissa walks in from out front, looking at both of us.

"Oh, I have these to ice, and Tommy—"

"Nonsense. The afternoon rush is over, so I can babysit Tommy. Maybe you should go have a chicken pie for lunch. You two haven't yet had a chance to celebrate your wedding."

I pause then, because Melissa's right. We haven't. It's not something we kept secret from anyone. But we haven't celebrated. There's been so much else going on it hasn't even occurred to us to throw a party or anything.

"Maybe she's right. Maybe we should take an hour and go relax?" Griffin adds, seemingly up for a lunch date with his wife. *His wife.* I'm still not used to it. But the ring sits firm on my finger, the ink now dry on the marriage certificate.

I look over at Tommy, my heart rate spiking at the thought of leaving him. He's been by my side every day. I don't want to leave him, but I know it's unhealthy of me to want him within eyesight at every moment. Everyone needs a little break. Including me.

"Just go for an hour, have some lunch. If he fusses, I'll bring him straight over," Melissa tells us, giving me a warm smile.

I look at Griffin and shrug. "It's kinda like our first date?" Because we didn't have one of those either. Sure, we went to Whiteman's Bar once, and he took me to the birthday party at Hudson's place, but that was with everyone, not a one-on-one date.

He huffs a laugh and nods. "Probably something we should've started our relationship with, rather than have it now, when we're already married."

I can't help but smile wider. Loving that we do life on our own terms and we're both so happy.

"Alright." I sigh, taking off my apron. "I have milk in the refrigerator if he needs a bottle, but I fed him thirty minutes ago, so he'll probably go down for his nap now anyway."

Melissa nods, already knowing our schedule. She's here every day. Outside of Griffin and me, she's the only one I'm totally comfortable with Tommy being with. "Sure, go. Enjoy. I've got it."

Griffin's hand slides into mine, and we walk out of the bakery and head straight across the road to the diner. I take a deep breath, blowing out my anxiety, basking in the sun that shines down on me.

"What's going on here?" I look at the diner at Griffin's words, and as I open the door and step inside, everything hits me.

"Surprise!" a chorus of people yell, and Griffin and I stand there at the door, dumbfounded.

There're decorations, balloons. People are blowing those highly annoying party blowouts that vibrate around the room.

"Congratulations, guys! We wanted to throw you a small wedding celebration party." Victoria comes forward with Tanner, the two of them embracing us.

I look up at Griffin, his body still, shock on his face.

"Are you alright?" I ask him quietly as people start passing around food and the music is turned up.

"Yeah, I just... I've never had a party before."

I frown. "Never?" My life at home was terrible, but I did have a few birthday parties when I was a kid.

He swallows roughly. "No. Never."

I squeeze his hand and smile, and he starts to relax as all our friends come forward, offering hugs and smiles and congratulations. We're engulfed. There's a table off to the side, which is overflowing with presents, and I shake my head in disbelief.

"I'm so glad Melissa managed to get you guys over here." Victoria grins, clearly happy that it all came together.

"Of course she would be involved." I roll my eyes at how easily Griffin and I were duped.

Rochelle has food aplenty. Aside from balloons, there's a big *Just Married* sign across the back wall, and everyone yells for us to cut the cake, which is a beautiful two-tier cake decorated in white icing and red ribbons. My heart is full. I can't believe I have people in my life who have gone through all this effort to show up like this.

"Speech, speech!" Hudson yells as the clink of glasses runs around the room, Sutton leading the charge and hitting his champagne flute with a spoon so hard I swear it's going to shatter.

"Well..." Griffin starts, and I stand proudly by his side. "We're surprised... so well done, everyone." His words cause the room to erupt with cheers before it quiets again.

"Savannah and I would like to thank everyone here today, all our friends, who for us are really our family."

I hear Daisy swoon over in the back somewhere.

"Savannah and I often say how our path to this point has been unconventional..."

"You can say that again!" Sawyer hollers out, gaining more laughter.

"But to be honest, there's been one constant in our lives, one supporter who has always been here, always had our backs, always been our comfort and that is this town and its people. Whispers is a special place. I've been coming here for years, and while not a local—"

"You're part of the furniture now, Griff!" Tanner yells, and I chuckle.

"I think I can safely speak on behalf of both Savannah and I when I say that we're glad to now call Whispers home. So again, thank you everyone. We really appreciate the effort. We're grateful to have so many amazing friends, and appreciate your support," Griffin finishes, and everyone cheers as we cut the cake, and before I know what's happening, the girls all swallow me up with hugs and kisses, passing me a small glass of champagne.

There's so much noise and chatter that I get caught up with it all, and when I look at the time, I realize I've been gone for an hour already. I look around to find my husband, seeing him sitting with Tanner and the guys at a booth in the back, a bottle of whiskey now opened.

"I'm going to go and check on Tommy," I tell him quickly.

"Bring him over. There are lots of people here wanting hugs," Tanner offers, and I grin, thinking I will do just that. It feels like the whole town's here, so I don't think I'll be getting many customers at Betty's this afternoon anyways. I can probably close early.

"I'll come with you." Griffin starts to stand.

"No. It's fine. I'll be five minutes, tops," I tell him, already walking out, wanting him to stay and enjoy this time.

I thread my way through the people and out the door, again basking in the sun as I cross the road and walk across to the bakery. The smile on my face is hard to remove. Life is good. I've met and married the man of my dreams. My son is loved and thriving. My business is booming, and we're surrounded by so many great friends. I couldn't ask for more.

Seeing the signs of my bakery, I feel pride at having my own little business here on Main Street. I've come so far. I wonder if Gran knew this was going to be the outcome. I think she did. I think she knew I needed to start fresh and get out of Williamstown. She would be happy for me, I know it.

I step into the bakery, the chimes ringing and announcing my arrival.

"Hey, I'm back!" I holler, seeing the front area empty and assuming they're in the kitchen. I'm still smiling, wondering how Melissa kept this a secret from me. I saw her talking to Rochelle yesterday. I should've guessed something was up.

"Melissa?" I call out as I step into the kitchen, my grin still wide, but then I pause, seeing it's also empty.

"She must be upstairs," I tell myself, and I run upstairs to the apartment. Tommy's probably asleep, and she must be watching him.

"Melissa?" I call out quietly as I reach the top step, not wanting to wake Tommy, but the apartment is empty, exactly how I left it this morning. Not a cushion out of place. I haven't lived here for months, but I do still spend time here, feeding Tommy or having a restful moment when needed.

"Where is she?" I run downstairs again.

"Melissa?" I walk to the back door, assuming maybe she's outside. It's a beautiful day and she might have taken Tommy for some fresh air.

"Melissa?" My eyes sweep over the small courtyard, but there's no one here, nothing out of place.

Panic sweeps through me, nearly toppling me over. Something isn't right.

"Sweetness? You alright?" Griffin calls from inside, and I rush back in.

"She's not here."

"What do you mean, she isn't here?" Griffin frowns and looks outside before running back in.

"I came in, looked everywhere, but Melissa and Tommy aren't here." I'm panting, heart in my throat.

"Are they upstairs?" He runs up before I can answer, but he's back in two seconds.

"They're not here." I can't immediately think something bad has happened. I can't let my thoughts spiral. "Maybe she took him for a walk?" That has to be it. "The sun is shining... It's a beautiful day. That makes sense." I look around, seeing her handbag and his baby bag gone.

"The bakery was left unlocked." Griffin looks unimpressed.

"Maybe she went to the toy store?" I try to think of where she would take Tommy.

"You go to the toy store, and I'll run back across to the diner to ask around," Griffin says, the two of us splitting up and rushing out to the street.

I run down Main Street, asking people as I move past, but no one has seen her. Their grins at seeing me fall the minute they see my panicked face. The toy store team hasn't seen her today either, and I barely have the chance to say goodbye before I run out and meet Griffin on the street, my heart now racing, and even more so when I see all our friends outside of the diner, everyone with a worried look on their face.

"I'll call the sheriff. Just in case." Rochelle goes back into her diner, and my stomach plummets. This can't be happening.

"Where can they be?" I plead with Griffin, feeling like he would know the answer.

"Have you got her phone number?" Tanner watches me carefully.

"Oh sure, I'll call her. Not sure why I didn't think of that." I shake my head, a weird laugh escaping me, feeling ridiculous that I'm jumping to conclusions. My mind is racing all over the place. Not thinking straight.

I call her, but the ringing continues. No one picks up.

"She isn't answering." I frown as I dial again, but she still doesn't pick up. I feel like I'm going to be sick.

"Do you have her address? Maybe we can go to her place? See if she's there?" Hudson asks.

"She didn't tell me where she lived, just that she was a local..." I tell him, and Tanner's head shakes.

"She isn't local."

Griffin and I look at him, eyes wide.

"What do you mean, she isn't local?" Griffin's voice has dropped an octave. His stance stiffens.

"I mean, no one here knows her. I thought Savannah brought her over from Williamstown. I thought she was a friend of yours or something."

Griffin's head whips to me.

"She walked into the bakery months ago, answering the help wanted sign I had in the window. She said she lived on the outskirts of town and was a local..." Without another word, driven by panic, I run back across the road to the bakery, wanting to dig out her resume, the piece of paper she handed me when she first turned up to apply for the job. Everyone follows me, and we stand in the bakery as the sheriff arrives. Sawyer talks to him out front, obviously bringing him up to speed.

Victoria, Lacy, Annabelle, Daisy, and Charlotte stand next to me, sorrow and fear lacing their faces.

I grab her file, my eyes searching, seeing her name, her phone number, her experience, or lack thereof. But no residential address.

"There's no address..." Griffin grabs the paper from me, scanning it quickly.

I've failed again. I've failed my son.

"Her number, nothing else." He passes the paper to Tanner and then the sheriff.

"I'll call my security team. They did a thorough check when they arrived. They'll have something." Griffin is straight on the phone, but all I feel is remorse, guilt, terror.

"It's all my fault..." I whisper, my hands shaking as Victoria's arms encase me.

"Don't say that. Tommy will be fine. She might have taken him for a walk in the sun. Maybe her phone is dead or she can't hear it," Daisy offers, and I look at her, knowing something else has happened. I can feel it in my soul.

I gasp for a breath, tears trailing down my cheeks. "If anything has happened to him... If anything..."

"Don't think like that. Let's get the sheriff to see what he can do. I'm sure we'll find her."

The fun afternoon all our friends planned has now turned into a ruckus.

Tommy could be anywhere. And it's all my fault. My parents were right all along. I can't look after a child. I don't deserve him.

43

GRIFFIN

I see the light leave Savannah and my anger grows. Not at her. She isn't at fault. But at Melissa. The one person who Savannah has been close with for months.

As I wait for my security team to email through what information they have, I pray that Melissa took him for a walk and will come through the bakery doors with him like nothing's happened. Like we're all crazy for overreacting.

But deep in my gut, I know that's not the case.

"I've requested an Amber Alert across the state," the sheriff tells me, and I pull my wife close to me, increasingly feeling her body sag with every new piece of information.

"It's only been a few hours, but it's best to get on top of these things early and be wrong than leave them to the last moment and lose precious hours." He looks at Savannah, and she nods. Her face is now pale.

My cell chimes, and I bring up the email from my security team.

"What do they have?" Tanner's on high alert.

My eyes skim the file. "No address, but they have the registration of her car."

"What is it?" The sheriff is on it. As I read out the registration, he gets busy calling it in.

"We'll find him. He's safe, he'll be fine," I whisper to Savannah, kissing the top of her head as I feel her shaking in my arms.

"I've got a contact at the FBI if we need it." Sawyer nods to me. I know he's already probably been calling and getting people on standby. I said it in my speech earlier, but these people right here are my family, and they're the best family anyone could ask for. Tanner and Connor stand ready and concerned. Sawyer is in full legal mode. Hudson is at the ready, thinking about everyone he knows. Sutton I know would step forward in a moment's notice for anything that we might need.

"Alright, got an address. A place on the outskirts of Williamstown."

"Williamston?" Savannah frowns, looking at him.

"67 Plentyville Drive..." the sheriff adds, and her frown deepens with knowing.

"Do you know it?" I see her come back to life a little. Anger swirling and replacing the helplessness and despair she had moments ago.

"It's in my old neighborhood."

I suck in a breath, and the sheriff curses. I see her thinking, trying to work out if she knows the exact place.

"I don't know the street very well. I can't think if anyone lives down there whom I might know..."

"Let's go," I bark to the group and pull her with me.

"Wait, you can't go banging on doors and..." The sheriff is talking, but I ain't listening. Pulling Savannah with me, Tanner and the other guys get in their trucks too.

"Jesus Christ, you boys... leave it to us!" I hear the sheriff yell, but it's too late; we're already on the road. Truck after truck in convoy, Savannah and I leading and speeding out of Whispers.

"We'll get him," I tell her, because I'm adamant we will.

"I can't think ... It has to be connected, though, right?"

"Where does Pastor Greg live?" I bite out, knowing that guy gave us the creeps in the hospital.

"He lives at the church house near the church..."

"Does he have another place?"

She shakes her head. "I don't know... I mean, I don't think so, but I don't really know..."

I clench my jaw and push the accelerator harder as I hear sirens from behind.

"If this is my family again, or someone from the church..." Her tone deepens, and her fingers tighten around mine with her anger.

"We'll get him." I want to swear to her that I will get our son back. But my own demons sit on my shoulders, telling me I'm too late. That, like my brother, Tommy will not be saved. I couldn't save my brother, and now I won't be able to save my son. The possibility has my stomach twisting and my eyes blurring, but I have to stay strong for my wife. Have to stay strong for our son who needs us.

We cross into Williamstown, and Savannah navigates me through the neighborhood streets until we hit Plentyville Drive.

"67... there it is!" she yells, pointing, and I pull up sharply, Tanner and Connor right behind me.

"Let's go." The two of us jump out of the truck fast, dashing across the road and opening the garden gate to the quaint house, all in under ten seconds.

"That's her car." Savannah points to the neat Honda Civic in the drive.

"There's a baby seat in the back."

"She doesn't have kids." Savannah frowns as I step to the door, as the police finally pull up behind everyone.

"Melissa!" I shout, not having the patience to wait.

The door opens, and a man answers.

"You need to get off my property."

Savannah gasps, and I look at her, seeing her eyes wide, her skin ashen, and she starts to shake.

"No... No, no, no..." she whispers. Clearly, she knows him for her to have such a visceral reaction.

I look back at him, and he feels familiar to me too. But I can't place him. Neat slacks, a shirt buttoned all the way up, his hair combed to perfection. His side part is almost comical. It hits me then. This is the guy I saw at Whiteman's Bar months ago. The one who was watching the ladies. He was also the guy I saw at the hospital when Savannah gave birth.

"Who the fuck are you, and where the hell is my son?" I bark out, trying to put the puzzle together.

"This is Tommy's sperm donor," Savannah whispers, and my heart stops. Tommy's bio dad?

The man looks at Savannah, I don't miss his eyes as they rake down her frame and back again before he swallows.

"And my son is now home where he belongs. With my wife," the guy states, as Melissa walks around the corner, holding Tommy, bottle-feeding him.

"Your wife?" Savannah yells, head rearing back in shock.

"I sinned by finding warmth in another body. I have repented." He says and I fist my hands, ready to knock out this low-life asshole.

"Give him to me!" Savannah screams, and I hear the police running up the garden path.

"Get off my property!" he shouts right back.

"Give me my baby!" Savannah screams again, and I step forward, about to walk in and take Tommy. That's our child, and I'm not doing this back-and-forth.

"Step back!" He produces a gun, and I pause, halfway in his door, the gun aimed squarely at my chest. Savannah whimpers beside me, her hand gripping the back of my shirt.

"This is the police! Lower your weapon!" the sheriff says from behind me. I don't move, but I grab Savannah and pull her behind me. She's crying, shaking, but I need her safe and out of the equation. I feel someone behind me grab her, Tanner, the police, who, I don't know, but I know she's safe as I look at this asshole who thinks he can get away with kidnapping my fucking kid and putting a gun to my chest.

"Give. Me. My. Son," I grit out as the barrel of the gun pushes into my skin. This isn't happening again. I'm not losing someone else I love. There's no way I'm stepping back. I look at Melissa as she cuddles Tommy tight, him oblivious to what's going on around him. But he can hear his mom's distress, and he's starting to fuss.

"I said step back! Unless you want a bullet lodged right into your chest." This asshole has the audacity to threaten me.

"Once I have my son, I'll walk out of here and never come back."

He shakes his head. "He's my boy. I heard God whisper. He told me I can make it up to my wife by giving her a child she couldn't have." I pull in a breath, this asshole cheats on his wife, gets Savannah pregnant then thinks he can live a life without consequence by kidnapping little Tommy and giving it to his wife? To Melissa? Anger swirls in me like it hasn't for a long time.

"No, he's not. You're not listed on the birth certificate and have no legal parental right, never once did you approach Savannah for the baby." I inform him through a clenched jaw, remembering asking Sawyer that same question. The legal information that's now stored in my brain is useful for once.

"I'm going to blow your brains out. Is the kid worth it to you? Is *she* worth it?" He looks at Savannah behind me, his face full of disgust and I explode.

I move quicker than I thought I ever could. I throw my arm over the gun, and it goes off. The gunshot vibrates around the neighborhood, and I feel heat searing through my shoulder. But I pay it little attention as I lift my other arm and throw it in his face.

His nose smashes into his cheek, blood spurts out instantly, and he falls to the ground with a resounding thud. Not dead but unconscious. Pity.

Melissa screams as I lunge at her next. But I'm not going for her; I'm going for my child. I hear steps, people running at me from behind, but I have tunnel vision.

"Give him to me." My vision is dark, my eyes on my son. Melissa's trembling.

"Please..." she starts to wail, but she doesn't hand him back. His face is covered by her sweater as she holds him tight. She's suffocating him and doesn't even know it.

"Release the baby, or we'll shoot..." the officer says from over my back shoulder. Melissa's eyes plead with me, tears falling, but I'm stone.

"Give me Tommy," I tell her in a gentler tone.

"But... he's my baby... I always wanted a baby..." she wails when I try to calmly reach out as I get closer.

"Melissa, give me Tommy," I say more urgently as the

police surround her. It's over. This is the end. She needs to let him go now.

She nods, crying, doing the right thing now that Tommy's wailing too, his cry the biggest I've ever heard as I reach out and pull him from her arms. The police surround her, pushing her to the ground, yelling at her as I step back, and for the first time, I look up and outside.

There are people everywhere. Neighbors, police, our friends. I spot Savannah, held back by Tanner, and I stride down to her, knowing she needs Tommy. Fuck, we both do. As I walk to her, I lift Tommy to my lips, kissing his head, my heart beating so hard I feel lightheaded.

"I saved you this time, buddy. I'm sorry I couldn't do it last time. I'm sorry I couldn't save you then. But I've got you now, little man. You're safe with me and your mama."

Tommy's screaming stops, and he snuggles into my chest as I finally make it to my wife, her cheeks tearstained as she reaches for him. I pass him over, seeing her cry into him and cuddle him tight.

"Thank you, Griffin. Thank you for saving our boy. Thank you for saving Tommy..." she chants to me through sobs, and I pull her close, the two of them held to my chest as we stand there with the ruckus surrounding us, knowing that they're the only ones who matter.

"Best get that looked at." Tanner nods toward my shoulder, and I look down, seeing my shirt coated in blood. I feel the pain now that he mentioned it, the burning.

"Oh my gosh! Griffin!" Savannah gasps, pulling back. In all the craziness, she must have missed who got shot.

"I'm okay, baby. We're all okay." I kiss her head, then turn to Hudson. "Do you know anyone who can stitch me up?" Adrenaline, shock, and anxiety are clearly making me sarcastic.

Savannah shakes her head, pressing a kiss to my chest, avoiding the blood, whispering how she loves me. I hold her tighter.

"You know how to give us all heart failure, don't you?" Hudson sighs as he walks over and peels back my shirt as the paramedics pull up.

"This is bigger than any movie I've ever done..." Sutton looks around before pulling his cap low.

"I'll see you back at Whispers," I tell him, because I know he and Charlotte have the media following them and don't need this extra drama, but I'm grateful that they came, ready to step in if needed.

I spot Victoria and Daisy on either side of Savannah, talking to her in hushed tones, rubbing her arms and Tommy's head as Lacy and Annabelle look to be getting things for her, water, a blanket. She'll need our friends. We both do, and I'm so glad we have them.

Our friends. Our family. Our home in Whispers.

44

GRIFFIN

I hiss at the cool contact.

"Oh, so now you're a big baby?" my wife remarks as she changes my bandages. My wound is healing nicely.

It was a straight through and through, the bullet missing all the important bits, slicing a bit of muscle, meaning my time on the hammer drill has been paused for now. It's been almost a week since everything went down, and Tommy hasn't left our sight since.

"Speaking of babies... Where did mine go?" I look at this child who sits happily on my lap, looking around the room, the chandelier above him taking all his attention.

"Hmmm, he's a strong boy, supporting his head already, basically a fully grown adult at this point." She humors me. God, I love her. I'm so proud of her. With the shit she's had thrown at her, all her life, to come out and be stronger, be a proud, strong mom to her son, and an amazing wife. We've both had a session with my therapist. Savannah's now going to start individual sessions too. There's a lot of baggage we both need to unpack from our past. Neither of us wants to bring any of it into our future. Into our new life.

"I probably should be putting a bit of whiskey on his pacifier... get him use to it."

She swats at me, and I grin. Clearly teasing her.

"You will do no such thing."

"No. I won't. But maybe we should start those swimming lessons? Get him in the water?" Hudson told me once healed, that swimming will be good rehab for my shoulder. Help get some strength back and things.

"You won't be going anywhere near that pool until this is healed."

"Here I was, thinking I was the bossy, grumpy one in this relationship. Thought you were all sweetness and spice and everything nice?" I murmur.

"That was before you purposefully put your body in front of the barrel of a gun."

"I put my body between you and the gun; there's a difference."

"Well, it was stupid. You could have been hurt even worse..." We've had this conversation numerous times since. It makes her emotional to think of what could have happened.

"I'd do it again."

"I know you would. That's one of the many reasons I love you." She leans down, pressing her lips to mine so sweetly I wasn't sure I'd ever get to feel a love like it.

We've endured a lot. More than most. Her family are still awaiting a court date, but by all accounts, they've now realized they failed her and went too far. But that relationship has sailed. They're not allowed anywhere near us, and I'll be making sure they uphold that.

As for Tommy's bio dad, he's being charged with kidnapping, endangering a child, and attempted murder. Sawyer's pushing for everything, and given Sawyer's contacts, and the fact that we had so many witnesses, I think he'll be locked away for a long time.

Melissa's currently helping the police with their enquiries and will be charged for her part in the kidnapping as well. It's been a complete whirlwind of emotions for everyone. But for the first time since we met, Savannah and I are free of all our past demons coming into our lives. We're now dealing with the memories and the damage to repair.

Savannah will start afresh at the bakery. Maybe hire someone new, and I already know that the process will be rigorous. Although Daisy, Annabelle, Victoria, Lacy, and Charlotte have all been helping this past week. One of them comes in each day, learning the ropes, helping with Tommy and supporting when and where needed.

Tanner and the boys have been making sure we have everything we need. They come over to talk with me during the day, ensuring that we're all good. This town rallies for its people, that's for sure.

"There. All done. Now let's go to the kitchen. I have something for you."

"What is it, buddy?" I ask Tommy, standing with him in my hold and following her, having no idea what she's up to. Tommy slaps my face with his little hand, and I squint at him and kiss him in return.

As I get closer to the kitchen, I start to smell an aroma I haven't smelled in a long time.

"Happy birthday, Griffin," she says as I round the corner, standing there with a small party hat on and a cake filled with candles. Putting a small party hat on Tommy, she puts one on me next as I look at the kitchen counter. There are a few gifts, all wrapped nicely with ribbons. I'm surprised.

Given everything that's been happening, acknowledging my birthday wasn't something I was expecting. Hell, I didn't even realize today was the day.

"What's all this?" I'm scared to breathe. It smells like my childhood.

"Well, today is your birthday." She smiles warmly.

"Is it?" I've never celebrated. For many years, my birthday came and went with no one knowing.

"According to the birth certificate we used at our wedding, it is." She nods before she continues. "And well, I remember you saying that your mom always used to make you apple pie..." She slides the cake across and, sure enough, under the three flaming candles is an apple pie. My eyes water, my heart pounds, and I pull in a breath.

"Help me blow out the candles, Tommy." I used to say that to my brother, and now I say it to my son. I lean in, blow out the candles, and Savannah claps.

"Make a wish." She grins as Tommy fusses.

"I don't need to. Got everything I could've ever wished for right here."

Savannah leans in, giving me her lips, and I kiss her quickly before she pulls back.

"I got the apples from Charlotte and some fresh cream from Annabelle's farm too... This is going to be delicious." She hums happily, heading to the refrigerator and pulling out a bowl of freshly whipped cream and a few plates.

"God, where did you come from?" I look at my wife in awe. Falling more in love with her every day we're together.

"My gran always used to tell me that she was making cookies one day and that she mixed the sugar and flour just right, and instead of cookies, I popped out. She always used to say that I was the sweetest treat she ever had."

I swallow, because that's exactly what she feels like to me.

"You are my sweetness. My everything."

As soon as the pie hits my tongue, I'm taken back. My last birthday with my mother, my brother running around and playing nearby. The apple still warm, the cream melting a little.

"So? Is it okay?" Savannah looks at me expectantly, eyes searching mine.

"It's exactly how my mom used to make."

And although my shoulder is sore, my heart is full. My family is whole, and I am now home.

EPILOGUE - GRIFFIN

The laughter from outside grows quieter as I walk into the house, my arms full of dirty cups and plates, the kids doing a fantastic job of making a complete mess.

"Oh, good. Tidy up as we go," Savannah says without looking at me. Instead, she's concentrating on putting the finishing touches on the cake.

"That looks amazing!" I'm honest, it does. If I didn't already know how talented my wife is, this birthday cake for Tommy is outstanding.

"You like it?" I look at my son's birthday cake in awe. It's a large cupcake. One that would feed over fifty people. Given there are about that many outside on the lawn, I'm glad she made a big one.

"Like it? I can't wait to eat it!" I tell her, as I step forward and curse.

"Motherfu—" I pause and hold my breath, and Savannah looks at me.

"What's the pain out of ten?" she watches me carefully as I lean over, picking up the little green army man from the floor.

"Seven." I grimace as I grab another two I spot across the kitchen floor, waiting to dig into my bare feet.

To say my house is now a family home would be an understatement. Not only is my kitchen a complete baker's delight, with ingredients, pans, recipe books, and food everywhere, but the rest of the house has toys scattered from one end to the other. And I couldn't be happier.

Right now, kids are everywhere outside, and along with a juggling clown, a jumping castle, and a small carousel, Tommy's giggling his little heart out as a new two-year-old.

We've come a long way, my little family and me. When we got through all our past family issues, I took Tommy and Savannah away. We all needed a break. A circuit breaker from the life we had, we needed to regroup, spend quality time without the heaviness of our past. So we spent a month at my house in Hawaii, where we picked fresh pineapples and Tommy splashed at the beach and ate sand almost every day. He's a water baby, for sure, and now the highlight of my day is an early morning swim with him here at the house when it's warm enough.

After that trip, we came home and got back to work. Savannah had help over the months from all the girls, but Debbie has been our saving grace. Annabelle introduced us to her months ago. Debbie was her boys' babysitter and she's known by every one of our friends who all vouched for her. She started coming into the bakery and watching Tommy in the kitchen while Savannah worked.

We then progressed to her taking him upstairs to the apartment while she worked, reading him books, singing him songs, feeding him, and putting him down for naptime. Now she's with Tommy almost every day while Savannah builds the bakery business and looking at a possible expansion.

"You know, they wouldn't be a problem if you didn't buy them." My wife gives me that look. The one that says *I told you so*. I grin. It's true. When I took Tommy into the local toy store a few months ago and saw the bag of green army men, I knew I had to buy them for Tommy. The way they're scattered around the house makes me feel good. Although my bare feet can barely take it.

"Okay, so the cake table is ready." Lacy and Victoria walk into the kitchen with arms full of dirty dishes, while the rest of our friends are outside watching the kids, eating all my food, and probably taking a bet on how long the clown will last in the heat.

"Wow. That's amazing!" Lacy sees the cake, her eyes widening.

"I need a photo of this." Victoria quickly grabs her cell and snaps a picture.

To say these girls have been a godsend is an understatement. They've been by Savannah's side for everything, becoming the true sisters she needed. I dart my eyes then, spotting the photo wall down the hall, now covered with framed photos of us, of Savannah, Tommy and me. And there, in the middle, is my brother. The toothy smile photo I kept locked away for years is now on full display. He would've loved to be here today. He would've been lined up for the first piece of this cake, that's for sure.

"You alright?" Savannah's voice is quieter as the girls clatter around in the kitchen behind us.

"Better than alright." I reach out for her, and she comes to me, fitting into my side like she always has.

"Can you believe our boy is two already?"

"No. I can't. He's growing so fast." She hugs me tight.

I have loved being Tommy's father. I make sure I'm there for every doctor's visit and nighttime wake up. I also continue to wake up early, spending breakfast time with Tommy. The little routine I started when he was a newborn, one I've carried on.

"You outdid yourself with this cake, sweetness."

Giving me a quick kiss, she smiles as she lifts the cake, and we take it outside.

I follow behind the women as the crowd starts singing "Happy Birthday" as we walk through to Tommy. He's perched at the kids' table, waiting, a look of glee on his face.

He's a little pocket rocket like his mom. Can't sit still for long, so I know this is killing him. Especially with all the activities spread out across our lawn. I remember dreaming of this moment. Of having a kid and having a birthday party here. Now to see it in full color, the feeling is surreal.

I've tried to give him and Savannah everything. Ever since I took them to Hawaii, we've traveled a little bit. So far, I've taken them to Colorado, Sonoma, and Sundown Valley —where Savannah and I tasted the most amazing wine ever at the Stonemore Estate—and we have a trip to New York planned for the holidays to see the snow. It was Savannah's first time flying, and now I have the jet stocked full of Tommy's things, like his toys, food, and blankets. I might as well rename the jet to Tommy's Second Home.

Tommy looks up at me with such happiness, I almost stumble. With the cake placed in front of him, Savannah and I stand nearby as the song comes to an end and he takes a big breath.

"Don't forget to make a wish!" Savannah says to him quickly, and he giggles and proceeds to blow out the two candles, causing everyone to cheer.

"Go play, and I'll call you over when I've cut it up," she

tells the kids before she starts cutting the large cupcake and our friends all gather around.

"This is great, guys. Who would have thought that you would have a kids' party here, Griff, when you hated attending ours so much?" Hudson teases, and Lacy laughs.

"I never hated them..." I mumble, only speaking half-truths. I didn't love kids' parties back then, but now that I have a child of my own, I could have a party here every week.

"Oh, by the way, I had a new mom come in this week. I gave her information on the new program." Hudson nods while lifting his beer, and I grin.

"That's good?" My eyes catch Savannah's, whose shine at me with pride. One of the things I did this year was work with Hudson on a new mother's program called *Forth Trimester*. It's an online and face-to-face program for new moms so they have support after delivery.

Experiencing pregnancy and birth with Savannah and going through all that we did when Tommy was born, made us realize that many others aren't as lucky with support, finances, and community. So we made it possible for them with the new program. We offer fully vetted nannies, food delivery services, Mother Maven products, and online support groups. So now Whispers has a prenatal support program that Tanner funds and a postnatal program that I fund. Meaning, kids in this town are thriving.

"Whiskey anyone?" Tanner walks up with a bottle of Builder's Arms. The only whiskey that I allow in this house. It's turning out to be one of Tanner's best sellers, alongside The Shadow Gentleman, which Sutton promotes, and Next Door, which was inspired by Victoria. It could be because I buy batches of it wherever I go, singlehandedly funding my own profit.

"About time," Sawyer says, stepping up with Annabelle.

"You boys and your whiskey..." Daisy shakes her head and grins as she and Connor join us.

"I need to get out of this suit..." Sutton says as we all look at him and laugh. He turned up today dressed in his famous superhero costume for the kids. They have all been begging him for months, and he finally did it.

"I can't believe you still have it on," Charlotte teases him, and I look at all our friends and smile.

"How about some cake to go with the whiskey?" Savannah starts handing out the pieces of cake and little forks.

"I hope it's good..." She watches me, waiting for my thoughts, but I'm not sure why. Whatever she makes is delicious.

I grab the plate and fork and shove a piece into my mouth. Red velvet, one of my favorites, with what I suspect is a strawberry icing.

My eyes widen as I chew, trying to school my features. I look at the boys, who have all stopped mid-chew.

"Well?" Her eyebrows rise.

I can't move. I can't talk. I stand staring at her with a mouth full of cake that tastes like day old socks.

"Oh..." Victoria says as I see her take a bite. Out the corner of my eye, Hudson stops Lacy before the cake gets to her mouth.

I finally swallow it down, and the realization dawns on me.

"We're having a baby?" I look at her in disbelief.

"Wait? What?" She looks confused before everyone around us starts spitting out the cake into their napkins and the kids all throw theirs away.

She quickly grabs a plate and spoons some cake into her mouth and chews.

"What? It's fine..." She looks at all of us like we're crazy before it dawns on her.

"I've lost my taste..."

"We're having a baby?" I smile as she takes it in.

"Oh my God... I mean, I am late..." Her hand slaps over her mouth, eyes wide, before a laugh escapes her.

"We're having a baby!" I yell, pure happiness overtaking me as I scoop her up and twirl her in my arms. She giggles, still in shock, but just as excited as our friends all holler and cheer and the kids run around, completely oblivious.

Yeah. Our life here in Whispers is going pretty darn well.

ACKNOWLEDGMENTS

Wow. What a journey.

The Billionaires of Whispers will stay with me forever. The town, the men, the women, the goats, the yoga, the butter-flies, the soap, the bees, the cupcakes... and, of course, the whiskey. That smooth burn of a Whitemans will live in my mind every time I see someone with a glass in their hand.

There are so many people who helped bring this world to life.

To my **family**. Thanks for putting up with the chaos, the deadlines, and the fictional men who keep stealing my attention.

To my editor, **Kenzie**. You've been with me almost from the beginning of my career, and I truly don't know what I'd do without you.

To my proofreader, **Kimberly**. Thank you for every single time I've hit you with a rush job. You always come through.

To my cover designer, **Angela**. Working with you on this series (and all the others) has been a joy. I can't wait to see what we create next.

To my author friends, **Sharon, Sam, Jade, and Sherri**. Thank you for the chats, the plotting, the support, and the sanity checks. I adore you all.

To my PA, **Treece**. Your ongoing support means the world. You are amazing.

To **Sara.** Thank you for wrangling my socials, my ideas, and my chaos with so much patience and skill.

To **Jodie and the team at Two Birds Audio.** Hearing these characters in my ears has been surreal in the best way. Thank you for helping me find the perfect voices.

To my incredible **ARC and ALC readers.** Your enthusiasm, your messages, your hype... you make this job magic.

To my **Skye's The Limit** Facebook group. Chatting with you each week is a highlight. I'm so grateful you love these books as much as I do.

And finally, to every reader who has spent time in Whispers. Thank you. This fictional town feels very, very real now, and I love that so many of us want to pack up and move there.

While Whispers will always belong to the Whitemans, I hear there's a little wine region called **Sundown Valley** that might be worth a visit...

For updates on what's coming next, join my newsletter or follow me on Instagram.

Join my newsletter here!

Follow my Instagram here!

ALSO BY SAMANTHA SKYE

The Billionaires of Whispers

Tanner

Hudson

Connor

Sawyer

Sutton

Griffin

SCROOGE: A Billionaire Christmas Story

Under The Mistletoe: A Billionaire Christmas Story

The Baltimore Boys

The Charming Billionaire

The Arrogant Billionaire

The Damaged Billionaire

The Secret Billionaire

The Bossy Billionaire

The Billionaire Babe

Men Of New York

My Legacy

My Destiny

My Fight

My Chance

Boston Billionaires

Coming Home

Finding Home

Leaving Home

Building Home

ABOUT THE AUTHOR

Samantha Skye is an international bestselling author. A country kid turned city slicker, she writes spicy and suspenseful contemporary romance novels that leave you hot under the collar and on the edge of your seat.

Samantha lives in Melbourne, Australia and when she's not plotting her next novel, she can be found travelling, drinking margaritas and enjoying a sunset or a stargaze somewhere.

To join in the conversation join Skye's The Limit Facebook group here;
https://www.facebook.com/groups/skyesthelimitbooks